The tableau was like something out of a story:
a proud, tragic queen; a druid foretelling doom;
a golden prince promising heroics.

But stories were by nature false—designed to fool the eye and twist the mind, to make us believe in things that couldn't ever be true. Stories gave us hope, and I hated them almost as much as I hated my stolen face, my uncertain origins, and my wild and wicked magic.

Real life wasn't like the stories. Real life ended in deception, betrayal, or tragedy. Which meant this pretty tale was either untrue or incomplete.

"So we're to use this Thirteenth Gate to rescue Eala?" I cut in.

Mother nodded. "The Folk have no reason to suspect we know of it. When the veil between the human realm and Tír na nÓg is stretched thin—during a full moon—it can be breached."

I cocked my head. "But to pass through, don't you also need the still-beating heart of— *Oh*."

The answer crashed over me like a winter sea, cold and inevitable. So *this* was why I'd been called here to stand beside Rogan and plot the princess's grand rescue—because my blood ran green and black as the dark parts of the forest.

A

FEATHER

SO

BLACK

Book One of the Fair Folk

LYRA SELENE

orbit

orbitbooks.net

Copyright © 2024 by Lyra Selene Robinette
Excerpt from *A Crown So Silver* copyright © 2024 by Lyra Selene Robinette

Cover design by Lisa Marie Pompilio
Cover images by Arcangel and Shutterstock
Cover copyright © 2024 by Hachette Book Group, Inc.
Author photograph by Alexis the Greek Photography

Orbit
Hachette Book Group
1290 Avenue of the Americas
New York, NY 10104
orbitbooks.net

First Edition: March 2024
Simultaneously published in Great Britain by Orbit

Orbit is an imprint of Hachette Book Group.
The Orbit name and logo are registered trademarks of Little, Brown Book Group Limited.

The publisher is not responsible for websites (or their content) that are not owned by the publisher.

The Hachette Speakers Bureau provides a wide range of authors for speaking events. To find out more, go to hachettespeakersbureau.com or email HachetteSpeakers@hbgusa.com.

Orbit books may be purchased in bulk for business, educational, or promotional use. For information, please contact your local bookseller or the Hachette Book Group Special Markets Department at special.markets@hbgusa.com.

Library of Congress Cataloging-in-Publication Data
Names: Selene, Lyra, author.
Title: A feather so black / Lyra Selene.
Description: First edition. | New York, NY : Orbit, 2024. | Series: Fair Folk ; book 1
Identifiers: LCCN 2023037933 | ISBN 9780316564960 (trade paperback) | ISBN 9780316564977 (ebook)
Subjects: LCGFT: Fantasy fiction. | Novels.
Classification: LCC PS3619.E4626 F43 2024 | DDC 813/.6—dc23/eng/20230919
LC record available at https://lccn.loc.gov/2023037933

ISBNs: 9780316564960 (trade paperback), 9780316564977 (ebook)

Printed in the United States of America

LSC-C

Printing 1, 2023

For anyone who has ever doubted
if they were the main character in their own story.
You are.

Part One

The Stolen Child

Where the wave of moonlight glosses
The dim grey sands with light,
Far off by furthest Rosses
We foot it all the night,
Weaving olden dances
Mingling hands and mingling glances
Till the moon has taken flight...
Come away, O human child!
To the waters and the wild
With a faery, hand in hand,
For the world's more full of weeping than you
    can understand.

—"The Stolen Child" by W. B. Yeats

Chapter One

Gort—Ivy
Autumn

I should not have drunk the blackberry wine. It slid violet through my veins and pricked sharp thorns at the nape of my neck. I'd thought it would calm me—focus my mind on the task at hand—but the opposite was true. I felt loose and reckless, jittering with nerves. I curled my hands tighter around my cup, fighting the brambles nettling at my fingertips.

Served me right for drinking on duty.

"More wine?" Connla Rechtmar, prince of Fannon, leaned forward in his fur-draped seat. He sloshed a carafe of purple liquid and flashed me an expectant smile. "Or do I need to offer you something stronger to make you take off that cloak you're hiding under?"

By now, the wine had traveled to my face, and I fought a flush—not of girlish embarrassment, but of fury. He had the audacity to speak to me like I was some timid strumpet? I could break his neck without breaking a sweat.

My wine-spiked blood pounded between my ears, hot with the prospect of violence.

I reminded myself that Connla didn't know what I was capable of. And if I had any sense, I'd keep it that way.

The tent was too warm, the fire roaring to ward off late autumn's chill. I would've preferred it cold—a bite of frost to keep me alert. I forced myself to count off the steps of my mission through the fevered muddle of my thoughts:

One. Get to the carafe of wine.

Two. Drug the wine.

Three. Smother Connla's unconscious face in his mound of seduction furs. (If I had time.)

Four. Find the prince's captive darrig.

Five. Bring the wicked creature to my mother.

I took a deep breath, even as I pressed a thumb against the bracelet I wore around my wrist, a woven circle of dried poison ivy, nettle, and bramble. It dug into the tender ring of irritated skin below it. The flare of pain untangled the snarl of my thoughts.

I undid the clasp of my heavy woolen cloak, dropping it to the floor before my skin could prickle with sharp thorns. Without the outer garment, the air was blessedly cooler on my bare arms and exposed collarbones. I looked up through my lashes at Connla, gauging his reaction to my kirtle—or lack thereof. The sheer forest-green silk was striking against my pale skin and did little to disguise my physique. The thin shoulder straps were unnecessary considering how tight I'd cinched the bodice, accentuating my modest curves and slender waist. The high slit in the skirt left little to the imagination.

It achieved the desired effect. Connla's eyes widened, then darkened. He shifted in his chair. I fought the urge to shudder at the vulgar anticipation slicking his gaze.

Truthfully, I could have worn a grain sack or a few judiciously placed oak leaves. Connla wanted me, with or without the clinging dress, and I'd known it since that morning.

For the past fortnight, all the under-kings and noblemen of Fódla had been camped near Rath na Mara—the high queen's capital—to participate in the Áenach Tailteann, funeral games held to celebrate and mourn kings of Fódla. This year's assembly honored the late under-king of Eòdan and crowned his heir.

For the first few days, the high queen, Eithne Uí Mainnín—my adoptive mother—had presided over the creation of new laws, followed by a great funeral pyre in the king's honor. Then the games had begun—trials of physical and mental prowess that allowed young warriors and poets the opportunity to prove their strength, valor, and wit.

Connla Rechtmar had represented his father's household in a few categories—archery, horse racing, blades. He'd won all his matches—an odd bit of luck, considering he was lazy and slow, even for a prince.

Mother had not allowed me to compete. No—I was her secret, her instrument, her *weapon*. Flaunting my skills before her nobles was of no use to her—not if she wished me to spy on them, tease out their secrets, hunt down their weaknesses. So, as always, she kept me beside her in the queen's box, demurely dressed and diffident. The queen's favored fosterling—a strange, quiet little mouse.

That was where Connla noticed me. It wasn't unusual to feel eyes on the side of my face—even though I looked chaste and obedient, there were the rumors. There were *always* the rumors—about where I'd come from, why I looked the way I did, why the queen took particular interest in me. But Connla's regard was different—an oily kind of interest I didn't find particularly flattering. I was debating whether I could surreptitiously give him the two-fingered salute across the ring, when Mother leaned over to me. She pretended to tuck an errant lock of sable hair beneath my veil.

"Rechtmar's son desires you," she murmured to me, too quiet for her other attendants to hear.

"I noticed," I grumbled. And then, hopefully: "May I kill him for it?"

"You may not." She almost smiled. "Cathair?"

Ollamh Cathair—the queen's druid, chief advisor, and long-term lover—moved from his place behind her. He slid onto the bench beside me as Mother returned her attention to the archery contest below. His unwanted closeness chased away my cheekiness, but I forced myself not to flinch.

Cathair was a slender middle-aged man with a mild bearing. But his looks were his best deception. He had trained me in many things these past eleven years. Folklore. Ciphers. Poisons. Espionage. But first and foremost, he had taught me never to show my enemy how much I hated him.

"Fannon has been exceptionally lucky in their border skirmishes this year," Cathair muttered. "Flash floods sweeping away enemy troops, falling trees blocking supply wagons. That kind of thing. My informants believe they may have captured a darrig."

Although the Fair Folk found ways to slink into our realm, it was expressly forbidden to consort with them. To keep a darrig was treason—the gnome-like creatures could predict events not yet passed and affect the outcome of simple occurrences. A tree falling, perhaps. The direction of a flood. Or even the outcome of a sword fight in a tournament.

"You believe Connla has the darrig?" I guessed, keeping my eye on the prince in question, who was celebrating his *lucky* wins by lazily swilling ale in the stands.

"Old Rechtmar is past his prime," Cathair told me. "Connla is his heir, his war advisor, and the captain of his fianna. If anyone has it, it will be Connla. Capture the thing for us, won't you?"

"You mean execute it." I glanced past Cathair to the queen. "Don't you?"

"Not this time." His expression held the kind of deadly intent I'd learned not to question. "We have a use for the creature."

I hid my uncertainty. Mother despised and distrusted the Fair Folk—they who had once ruled this land as gods. They were wicked, fickle, violent creatures who did not belong in the human realm. During a diplomatic delegation twenty years ago, the Folk had assassinated the high king, Mother's husband. The unjustified execution had incited the Gate War. The fight had been savage and bloody, until the Folk had effectively ended it by stealing away twelve human girls—the last, the queen's own daughter.

Mother *never* utilized the treacherous Folk for her own devices. Except me, the changeling child who had been left in her daughter's place twelve years ago. But after so much time in the queen's household, I was far more human than Folk. And everything I did for Mother, I did willingly.

Including this.

I refocused my attention on Connla, who was still staring brazenly at me from below. "How am I supposed to find the darrig?"

"You've demonstrated your tactical skills to me, little witch. And you've been developing an adequate head for subterfuge." Cathair's voice was sardonic. "But you have not yet proved yourself adept at seduction."

I wasn't thrilled by that idea. But what Cathair—and by extension, Mother—asked of me, I obeyed.

So here I was—a little drunk, sweating my arse off in a gown that left nothing to the imagination, as an overfed prince beckoned me closer with greedy fingers. Again, I fought a shudder of disgust.

I reminded myself this face did not belong to me. Nor the body, most likely. Who cared if I used them as tools, as *weapons*? They were nothing but what I made of them.

I swayed toward Connla, pasting on a slow smile and swinging my hips more than was strictly necessary. He patted his knee and I lowered myself onto his lap, gritting my teeth as his hand slithered around my waist.

"Yes, more wine is exactly what we need," I murmured, leaning into him. "But won't you allow *me* to serve *you* this time, my prince?"

I reached for the carafe of wine. But Connla caught my hand with one of his own, gripping my wrist. His eyes raked me from head to toe, bright with a canny light.

"I didn't expect your message tonight, *my lady*." His breath was hot and sour on my cheek. "Nor did I expect you to show up in my tent, half-dressed and eager for wine."

"What can I say?" I clenched my jaw harder behind my smile. "I couldn't take my eyes off you. Besides, it's hard to find a decent drink up at Rath na Mara."

"Perhaps. Or perhaps you had some other reason." His eyes glittered. "You see, after your unexpected note, I confess I told a few local lads about it. I maybe even bragged a bit. And what they had to say about you was . . . *interesting*."

His hand tightened around my wrist, sending pain flaring up my arm.

"The thing is, *Fia Ní Mainnín*, everyone says you're not actually a cousin of the queen. They say you're a little witch. A cailleach, if you can believe it." His voice took on an unpleasant note. "Now, I've lain with a witch or two before, so I couldn't care less about that. But they also say your power comes from the Folk. They say you're a *changeling*."

Shite.

"Changeling?" I forced a laugh, which came out reedy. "The wine must have addled your wits, my lord. I'm the queen's *foster*ling."

"I know what I heard." His expression was implacable. "You're unnatural. Look at you—your hair is dark as deep water. Your mismatched eyes are strange enough to give a man nightmares. You're small enough to snap like a twig in the forest. I'd wager money on it—you're a filthy changeling, like they said. Where did the high queen find you? How does she keep you? And what must I do to take you from her?"

I froze at the menace—the *hunger*—in Connla's voice. His grip on me tightened painfully. My options were narrowing by the moment. My veins itched with brambles, and I fantasized—brilliantly, achingly—of wrapping my fingers around his throat and choking him with thorns. Filling his mouth with sharp leaves, blanking his eyes with wet berries until I returned him to the land as a creeping, stinging blackberry bush.

It would be so easy.

But mother would eat my liver for breakfast if I Greenmarked one of her under-kings' heirs without her say-so. With more willpower than I knew I possessed, I calmed myself.

Still, his words crept into my mind on serrated little feet.

You're small enough to snap like a twig in the forest.

The words rankled me, although they were half-true—I *was* small. I'd always been small. When Mother first sent me to her weapons masters to learn to ride and shoot and wrestle and fence, I was nine, and small even for my age. I couldn't draw the longbows favored by Mother's fianna; I couldn't reach the backs of their fine tall stallions; I couldn't even begin to lift the broad, straight claimhte carried by proud fénnidi into battle. So I fashioned my own bows out of young saplings I found in the wood, and I taught myself to ride bareback on fleet marsh ponies too small for grown adults and to fight fast and dirty with a dagger in both hands. Even now, at twenty, I was small—shorter than most and lean from strict exercise and rigorous sparring.

But size wasn't everything. The height of a bow was worth less than the aim of the archer. The stride of a horse was worth less than its will to run. The length of a sword was worth less than the edge on its blade.

I was small. I was a changeling, although I'd be damned if I admitted it to this fatted prince. But I was fast and fierce and unrelentingly trained.

Screw the revealing dress and the subterfuge. I was going to have to do this my way.

Without warning, I jabbed my free hand inward, catching Connla's bicep above his elbow. He grunted as the muscle spasmed. His grip on my wrist relaxed—I wrenched my hand free and sucker punched him in the face. He reeled away, dumping me out of his lap. Blood dripped down his chin, staining the expensive rug under his feet.

"You bitch," he gasped wetly.

"Bitch, witch." I shrugged. "Just don't ever call me changeling again."

I climbed him like a ladder before he could so much as make a fist. Wrapping both arms around his head, I swung my legs around his neck—the fabric of my dress audibly ripping—and threw myself backward. My weight jerked Connla forward, cartwheeling him head over arse. He landed hard on his back, the wind visibly gusting out of his chest.

I landed neatly on my feet. I crouched over him where he flailed like a gutted fish, planting my elbows on my knees and staring into his blood-drenched face.

"Tell me where the darrig is," I demanded.

It took him a long time to draw enough breath to say, "*No.*"

"Fine," I told him. "I'll find the wretched creature myself."

I slammed his skull against the edge of the fire pit. His eyes rolled and his head lolled sideways.

The tent was large, but it wasn't endless. There were only so many places you could hide one of the Fair Folk, especially if you were keeping it captive. Somewhere out of the moonlight, which lent them power. Within a cage made of iron, which sapped their strength. I skipped the bed—mounded with soft furs, its purpose was revoltingly clear—and turned to Connla's war trunk.

Locked, of course. I could pick it, but that would take precious minutes I didn't have. Connla wouldn't be out for long.

I laid my hand against the mechanism, then hesitated.

Little witch.

When I was ten, I'd found an injured hedgehog at the edge of the forest. I snuck it into my chambers, hiding it beneath my bed. I'd come to adore it, nursing it back to health and naming it Pinecone. But I'd let it get too close to me. One day, I'd fallen asleep with it tucked against my chest, beneath my shirt. When I woke, my magic had taken Pinecone from me—all that remained were clods of dirt and flecks of blood held together by pine needles and wood sap.

Some people—Mother in particular—saw my magic as a gift. I knew it to be a curse. It never gave, only *took*.

Blood throbbed against my palm, dark with shadow and hot with wine. I hesitated a second longer, then closed my eyes. I imagined thick brambles studded with dark fruit and capped with sharp thorns. When I opened my eyes, tough briars had snaked into the mechanism.

The metal groaned, bent. Snapped. I threw the trunk open.

At first, it looked like Connla's trunk was full of jumbled sticks. But I blinked, and it was the darrig—a hunched and broken creature, with a body like a stump and limbs like gnarled branches and eyes like glossy pebbles. The iron cage Connla kept it in was too small—the darrig's legs didn't have room to bend without touching the metal, and ugly welts vied for space with bruises on its tree-bark skin. The sickening stench of burnt wood and rotting mulch wafted out of the trunk.

"Help," the darrig croaked.

Sympathy pulsed through me, warring with my purpose for being here. The darrig might be a wicked, deceitful creature from Tír na nÓg. But not even fiends deserved the treatment Connla had given it. Stuffed into a tiny cage, starved and beaten.

I steeled my emotions. The Gate War had been fought with battle metal and mortal blood, nightmares and stolen fears. It had claimed countless lives. The war might technically be over—the Gates closed and buried, Mother's vast fianna disbanded—but it had never *ended*. It was now simply fought on different fields.

I turned away from the creature, casting about for where I'd left my cloak. I needed something to wrap around the cage, to—

Fingers brittle as twigs wrapped tight around my wrist. I whipped around. The darrig had squeezed its wizened arm through the bars of its cage, ignoring the metal searing its flesh. It was surprisingly strong—although I shook my wrist in disgust, it held on to me with grim determination.

"Help." An inexplicable glimmer of hope touched its depthless eyes. "Mend the broken heart. End the sorrow. Give what life is left, so we may see the morrow."

"What are you talking about?" I twisted my arm, but the thing wouldn't let me go. "Are you asking me to put you out of your misery?"

There was a thud behind me, drowning out whatever response the creature would have made. A hand wrapped around one of the braids coiled at my crown, brutally yanking my head back. Through watering eyes, I saw Connla looming behind me. His arm snaked around my throat and squeezed, sending pain spiking from my neck to my skull.

"Dishonorable bastard," I croaked. I had severely underestimated his recovery time.

"Treacherous changeling," he growled.

My vision blurred.

Wrapping my hands around his elbow joint, I pivoted, swinging sharply away and breaking his hold. I slid one hand to his wrist, still gripping his elbow in the other, and cranked his arm sharply. He cried out, leaning back to avoid my breaking his arm. One swift kick to his leg sent him to his knees. Another returned him to the floor.

This time, I was angry. I flung myself down on top of him, clamping my legs around his arms and torso. One of my hands found the hilt of my razor-sharp skean; the other, jammed into the soft space where Connla's throat throbbed, began to change. My veins went green. The tracery of serrated leaves was lace on my skin. And little thorns—sharp as a blackberry bramble—prickled my palm and fingertips. A trickle of blood dripped down Connla's neck, and his throat worked, fear muddling his gaze. Some corner of my mind screamed at me to release him, to shake out the fury bruising my blood.

But it was too late. I hadn't wanted to kill him before.

I did now.

Black and red and tumultuous green flared behind my eyes. I lowered my knife toward his throat.

Hands clamped down on my shoulders.

I cursed—yet again, I'd forgotten to watch my back.

Chapter Two

My attacker was strong—they lifted me like a rag doll off Connla's supine figure. I kicked back and struck flesh, earning a male grunt for my efforts. I took quick advantage, seizing the wrist of the hand gripping my shoulder. Twisting under the man's arm, I grabbed a fistful of his thick cloak and sliced my skean toward his throat.

He blocked my blow with a gauntlet, sending a shock of impact blazing up my arm. His hand folded over mine where it gripped his mantle. He leaned forward.

"The joy is in the thrill of the fight," he murmured, too low for Connla to hear. A trace of inexplicable amusement varnished his low tenor. "Not the promise of a kill."

I froze. The voice might not be familiar, but the words were. They conjured a morning swathed in mist—the training yard at dawn. The clack of wooden training swords. Cold sweat puddling along my collarbone and my breath like a knife in the throat. I'd been thirteen and livid with righteous indignation—my sparring opponent, a trainee in one of Mother's fianna, had beaten me a dozen times in a row. But he'd won badly each time—whacking me over the wrist so my numb hand dropped my claíomh; jabbing my throat with his fingers so I doubled over coughing; pulling my hair until my neck ached. Each time, I'd looked to the rígfénnid for support, but he was never watching when my opponent cheated. Anger had spiked hemlock through my veins. Finally, I'd snapped—I'd thrown myself at the young man, play-sword forgotten, throttling him and pummeling him and kicking him. I'd wanted to kill him, and nothing had ever felt so good.

But *he* had been there to pull me off—Rogan Mòr, prince of Bridei, one of Mother's noble fosterlings. My best friend, two years older than I was. My only confidant.

That day, he'd gripped me tight until my rage had faded, and he'd whispered those words in my ear, as he would many times after: *The joy is in the thrill of the fight, not the promise of a kill.*

But Rogan had been gone for *years.*

The last time I saw him, he'd been a gangly youth. Now he had the face of a man—hard jaw, soft lips, bold brows. But the boy I knew was still there—in the waving golden hair kissing his brow, in the laughing set of his mouth, in eyes the same shade as the ocean below the hill at Bré.

I unwound my hands from his mantle. Not because I didn't want to touch him, but because I did. I had to remind myself—it was *he* who had left four years ago.

He is not meant for you.

"Princeling?" I ground out through clenched teeth. "What in the Morrigan's name are you doing here?"

"Saving your hopeless arse." Despite my tone, he smiled—warm wind and spring green. "Or more accurately, *his.*"

Connla had taken advantage of our distraction to scoot backward across the floor, clamber over his mound of seduction furs, slam the top down on the darrig's chest, and rip open the door to his tent.

"Guards!" he hollered into the night. "*Guards!*"

The response was immediate—shouts rang out across camp, along with the clatter of metal and the keening bay of hunting dogs.

"*Shite.*" I lunged for my discarded cloak, glancing regretfully at where the darrig was hidden. Maybe there was still time—

But a long, sharp claíomh had found its way into Connla's hand. Blood still dripped from his nose—the triumphant grin he gave me was red and gruesome as he blocked the doorway.

Swiftly, I glanced around Connla's lordly tent. The canvas was thick and new—there was no way I'd be able to slice through it with my slender skeans. No claíomh hung from Rogan's hip.

And I had a feeling Connla would rather kill me than let me get past him.

Which left only one option.

I laid my hand against the fabric of the tent wall and closed my eyes. The fibers were fine woven and dense. Lifeless. I pushed through the haze of purple wine and sharp thorns still clouding my mind, seeking the spark, the life, the *growth*. Finally—a glimmer of green. A flash of pale sunlight between high rows of plantings. Comb-toothed leaves swaying in a damp breeze. Mud and rot and earthworms pushing between roots.

The hemp had nearly forgotten what it was to grow, to *live*. It had been plucked and retted and combed and spun and woven. It had grown accustomed to being inert, being dead, being *cloth*.

But nothing could forget what it truly was. Even those things that might wish to.

I latched onto the hemp, anchoring it to my own moss-stained blood. The fine-woven fibers burst to life. Green rippled along the canvas. It split apart, broad leaves waving us through. I dashed out into the chilly evening, Rogan close on my heels, then closed the gap behind us. Regret slid through me as the hemp reluctantly became cloth once more.

I let my hand drop, then glanced at Rogan. A trace of unease touched his face before smoothing away.

"Now what?" he asked.

I set my jaw and glanced up. Perched on the neighboring tent were a few curious starlings, their glitter-black plumage nearly invisible against the night sky. I signaled to them, and they dispersed with a trill.

Tonight was not yet lost. I might not have retrieved the darrig myself, but I wasn't the queen's only spy. After the offenses I'd done him, Connla would feel honor bound to pursue me if I ran. And with his fiann on my tail, his tent would be unguarded.

Cathair's witch-birds would pass along my message.

"Now? I'll lead them in a merry chase." I smirked at Rogan, giving in to the pulse of new life shading my blood green and gold. "See if you can keep up, princeling."

❧ ～❧

The fields below Rath na Mara were dominated by the vast hunching tents of the four under-kings of Fódla, their households, and their retinues. But theirs were not the only encampments. Despite plague in the south and famine in the north, many had made the trip to the capital for the funeral games—merchants, beggars, bards. Hopeful farm boys with their granddad's rusted swords. Tents and lean-tos and caravans dotted the plain, with a cobweb of makeshift roads and pathways churning to muck between them.

It made for bad, slow going. And with every step we took, Connla's men and dogs circled closer.

"It's too far," I gasped out. My bravado was beginning to leak away as we crouched down behind a makeshift privy reeking of shite. The high wooden palisade ringing Rath na Mara was barely a quarter mile away, but the improvised city hemming us in was like a maze. "What if you led them off? Connla's looking for me, not you."

I turned to Rogan. It was hard for me to look at him without staring—I reveled in the familiarity of him, even as I ogled at the changes. And there were a lot of changes. He'd filled out, for one— his arms, bare beneath his cloak, rippled with thick muscle, and the cut of his shoulders was far broader than I remembered.

"Me?" He huffed a laugh. "Fannon hates Bridei. If they catch me lurking in their camp, they'll cut an eye out, then tell my king father it was an unfortunate accident."

"Good point." I looked at the eyes in question, which even in darkness shone a deep blue-green. "Although you only really need one of your eyes."

"I would look dashing in an eye patch."

A dog barked, too close for comfort. Some decision sparked on Rogan's face, and he began slinking away.

In the wrong direction.

"Where are you going?" I hissed at his receding back.

He paused. "Have I ever led you astray?"

"Frequently."

"Maybe I've changed."

I opened my mouth to retort, but smoking torches flamed in my periphery and for a moment I felt the bite of phantom teeth. Following the prince who had broken my heart deeper into the camp of a man who wanted to kill me wasn't my favorite idea. But I was running out of other options.

I crept after Rogan.

After what felt like miles—Connla's men gaining ground with every step—the tents and lean-tos thinned out. The light of a bonfire rose up. A scattering of derelict outbuildings appeared—a crofter's hut, long abandoned, and what looked like an old barn. Torchlight glittered from dilapidated windows ringing with loud laughter and song. Men and women stumbled drunkenly around the fire. Tapped barrels were stacked beneath the eave of the hut.

A makeshift tavern? "I don't think—"

"Trust me." Rogan held out his hand. I hesitated, then gripped his palm, even as I cursed myself for a fool.

He pulled me toward the hut, pushing through the crowd. A narrow alley cut between the hut and the barn—barely any light filtered through. He pushed me in first, then glanced back the way we'd come.

Connla's fiann had cleared the last few tents and marched on the bonfire. Metal glinted red in the firelight. Huge dogs strained at collars. The rígfénnid stopped one of the drunks by the fire, who shook his head. The rígfénnid waved his men toward the ring of barrels. I swallowed fear and tugged Rogan's hand, wanting to move deeper into the alley. He shook his head.

"Dead end," he whispered.

My heart thundered in my chest. "Then why—"

Over his shoulder, one of the men by the barrels pointed in our direction.

Rogan spun toward me. He slid both hands around my waist and lifted me like I weighed nothing. My back struck rough stone as Rogan pinned me with his bulk. I inhaled sharply, gripping his shoulders for balance. His muscles flexed beneath my palms as one of his hands slid along my bare leg, lifting it up around his hip. The leather armor covering his torso slid hard against the inside of my thighs. Warmth sparked in my core and sizzled through my veins, tangling with my rising panic.

"What are you doing?" I breathed.

His other hand rose to my face, tugging the hood of my cloak further over my forehead. His fingers splayed against the side of my cheek. He bent his face toward my neck. "You can thank me later."

Rogan's lips brushed my throat, sending delicate vines of heat to climb my face. His breath was ragged. My own breath rose to the same cadence as nerves and adrenaline and his overwhelming closeness sent my pulse ratcheting. I dug my fingertips deeper into his mantle, praying to any gods who might be listening that this wasn't the stupidest plan my handsome, idiotic prince had ever devised. But it was hard to focus on impending doom with his kiss teasing my neck, his large hands circling my waist, his belt buckle pressing into my lower belly. I shifted my weight, hooking a leg into the small of his back to brace myself. He exhaled roughly, sliding his hands lower to cup my rear. His eyes dragged up, collided with mine. His lips were mere inches away, and I—

The thud of boots made every muscle in my body tauten. The scrabble of claws on stone scratched my ears. The *shink* of metal being drawn pulled ice down my spine.

There was a rough male chuckle from five paces. A mocking whistle.

Without pulling his mouth from my throat, Rogan lifted two fingers and flipped off the guards.

Who laughed. Yanked at their dogs. And miraculously moved on.

I closed my eyes and followed them with my ears—boots tromping back toward the bonfire, armored men shoving into the crowded crofter's hut. Shouts of annoyance. Muffled conversation. And then—at last—nothing but the nonthreatening sounds of laughter and singing and someone puking up ale in the gorse.

It felt like a long time before Rogan released me—and yet not long enough. We were both panting, and I was trembling—the aftereffects of fear and adrenaline and desire skating hot along my bones. Rogan stepped away from me, but one of his hands lingered at my waist. The buckles on his armor had shredded the silken dress, and his palm was warm through the tattered fabric.

"You're insane," I ground out.

His shrug was carefree, but relief pooled in his eyes. "Better than dead."

"Debatable." Connla's fiann was nowhere in sight, but it wouldn't be gone long. "We need to get back to the fort before they double back."

"Lead the way."

The high palisade surrounding Rath na Mara was studded with fortified gates. The night watchmen waved me through without question—they were sworn to Mother and accustomed to my odd hours. They studied Rogan more closely but allowed him to follow me across the courtyard into the main hall. We stumbled inside the arching doors, our panting breaths loud in the echoing, silent room.

"What are you *doing* here?" I choked out. It was late—although Mother had feasted with her under-kings earlier, all that was left of the revel were carcasses on platters, empty flagons of mead, stinking rushes beneath our feet, and a few drunks snoring in the corners. "And what in the Morrigan's name were you doing in Connla's tent?"

Rogan shook out his golden hair and unfastened his bold-checked cloak. The candlelight caught on the brooch at his shoulder—a cracked gemstone polished to a sheen that perfectly matched his eyes.

No—not gemstone. *River stone.*

My breath caught. I'd been about eleven the day we'd found it. Rogan and I had gotten separated from a boar-hunting party. Not particularly disappointed, we'd spent the warm afternoon chasing rabbits through the forest and splashing in the wide brook winding between the trees. I'd been the one to find the glittering blue-green stone—as large as my fist, with a narrow crack through its center. But it was Rogan who'd fallen in love with it. He'd held it up to sparkle in the light and claimed it was an enchanted emerald from far-flung lands. I'd laughed at him, saying we were too old for such fanciful stories. But when the sun rode low and Rogan tried to hand the pretty stone back to me, I'd told him to keep it.

"Perhaps someday you'll use that enchanted emerald to break a Folk curse," I'd told him, teasing. "Besides, it matches your eyes."

But the truth was, I'd never been able to refuse Rogan Mòr anything he wanted.

And all these years later, he still wore my gift like a talisman.

I gripped my wrist beneath my mantle, driving the bracelet of nettles and thorns deeper into the tender skin.

He is not meant for you.

"I arrived at Rath na Mara earlier tonight," Rogan was saying. "I was supposed to present my father's tributes to the queen at the feast. But then I saw you—or who I *thought* was you—leave through the gates. I tried to catch you, but you were long gone. And honestly, I got kind of lost. I wound up at that tavern where we—"

He trailed off. His eyes darkened, and I didn't think it had anything to do with the tapers dying on the table. A traitorous dart of heat tangled with wariness in my belly.

I kept reminding myself *he* left *me*, four years ago. His choice. No one had made him go.

"Anyway. I was thirsty. While I was there, I heard some of Connla's cronies gossiping—about a witch, a *changeling*, some dastardly plot afoot. I thought you might need saving."

"I didn't."

"I know that now." He grinned. "I'm pretty sure it's that hog Connla who owes me his life."

Silence settled between us.

"Amergin's knees, Fia!" he finally said, whistling low. "You've changed. How long has it been?"

I knew exactly how long it had been, down to the hour, minute, and second, although I wasn't going to tell him that. The memory of the day Rogan left haunted me. A cool blue morning at the end of summer. The courtyard of Rath na Mara ringing with the hooves of his soot-black stallion, a gift from Mother on his eighteenth birthday. Cairell Mòr's fiann, come to escort their prince home. And Mother's hand on the back of my neck, fingernails grazing my skin just enough to remind me she'd been right all along.

Princes were nothing but trouble. And no one—especially not Rogan—could ever love me more than she did.

"Four years, more or less," I answered carelessly. "What are you doing back in Rath na Mara? Mother will be displeased when she hears you've returned without her permission."

"Displeased? Don't you mean she'll have my skull as a paperweight?" He grinned. "I'm not so stupid, changeling. She's the one who summoned me."

Traitorous hope bloomed inside me. "Why?"

"Why else?" His eyes softened with dreams unfolding—dreams

I knew him well enough to recognize. Dreams that had never included me. "The queen and her druid have solved it at last. They've found a way to save the princess and bring her home."

The unspoken end to the sentence hung in the air between us.

Bring her home...to marry me.

Rogan Mòr had been betrothed to Eala Ní Mainnín since the day she was born. And although I had been raised by Eala's mother and wore Eala's face, I was not Eala. Would never be Eala. Not in any of the ways that counted.

I was made of rocks and bones and stinging things. I was not destined to wed princes. Admire them. Lust after them. Maybe even bed them.

But never wed them.

"It's late." He yawned. "I'm to bed. Coming?"

I swallowed, trying not to think of him in his bed. "As tempting as that sounds, I think I'd rather snuggle up with the drunk in the corner."

Rogan forced a chuckle. "I meant *your* bed, you wanton woman. But don't let me dissuade you from your choice of a vomitous bedfellow."

I watched his back recede through the smoky feasting hall. Memories twisted in my head like a thicket of briars—Rogan Mòr's hands on my hips, my legs around his waist, his lips on my throat. How he always called me *changeling*, in a way that made me feel like I might be something precious, something *wanted*, instead of a fell creature of the forest, with a stolen face and a borrowed mother and an unrequited love.

Because precious or not, *changeling* was what—and *who*—I was.

Of the twelve daughters stolen by the Folk, only Eala had been replaced by a living changeling. The first girl had been replaced by a bundle of twigs held together by a baby's swaddling cloth—a silent manikin who withered away to rotten wood. Another disappeared into a meadow of flowers, replaced by a swarm of angry bees. One mother put her child to her breast only to find a ravenous piglet suckling in its stead.

But in Eala's place had been left a little girl. A girl who looked just like the princess, but with night-dark hair and strange, mismatched eyes.

Me.

I'd woken one morning in a plush feather bed with green magic at my fingertips, the dark forest in my heart, and no memory of where I'd come from. I'd been as confused as the princess's nursemaid, who'd taken one look at me and screamed loud enough to wake the whole castle.

For months, Mother expected me to burst into a cloud of butterflies or rot into piles of mushrooms. But I stayed, although no one could say why.

I was not born of these human realms. I was not human.

But neither was I one of *them*. Iron did not scald me; rowanberries did not blind me. I aged and sickened like a human. I could not survive on moonbeams and flower pollen—I needed bread and meat to nourish me.

Too much of each, yet not enough of one to be accepted by either.

Whatever—whoever—I was, I belonged here now. If the Folk had ever had a claim to me, they had renounced it when they gave me up, *abandoned* me in exchange for Eala Ní Mainnín. They had stolen a princess and left *me*. She was valuable—I was something they bartered away without care and without my consent. I hated them for it—hated them almost as much as I adored the queen who gave me a home, raised me with a purpose, loved me as she would her own daughter. Despite the mockery of my appearance, a constant reminder that the same vengeful Fair Folk who left me had killed her husband and stolen her only child.

She could have easily executed me. And not even I could have blamed her if she had.

I sighed and squared my shoulders. I would do anything for Mother. Including helping the man I loved find the woman he was promised to marry.

Chapter Three

The high queen's summons came early the next morning. Too early. My head pounded from wine, adrenaline, and too little sleep. My limbs ached from using my Greenmark—as though I had knotted branches for bones and tough vines for muscles.

But one did not ignore an invitation from the queen. So I braided back my tangled hair and chugged a cup of water to sweep away the tastes warring in my throat—muck, disgust, desire, resentment.

Rogan was waiting at the door to Mother's audience chambers. He didn't say anything, only flashed me a private smile.

My head throbbed like a swollen river. I didn't smile back. Instead, I shoved the door open.

I should have knocked.

Mother's throne room was austere. No bronze cups or carven shields or glittering weapons adorned the walls—only a handful of simple tapestries depicting the patron gods of Fódla's four kingdoms. The Morrigan, goddess of sovereignty and war, surrounded by her prophetic ravens. Donn, god of the dead, framed by the black gates of his realm. Brighid, goddess of husbandry and healing, flanked by her prized cattle. Amergin, god of poetry and law—and founder of Fódla and its peoples—standing proud with his harp and his staff.

But there was nothing here to flaunt Mother's wealth, power, or reputation as a brutal war queen. I happened to know she disdained such ostentation. She considered golden embellishments, elaborate hairstyles, and extravagant surroundings vulgar—even dangerous. Such things echoed the insidious glamours of the Fair Folk, hiding the truth behind glittering masks. No—she kept all her treasures locked away in a narrow antechamber off the main reception room. A room known only to a few close allies.

A room whose door was thrown wide open, revealing shelves choked with strange objects and misshapen artifacts. Shards of fallen stars. Vials of onyx sand and argent blood and ruby heartbreak. Blades swirled with shattered glass and hammered nightmares. Relics, all of them—relics from Mother's violent forays into Tír na nÓg during the Gate War. Relics she kept and studied with hateful, careful, obsessive scrutiny, trying to understand an enemy who was unknowable.

But it wasn't any of those objects that caught my attention now. It was the spindly gnome strung up from the ceiling, shackled in iron and garlanded with rowan, flanked by Mother and Cathair.

The darrig.

Its arms were like broken branches; its legs, unearthed roots. Green and brown liquid spattered its torso and the floor below it. Its depthless eyes stared at me as they had last night, but now they were blank and flat.

Lifeless.

My stomach bottomed out with regret, chasing away any satisfaction I might have felt at its successful capture. I ran a finger over my bracelet of thorns and nettles, spiking fire against the angry skin beneath it.

What had the darrig said to me? Something about a broken heart. About ending its sorrow. It had asked me for help. And I— I'd done nothing. Not even to put it out of its misery.

I willed my spine straight as hardwood. The creature was beyond anyone's help now. And maybe that was for the best.

Beside me, Rogan coughed. Mother's head snapped up. An iron spike disappeared behind her skirts. She said something to Cathair, who kicked the door shut. A few moments later, they both emerged with clean hands and calm faces. The queen climbed the dais to her throne, Cathair a few steps behind. I swallowed the revulsion still crawling its way up my throat and looked up at Mother.

Eithne Uí Mainnín was—in the way of old stories and tall, twisted tales—a *queen*.

She looked down at Rogan and me, her beauty a kind of spell. Although she dressed in a simple blue kirtle, wore no jewelry but a plain golden torc around her neck, and sat upon a wooden chair in an unadorned room, she was radiant. The streaks of gray in her long blond hair gleamed like strands of silver amid gold. Her pale blue eyes glittered like diamonds. The set of her mouth hinted at a jeweled tongue.

Mother was never intended to rule. Although she was beautiful and shrewd and the blood of kings coursed through her veins, she was merely banfhlaith. A princess. Her fate was to marry, for the dowries of princesses have always been the alliances of kingdoms. Her bride-price—when she wed Rían Ó Mainnín, the last high king—was peace and unity in Fódla.

But her destiny was always war.

"Rogan Mòr," Mother said with a hint of a smile. She waited for him to bow to her before rising and embracing him. "You have grown tall and broad as an oak! How is your father?"

"Grumpy as a goat in his dotage." Rogan laughed. "And his temper is not improved by my brothers surrounding him like stray dogs begging for scraps."

"So he has not yet named an heir?" Mother already knew the answer to this—she kept abreast of the affairs of all her under-kings.

"No." Although his smile didn't fade, I remembered Rogan's

face well enough to notice the way his eyes tightened. "And he will keep us all guessing until his sickbed becomes his deathbed, my lady."

"I don't doubt it." Small talk finished, Mother nodded to me. "You did well last night, a stór."

My treasure. The pet name she used only for me. Hearing it loosened my tension, and I gave a small bow. "I am only sorry I could not retrieve the darrig myself."

"You followed procedure, little witch." Ollamh Cathair glided like a shadow from behind his queen. "We must take our successes where we find them. We cannot all be heroes."

I glowered at the druid but bit my tongue. Cathair did not share his queen's disdain for ostentation. His fingers dripped gems, and his mantle was edged in gold thread. His hair and beard were braided with little bronze trinkets that clinked when he talked. Some considered his features handsome for a man of his age. But he had said and done too many ugly things for me to see any beauty in him.

I dragged my thumb over my jagged bracelet.

Cathair's canny eyes did not miss the action.

Pain is useful. But only if you're the one choosing to inflict it. That was what he told me a few months after Rogan had left. He'd seen the way my eyes welled with tears every time Rogan's name was mentioned. So he'd shown me how to turn that despair into strength.

Oh, yes. Cathair had made me very strong.

"Tell them what you've seen, Cathair," Mother was saying. "And how it pertains to what we discovered from the darrig."

"For many years, the Book of Whispers only showed me what I had already seen," Cathair said with a flourish of his hands. "The Gates between the human world and Tír na nÓg, twelve in all. Opened in a time of war, then closed in surrender."

Like Mother, Cathair possessed many arcane objects. The Book of Whispers was the most powerful. Found buried beneath a fairy hill, papered with birch bark and bound with human hair, the tome was written in the language of dreams and spoke to the druid only as he slept.

After the Fair Folk murdered the high king, Cathair had tried to solve his grieving queen's first and greatest problem: how to wage war upon the Folk when they lived in Tír na nÓg, a place beyond mortal knowing. How could she march upon castles in the clouds? How could she ambush starlight? How could she slay armies of wildflowers?

It took five years for Cathair to discover how to open the Gates to Tír na nÓg. Beneath the light of a full moon, an incantation must be spoken in the tongue of the ancients. A knife of pure iron bound to ash wood must be forged. And blood must be spilled upon the thirsty earth from the still-beating heart of one of the Folk.

One by one, the twelve Gates to Tír na nÓg had been opened this way. Many died in the ensuing war, and many met fates worse than death. It was only after Eala was stolen that the queen refused to carry on with the war—she thought if she ended it, the Folk might take pity and give her daughter back. She dispersed her fianna and ordered the twelve Gates closed and buried beneath great mounds of earth. She swallowed her defeat like the cup of poison she knew it was. She waited for her daughter to be returned to her.

But none of the stolen girls returned. Only I remained.

"A fortnight ago," Cathair continued, "I had a new vision as I slept. There is a Thirteenth Gate to Tír na nÓg, one that has never been opened. Beyond its threshold, I saw a lough of darkness. And upon that lough were twelve white swans. And in the fort above the lough lived a shadowy tánaiste—an heir among the Folk. One of the Gentry."

Disgust burned through me, and I clenched itching fingers tighter around my wrist. In the past few years of acting as Mother's spy, I'd encountered a fair number of the Folk. But never the Gentry, the dreaded aristocracy of the Folk.

Where the Folk were fickle, the Gentry were treacherous. Where the Folk were dangerous, the Gentry were murderous. They were hollow-hearted predators, worse than their smaller brethren by far.

Cathair paused significantly, not because the story was finished, but because it wasn't. But Rogan didn't know Cathair as well as I did.

"So there's a Gate we didn't know about," he said. "But swans? I don't understand."

Though Cathair looked annoyed at the interruption, he answered the question. "The swans are not truly swans—a powerful geas has been laid upon them."

This only bemused Rogan further. "A geas?"

I knew the word. It meant something like *binding* or *obligation*. In the Folk's uncanny stories of broken promises, stolen lovers, and backstabbing treachery, it was a common theme.

"You've heard of geasa," I said to him. "Our great warrior Cuchulainn was said to have been placed under two. One geas forbade him from ever eating dog flesh. The other forbade him from refusing hospitality. When a host offered him the meat from a hound, he was forced to break one of the two geasa upon him. His strength was shattered, his love was lost, and soon after he died in battle."

Rogan nodded, although he still looked confused.

"The little witch speaks true," said Cathair. "This geas fades at night, when the moon sails high above the lough. Then, and only then, do the swans return to their true forms, as twelve human girls. And around the throat of the twelfth and loveliest girl is a golden torc—the weight of royalty carried in precious metal. She is banfhlaith—a princess."

"Eala." Rogan looked stunned.

"Yes." Mother's sudden smile brimmed with gladness, and the rare unguarded expression knocked me off-balance.

Mother had long suspected her true daughter was alive. For years she'd believed the Folk mocked her with insolent signs. Cornflowers—Eala's favorite—growing like weeds in the kitchen gardens. Skylarks singing in the pink of morning, as they had the day the princess was born. A child's giggle echoing through the castle in the dead of the night. But it occurred to me now that part of her had not believed she would ever see her daughter again.

Rogan shook off his dazed expression.

"If this is true, then she's been suffering at the hands of our enemy for twelve years. We must do everything in our power to rescue her." His quiet conviction sent a sharp splinter to pierce my heart.

"That's very noble, boy, but she is trapped," said Cathair impatiently. "Imprisoned in both body and soul, within deceptive Folk magic. The task will not be easy, and the price of her freedom may be high."

"There is no cost too high, nor risk too great." Determination hardened on Rogan's face.

The tableau was like something out of a story: a proud, tragic queen; a druid foretelling doom; a golden prince promising heroics. But stories were by nature false—designed to fool the eye and twist the mind, to make us believe in things that couldn't ever be true. Stories gave us hope, and I hated them almost as much as I hated my stolen face, my uncertain origins, and my wild and wicked magic.

Real life wasn't like the stories. Real life ended in deception, betrayal, or tragedy. Which meant this pretty tale was either untrue or incomplete.

"So we're to use this Thirteenth Gate to rescue Eala?" I cut in.

Mother nodded. "The Folk have no reason to suspect we know of it. When the veil between the human realm and Tír na nÓg is stretched thin—during a full moon—it can be breached."

I cocked my head. "But to pass through, don't you also need the still-beating heart of— *Oh.*"

The answer crashed over me like a winter sea, cold and inevitable. So *this* was why I'd been called here to stand beside Rogan and plot the princess's grand rescue—because my blood ran green and black as the dark parts of the forest. Not because I'd been raised by Mother and she wished me to be the first to welcome home her true daughter. Not because of my childhood rapport with Rogan. Not even because I'd been unflinchingly trained as a queen's warrior and spy.

They didn't need me. They needed my death.

I forced the painful blossom of my resentment to die on the vine, where a thousand small bitternesses hung like corpse flowers. I'd never belonged in this world. Maybe leaving it would be easier than staying in it. If this was what Mother required of me, I would do it. She'd given me so much over the years—not least, her love. I wouldn't deny her something as little as my life in return.

Rogan was studying my face, and I saw the instant he understood. I loved him for the way he squared his shoulders and set his mouth, willing to defy a queen on my behalf.

"No," he said firmly. "There must be another way."

"Calm yourself, Mòr," Mother said with a touch of amusement. "We are not the Folk. Do you really think I would sacrifice one daughter for another?"

Relief dragged me up from the cold, choking sea of my compliance—relief so profound it forced a sigh from my throat. Mother glanced at me, her brows drawing together as she realized I had leapt to the same conclusion as Rogan. Hurt pooled in her pale eyes, her injured stare wordlessly chiding me for ever believing she would demand such a thing of me.

How could I sacrifice you? it seemed to say. *I have only ever loved you, when no one else could. How could you think so little of me?*

Contrition and shame bowed my head. I blamed that damned blackberry wine—it must still be lingering in my veins. Only alcohol and wild fruit could grow such sharp, dark thoughts inside me.

"Then how?" Rogan asked.

"The darrig was helpful in that regard," Mother said. "The Gates are all linked by the same powerful Folk magic—a magic that has been damaged. The integrity of the Gates has weakened, the Thirteenth Gate included."

"The queen speaks true." Cathair narrowed his hazel eyes at
me and smiled. "The boundary is beginning to come apart at the
seams. Something might find a way to *slither* through the cracks."

I bared my teeth at him. "I suppose a snake would know."

His smile only widened.

"Folk heart-blood and a full moon are still required to pass
through," Mother explained, glancing again at me. "But it need
not be more than a few drops. That should be enough to prick a
hole big enough for you—*both* of you—to cross over into Tír na
nÓg. Once there, you will find the dún on the hill, above the lough
of shadow. You will find the swan girls—you will find my daughter. And you will bring her back home where she belongs."

It seemed very neat. But when it came to the Folk, things were
rarely as simple as they seemed.

"Why now?"

"The Book of Whispers speaks to me whenever the balance
between our worlds shifts." Cathair said this with the air of a
prophecy. "These past few years, we suspected the Gates were
weakening, but had no way to pass through them without exposing
ourselves."

"I grieved, thinking we had missed our chance to strike against
the Folk and rescue Eala," Mother said. "The discovery of the hidden Gate changes things."

"We will not fail you, my queen," Rogan interjected solemnly.

"Good." Mother didn't wait for my response. She simply
passed a rolled map to Rogan. "In Bridei, beyond the town of Finn
Coradh, you will find a half-ruined fort—Dún Darragh, it is called.
It is close to the Thirteenth Gate. It will not be luxurious, but it will
keep the rain and wind off your backs."

"I know of it," Rogan said with an odd expression.

"And how are we to find the Gate from there?" I asked.

"I have seen it," Cathair said portentously. "In the forest beyond
the lough, in a place called Roslea, where monsters lurk in shadows
and the trees have silver boughs."

Unhelpful, dramatic nonsense. I tried a different tack.

"How will I know if I've opened it? How will I know if we've passed through into Tír na nÓg?"

Mother's eyes were heavy on mine. She had told me about the strange land the Folk called home, when she was drunk enough to lose herself to the memories. She described birds who sang with the voices of the long dead. Multicolored seas of hope and honey. Palaces thatched with leaves of glass. She told me how those who returned from the battles came back different—their tongues no longer possessed the power of speech, or their eyes saw only in darkness, instead of light. Wounds bled vines instead of blood, until flesh became bark, branches sprouting where limbs once grew...

"You'll know, a stór," she said with flat finality. "You'll know."

She looked away so suddenly I flinched. Then she made a dismissive gesture, and I knew the conversation was finished. Rogan tossed his mantle over one shoulder and strode toward the door. I moved to follow him, but Mother's voice stopped me.

"A moment, Fia."

I stopped. Mother waited until Rogan passed out of her chambers before turning to me.

"Rogan will retrieve my daughter." The queen's face was silk but her voice was iron. "Eala may be bewitched as well as enchanted, snarled in Folk magic. But Rogan is handsome and tall and good—he will be able to break the spell and beguile her back to where she belongs."

I agreed wholeheartedly. And part of me hated him for it.

"Fine," I said easily. "But I know you have not raised me by your own hand, training me in the ways of war and educating me in the ways of the Folk, for me to guard a Gate and wait for a prince."

"You're right." Mother almost smiled, and my spirit lifted, like a flower turning toward the sun. But the smile faded before I could feel any hint of warmth. "I did have another task for you, a stór. One nearly as close to my heart as my daughter's rescue, yet twice as difficult." She hesitated. "But after you believed I would willingly call for your death in service of this mission, I am loath to tell you of it. I would hate for you to believe that I would so easily risk your precious life. Perhaps it would be easier for all of us if I asked Rogan instead—"

"Tell me." Renewed contrition and a desperate desire to prove myself sent the words tumbling from my mouth. "Anything you ask of me, I will do. No matter the difficulty—no matter the cost."

The queen appraised me, as though weighing the meaning behind my words.

"Very well," she said at last. "Cathair will tell you the details while I attend to my other duties. Tonight, you'll join me at the feast, and we will discuss it further. Tomorrow, you leave for Bridei with Rogan."

I bowed to my queen and mother, then followed Cathair from the throne room.

The druid's chambers were unpleasantly familiar. Sandwiched between the dungeons and the scullery, the sprawling, low-ceilinged rooms were lined with shelves and trimmed with cluttered workbenches. The air reeked of black walnut and cheap mead. Starlings roosted noisily in the beams. Manuscripts and grimoires fought for space with magical artifacts and grisly souvenirs stolen from Tír na nÓg: jars of pickled mandrake root, broken ollphéist fangs, vials of unknown toxins.

I crossed my arms against the permanent dank chill of the vault, wondering how many years of my life I'd wasted down here, learning the history of the Gate War; the lore of the Folk; espionage and poisons.

"Why did the high king travel into Tír na nÓg some twenty years ago?" Cathair's voice echoed over his shoulder as he reached a few heavy books down from a high shelf.

"Fódla was in peril," I responded automatically. Though humans and Folk had never been friends, before the Gate War there had been careful amity between the realms. Diplomacy was not unheard of. "Plague had taken root in Delbhna. Blighted grain threatened famine in Bridei. Raiders sank ships along the eastern coasts. The high king went to the Fair Folk to ask for aid." And the Folk had killed him for it.

"He went to ask for *magic*," Cathair corrected, slamming a heavy volume on the table. I'd pored over the tome countless times—*The Book of Beotach*, a bestiary of the Folk. "Half an age ago, in the time of Amergin, the Fair Folk stole all the wild magic from the human lands. It weakened our world, like carving organs from a body. All so they could hoard that magic in Tír na nÓg for their own use. They channeled it into four precious Treasures, objects of immense power wielded by their ruling Septs."

"The Septs, I remember—they are the four noble clans of the Folk." I stared at him. "But you have never told me of these Treasures."

Cathair flipped open the book. I glimpsed diagrams: a hairy, moon-faced gruagach, amusing itself by dispersing herds of cattle after stealing milk. A shrieking bean sidhe, clad in grave shrouds, bringing death with her keening. A bloodthirsty dearg due, with its gore-tipped claws and teeth. A shapeshifting aughisky, with its slender equine features and rows of shark teeth. Aquatic murúcha, solitary brùnaidhean, malicious púcaí. But Cathair riffled past these drawings of the lower Folk, stopping only when he reached the last chapter. The chapter about the treacherous, bewitching aristocracy of the Folk.

Trepidation prickled along my spine. I'd been young the first time I'd read that chapter. Nightmares had plagued me for weeks after—delicious, devious dreams of bladed tongues and bejeweled talons and indistinct voices calling me deeper into the forest. Even now, the lure of those drawings set my teeth on edge. But when Cathair tapped on an open page, I dutifully dropped my gaze.

He was pointing to a circular design, cross-sectioned into four— almost like a coat of arms.

"I have spent half my life unraveling this, the Folk's best-kept secret." Cathair's smile was self-satisfied. "Each clan corresponds to the wild magic they funneled into their Treasures. The Sept of Fins wields the Un-Dry Cauldron. The Sept of Antlers, the Heart of the Forest. The Sept of Scales, the Flaming Shield. And the Sept of Feathers claims mastery of the Sky-Sword."

My eyes followed the diagram as he spoke. Intricate geometric designs braided across it, layering into a dense pattern of illuminated flora and fauna. Color swirled in a gradient around its face— the azure of the ocean deepening to the emerald of the forest; the crimson of fire cooling toward a violet twilight.

I didn't understand why he was telling me this now. "So?"

"These Treasures are capable of vast magic, little witch. The power to raise mountains or drown cities. Burn forests or reroute rivers."

"Cure plagues." I was beginning to understand. "Improve harvests. Defeat raiders."

Cathair inclined his head. "And this Gentry lord who keeps Eala prisoner? Your darrig friend said he is tánaiste to one of these Septs. Heir to its Treasure. The queen wishes you to steal it from him, little witch, and return magic to its rightful place in Fódla."

I stared at him, a thistle of dread growing in my chest. I had sparred with warriors and slain Fair Folk and spied on drunken lords and seduced princes (the last, somewhat unsuccessfully). But I had never even met any Gentry, much less plotted against them. To steal a potent, precious Treasure from one of them? Mother had been right—this was a far greater task than I'd ever been set before.

"Which Treasure am I to steal?"

"He is said to be tánaiste of the Sept of Feathers," said Cathair. "The Sky-Sword."

"What does it look like?"

"That, I cannot say."

"Then how am I meant to find it?" Frustration and fear made my skin tight. "How will I know it from any other Folk-damned sword?"

"I've given you many tools these past twelve years." Cathair's voice was passionless. "Use them against this Gentry heir. Stalk him, lie to him, ingratiate yourself with him. You've grown into a pretty little thing—perhaps you could seduce him. It matters not how you ferret out his secrets. All that matters is you bring us back the magic this land so desperately needs. Do you understand me, little witch?"

"I understand." The tender skin of my wrist itched like ant bites. "But I'm not ready—I'll need weapons, tinctures and poison, books—"

Cathair set a large oilskin bag on the table with a thunk. Inside were sheaves of parchment, bundles of herbs, glints of metal.

"I have already prepared some things you'll need. Incantations to cross the Gate. Iron spikes dipped in antimony, although those will only protect you against the lower Folk." Cathair made a sweeping gesture toward his chamber. "Take whatever else you need."

I rose to my feet, eager. But the druid's cool palm gripped my elbow, stealing the nervous energy propelling me away from him. "One more thing."

What more could he possibly ask of me?

"I have not forgotten what happened with the prince, all those years ago." His hazel eyes were shrewd on my face. "Neither have you, I think."

I had certainly tried to forget.

It had been a blazing hot summer day when I was sixteen. Rogan and I had run away from our archery practice, snuck down to the swimming hole while the rest of the fiann sweated in the training yard. Dizzy with mischief, we'd dived deep and swum until our limbs trembled, then sunned ourselves on the grassy banks. As afternoon burned into evening and fireflies flickered in the dusk, he'd kissed me. His lips on mine had tasted like all the things I'd told myself I didn't want. And even though I knew—I *knew*—I could never have him, I kissed him back. When his hands roamed lower, I'd arched myself to meet him. We'd slid together, wet and hot and wild with wanting, until we came apart at the seams in a way that made me never want to put myself back together again.

He'd been my first. And much as I'd tried to convince myself it had been nothing—two striplings playing at passion—I knew I'd loved him then. As I loved him now.

I still don't know how Mother found out. Maybe she'd already been watching us, sensing our relationship begin to shift. Maybe Cathair's birds saw us, and he snitched on us for his queen's favor. Regardless, soon after, Cairell Mòr called his eldest son home to Bridei.

"What of it?" I ground out, shaking off Cathair's grip. "I do not love him—not anymore."

"You must think me daft, little witch. I see how you look at him." He cocked his head like one of his pet starlings. "You should know, no matter how much you might wish it, he will never be yours. He will marry a princess—if not Eala, then some other king's daughter. Perhaps you'll get lucky, and she will die in childbirth, and he will choose not to marry again. Then, at least, you will be first in his heart." His casual malice churned nausea in my gut. "But most likely, he will never choose you—you will never be more than an afterthought to him. And you will spend the rest of your miserable life being nothing more than his mistress. His shadow. His whore."

"Is that what you are to the queen?" I lashed out, thorns of fury prodding me to recklessness. "Her whore?"

"Perhaps I am." Cathair's smile was born from a malevolent kind of pride. He enjoyed it when I lost my temper—enjoyed it like a smith might enjoy cutting his finger on a newly forged blade. It proved to him how sharp he'd made me. "Be glad you are not. You are a weapon, little witch. You were made to hurt. And men only know how to use weapons—they do not know how to love them."

"Are you sure? I've certainly known men who were a little too fond of polishing their swords." I painted honey over my grimace and didn't care if it looked like a smile. "Now if you'll excuse me, I need to pack."

I grabbed the oilskin sack off the workbench and fled Cathair's dungeon, taking the steps two at a time. His laughter chased me into the light of the morning, but so too did his words, although I'd never let him know it.

No matter how much you might wish it, he will never be yours.

Much as I hated him for saying it, he was right. And to the two near-impossible tasks I'd been set today, I mentally added a third: to steal back my own heart from someone I should never have entrusted it to.

Chapter Four

Abrisk tap on my bedroom door dispelled my concentration. Irritated, I looked up from cataloging my socks and calculating how many times I'd reasonably be able to wear each pair before having to wash them.

Candlelight haloed Rogan as he pushed open the door and ducked beneath the jamb. Even when he straightened, the top of his head almost brushed the low ceiling. I stepped away from my pile of socks, fighting a burst of ancient embarrassment.

It wasn't the first time the prince had been in my room—not by a long shot. But I'd never liked having him here. After my unexpected arrival in the castle twelve years ago, I hadn't lasted long in the princess's bedroom. Mother had reserved those spacious chambers for Eala's awaited return—each doll carefully placed, each pillow regularly fluffed. Me, she'd moved to a higher floor—a floor for high-ranking servants; merchants without titles; secret changelings. I normally didn't mind the drafty shutters or the tallow tapers or the chinks that let the mice in. But with Rogan looming here, the walls seemed unpleasantly bare, the bed unconscionably narrow. So unlike Rogan's own royal guest chambers, which boasted rich tapestries and beeswax candles and feather mattresses.

"There you are." His mouth quirked up in a smile that tore at my heart. His hair had gotten long in the years since I'd seen him— it fell in golden waves past his shoulders, braided and knotted back from his face as was the fashion among young warriors. "What are you still doing up here? You're going to be late for the feast."

"Packing." My voice was stiff. "You may have heard of it?"

Rogan sat on the edge of my bed without asking, his weight sinking deep into the straw mattress. He examined my haphazard piles of spare armor, fletching supplies, unlabeled vials, and dog-eared books.

He whistled. "Brighid's forge, Fia! Are you really bringing all this?"

"Most of it. There's no telling how long we'll be away or what we'll face, and I like to be prepared." Rogan plucked up a wrinkled apple I'd earmarked for my horse, examined it, then sank his teeth into it. I folded my arms. "Why? What are you bringing?"

"My sword, of course," he mumbled, mouth full. "And I'll be wearing my mantle, my armor, and my boots. All I'll really need is a spare change of clothes, I reckon."

My eyebrows shot up. "A single change of clothing? No food? No medicine?"

"There's a village three leagues west of Dún Darragh." He shrugged. "No point in bringing loads of stuff when we can buy what we need. I'll carry plenty of coin."

I almost laughed. Only a prince would assume there'd be food to be bought in a rural village at the beginning of winter, when a poor harvest meant hunger already nipped at farmers' stomachs. But I wasn't going to waste my breath trying to convince him otherwise. I was simply going to have to pack enough for both of us.

No surprises there.

"You know the area, then?" I remembered his odd reaction to the fort Mother had named. "You know Dún Darragh?"

"I do." Rogan took another bite, whittling the apple down to its core. "They say it's haunted."

I shoved a spare pair of boots into my pack. "Really?"

"It's a strange story." Finished with the apple, he crossed to the window and tossed the core from the casement. He leaned back against the sill. "Long ago, when Folk wandered these lands freely, they say a human fénnid fell in love with a bewitching Gentry maiden. He broke his oaths, abandoned his lands, and followed her to the edge of Tír na nÓg. But he could not cross over into the otherworld. So he built Dún Darragh himself, from stones he quarried by hand, and never stopped trying to find a way to his love."

My hands had stilled as he spoke. I busied them again, forcing my eyes from the golden prince framed in twilight. "And did he?"

"I have heard it said he found a way to cross realms and win back his love." Rogan chuckled. "But most say he died in Dún Darragh of a broken heart, his fort unfinished and his love lost, and his spirit haunts its halls to this day."

I suppressed a shiver. "Thanks for that delightful image."

"Always happy to help." He glanced back out the window—below, the courtyard rang with the sound of hooves and merry laughter. "We really are going to be late."

Ire fisted my hands. If Rogan hadn't barged into my room uninvited, I wouldn't be late, and I would've already finished packing. But I was determined not to let him affect me—for good or bad. So I simply set my pack to one side and made my expression neutral.

"I'm almost ready." I gestured at the rough-spun tunic I wore over leather trousers. Hardly feast attire—Mother would not approve. "I need to change."

Rogan didn't budge.

"Change my *clothes*," I clarified.

"Modesty, changeling?" The candlelight caught the edge of his grin. "Since when do you care if I see you change?"

"Since we grew up, *princeling*." The rush of warmth to my cheeks made me mulish. "We're not children anymore."

He finally took the hint, pushing off the sill and crossing the narrow room. But he paused at my shoulder, reaching out to gently flick the end of one of my braids.

"No, changeling." In the shifting light, his blue-green eyes were opaque as the cracked river-stone brooch winking from his breast. "Indeed we are not."

The door clicked shut behind him. I exhaled and swiftly jerked off my tunic, wishing I could pull off my hot, tingling skin with it. Instead, I dressed dutifully in a modest woolen kirtle Mother would approve of, coiling my braids artlessly at my nape. I shoved my feet into embroidered slippers, then plucked a few pieces of jewelry from the fine little box I kept hidden in the wardrobe—all gifts from Mother. The jewelry did not suit me—the silver rings looked strange on my sword-calloused hands; the ruby earrings did not flatter the wan tone of my skin. But Mother would want me to play the part of her meek fosterling tonight, and I did not wish to disappoint.

Rogan waited for me outside the door. He set a rapid pace through the fort, whose halls and staircases he seemingly had no trouble remembering. Old resentments made a muddle of my thoughts as I trotted to keep up. Why was he acting like nothing had changed between us? When it was he who'd left me four years ago. When he'd come back only to rescue his promised bride. I would never forget what he said to me that dreadful morning—

I shoved the thought away as we approached the great hall through a narrow corridor. A single guard stood at its terminus, torchlight glinting off his helm. He saluted to Rogan, but when he saw me following a few paces behind, his expression shifted. I paid him little mind until he sidestepped unexpectedly and body-slammed me into the wall.

The impact knocked the breath from my lungs, but the shock hardly slowed my reaction. My muscles were already coiling to fling myself forward—

Rogan stepped in front of me.

"Donn's black gates, man!" The rebuke was critical yet jovial, with a bare note of condescension. It was Rogan's prince voice—the one he used to command underlings and disarm his peers. I hadn't heard him use it in years, and it fanned my smoldering discontent hotter. "What do you think you're doing?"

The guard glanced swiftly between Rogan and me. He hadn't realized we were together—he'd thought we were merely walking nearby. He stepped back to his post, hung his head.

"Sorry, m'lord." His eyes flicked to me before fixing on the middle distance. "A mistake. These halls are awful narrow, y'see."

"Apology accepted." Rogan didn't hesitate before clapping him on the shoulder. "Just see it doesn't happen again."

Rogan stepped aside and gestured for me to precede him into the feast. But I couldn't help glancing over my shoulder at the guard, who—behind Rogan's back—was making the sign against the evil eye. I fought the urge to bare my teeth and hiss at him.

But Rogan wouldn't understand. Rogan never understood—not any of it.

The joy is in the thrill of the fight, not the promise of a kill.

Easy for a prince to say. How many walls had he been thrown into? How many feet had tripped him as he rushed through the halls? How many curses were whispered at his back? And for what? Simply being born who I was.

The hall was already raucous with food, firelight, and alcohol-fueled conversation. Rogan bowed me to my seat at the queen's left hand, then sauntered over toward his own family's place, greeting fellow lords and warriors as he did. I readied myself to apologize to Mother for my tardiness, but she was deep in conversation with her brother, the under-king of Delbhna, who sat on her other side. A servant placed food and drink before me, but I didn't touch them, sweeping my eyes over the gathering instead.

The high queen's table was U-shaped, dominating the feast hall. On one end, Rogan sat with his half brothers, Cillian and

Callum, and a handful of their oath-men and vassals. They represented Bridei, the southernmost kingdom of Fódla, best known for its rich grain. Beside them, on my left, sat Derg O'Breithe, underking of Eòdan. Middle-aged but hearty, he doted on his daughters and bred the finest cattle on the isle. Delbhna's delegation sat to Mother's right. Known for its fine steel, finer warriors, and rocky landscape, the birthplace of the queen relied on other kingdoms for most of its food—through either trade or raid. Last came Fannon, Connla Rechtmar's birthright and the longtime rival of Bridei.

My eyes slid reluctantly to Connla, and I was not entirely surprised to find him already watching me. He boasted a livid broken nose and a huge bruise on one side of his head. He caught my eye and smiled—slimy and savage—over the lip of his cup. Then he bent to whisper in the ear of his rígfénnid drinking at his side. A moment later, the other man stared over at me too. Briskly, his fingers made a sign—the same sign the guard outside the hall had made. The sign against evil.

A thicket of dread closed around my heart. Connla had neither forgotten nor forgiven what had transpired last night. No—he had only realized that as I was the queen's favored fosterling, he would not be able to attack me directly. He would have to undermine me more cunningly—by poisoning hearts and minds already disposed against me. There were always the looks, the whispers, the rumors. But tonight I swore more eyes trained toward me, more hands raised to cover gossiping mouths...

A palm fell on my arm. I jumped, nearly spilling the wine goblet at my elbow. Power embroidered green through my veins and pricked thorny needles along my wrists—

"A stór?" Mother was looking at me askance. "Is something wrong?"

I wrapped my hands together in my lap and willed my Greenmark away. "No, Mother."

She stared at me a moment longer before sipping her wine. "How was your conversation with Cathair this morning?"

She was talking about the Treasure, in terms she did not mind being overheard. I glanced around for the druid—her shadow, her *whore*—but didn't see him. Cathair must have made himself scarce for the evening—the queen's brother did not approve of the druid.

"Illuminating," I replied carefully, remembering the intricate drawings of eerie Folk and elemental magic. "I will endeavor not to fail you in this, as in all things."

"I know you won't." She leaned forward, squeezed my shoulder with a cool palm. She lowered her voice. "You have never complained about being kept to the shadows, although I know you do not enjoy it. Return my daughter to her home and return magic to our lands. Then you will no longer have to keep your talents hidden. You will be publicly sworn into my fiann as an honored fénnid, and when your beloved sister someday succeeds me as queen, I promise you will be her respected war advisor."

Mother's words thundered through my chest, jolting my heart out of its thicket of dread. They were the antidote to Connla's toxic whispers and venomous glances.

Fiann. Fénnid. Sister. War advisor.

If I succeeded in Mother's tasks, I would no longer be the strange little mouse who sat silent behind the queen. I would no longer even be the little witch—the *changeling*—who gathered whispers wherever she walked. I would be part of the queen's army. Her household. Her family.

Beloved.

I bowed my head. "I want that, Mother."

"One other thing, a stór." The queen's fingers tightened around my arm. Her ice-blue eyes pierced me. "Know this—were there any other way, I would not have paired you on this mission with Rogan Mòr. But you both must go to Tír na nÓg to save my daughter. To save Fódla. It is the only way, but know I am sorry for it."

Not as sorry as I was. Almost against my will, my eyes sought Rogan down the length of the table. He was laughing at some story his younger brother was recounting, his head thrown back and his shoulders easy.

"Do not tell him of your secondary mission," Mother continued. "Princes are weak—their heads easily turned by thoughts of power. I don't need notions of powerful magic distracting him from saving my daughter. Rogan may one day be king, but only when I am done with the throne and ready for Eala to become queen."

I hated the thought of keeping such a secret from Rogan. But I agreed nevertheless. "I understand."

"And keep your head around that boy." She paused. "Do not let him fool you into giving him your heart again, Fia. He doesn't want it and wouldn't deserve it if he did."

Her words were so close to Cathair's—although much gentler—that I knew they must have discussed it. Shame crept through me on greasy feet. I longed for this conversation to be finished, but Mother was looking at me like she expected an answer.

"He is not meant for me. Even if I still loved him—which I don't—I know he could never love me back." My lips felt numb as I repeated the words she'd said to me—once, twice, a hundred times. "I was made of dusk and leaves and hidden places. I was not made to be loved by men."

Mother nodded. She cupped my chin with her hand and stroked a loose strand of hair back from my face. I closed my eyes, reveling in the brief, rare touch.

"Only I know how to love someone like you," she reminded me. "And no one will ever love you more than I do."

She released my chin and turned away. Below the high table, a bard had taken his place, harp in hand. The lesser nobles and wealthy merchants had already pushed the lower tables aside, crowding close to listen and dance. The rest of the night would be passed in music and merriment. But one last question collected on my tongue like brugmansia, a poison only I could taste.

"Mother?" Her gaze returned to me, surprised but genial. "What happens—what happens if I fail?"

All the warmth in my queen's gaze bled away. For a moment, her eyes were rigid as tempered steel. Then, just as quickly, diamonds of tears threatened to fall.

"You cannot fail me, a stór." If it hadn't been nearly inaudible, I thought her voice might have trembled. "Have I not already lost everything? My dear husband. Countless battles against the Folk. Mastery of the Gates. My own precious daughter. Would you have me lose this too? My last shred of hope?"

Horror drained the blood from my face. "I would never purposefully—"

"Were I not the daughter of kings," she whispered, still holding back her tears, never letting them fall, "I might already have died of grief. Do not be the thing that breaks me, a stór."

I hung my head. She was right—though she had lost almost everything, she had still given me all she had left. I would do what she asked of me. I would be her weapon.

And no matter what obstacles stood in my way, I would not fail her.

⁓

As soon as I was able, I fled the feast. Outside, the night air was brisk against my bare arms. I pulled off my jewels and kicked off my tight slippers, running barefoot across the chilly cobbles. No one accosted me as I made my way to the stables—this late, only a small complement of guards would be manning the walls. The rest would be in the barracks, enjoying their rations of ale or dicing away their meager stipends.

The stables were dim, and warm with the scents of hay and sleeping beasts. I made my way toward a stall where a dappled gray mare dozed. I leaned my arms over the gate and whistled softly. She roused, ears perking forward.

"Eimar." The mare whickered and stepped forward to push her velvet nose into my chest. "Hello, swift one."

The horse had been a gift from Mother on my eighteenth birth-day, and I loved her—loved her for her strength and agility, for her calm steadiness, for the way she accepted me without caveat. I fished in my kirtle for a piece of sugared violet I'd nicked from the feast—Eimar gobbled it greedily, her whiskered muzzle tickling my palm. She stomped an impatient foot.

"Not tonight, Eimar." Sometimes—when the moon was high and restless greenery tangled in my veins—I'd bridle the mare and ride her bareback down to the stream, where the forest sang its woodwind song. "There are too many people about. Besides, we have a long ride ahead of us tomorrow."

Again, she bumped her nose into my sternum. I stroked her forelock.

"It's a long story. But the queen is sending us to rescue her daughter, the princess. Eala. My—"

I stopped myself before I said *sister*. Still, the word rippled through my mind, dredging up disquiet in its wake.

My whole life, Eala Ní Mainnín was the light that cast my shadow. Distant, untouchable, yet shining so much brighter than I. My looks, my behavior, my personality—all measured against her perfect absence. But I was flesh and blood, all flaw and feeling. I could never compare to an ideal, a myth.

Yet before long, Eala would no longer be a glittering void, free to be colored in by others' imaginations. She would be real. And I...I would *meet* her.

The prospect seeded uneasy questions inside me. How would Eala feel, to know I had been left in her place twelve years ago? What would she think, to learn I had been raised by her own mother? How would she react to witnessing our uncanny physical resemblance? I'd heard the tales of Eala's great beauty—her milk-and-honey coloring, her spun-gold hair, her lovely sky-bright eyes. I was her dark mirror: wan skin, sable hair, mismatched eyes. One green as moss, the other brown as dirt. Would she think I was a monster—a fetch, an omen of death, come to steal her soul? Or would she know me as a sister, knitted to her by love if not by blood?

Eimar stuck her nose in my hair and blew out her breath, tickling my ear.

"You're right." I laughed. "I am overthinking things."

She snorted again.

"No, we won't be going alone. Mother has sent Rogan, prince of Bridei, to join us. He—ah—he has a very handsome stallion. But with any luck, we won't have to see much of them."

I trailed off. Lulled by the dim warmth of the stables and Eimar's comforting presence, my heart's careful cage of sharp thorns and rigid branches began to crumble, exposing my hurt. The memory I'd been keeping at bay closed like a sprung trap, seizing me with razored teeth.

Four years ago, Rogan had tried to leave without saying goodbye—without saying *anything*.

Mother had broken the news to me. Cairell Mòr had discovered what had passed between us, and ended Rogan's fosterage. Rogan had reached his majority—it was time for him to go home. But that had been nothing compared to what she told me next. How she'd offered Rogan the chance to break off his engagement with Eala, in order to wed me instead. How he'd declined.

He'd chosen Eala. The storybook princess. The fantasy.

Instead of me. The changeling. The girl standing in front of him, beating heart and willing body.

I hadn't wanted to believe her. But three days passed, and Rogan was nowhere to be found. I'd waited for him to come to me, desperate for some explanation, some repudiation, some excuse. Anything to salve the gaping wound slowly festering inside me. But he never came. Whatever I'd imagined between us was over. Or perhaps, worse, it had never existed in the first place.

I'd tried to stay calm, that cool blue morning, as horses wheeled in the courtyard and gulls circled overhead. Mother's hand had been heavy on my neck—the faint brush of her fingernails reminding me not to show weakness. Not to show Rogan how fragile my love for him had made me.

I'd tried to be strong. But I'd failed.

At the last moment, I'd wrenched out of Mother's grip and dashed out across the courtyard. My reckless run had startled Rogan's stallion, Finan—the tall black horse had shied from me, snorting. But I'd grabbed for his stirrup, hanging on for dear life as the stallion sallied. Rogan had finally reined him still, and I'd looked up at him.

His face had been pale. His expression, harsh.

"Fia," he'd ground out. "What are you doing?"

I'd almost lost my nerve beneath his unforgiving stare. But I still couldn't believe that he'd really leave me—not like this. Not silently, in the blue of dawn. Not without saying goodbye.

"Tell me it wasn't real," I'd pleaded up at him, my voice pathetic with tears. "Tell me none of it was real, Rogan, and I'll let you go."

His river-stone eyes had gone flat in the pale sunlight. His fingers had tightened on the reins, white at the knuckles.

"It doesn't matter," he'd said. "I am not meant for you. We are not meant for each other."

"*Meant?*" The word had ripped jagged from my throat. "What does that mean?"

I'd thought he might relent. But when he spoke again, it was as if his voice had been stripped clean of all emotion, leaving him blank and wooden.

"It means I am a prince." Dispassionately, he'd reached down and unhinged my fingers from his stirrup. "And you—you are..."

A *changeling*, I'd thought he would say.

"You are no one."

He'd turned his back to me and galloped away without another word.

I wrapped my arms around Eimar's neck, burying my face in her mane as I had many times before. But although I squeezed my eyes shut against the anticipated burn of tears, they did not come.

Tonight, after four years and a thousand nights of weeping, I was finally empty. The day Rogan left had nearly broken me. But I'd patched the cracks with knotty vines, sewn them up with thorny briars, hidden them behind poison flowers.

And if his leaving couldn't break me, neither could his return.

Chapter Five

Morning dawned sullen as Rogan and I set out. After last week's crisp autumn splendor, the rotten weather felt like a bad omen, and neither of us had much to say as we turned our horses toward Bridei, Rogan's home kingdom. The first hour was slow going—the roads were choked with the Áenach Tailteann's exodus from Rath na Mara. Slow wagons rumbled over packed dirt. Sluggish packhorses dropped dung. Restless children played chase beneath the mounts of their hungover parents. Beggars held out their dirty hands for the mercy of others.

Too many beggars. Old, young—they lined the roads outside the fort. Many bore the hallmarks of the wasting sickness plaguing the west—raised lesions on the skin, fevered gazes. Others wore missing limbs, wounds suffered in the Gate War or inflicted by the pirates who raided our eastern waters. But most just looked hungry.

Shame rose in me when I remembered last night's feast—the imported wine sipped from gilded goblets, the fatted calves roasted in crackling hearths, the rare fruits piled beside rich honey cakes. Perhaps, if we had dined on a little less, these people might have had a little more.

I tossed what coin I had in my pocket to a skeletal girl no older than I. Cathair's voice rang in my ears: *Bring us back the magic this land so desperately needs.*

With a Folk Treasure at Fódla's disposal, perhaps all this sorrow could be ended.

Beyond the outskirts of the city were rough lanes bordered by hedges and muddy fields. The clouds spat icy rain, and Rogan and I both drew up our hoods. By midday, the drizzle became a downpour. An ancient beech tree provided some shelter from the wet. We ate a cold lunch while the horses cropped at the grass and shook out their manes.

"I'm freezing," Rogan said. "There's a village half a league west—what do you say we stop at the inn? We'll find a table by the fire, and I'll buy you a pint of ale and a proper meal. And then two warm beds...or maybe just one." He quirked a golden eyebrow at me, sending a fist to squeeze my heart.

The image of us tangled together—the memory of how he'd pressed me against the stones of the crofter's cottage in Connla's camp—flooded my mind. The weight of his hands at my waist, the press of his hips between my legs, the brush of his lips on my throat—

"I doubt such humble fare could satisfy your royal tastes, princeling." I tossed an apple core to Eimar and cut him a cold look. I would not be so easily swayed. "And if it gets around you're buying girls' drinks, I daresay we'll be there all night."

Hurt flickered across Rogan's face. I forced myself not to care. I had to learn to quell any feelings I still harbored for Rogan Mòr.

"Does the queen ever speak of Tír na nÓg?" Rogan asked, blessedly changing the subject around doleful bites of his crust of bread.

"Rarely."

For Mother, the Gate War was a mistake flanked by tragedies. On one side, the Fair Folk senselessly slew her beloved husband mere days before Eala was born; on the other, the Fair Folk stole that treasured daughter away into Tír na nÓg. Between, she had fought battle after battle against an enemy who could not be beaten.

"She said—" I struggled to remember her words. "At the Battle of the First Gate, when Cathair slew the leipreachán, trees of night sprang up where its heart-blood fell, and beyond them rose the morning sun, if morning were music and the sun were the sound of being alive."

"That sounds more like a dream than a memory." Rogan's words were taut with unease.

I looked down at my hands clutched in my lap. When I spread my fingers, I imagined each one was a comb-toothed leaf, bowing beneath the drizzle.

Dreams didn't always happen while you slept. And things didn't have to make sense to be real.

I stood abruptly. "We should move. We don't want to lose the light."

The rain stopped after noon, stacking banks of heavy clouds above the rising hills. We passed Finn Coradh, the village closest the fort, and kept riding, despite Rogan begging for a flagon of ale and a roast. At last, we saw it—the unfinished dún hunching dark against an iron sky, towers jutting jagged as broken teeth. Hills dotted in violet and gold tumbled down toward a glassy lough, beyond which a dark line of trees disappeared into the coming dusk.

Rogan reined Finan, who stomped and snorted, his breath a cloud of white.

"Home sweet home, I suppose." Rogan whistled, rueful. "You're sure we can't stay in Finn Coradh? The Muddy Ram is famous, although I can't remember whether it's for the wine or for the women."

"Perhaps we should." I grinned and tossed my head. "Where there are women, there are always men. Shall we wager which of us can fall into our *one* bed with someone faster?"

Rogan frowned, shook his head, and spurred his stallion forward.

The fort's shadow tasted like winter. The path sloping upward was edged in trees gnarled like broken harp strings. Two tall, pitted standing stones loomed stark as sentinels at the base of the hill, their time-smoothed surfaces sloping like old men's shoulders. In the fading light, I imagined the patterns of lichen and moss were human features. A giant eye. An open mouth, its ancient words lost on the wind.

It felt like a warning.

I nudged Eimar toward the standing stones. She balked and sallied, forcing me to rein her tight.

"Something has them frightened," Rogan said, apprehension shadowing his face as he tried to control his own horse.

"I can see that." I eyed the sky. Red mottled the horizon and stained Dún Darragh's towers with blood. Night was coming, and the fort was still half a league's ride. I made my voice soft and murmured to my mare, "Come, girl. There's nothing fearful here."

As I guided her between the standing stones, time stopped and the world tilted. I raised my eyes, somehow knowing what I would see before I saw it: two standing stones looming over a path edged in flowers, leading to a castle atop a rise. But the stones were giants with granite faces, and the flowers bloomed with black-and-white petals, and the fort was built of jewels and dreams and strange wishes. The sky sang with light and the earth sang with life. My bones hummed.

Eimar passed beyond the stones. The edges of my vision blurred, as though objects out of sight were twisting into new shapes. The world stretched thin as silk, then righted itself.

I wheeled to look back at Rogan, who was passing through behind me. But his face didn't change—his eyes didn't dazzle with impossible visions. He gave me a questioning look.

A flock of ravens burst squawking from a nearby tree, sending rust-colored leaves fluttering to the ground, and filling the sky with black feathers. Eimar whinnied and reared, nearly crashing into Finan. I struggled to keep my seat, gripping the saddle with my knees and grasping for the reins. My hands found her withers. I buried my fingers in her white mane as she tried to throw me. Panic stomped my heart, and the shadowed forest within me lurched out without my permission.

Greenery burst along Eimar's neck, leaves rustling toward her ears. Vines twined her head like a second bridle. Instantly, the mare settled, all four hooves dropping to the ground. Her gray hide twitched, and she bowed her head to crop at the grass.

I gripped my hands into fists and swore. Behind me, Rogan inhaled in shock. Regret pulsed through me as I examined the threads of green writhing beneath Eimar's hide, twisting slowly toward her heart.

"What did you do?" Rogan asked softly. "Your magic—"

"Don't call it that!" Tears pricked my eyes, and I fought to control my voice. "Please don't call it that."

But it didn't matter what he called it. Mother called it my Greenmark; Cathair called it something uglier. I tried not to name it at all. But it lived within me, like a set of green fingerprints on my heart. Folk magic—wild growth and rot and rebirth. I *hated* it. I hated the way it slid through my veins like dark water and thronged my thoughts with shifting leaves.

I forced myself to look up, to meet Rogan's eyes. I swallowed my remorse and confirmed what he was already thinking.

"My Greenmark—it's stronger here. The moment I passed between those stones..." I trailed off. Below me, Eimar cocked an ear and lifted her delicate head. Her eyes had already turned to leaf-glass, glossy as a pond beneath trees. I thought of my beloved Pinecone, crumbling to dirt beneath the hem of my shirt. "My poor girl. I loved her."

Rogan's eyes were hard to read in the dimming light. "What will happen to her?"

"By morning, she'll be another tree in the hungry forest."

I dismounted, pressing my face against Eimar's neck. Her mane was already braided through with fast-growing ropes of flowering vines. Her familiar scent of hay and warm, dark stables had disappeared beneath the smells of turned earth and rotting wood. I unbuckled her bridle, the leather crumbling to brown ash between my fingers. She stamped a leaf-draped hoof. I stroked her soft muzzle, one last time, my eyes burning.

"Go on, then." I slapped her rump. She trotted away, the dusk swallowing her velvet ghost. "Goodbye, swift one. I'm so sorry."

I would never see her again. Time and again, I forgot that my love only destroyed. Time and again, I was cruelly reminded. I bit down fury and self-loathing and turned to face Rogan. His eyes were shadowed, high upon his stallion.

"I'll walk the rest of the way." I summoned false nonchalance. Finan was strong enough to carry both of us, but Rogan wouldn't want me near his prized horse after what I'd done to Eimar. He wouldn't want me near *him*. "It'll be hard to rescue the princess if I accidentally turn you into a shrub."

For a split second, his wary expression lingered. Then: "Don't be stupid." He leaned down, offered his hand. "I do all my best work as a shrub."

Oh, how I loved him for it.

I exhaled and reached up. Rogan's hand gripped mine, warm in the brisk twilight. I swung up behind him and slid my hips flush against his backside. I curled my arms around his hard torso and pretended I didn't notice when his muscles jumped at my touch. Rogan urged a snorting Finan forward. I buried my hands in his mantle and laid my cheek against his shoulder. I wanted to believe I was made for this. To hold—to be held.

But I knew I wasn't.

Our stories had all begun the same way—with a queen and her enemies, with war and magic, with stolen girls and vengeance. But this moment—a prince on a fine steed, riding into strange lands to deliver a damsel—was where Rogan and Eala's story diverged. They would get their tale of rescue, redemption, and true love.

I would never be part of their story. And whatever might happen in mine, I feared it would have a darker end.

❧ ～❧

Dún Darragh loomed into view, feverish with sunset. Half the fort was crumbled to nothing, roofless arcades gaping at the sky. Other wings were barely begun, a miscarriage of pale quarried stone and empty windows. Rogan's ghost stories had unsettled me. I shuddered against the sense of unseen eyes surveying me from the shadows.

The last of the sunlight slipped away as we dismounted in the courtyard. The air smelled of a world on the edge of winter: fallow fields and rotting flowers, woodsmoke and wooden hearts.

"Finan needs water and grain," Rogan told me. "I'll see if there's a stall for him. Fancy finding a way into the fort and scouting a place for us to sleep?"

Dún Darragh's heavy doors were carved from dark oak and studded with twisting skeins of metal. They swung open at my touch, hinges groaning. I squinted into the murk, musty smells of old stone and dust tickling my nostrils.

"Hello?" The irrational sensation of being watched lingered. "If anyone's in here, you should know I'm extremely well armed. And, um, really, *really* big."

Fragments of my own voice echoed back at me. But no one else answered. I grabbed for a cobwebbed torch in a crumbling sconce. A spark from my flint caught on the dry wood, and the firebrand flared to life.

The torch smeared gold against the edges of things: a spiraling staircase, a doorway, an arching ceiling. Another sconce holding another torch. The stone leached cold through the soles of my boots as I touched flame to the second taper. Shadows ebbed, lapping at the base of the staircase. I climbed, searching for more torches.

Finally, the vast hall sighed with light. Four pillars broad as ancient oaks reached toward a ceiling carved with intricate shapes. No—*everything* was carven, from the pocked stone walls to the contoured stairs. The engravings gyrated in the dancing torchlight, reminding me of nothing so much as Cathair's illustrated bestiary. Fawns with the heads of wolves; birds with too many beaks. Growling, howling, leering faces with beards of hawthorn leaves and acorns for eyes.

I grimaced, suddenly more inclined to believe Rogan's far-fetched tale of the human fénnid driven mad with love for a Gentry maiden. This place had too much of the Folk about it for my tastes.

A cough came from over my shoulder, shattering the silence. I shrieked and swung the torch, jabbing it toward the sound. It was a carved face—mournful eyes looked out over a long, drooping nose. Broad hazel leaves choked the figure's gaping mouth, spilling over its cheeks and chin.

The muffled cough came again. I jerked back a step, then gritted my teeth and leaned closer. *Surely* the goblin was only a carving. I reached out and touched the tip of my finger to its nose.

Green flashed—sunset through summer trees—and the shadows striping the wall lengthened and deepened. I stood in a forest at night, full of grasping branches and rough black trunks knobbed with faces. A breeze brushed my hair from my nape.

I blinked, and dim torchlight kissed my cheeks once more.

The dour face spluttered as it worked its thick stone lips, spitting foliage until its wide mouth gaped empty. Then it cleared its throat. And *spoke*.

"Hello, chiardhubh!" it said. "You're late."

I stared. The archaic word—*chiardhubh*—thudded in the back of my mind with strange familiarity. *Sable-haired.*

"Or early." The froth of hazel leaves surrounding its face rustled and shook. "We tend to stray as time slips away—centuries, years, and minutes at play. No one to talk to. Well...no one who'll stay."

The realization of what this *thing* must be cut through the babble and brought me back to my senses. I swiftly made the sign against evil, invoking the goddess Brighid's protection.

"Restless ghost," I hissed. "Begone from this place!"

"*Ghost?*" screeched the head, sounding amused.

I waved the torch. "Whether wight or sprite, I said begone!"

Its amusement turned to indignation. "You offend us with such erroneous monikers."

"Are you a Folk beastie?" Curiosity tangled with instinctual loathing. I'd never encountered a Folk creature like this—neither in the flesh nor on parchment.

"*Beastie?*"

"Well?" Now that I knew I wasn't being haunted, I regained some measure of my composure. Compared to a restless spirit, the Folk were a known quantity. Something I hated but understood. "Are you the brùnaidh of Dún Darragh? You'll find no crusts of stale bread nor rancid cups of wine here."

"Brùnaidh? Oh, no. Horrid, meticulous little creatures."

"Then what are you?"

"We are broken hearts and old sorrows," said the carving, with some glee. "We are crumbling rocks and empty glasses and forgotten hallways and the tolling of the bell in the highest tower."

Riddles and nonsense—it was like talking to Cathair, but worse.

"It doesn't matter," I said, brisk. "Leave me alone, and I'll try not to kill you."

I made my way back toward the main door. The carved face gave a small wail, then went silent and still. A flurry of motion leapt from carving to carving, animating a thick-tusked boar, a moon-faced gruagach with crystals for eyes, and a squirrel with its heart gripped in its paws. I watched the... *sprite* out of the corner of my eye as it followed me along the walls.

"Alone?" The sprite bellowed from one of two twin heads carved in bronze on the door, squat and puff-cheeked, haloed with ivy. "But we've been too long alone as it is! We long for a sweet, dark-haired maiden to sing us lullabies and pick us posies of flowers."

I snorted. "You've got the wrong maiden."

"Fine," said the other head, sly. "Then we long for a foul-tempered, sharp-tongued wench to plague and torment us."

"*Wench?*"

I opened my mouth to tell the sprite I'd show it what torment was, but Rogan chose that moment to tromp through the door, carrying an armful of firewood. He threw it down into the cold hearth, then stretched out his back and looked around.

"This place is a dunghill," he grumbled.

"And bedeviled by spirits," I added, gesturing with my torch at the living carving, who winked at Rogan more salaciously than strictly necessary.

"The carvings are eerie." Rogan huffed a laugh, his eyes barely skimming the animated head before traveling along the walls and toward the ceiling. "But not all stories are true, changeling."

He ducked back out into the night for more firewood.

I looked at the carving. "He can't see you?"

"He wasn't looking at the right time," said the sprite, sticking out a long tongue studded with new leaves. "He might have seen us yesterday. Or tomorrow."

"So you intend to harass only me?" Frustration scored my words. "What *are* you?"

"We are just us. When we're cross, we call ourselves Corra. You can do the same, if you fancy."

Corra. The name seemed innocent enough. All the Folk were deceitful and wicked. But other than possibly annoying me to death, it was hard to imagine what harm this strange spirit could do me.

All I could do was tolerate it. Or ignore it.

I chose the latter.

I bent to the firewood, arranging the haphazard pile into a neat stack. I struck golden sparks with my flint and steel, then blew across the smoldering kindling. But the light fizzled out. I lifted my flint to try again and—

Whump!

Hungry blue flames burst crackling from the hearth, rushing over the firewood and collecting yellow edges. I jumped away from the blaze, careful with the ends of my braid and the fringe of my mantle.

"I didn't ask you to do that!" I shouted at the air. "It's cheating!"

A muffled laugh climbed the walls and spiraled toward the ceiling. "Whatever works, chiardhubh, works!"

"Who are you talking to?" Rogan asked from behind me. He threw down another armful of firewood, then unpinned his riverstone brooch, forearms flexing as he hung his mantle over a bare sconce. "I'm impressed. How did you get the fire going?"

I didn't know whether to laugh or cry. So I just shrugged.

"I cheated."

Rogan chuckled. In the firelight, his eyes were gemstones. "Whatever works, changeling, works."

Chapter Six

Dirty-dishwater light splashed across my face. I scrubbed at gritty eyes and wished for more sleep.

Last night, Rogan and I had briefly explored the fort. We'd found a dank rabbit's warren of hallways with their roofs caved in and staircases ending in empty air, festooned in moldy tapestries and rat droppings. We'd eaten a cold meal of bread, salted fish, and pickled vegetables, Rogan bolting down two days' worth of my supplies in one go. We laid the bedrolls—which I'd also thought to pack— in front of the fire and slept beneath our mantles. Bad dreams had plagued me—mud-caked vines latching around my wrists and dragging me underground, a carven face laughing as I smothered to death in the dirt.

I kicked off my cloak and looked over at Rogan. He was still sleeping, his cheek pillowed on one hand and his golden hair mussed. I stared at him a moment too long; in sleep, it was easy to see the echoes of the boy I'd once loved.

But much as I wanted to hate him for the man he'd become, he wasn't making it easy. Last night, after we'd snuffed the torches, banked the fire, and lain down, his voice had found me in the dark.

"You're very far away, changeling," he'd murmured.

I'd bit my tongue and curled deeper into my mantle. There had been a time when we'd slept on top of one another, piled like puppies for warmth and comfort. But we'd been children then. Even with an arm's length of distance between us, I'd been able to sense his warmth, smell his sharp male scent of sun-warmed rock and vetiver. I'd ached to move closer to him, to fit myself against his chest and pillow my head on his arms. But I'd stayed where I was, silent and unmoving. Perhaps he would think I was already asleep.

He hadn't said anything else.

I dragged my eyes from his face and shoved my chilly feet into boots. I reached for my pack, searching for a leftover crust of last night's bread.

Something sharp pricked my thumb. I snatched my hand away, hissing as a droplet of dark green blood squeezed from the pad of my finger and dropped to the floor. Where it landed, a tiny black flower sprouted.

I glanced at Rogan, who stirred but didn't wake. I ground the blossom beneath my boot. Then I reached more carefully into my pack.

It was a feather. Black as the space between stars, its glossy vane gleamed with a hellebore luster. I twirled it, watching it glide and flash in the dim. It reminded me of a raven in flight, or a night before dawn.

More vile Folk magic.

I tossed it onto the banked fire, sucked blood from my thumb, and snuck out into the cold morning.

Dingy sunlight painted the estate in shades of gray. With its back against steely moors, the fort looked out across a lough surrounded by fields. They might once have held crops or livestock but now stood empty and brown. A rocky trail coiled down the lee side of the hill, winding through an orchard of gnarled apple trees. I craned my neck, glimpsing a cluster of outbuildings. A stable, maybe; a dilapidated shed; and—

The glint of dull sunlight on distant metal. The gleam of broken glass. The burnt tones of dying foliage draped around thick arching windows.

A *greenhouse.*

Dusty longing climbed my throat. After Rogan left Rath na Mara, I'd had no one. I used to sneak into the royal greenhouses between training sessions, seeking the companionship of growing things. I'd loved the warm, damp kiss of the humid air, the clusters of hothouse flowers pressing rosy faces against the glass, the heavy smell of dirt and mulch and growth. The gardeners had taken pity on me, taught me how to mix compost with dirt, how deep to push seeds, how to train vines onto stakes, how to prune fruit trees. They'd marveled at how quickly seedlings took root when I planted them, how early roses bloomed when I fertilized them, how large vegetables grew when I weeded around them.

I had a gift, they'd said. They were right, of course. But I hadn't told them about my Greenmark. They wouldn't have understood, and I needed their companionship like a flower needs the sun.

Then, one day, Cathair had summoned me to his grim, vulgar chambers. The druid's workbench had been cluttered with herbs and tinctures I'd recognized but always avoided: black walnut, foxglove. Sweet rue, belladonna.

"Your Folk stain is not a hobby, but a weapon," he'd said without preamble. "What use is growing silk blossoms out of granite, or roses blue as birds' eggs? You should be learning which plants are dangerous, which plants will make you deadly."

I'd balked. "I don't see what's wrong with learning how to grow all things."

"You were made of bloodroot and mountain laurel, little witch." He'd laughed and tossed me a vial of something murky. "You were made to destroy."

His words had taken root inside me and poisoned the love I had for green, growing things. I'd never returned to the greenhouses. But perhaps, if there was one at Dún Darragh—

I marched down the ridge.

The outbuildings were set in a grotto behind the fort, through a copse of blackthorns netting slender branches against a chalky sky. The sharp air crackled in my lungs, and my boots squelched through russet slime studded with acorns and pine needles.

The clearing might once have been beautiful. Only weeds and tight-curled ferns grew here now, but the ground was scored where rows of flowers once flourished, the stone walls scarred by the outlines of fallen trellises. A fountain spluttered sadly beneath an ancient willow. And at the center of it all stood... well. I wasn't sure the name *greenhouse* still applied to this... *structure.*

Archways of rough iron swooped gaunt as a skeleton's ribs. Huge walls of tempered glass hung shattered in their panes, like gaping mouths full of broken teeth. Delicate finials of hammered brass dangled askew; bronze sconces cupped shadows instead of flames.

And what time hadn't ruined, wild nature had reclaimed. Birch and alder trees burst through the ceiling, reaching for fresh air and sunshine. Knotted vines older than I coiled greedy fingers around metal frames, crushing as they climbed. Shrubs and undergrowth fought for space with grasping weeds.

I shoved at an iron door hanging off its frame. The hinges squealed in protest, but the door shuddered inward.

The warm-rot scent of loam slapped me in the face. Daggers of sunlight slashed down over long rows of tables whose lame legs sagged toward the ground. Potting supplies were scattered—trowels, vats of dirt, baskets of desiccated seedlings.

"You're back, chiardhubh!"

I jumped back from the shouting voice, steadying myself against one of the tables. I glared up at an ancient topiary, so old and disheveled it looked more like an unshorn sheep than whatever prancing steed it was meant to be.

"Stop sneaking up on me, foul beastie," I growled.

"Wasn't sneaking!" Corra swiveled a bushy head to peer at me with spindly shoots for eyes. " 'Twas only peeking."

"More like spying."

"What would we see?" It was hard not to laugh at Corra trying to make an overgrown topiary look innocent. "And who would we tell?"

"I told you to leave me alone." I wagged my finger with as much menace as I could muster. But my curiosity won over my contempt. I gestured to the ruined greenhouse. "How long has it been like this?"

"Has to be decades." Rogan's voice drifted through the door.

I spun. The broken door framed him, lending him silver edges and casting his face in shadow. I swiftly quelled the shiver of elation the sight of him still elicited.

"You're up," I observed.

"I am." He kicked at a pane of glass. It splintered around his boot. "I came looking for breakfast. But I don't suppose there's anything."

He looked like he'd slept about as well as I had—purple circles bruised the skin below his eyes, and his golden curls made a disheveled halo around his head. It did little to dampen his light—if anything, it made him look more real, more tangible. Less a prince and more a man.

Princes were meant for princesses. But men—men could be touched. Men could be had. Men could be loved.

"Not unless you're fond of eating dirt." I pushed past him, out into the clearing. I gestured to the pool beneath the willow. "But there's fresh water, at least. This looks spring fed."

Rogan stared askance at the scummy surface strangled with reeds and clogged with dead leaves.

"It just needs a little clearing out." I rolled my sleeves to the elbow and dunked my hands in the frigid water. Dredging the slime with my fingers, I brought out handfuls of muck. The water churned with dirt, flinging shards of my own reflection back at me. One green eye, one brown eye. Finally, the struggling fountain spat a stream of clear water.

I rinsed my hands, then cupped the clear liquid, bringing it to my lips. It was so cold my teeth ached, but the water was sweet, tasting of new honey and winter melt.

As I drank, the water leapt and splashed with such vigor I imagined it was laughing.

No—the fountain *was* laughing.

"Spluuuuurgle!" chortled the fountain. "Rrrrghghgurgle!"

The spray spurted higher, taking on shapes. A clear-glass goblet. A fat-bellied fish. A dancer in pirouette, elegant arms draped in diaphanous veils.

I gritted my teeth. This Folk beastie would drive me mad.

"Gurgle," said the water more clearly. "Murmur! Splash!"

"Shut up!" I hissed.

"Did you say something?" Rogan asked me.

"No," I replied, hauling myself to my feet. "The water's safe to drink."

He bent and sipped some of the water. He didn't—*couldn't*—see the crystalline otter doing somersaults around his hands. When he looked back up at me, his blue-green eyes were intent.

"You used to talk about growing things when we were younger," he said. "You planned to ask the queen for a plot in the kitchen gardens, I remember. Did you ever?"

"No." Cathair's vile tinctures and rude poisons had dissuaded me from that notion. "That was a long time ago. It was a child's dream."

Rogan looked at the derelict greenhouse, the overgrown beds, the broken stone walls. A spark of inspiration danced across his face. "Maybe, while we're here—"

Moments ago, I'd been guilty of the same thought. But creeping beneath that thought were terrible memories of what my growing magic had done. Pinecone, crumbling to dust. Eimar, trotting into the dusk. Caitríona—

No. My magic was dangerous—I couldn't allow myself to love anything else, not even a garden.

"We have other things to focus on. Starting with finding the Thirteenth Gate. The full moon is only a few days from now. We need to be ready."

"Right." Rogan shed his morning's softness, turning hard as battle metal. From his mantle, he unfolded the map Mother had given him. "It's supposed to be somewhere in those woods—the map here calls it Roslea."

A chill stroked my spine, and I glanced over my shoulder into the forest. Blank eyes stared from beneath bushes. Faces frowned from tree trunks. Grasping arms—

I blinked. Nothing more than the undersides of pale leaves, the gnarled bolls of ancient oaks, the branches of tall trees. I squared my shoulders, rubbed my thumbs over the twin hilts belted at my hip.

"I don't think I need a map," I said. "But we should go now, before the morning passes. We don't want to be caught in the forest after dark."

Rogan gave me a questioning look. But I didn't know how to explain to him that the forest was watching.

And I wasn't sure it liked what it saw.

❧

The forest was somber this time of year. Last week, these trees would have worn gowns of russet and gold. Now their bare branches grasped at leaden skies, and brown leaves crunched beneath our feet. We walked until we could no longer feel the weight of Dún Darragh at our backs. The trees grew huge and widely spaced, their thick ancient branches sifting gray light.

A crash in the underbrush broke the silence. The weight of watching eyes pricked the hairs at the nape of my neck. I spun on my heel, scanning the forest.

"What do you see?" asked Rogan softly.

I squinted into the twilight hush. I glimpsed the outline of a stag—noble head, muscular legs poised for flight, great arching antlers scraping the sky. But no—the light shifted, and it was brush and branches.

"Nothing," I said.

I turned and nearly walked into an ash sapling in the middle of the path. I sidestepped the tree, but something about its shape made me hesitate. Four slender roots pushed into the ground, almost like legs. Something pale was caught in the tree bark—I brushed my fingers across it. Animal hide. Dappled gray, like—

Realization punched me in the chest. A half second later, I saw the horse's skull embedded between the sapling's branches, twined with vines and staring with unnatural blossoms.

"Eimar," I gasped. From the moment I accidentally Green-marked the mare, I knew this would happen. But it was another thing to *see* it—to see something so alive become *death* and, in that death, become a different kind of life.

I stumbled back. My heel smacked against something hard lodged in the earth. I fell onto my arse, graceless. Rogan reached down to help me up, but I batted his hands away, reaching instead to brush layers of old leaves off whatever tripped me. It was quarried stone—odd for the middle of the forest. I stood, eyes scanning the ground.

Another stone humped a few paces away. Rogan intuited my intention and bent, clearing moss and dirt from its base. Time-smoothed contours gave it a familiar shape. A *face*.

Rogan's river-stone eyes were unnerved. "What is this place?"

I shook my head.

Together, we moved deeper into the forest. We threaded between battered rocks and listing statues bent in shapes and angles nature didn't make, beginning to see this ancient place for what it was.

A graveyard for monsters.

The huge fangs of a scaled and twisting ollphéist pierced upward from the loam, hungry for long-forgotten flesh. A bare-breasted bean sidhe screamed into eternity, her marble bones melting into

dust. Giant Fomorians wrestled between primeval oaks. A massive
dearg due reared up from the earth, dark maw yawning like death.
Reclining Folk evanesced into moss and lichen, their names lost to
time and earth.

Disgust mingled with awe as we walked. This place reeked of
Folk magic and yet seemed somehow unbearably human. These
statues were old—as old as the Folk, who were said to live forever.
And yet they were lost. Forgotten. Mortal, if only in the way they
dissolved into the forest. Grotesque yet beautiful. Profane yet silent
enough to be sacred.

"Do you—" I turned toward Rogan, thinking suddenly of
Corra, who'd been invisible to him. "Are you seeing this? Are you
seeing them?"

"Yes," Rogan whispered, stricken. "Do you think she— Has
Eala been trapped somewhere like this for all these years?"

"I don't know," I told him honestly. "Some say Tír na nÓg is a
paradise. Others believe it to be a tortuous underworld."

As if in response, a breeze lifted the edges of my hair. Leaves
spun away like birds. A flat path paved in stones appeared, curving between the trees. A beam of weak sunlight filtered down and
transmuted the stones to gold.

"They must be flecked with mica," I murmured.

"What?" Although Rogan's eyes followed mine, his gaze was
unfocused. He'd been able to see the statues, but he couldn't see
this?

I didn't have time to question it. Quickly—before the path
disappeared—I followed it to a stone bridge arching over a rushing stream. A willow tree combed her hair across the glassy swirl.
I tested the arch of the bridge with my boot—despite its age, the
stones were sturdy. I stepped to its center.

Beyond, ancient trees reached silver branches over the path. I
glimpsed a sunlit glen ringed in jewel-bright flowers. Flaxen leaves
crowned trees swaying like sheaves of wheat. The distant swell
of lively music teased the edge of my hearing—a familiar melody

sweeping away my unease. A sweet breeze dragged me through roots and branches and vast skies all the way to a place I'd never known.

Home.

Wonder and hope and everlasting melancholy pushed me over the bridge. And for an aching, unbearable, unbreakable moment, I knew where I came from. I knew what I was made of, and what I was made *for.*

"Changeling."

A rough hand caught my wrist, wrenching me around. I thrashed, fear bursting hot in my veins as I fought to free myself. Another palm closed over my other wrist. I snarled, throwing back my head and kicking out with my legs. We both went down, thumping onto cold, hard earth beneath silent trees.

"Fia!" Strong arms wrestled me against a broad chest. Stubble rasped my cheek. The scent of warm steel and spiced soap filled my nostrils. "Fia, get ahold of yourself!"

My eyes snapped open. I shivered against the cage of hot skin. Finally, I recognized the voice, recognized Rogan. He loomed over me, the weight of him pinning me against the cold ground. We were both breathing hard. After a moment, he released me and rolled away. I heaved up onto my elbows, tried to get my bearings.

"Amergin's knees, changeling! My nose!" Rogan grunted wetly, raising a hand to his face. Blood gushed over his mouth and chin.

"Here." Embarrassment came in a hot flush. I sat up, tried to press the edge of my sleeve to his face. He pushed me away, continued pinching the bridge of his nose. "What happened?"

"You went mad, is what happened." His voice was tight with pain and panic. "You stepped over that bridge, and—I don't know. Your eyes were wild as the forest and I heard—well, *heard* isn't the right word, but you were singing or laughing or—" He took his bloody hand from his nose and pressed it to his forehead. "No, it's all jumbled now. But it looked like you were going somewhere I couldn't follow, and I...I couldn't let you." His voice cracked on the last words.

I sat back. Mother's remembrances of Tír na nÓg sounded much the same—a confusion of sight and sound. Feverish images like half-remembered dreams.

Which could mean only one thing.

"I think we found it," I told him. "This is the Thirteenth Gate."

Rogan cursed, rolled to sit beside me. His arm brushed mine; steam rose from the blood clotting his nose. He faced me. "Is it broken?"

"Just bruised," I said, still a little abashed. "It's still a nice nose."

Rogan's eyes flicked to mine. So close to the gate, they glowed with strange intensity. The green around his pupils was like calm seas; the blue flecks, like clear skies.

"Lucky me," he said with a snort. "I'll get to meet my future wife with a bruised nose. But at least it won't be crooked too."

The mention of Eala as his *future wife* burned away my lingering embarrassment. I jerked my arm from his. Stood, brushed off my trousers.

"If she can't handle her future husband looking like a common brawler, then she probably shouldn't marry you."

Rogan got to his feet, more slowly. "You pick far more fights than I do, changeling."

"And endeavor to win them." I made my voice sweet. *"Princeling."*

Rogan flushed. We looked back toward the Gate at the same time.

The path was now dingy and overgrown. The bridge, a sagging ruin. Even the stone monsters were nothing but ancient relics.

A chill of frost raised the hair along my forearms. Like all Folk magic, this place was determined to beguile the mind and fool the senses. Next time we came here, I'd have to be more careful not to let myself be tempted by the pretty fantasies of the Fair Folk.

"We'll come back when the moon is full." Morning was bleeding into afternoon, and it was a long hike back to the dún. "We'll cross into Tír na nÓg, and we'll find Eala together."

If the prospect of Tír na nÓg frightened Rogan, he hid it well. He nodded, and together we headed back to the fort.

⌁

"I'm hungry," Rogan grumbled to me as we hiked through a copse of aspens.

"So you've mentioned." I sighed, more amused than annoyed. "You were hungry this morning; you were hungry at lunchtime."

"I should have packed more food."

The urge to say a vicious *I told you so* nearly overwhelmed me.

"I have dried meat and cheese left in my pack," I told him instead. "We'll share it when we return. Tomorrow we can send to the village for supplies."

He muttered something unintelligible.

"What was that?"

"I said, *I'm bigger than you.* I need more than bits of cheese to survive."

"You are bigger than me." I reached out, pinched his well-muscled abdomen. "What's this if not stores for the winter?"

He squawked, batted my hand away. But mercifully stopped complaining about food.

We reached the dún before the light faded. Rogan trudged straight through the doors, silent and morose without any promise of a warm dinner. But I paused at the top of the ridge. The land spread out like a tapestry, warp and weft woven in fallow fields and shades of frost. The lough was a circle of slate. On its far edge, dense forest pressed close.

An icy wind gusted by, bringing a wave of longing with it. I suddenly missed Rath na Mara. Missed Mother, despite her hardness. I tried to imagine what she must be doing now, with a fire blazing in the hearth and sunset chasing the horizon. Drinking with Cathair, perhaps. Entertaining one of her under-kings with a tale of heroism or hubris.

I hoped our own tale would have the ending she demanded. For all our sakes.

Wearily, I trudged into the dún—then stopped in my tracks.

A fire crackled in the hearth. A low table offered up a hearty meal—hunks of crusty black bread, a steaming vat of pottage, a roast pheasant. For a moment, it seemed another trick of the Folk—a vision meant to torment me. But Rogan had already availed himself of the spread; crumbs and small bones littered the table in front of him.

"What's this?" I asked, shedding my mantle.

Rogan shrugged contentedly. "Someone must have sent it up from the village."

"No one knows we're here." I frowned. "Much less who we are."

"Who else could it have been?"

He had a point. But I hadn't been raised to devour food of uncertain provenance. I dipped a finger into the pottage, brought it to my lips. I didn't taste any poisons. At least, none I was familiar with.

A flurry of motion on the wall caught my eye. I stalked over to inspect the carvings. The firelight sharpened on a furred mouse with vast whiskers, rubbing tiny stone paws over its quivering nose.

Corra. Damned creature.

"Did you do this?" I accused, too loud.

"Obviously not." Rogan spoke around a full mouth.

I considered telling him he was likely dining on cobwebs and bog mud, but couldn't quite muster the energy to explain how I knew. Instead, I glared at the Folk sprite, who twitched its round ears.

" 'Tis but a taste of what we can conjure," Corra said. "No need to send for supplies, to build your own cook fires, to learn how to roast your own meats. Let Corra provide."

"That's awfully generous of you," I hissed. If Rogan kept catching me talking to myself, he was going to think Tír na nÓg had addled my brain.

The mouse blinked its adorably huge eyes. "We ask but one small favor in return."

"Of course you do." I turned on my heel. "You can keep your food, which will likely prove to be dust or sewage instead of nourishment. I have no intention of doing anything for you."

Corra followed me, jumping one by one into the myriad carvings etched on the castle wall: a writhing sea monster, a honking goose, a crow with a beak carved from polished mica.

"The food is real and nourishing. We would not endanger you—if you wither away, you'd be no use to us!"

I waved a hand at the sprite, dismissing it.

" 'Tis but a trifle! All we ask is you tend the garden for us."

I stopped in my tracks. A vision of the ruined greenhouse and its surrounding gardens crept into my mind. Once upon a time, it must have been magnificent. Rogan and I could travel into Tír na nÓg only at the full moon, leaving twenty-eight days out of the month that had to be filled with something. And who knew how long it would take to rescue Eala.

Perhaps—

I narrowed my eyes at Corra. "Why?"

The glittering bird flapped incised wings and gave me a shrewd wink. "The days are long, chiardhubh. Being busy is better than being bored."

"I'll take up knitting."

"As the willful mistress pleases."

"Hmph." My stomach rumbled at the smells wafting from the table—tempting aromas of fresh bread, warm stew, roast meat. "I'll think on it."

"Mind you do, chiardhubh."

I sat and made myself a plate, mouth watering. But I continued glaring at Corra, not wanting it to know how hungry I was. "Next time, I want pie."

"That's awfully demanding of you." Rogan chuckled. "I imagine the villagers will bring us whatever they have on hand."

I bit my tongue and ate. Everything was delicious. I had to remind myself none of this was real. This food was made with Folk magic. Rogan and I were dining on lies.

And if I was going to take on a thankless project in return for such dubious provisions, then I might as well demand pie.

Chapter Seven

Crouched low between the trees, Rogan and I waited for the full moon to rise. The dim wood was eerie at dusk, the stone monsters' shadows quietly lengthening. My unease was polished to a hard sheen, although I wasn't sure whether my nerves were born from fear of what lay beyond the bridge...or *longing* for it.

What waited for us beyond the gate? Lost love and magic? Or cold heartbreak and sorrow?

Rogan elbowed me through my cloak.

"Ow!" I scowled at him. "What was that for?"

"You're making one of your grim, dire faces, changeling." Rogan smiled, a sharp dazzle of nervous humor. "What are you thinking about?"

"Your bruised, crooked nose."

Rogan made a face and gingerly patted the nose in question, which was neither crooked nor particularly bruised.

I was quiet for a long minute. And then: "The Gentry tánaiste beyond the gate—the one who holds the swans captive. What must he be like?"

"I've heard many stories of the Folk Gentry." The twig Rogan had been idly scratching in the dirt took on a purpose, scoring the hard earth with deft lines and curves. A rough picture began to take shape—staring eyes, hooked claws, crooked limbs.

Once upon a time, Rogan had talked about drawing the same way I'd talked about gardens. When his hands hadn't been busy with swordplay, they'd been stained with paint or blackened with charcoal. But that had been a long time ago.

"Some say their bodies are twisted and deformed, tortured into strange shapes by the dark magic they flirt with. Others say they are beautiful enough to drive a person mad." He finished his drawing with a flourish of his stick. A monster stared up at me with venomous eyes. "Perhaps this Gentry heir will command his cursed flock of swan maidens to peck out your eyes and dance on your bones."

I snorted to hide the chill caressing my spine.

"Or perhaps they're just stories told by mothers to frighten children. Or by drunkards to stave off the chill of the night." Rogan erased the crude drawing with a swipe of his palm. "And he'll be no different than you. Or I."

Perhaps. But I'd learned that no stories were ever *just* stories. Stories had their lies but also their truths. Stories were how we taught ourselves to fear the things we secretly desired.

Dark forests. Beautiful monsters. Broken hearts.

"And Eala?" I conjured the specter of my adoptive sister between us. "What will she be like?"

"They say you looked exactly like her when you first came to Rath na Mara, except for your coloring." Rogan brushed dirt off his palms. "If you two have grown up alike, then I imagine she will be beautiful."

I looked at him, startled. In the dimming light his eyes were less like the ocean at dawn and more like the forest at dusk. His arm brushed mine, and I imagined the heat of his skin even through our cloaks. I couldn't stand his closeness yet couldn't bear to be farther away from him. Brusquely, I stood and gestured toward the veins of silver netting the trees.

"The moon's rising," I said. "It's time."

We climbed the stone bridge in silence.

Voice uneven, I sang out the incantation Cathair had given me before we left Rath na Mara. Although it was written in the ancient tongue, the moment I said it aloud, its words etched along my bones and its rhythms rooted behind my teeth. The stones below our feet began to glow, taking up my melody and carrying it onward, like a forgotten lullaby. At first, it sounded sweet, but when I listened more closely, it rang discordant.

It told me if I climbed out of my skin and followed it into the keening twilight, it would carry me home.

"Changeling." Rogan gripped my hand. "*Fia*. Don't get distracted."

I shook my head to clear the dream-haze of music. Swiftly— before I lost myself to the terrible magic again—I drew out my skean and pricked my finger. Mother had said only a few drops of blood would be demanded of me, but I suddenly knew how many would be required. I counted silently, drawing my hand back when thirteen green-black droplets had stained the earth.

Moonlight blazed above the trees, limning the path in silver and sparking cold flames among the trees. Rogan lifted an arm to shade his eyes. He flew far away, caught somewhere between time and place, and I went with him.

I saw geese flinging themselves in a wide V against the wind. Heard blue water laughing nearby, and the singing of bells. Smelled woodsmoke. Autumn's chill swept my hair, tinged with the metallic gnaw of dying leaves, and there was a tree, iron-boughed and crowned with fire...

I fell through the sensations until darkness swallowed me up, then birthed me again.

I stumbled, jerking my head up and gasping. Beside me, Rogan put his hands on his knees and doubled over, as if he might vomit. The forest was bright and dim; the moon had sailed high, painting the earth with bands of silver.

But it was not the same forest. The trees seemed to grow down instead of up. The willow was in the wrong place beside the bridge. Everything was backward, like we'd stepped through a great mirror and were looking at our world from the other side.

Tír na nÓg.

"You did it." Disbelief and awe jumbled on Rogan's face. "We're here."

Sudden hesitation stayed my limbs. Part of me had always doubted we would truly be able to cross over. And yet here we were. Which meant we actually had to *do* the tasks we were set. Find the princess, break her geas, bring her home. Find the Gentry tánaiste, steal his Treasure, save Fódla.

Relinquish the tiny shred of hope that I might be the one to end up with Rogan.

"Let's find the dún above the lough," I said softly to Rogan. "Let's find your princess."

White-faced, he nodded. I raised the hood of my cloak and stepped deeper into the woods.

e～～๑

Time and space ran strange in Tír na nÓg. As Rogan and I set off in the direction we hoped would lead us to the lough and the shadowy dún and the swans, the trees shifted and warped in the corner of my eye. Yet when I turned to look directly at them, they were nothing more than bark and brittle leaves. We trudged through the forest for what felt like hours, yet when we at last saw the ripple of moonlight on water, it seemed mere moments since we'd left the Gate.

As we crouched down at the edge of the wood beside the lough, I gritted my teeth. Nothing in this land was real. Already the spells of this wicked place twined between my bones and behind my eyes. I wanted to go home.

A voice soft as moss whispered in my ear, *What if this is your home?*

We'd arrived at a place that looked like Dún Darragh, if Dún Darragh had been crafted from dark dreams and sharp wishes. The sky was black but pricked through with too-bright stars. The moon burnished the unruffled lough into a mirror. A field of glittering white flowers sloped up to a great fort—although calling it a *fort* felt wrong. It was both more monolithic and less substantial than anything built by human hands. Its bricks were shadow; its windows, tempered starlight. Towers wrought from melancholy loomed above crenellation-fanged walls. To look at it was to look *inside* it, to see staircases twisting like broken spines and ceilings dripping with diamonds.

Motion along the shore captured my gaze. In the moonlight's spell, a bevy of swans were gathered by the water's silver edge. My breath froze in my throat. Without looking away, I grabbed Rogan's arm, directing his attention toward the lough.

The swans ruffled bone-white feathers and unfurled powerful wings as they gathered on the pebbled beach. Their movements took on a swaying, hypnotic quality. They surged like ghosts against the darkness of the lake.

The moment fractured. Feathers drifted down to reveal soft, supple skin. Beaks became delicate noses and laughing mouths. Wings unveiled waving arms.

Where the swans had been stood twelve human girls. There was a brief frenzy of activity—sisterly embraces and muted exclamations. Then, almost as one, they danced away along the shore. Their feet seemed to skim the water, held aloft by night's strange grace. The roaring moon bleached their limbs white as the swans they'd been mere moments before.

Neither Rogan nor I spoke as we crept after the swan maidens. Though they were far from identical—their heights varied, as did their hair, skin color, and features—each carried herself with the poise of a dancer and the air of a mirage. They were sisters—if not in blood, then in the strange curse binding them together.

The maidens paused at the base of the hill beneath the fort.

Rogan and I inched as close as we dared, blinking against the brilliance of the flowers carpeting the rise. They shone like fallen stars, and I felt a sudden desire to pluck one, to pluck them *all*, to weave them into a garland and wear them in my hair and—

I pressed hard against my bracelet of thorns. The flash of pain cleared my head.

I would *not* let this place seduce me with illusions and fancies.

The girls crouched down among the flowers, gathering them up. Their fingers began to bleed, droplets of crimson spattering across the ivory blooms. Revulsion scraped up my throat, but the girls only laughed and chattered as they twisted the flowers into necklaces and tucked them into each other's hair.

One girl didn't join them. She stood proud, waiting for the other maidens to bring the flowers to her. Before long, they did so, tangling them in the blond waves skimming her spine down to the back of her legs. Soon, she wore a luminous crown of bloody stars.

Rogan shifted in the undergrowth. A twig snapped.

The girl turned at the sound.

Vertigo washed over me. I knew what I would see before I saw it.

My skin, blanched white as a swan's feather. My mud-dark hair, but frothing pale as fairy flax. My green-and-brown eyes, but blue as dawn. My petite frame, but soft instead of hard, elegant instead of brutal.

She was I, and I was she, and we were neither one of us each other.

Eala. The queen's true daughter, alive and breathing. She stared a moment longer into the forest as the other maidens blithely continued braiding their glowing garlands.

Rogan was rapt, his attention fixed on his long-awaited princess. He started forward. But I gripped his arm, digging my nails into his skin. He turned, moving as if he were underwater. His eyes glittered deep within the hood of his cloak.

"You're going to march out there?" I hissed. "Just like that?"

"Isn't this what we're here for?" Rogan gestured to Eala.

"What if you frighten her? What if she's loyal to the Gentry tánaiste? What if she's on her way to him right now?"

Rogan frowned—clearly none of this had occurred to him. "How am I supposed to convince her to come home if I can't speak to her?"

"You don't have to spirit her away tonight," I reminded him. "She's been here since she was eight years old. She may not remember you. She may not even remember Mother—*her* mother."

Rogan's shoulders bunched, and his face grew frustrated. "Then what am I supposed to do?"

"Why don't you follow them—just for tonight?" The twelve maidens finished picking their bladed posies and started toward the forest. We edged deeper into the shadows, letting them sweep by us like a river of starlight. "See where they go, watch what they do, get to know them better from afar. Then next time, you'll have a better sense of how to approach them."

"Fine." Rogan rose, but when I didn't get up with him, he paused. "Aren't you coming?"

Mother had forbidden me from telling Rogan about my half of the mission. I didn't like the idea of lying to him outright—instead, I flashed him a small smile in the dim.

"What, princeling? You need my help following a dozen pretty girls into the forest in the dead of night? You were born for this."

His eyes flickered.

"Be back at the Thirteenth Gate before the moon sets," I reminded him. "Otherwise we'll be trapped until next month."

"Would that be so terrible? We'd have more time to save Eala."

I shook my head. "We can't risk eating or drinking in Tír na nÓg, lest we become bewitched. I might be able to survive here for a month—but you can't. And if we were discovered by the Gentry? We would be killed on sight. We must go back to Dún Darragh when the night is done."

Rogan nodded reluctantly, then disappeared into the forest.

I waited until I no longer heard his footsteps. A breeze rattled the branches above me. I swore I heard words in the sound, but though I strained my ears, I couldn't understand them. I tugged my hood higher, then gingerly stepped out into the open. For a place of such darkness, Tír na nÓg was unnaturally vivid. I crouched down at the base of the slope leading to the shadow fort, studying the blossoms growing closest to my boot.

They were tiny, ethereal flowers with white pointed petals. A strange throb pulsed in the pit of my stomach, and I reached for them...

Pain burst hot against my fingertip and darted toward my elbow. I snatched my hand away, even as a drop of green-black blood stained the silken bloom.

A memory from three days ago burned behind my eyes: Another drop of blood. A razored ink-black feather tucked into my pack.

Something dark and brilliant flashed at the corner of my vision. I whirled. And looked straight into the face of a man about to kill me.

Chapter Eight

The arrow trained on my heart gleamed bright from twenty paces. But the man holding the bow was harder to see, as though the moonlight couldn't bear to touch him, and so bent away, leaving him in shadow. I held my body utterly still, squinting from beneath the shadow of my hood. I saw only edges—night-black hair; charcoal smudged in the hollows of angular cheekbones; a jaw like metal.

Only his eyes shone distinct, and they were savage. Bright as moonlight, dark as a nightmare. I knew then—he was no *man*.

"Good evening," I said inanely. As if we were guests at a feast, partners in a dance.

He tilted his head—a tiny yet threatening gesture. Dread weakened my limbs and muddled my thoughts.

I steeled my emotions. I was made of frost and rot and endless things. I was not made to fear the Folk.

"State your business, ghillie." The menace in his voice raised the hairs on my arms. "Then begone."

"I'm no ghillie," I said clearly and pleasantly. "Although I've always wondered what it would be like to have birch bark for skin and moss for hair."

His silence was sharp.

"It seems like it would be...*itchy*," I clarified.

He moved closer, although neither bow nor arrow dropped. He was without question a warrior—I knew the look of a man acquainted with violence. It was there in the measured rhythm of his feet against the earth. The angle of his head. The easy slide of lean muscle over bone. The sheen of danger in eyes silver as far-away stars.

The blade of his jaw lifted, and he scented the air.

"You stink of the human realms. You speak like a human." He glanced down at the shimmering petal I'd stained with my green-dark blood. "Yet you bleed like the forest. Tell me what you are."

He took one final step toward me, and I finally saw the whole of him between the twisting shadows that wreathed him like great black wings.

He was *beautiful.*

He stood more than a head taller than I, narrow at the waist but broad through the shoulders. Unlike the men of Fódla's long braided styles, his hair was cropped brutally short, the strands the shining black of a raven's wing. In contrast, his skin was pale as marble. And oh, his *face.* His striking features were carved in clean, austere lines—chiseled cheekbones, stark frowning brows, a hard sculpted jaw. The only soft thing about him was the bow of his incongruously sensuous mouth. And those *eyes*—like metal, like moonlight, like...

For a long moment, I was taken in. Bewitched. My shoulders relaxed; my mouth curved into a smile; my mind loosened.

Then I remembered where I was. Who he was. *What* he was.

His was the beauty of the night—dark moons and dark deeds. His was the beauty of the forest—hiding teeth and hiding monsters. His was the beauty of black ice—slick and thin and masking death.

I knew him then by his treacherous beauty. He was one of the Folk Gentry.

My hands trembled with the urge to defend myself, to snatch up my skeans and fling them at his heart. But I suspected my blades would not find their mark, no matter how true my aim.

"I am—" I hesitated, a mouse in a trap. There were many things I could tell him. Many truths. Many lies. There were also many ways I could die, here, tonight. "I am lost."

"This is no place to be lost." He circled closer. "Nor found."

"The pleasure of the losing is in the finding." I refused to show fear. "Or so I've been told."

He stopped an arm's length away. He appraised me calmly, like a falcon who had caught sight of its prey but was in no hurry to stoop.

"You hide your face." His voice was husky, as if he didn't use it often. "Which makes me think you are not lost at all, but rather wish not to be found."

"Maybe I'm unbearably ugly."

His expression shifted.

"Loathly or not," he said, "this is no place to be found—nor lost."

"You already said that."

"I did not think you were listening."

I dared a sideways glance, meeting eyes cold enough to freeze my blood. Silence strung a bow between us.

"Tell me what you are," he offered, without lowering the arrow still trained on my face, "and I will consider letting you leave this place alive."

"If I knew," I honestly said, "I'd tell you. But as far as I know, I'm just a girl. I'm just *me*."

He considered this.

"And you?" I dared to ask. "What are you?"

My boldness made him smile. His teeth glittered white in the moonlight, his canines a little longer than they ought to be.

"When this place needs guarding, I am its guardian. And I am not fond of intruders."

My fear lurched toward terror.

The Gentry guard reached out to grasp a dark curl falling out of my braid, sliding it between his fingers. Tattoos twined above his leather vambraces toward his sculpted bicep. In the drifting moon shadows, they looked like the pinions of a great black bird.

"Perhaps I should have been more clear." His voice rasped with pitiless amusement. "When I said I do not like intruders, what I meant was: I promise to give you a head start."

A lifetime of training had taught me many things. It had taught me the value of my instincts. It had taught me when I was outmatched and outwitted. It had taught me the surest way to entice a predator to pounce was to turn my back on it.

It had also taught me that sometimes, all there was to do was run.

I had never run like I ran now.

There was no thought for form or style, only speed. My legs pumped beneath me; my breath gulped in my lungs; the world went black and silver as the forest swallowed me up. The crash of my steps in the underbrush was too loud. Strange specters and phantoms paced me in the dark.

Emaciated foxes creeping on elongated, soot-stained paws. They carried bloodied scalps between their teeth, matted hair trailing through silver leaves.

Skeleton birds with smoke for feathers and daggers for beaks.

Men without faces, girls without eyes, beasts without mouths.

But though I strained my ears for the sound of my pursuer—his footfalls, the twang of an arrow on a bow, the *shink* of steel leaving a scabbard—I heard nothing.

After what felt like an eternity—or, perhaps, mere moments—I reached the stand of ancient ash trees. The bridge over the stream. The willow, with her tangled tresses. The Gate, its borders a sullen shimmer.

I slowed. And finally heard the footsteps I'd listened for—the crash of my pursuer through the undergrowth. Fear burned away my exhaustion. I closed my eyes, lunged for the bridge.

A hand on my shoulder gripped me, stopped me. Spun me.

Rogan.

Relief liquefied my limbs. He was everything that Folk monster wasn't—rugged and familiar and so perfectly imperfect, so *human*, I nearly wept. I reached out, gripped his warm, rough, freckled hand. His eyes found mine as pink dawn kissed the trees, all the things we had seen and done this night lingering between us, unsaid for now. As the light changed from silver to gold, the Thirteenth Gate swept us up and carried us home.

But I couldn't unhear the faint note of nightmare laughter that chased me through the Gate.

Chapter Nine

I woke that afternoon to thorns in my skull and a mouth choked with weeds.

I turned over in my bedroll and groaned. It felt like a hangover, only worse—my head hollow as a rotten log. But beautiful thoughts and seductive images also teased the back of my eyelids. I reached for them, struck with a sudden awful longing, but they were slippery as green algae.

Mother's voice echoed through my thoughts. *When you are there, Tír na nÓg will take every opportunity to remind you that you do not belong. Once you are gone, it will make you wish you could return.*

I gritted my teeth and forced my eyelids open. I was almost *glad* to experience the aftereffects of my journey into Tír na nÓg—it meant I did not belong there. It meant I was more human than Folk. It meant home was here—not *there*.

Rogan's bedroll was empty, which meant he must have either woken before me...or not slept at all.

As we'd hiked back to the fort earlier, I'd asked Rogan what had happened with the swan maidens. With Eala.

"I went—" He'd shaken his head, his mouth narrow as a blade. "I followed them to a party. At least, that's what I think it was."

I'd stared at his profile in the dawn, fighting a burst of confusion. I'd spent less than an hour in Tír na nÓg—of that, I was almost certain. How had Rogan had time to follow the swan maidens to a *party*? Did time run differently in the Folk realms?

"And you?" His expression had shifted. "Something sure had you frightened."

"Oh." I'd tossed my head and tried to suppress the panic rising in my chest, the adrenaline burning through my sluggish limbs. The dark amusement in the Gentry guard's voice still nipped at me like fangs. *I promise to give you a head start.* "I went for a walk in the woods. But the wildlife was unpleasant."

Rogan had frowned but hadn't pressed me. And we'd walked the rest of the way to Dún Darragh in silence.

Now I scrambled to my feet and tugged at my rumpled tunic. It smelled like cold water and caged joy and the moment before lightning struck. I resolved to throw it on the fire.

"Corra!" The formless wight might as well put themself to use. "Corra, where are you?"

A stout hedgepig with brambles for spines and a blackberry for a nose rustled to life on the wall.

"Have you decided to renew the gardens, chiardhubh?" queried the little creature adorably.

"I certainly have not," I scoffed. "Did you see where Rogan went this morning?"

I got a blank stare in response.

"You know." Annoyance rose in me. "Big, handsome, human? Looks like a prince? *Rogan.*"

"The one with oatmeal for a face and mushrooms for ears and rocks for feet?" Corra responded uncharitably. "Him?"

"Him. Where is he?"

"He left. But then he came back."

"So he's in the fort?"

"He'll leave again," Corra warned, leafy spines bristling.

"I'm sure he will." I sighed. "You're going to make me open every door on every floor until I find him, aren't you?"

"Not if you give us your boots."

"My—" I looked down at the footwear in question, which was several years old and caked with muck from tromping in the woods all night. "Why?"

"Our toes are cold."

"You don't have toes. Even if you did, you can't have them. They're my favorite pair."

"Willful wench," Corra hissed. "The brute is in the tower. But you should know he has vinegar for blood and rotten leaves for skin and spiders for hair and—"

"Thanks so much," I interrupted. "Oh, and Corra?"

"Yes?"

"Shut up."

Corra keened a curse, then rocketed out of their spiny host, whizzing between carvings and muttering epithets. I heard what sounded suspiciously like *puke-stockinged maltworm* and *beef-witted baggage* before the sprite disappeared into the ether.

I swallowed a smile. I'd grown up an unwanted changeling in the court of a queen at war with the Folk. Corra was going to have to do better than that if they wanted to pierce this beef-witted baggage's thick skin.

❧ ～ ❧

The staircase to the tower left me panting, sweat beading along my upper lip and down my back. At the landing, a plain wooden door stood slightly ajar. I knocked. No one answered, so I pushed inside. The vaulted tower chamber was dim, unlit save for the small strip of gray light filtering in from a drizzly afternoon. My eyes dredged the shadows.

"Rogan?" I called, even as I caught sight of him.

He slouched in silhouette against the window, which was open to the elements. Rain splattered against the stone sill and dripped onto the floor by his boots. A gust of wet wind lifted the ends of his golden hair. He'd somehow acquired a bottle of ruby-colored liquor and already made his way through half of it.

He was up here brooding. I should have guessed.

"Afternoon, princeling." I managed to sound only slightly sarcastic.

A muscle in his arm jumped, and the leg propped up on the sill twitched. He kept his face resolutely slanted down toward the iron lough.

"Do you have to call me that?" he said after a beat.

Hurt spangled through me. *Princeling, changeling*—these were the names other people called us. Names they used to fit us into tiny boxes we didn't like and hadn't agreed to. Names they used to hurt us. But when we were children, they had become like our own personal language. Between the two of us, the names were a reclamation—of the things we were and weren't, of the things we wanted but couldn't have. Of the things we meant to each other.

At least, that was how it used to be.

"I don't *have* to." I made my voice blasé. "But what will do instead? *My lord? Conqueror of towers? Slayer of wine bottles?*"

He didn't take the bait. He didn't even look at me. "How about my name?"

"Fine, *Rogan*. What's going on?"

"I met her once, you know." He drummed his fingers against the neck of the bottle. "When we were children."

He was talking about Eala. Curiosity rose up to meet my simmering bitterness. When we were young, we'd rarely spoken of the princess. Neither of us had known her; she was little more than an abstract concept. As we'd grown, so too had Eala's specter, haunting the spaces between us. But discussing her had given form to the ways we were shaped and bound by her—had given name to her presence, even in her absence. So we'd rarely mentioned her.

"I was six or seven. She, four." Rogan took a pull from the bottle. "She was a tiny, pretty thing, sitting prim and poised at her mother's knee. I remember thinking how different she was to my snot-nosed, grubby little brother, who was about her age. Our parents made us play together. She wanted to play dolls. Suffice it to say, it was not my idea of fun. I grew bored, kicking ashes into the fireplace and ignoring her." He paused, his eyebrows drawing together. "But then she stuck one of her dolls in my face. 'Rogan,' she said to me, 'I hate this dolly. But Mother won't buy me a new one unless she breaks.' It seemed a straightforward scheme to me—I obliged the princess by ripping her doll's head off. But then Eala... she went screaming to her mother. The queen was furious at me. I tried to explain, but that only made things worse. She ordered my father to punish me for the offense. I still have scars from the caning he gave me."

Sympathy pulsed through me. Cairell Mòr was not a kind man—especially not to his eldest son. "Rogan—"

"It's been sixteen years." Rogan finally looked at me, his blue-green eyes hazy with memory. "And I still can't figure out why she made me break that doll."

An uneasy silence stretched between us. I had no answer for him. I could picture that little princess easily—now that I'd seen Eala grown, I had no trouble believing her younger self had been just as bright and lovely. No wonder I'd been such a disappointment when I'd awoken strange-eyed and wild-haired in her bed. But I had no insight into that child's mind or motivations. Nor did I understand why Rogan had brought it up. If Eala had been such a horrid menace to him, then why had he chosen her over me, four years ago?

I pressed my wrist against my thigh, letting the new pain chase away the old.

"Perhaps it was a misunderstanding," I suggested diplomatically. "Rogan... did something happen between you and Eala last night?"

My words pulled Rogan's rain-washed gaze back into focus. He stood up from the windowsill and set the bottle down.

"You should have warned me we were going to split up." His voice was rough with accusation. "In Tír na nÓg. Instead of sending me off into the forest alone."

"Why?" The displeasure in his voice raised my hackles, and the sudden change in topic made me think he didn't want me to know what had happened between him and Eala. "Did you need me to hold your hand?"

"No. I needed to know where you were. I needed to know you were safe."

"I don't want your worry." Annoyance pounded through my head, joining the cacophony of my otherworldly hangover. He'd given up the right to worry about me when he chose Eala over me. When he left me alone with Cathair's merciless ministrations for four long years. When he told me I was nothing to him. No one. "I can take care of myself."

"Can you? Last night I found you sprinting through the forest like the hounds of the Morrigan were snapping at your heels." He paced toward me, then stopped a few inches away. Too close. Not close enough. "You were terrified of something. You jumped out of your skin when I touched you."

"Maybe that's because I don't welcome your touch."

The words sounded crueler than I intended them to, but they had the desired effect. Rogan's blue-green eyes narrowed to furious slits. He rocked back on his heels, crossed his arms over his chest.

"Tell me what task the queen has set you."

"I don't know what you're talking about."

"I'm not stupid," he growled. "I know you weren't hanging around that shadowy fort picking flowers. Just tell me. Maybe I can help."

Mother's warning pricked brambles through my mind.

"You're right—I do have a task. But it's a secret."

"We don't keep secrets. Not from each other."

"We *didn't*. That was before you—" The old wound throbbed. "Before you left Rath na Mara. You don't need my help wooing your swan princess. And I certainly don't need your help fulfilling Mother's demands of me."

"You always did before."

My hurt must have shown on my face—Rogan's river-stone eyes widened in apology. "Changeling—"

"How about my *name*, Rogan?" I threw his words back at him with all the venom I could muster. "Or are you the only one who deserves that privilege?"

I didn't wait for him to respond. Taking the winding stairs two at a time, I fled out into a sullen afternoon.

My aimless steps had nearly carried me to the greenhouse when I thought of Corra's bargain. If I was honest, I had little desire to pour my time and effort into the garden—it would be thankless work. But Corra had been right. We needed food and supplies. And I needed something to occupy my time between full moons. Otherwise I was going to murder a prince.

Or cry.

I wasn't sure which was worse.

⁓

Wind whipped the lough to froth beneath a ragged sky. Mud squelched at my boots, and cold seeped through the seams of my woolen cloak, but I didn't care. I was nearly to the grotto when my eye caught on a scrap of black. I bent, reaching for the bedraggled feather wedged between two clumps of weeds.

Even dull and wet and missing half its barbs, the slender vane was beautiful. I glanced at my fingers, thinking of the first feather I'd found—the prick of its quill. Then I looked at the sky. Ravens chattered in the wood, and rooks roosted beneath the eaves of the dún. But these stiff pinions were nearly as long as my forearm.

The drizzle became a downpour as I dropped the feather, feeling mutinous. I'd never expected this to be simple. But back at Rath na Mara—back in the *real* world—I *knew* things. I knew a claíomh swung at the wrong angle with too little force would cripple a man instead of kill him. I knew milk thistle, when brewed into a tea, could counteract the effects of many mild poisons. I knew Mother loved me, and her love was stronger even than her hate for the Folk.

But here, in this moldering haunt of a dún atop ruinous lands at the edge of Tír na nÓg, I knew nothing. I was full of answers without knowing any of the questions. A maple seed spinning endlessly through the air, not knowing where I might land, only knowing I could never return to my branch.

I swiped moisture from my eyelashes, then marched into the greenhouse.

The cracked glass and busted metal did little to keep out the elements. Water pattered on my head as I trailed my fingers along one of the dilapidated tables. Dirt clung to my hand, smelling of manure and rotten leaves and rich clay. This had been good dirt, once—the kind of dirt that nourished life. The kind of dirt that made green things flourish and grow.

At the end of the greenhouse, a creeping vine had been left to spread. I didn't recognize its spiny leaves or long sharp thorns. Its flowers were past season, petals hanging like shrouds. I stared at the plant. Something venomous cast a shadow over my heart. My foul mood blossomed.

I thought of Rogan, whom I'd always loved but who'd left me.

Mother, who praised me but then set me a nearly impossible task.

Eala Ní Mainnín, my sister, a beautiful stranger, whose life was valued higher than mine.

My Greenmark, which turned hedgehogs to dust and gray mares to wild trees.

I grabbed the ancient shears propped against the workbench. The blades were dull and grimed with rust. They shrieked as they sliced through the vines. Ichor spurted from the tendrils, thicker and darker than blood.

I hacked at the vine until my hands were covered with clinging ooze and my arms were lacerated with tiny scratches. I plucked sharp thorns from the pads of my fingers with my teeth and spat them into Dún Darragh's dead gardens. I stepped back, breathing hard.

The vine lay utterly destroyed at my feet. And where it once sprawled—creeping and digesting and ruining—something grew.

A tiny flower with pointed petals. But instead of being bright as a star, this flower was black as the space between them. I knelt, reaching for it.

Brilliance flashed at the corner of my vision. I whirled, but there was only a chime of distant music and the aching sensation of forgetting something I was meant to remember. When I turned back, the small black flower was gone.

A crash echoed through the greenhouse, followed by an audible yelp and a round of inventive cursing. I whipped my head around to see Rogan wrestling with a plank of wood that might once have been a potting table.

I stalked to the front of the greenhouse. Rogan tensed, lowering the massive board. When he looked at me, his blue-green eyes crackled with a desperate hope that made my heart feel too big for my chest. I willed it as vicious and sharp as the vine I'd just butchered.

"What are you doing here?" I snarled.

"*Helping.*"

I crossed my arms. "Looks more like an exercise in futility."

He huffed. "My specialty, apparently."

He hefted the slab of wood he'd been lugging. I inhaled—even for a man of his musculature, the board was enormous. He grunted, taking the weight onto his back, then heaved it to the side, out of the center of the room. It hung in midair before crashing directly into the risers, taking a row of clay pots, a handful of seedling jars, and half a wall's worth of clouded glass with it.

"Rogan!" Green fury blazed up around my heart. If I decided to take Corra's deal, those jars could have held dormant bulbs for the spring—bulbs that would one day be tulips, allium, maybe even magenta lady's slippers. The seedling jars might have held herbs—rosemary, thyme, sage—for Corra's stews. And Rogan had crushed those possibilities with his carelessness. "What do you think you're doing?"

"I was just—" Confusion and remorse muddied his gaze. He scraped tangled golden hair off his face. He looked exhausted. Violet hollows ringed his eyes and carved out his cheekbones. Had he slept at all this morning before spending half the day drinking? "I just wanted to help—"

"Get out." I shoved him in the chest, hard. My control over my magic was starting to slip. "Get out of my greenhouse!"

"*Your* greenhouse?" Rogan caught my fingers in his large, rough hands. "What are you going to do, changeling? Greenmark me?"

"Maybe I will," I snarled. "I'd like to see you try and rescue the princess with ferns growing out of your big ugly ears!"

For a long moment, we stared at each other. Then Rogan bent over, put his hands on his knees, and started wheezing. Concern jolted through me, followed by indignation when I realized he was *laughing.* He straightened, still chuckling, and pulled me against him, wrapping his arms over my shoulders and tucking my head under his chin. I tensed and almost pushed him away. But he was warm and solid, and the laughter rumbling through his chest vibrated through me, and everything suddenly seemed...*all right.*

Morrigan, but I'd *missed* him.

For a long moment we stood like that, me tucked close against his chest, his arms enveloping me. Eventually, I pushed back enough to look up at him.

"Was that our stupidest fight?" I asked.

"Not even close." He lifted one burnished eyebrow. "Remember when you punched me in the throat so hard I couldn't eat solids for a week?"

"It was *three days*," I countered. "And you didn't have any problem using said throat to complain about how horrible your life had become without regular access to bread and cheese."

"It was genuinely horrible," he said ruefully. "Remind me what I did to deserve it?"

"I don't actually remember," I admitted. "I wasn't even trying to punch you in the throat. I was aiming for your jaw."

He grinned down, his crooked smile disarming me. "What went wrong?"

"I missed. You were so—" The words came out softer than I meant them to. I cleared my throat. "You've always been . . . so tall."

Something in my voice chased the smile off Rogan's face. He looked down at me with sudden intensity, his gaze darkening. Awareness spilled over me like rain, touching my skin with a thousand sharp thorns as I registered how tightly I was molded against him. How close my face was to his. How warm his palms rested at the curve of my waist. I tensed and made to move away, but one of his hands lifted to the nape of my neck and sank into my loose hair. Gently, he tilted my head back until I had no choice but to lift my eyes to his.

"Changeling." His voice was heavy with all the memories we'd shared, the years we'd been apart, the words we'd never dared say to each other. "I've missed you."

Briefly, as I met eyes warm as a summer sky, I allowed myself to remember. Remember what it had been like *before*. When he was only mine, and I was only his. When we'd been so close no one had a name for what we were. Best friends. Lovers. *Family*.

I forced myself to remember. He'd chosen *her*. Left because of her. Returned because of her.

You are no one.

Gently, I disentangled myself from his arms and walked out into the rain.

If I looked back at him even once, I would keep looking back at him forever. So I didn't look back.

Dún Darragh's great hall flared with torchlight. The massive hearth crackled with badly cured logs, spitting green sparks across the rushes.

"Corra, are you here?"

I scanned the carvings for motion. After what felt like a long time, a chiseled crow with an onyx beak ruffled indignantly to life.

"We weren't but seem to be now," said the sprite, with some asperity. "How may we wet your whiskers?"

"I'll do it," I said without preamble. "But I'll need things. And not only for the garden."

"Things," Corra agreed noncommittally, scraping their crow's feet on the ancient stone walls.

"First, a bed." I'd made a decision on the mucky walk up from the greenhouse. I didn't want to do any favors for the formless sprite haunting this fort. And reviving that corpse of a garden would be hard, thankless work. But if I was going to spend however many months *not* falling back in love with the infuriatingly handsome prince who knew me too well, I was going to need something to occupy my time. And despite my threats, I didn't know how to knit. "And some blankets. Simple clothes, or fabric I can sew. Supplies too—tools to repair the greenhouse, and trowels and spades and dowels and dibblers. I'll need bulbs if we want anything to grow next spring, and plenty of seeds. Pots to replace the ones Rogan broke. Compost. Burlap. And a hot, steaming, utterly *scalding* bath."

"Will that be all, *mistress?*"

"Not quite. I also require…*intelligence.*"

"We fear only the gods can help you with that."

"*Information.*" I huffed, crossing my arms over my chest. "All I know of Tír na nÓg I learned from stories and legends. I need to know about the geography. The social and political structures. The…people."

The crow gave me an aggrieved look. " 'Twasn't part of our bargain."

"Name something more you want from me in return."

For a long moment, the only sounds in the hall were the snapping of the green logs in the fireplace and the distant howl of the wind over the moor.

"You must celebrate the high holy days." Corra's crow gave me a sly look. "And you must promise not to tell that long-tongued canker-blossom anything about us."

I'd never had any intention of telling Rogan about Corra, lest he think me madder than an outhouse rat. Better he believe in generous villagers than invisible sprites. So I said, "Done."

Corra shot out of their crow, leaving it motionless on the wall, and scuttled off to disappear somewhere near the ceiling.

A row of torches flared to life against the far wall. I hefted my pack—much lighter now than when we'd left Rath na Mara, thanks to Rogan's ravenous appetite—and followed, determined to be unsurprised by whatever trickery Corra might submit me to.

But I was surprised. Because down a long hallway, up a crumbling flight of stairs, and nestled between two molding tapestries was a small, snug bedroom. A fire crackled merrily in a hearth. A bed was mounded with coverlets and furs and—oh, glory—*pillows*. And a huge brass tub foamed with hot, lavender-scented water.

I undressed quickly and bathed slowly, reveling in the feeling of hot water sweeping away a week's worth of grime. I lowered my head beneath the suds and imagined all my resentments and shames and wants melting off with the dirt. Slowly, my body relaxed; my mind calmed.

When I surfaced, I smelled food. A low table had appeared, piled with my favorites. Flaky scones, fresh butter, autumn squash, stinky cheese.

And pie.

Chapter Ten

Ngetal—Reed
Late Autumn

Tell me of the Thirteenth Gate," I said to Corra, frustration grinding between my teeth as I fought a losing battle with a tangle of weeds. "How was it never discovered before now?"

"The Gates have not numbers." Corra shot me a sullen look from the frowning knot of an overgrown alder.

The first week after the full moon had been fine, if boring. I'd explored the fort while Rogan brooded in the tower, which he'd chosen for his room. By the second week, we were both stir-crazy. Rogan took to roaming the edge of Roslea with his claíomh, hacking at rotten stumps and leafless saplings and chasing small woodland creatures back into their burrows. This irritated me enough to start work on the greenhouse, if only to hack at something myself.

"Then how should I refer to them?" I asked, yanking at a particularly stubborn root. Corra had attempted to make good on their promise of tools by leading me to a falling-down shed boasting exactly one rusty shovel and one gap-toothed rake. I'd reiterated my demands, then made do with what I had. But for all my hours of hard work—all the scraping and raking and struggling—the gardens looked barely better than when I first saw them.

"They are named after trees—one for each moon of the year. Birch, ash, rowan. The like."

I tilted my head toward Roslea. "The Gate here?"

" 'Tis the Willow Gate," said Corra. "And sorrowfully so."

I waited for more information. "Is that all you're going to tell me?"

"We have no more to offer," said Corra. And then, wickedly: "Though many a word has been left to collect dust where rats and weevils like to play. But your skills at reading, you'll have to trust. A rather large gamble, wouldn't you say?"

"Are you telling me there's a library of some kind?" But the sprite had seemingly vanished. Still, I remarked to the air, "As far as attacks on my literacy go, Corra, that one was rather tortured!"

❧ ～❧

By the night of the next full moon, the gray drizzle had given way to a bone-cracking cold.

Neither Rogan nor I had particularly wanted to leave the dún. Although the fort was drafty, it had huge hearths and crackling fires and hot beverages. But after weeks of impatiently watching a lazy moon slide through her phases, there was little chance of either of us sitting on our hands tonight.

"It's time," I said.

Rogan nodded, his face shadowed beneath the hood of his cloak. He'd kept his distance from me since that day in the greenhouse. But now a quick cascade of emotions rippled across his expression. Hurt...bitterness...resignation.

I looked away first.

The ritual was easier this time. The words of the incantation tasted less foreign; the transition over the boundary felt less like being flung by a giant hand and more like a wave lifting us across an ocean. My stomach twisted; my eyes ached. And then we were in Tír na nÓg, with its melting trees and blooming sky.

We set off toward the fort without a word—now we'd been here before, we knew our roles. It was mercifully easy to fall into them.

By the time we reached the edge of the trees, the swan maidens had completed their trek to the base of the fort and already wore garlands of bloody starflowers. Chattering and giggling among themselves, they circled back toward the lough. They paused at the edge of the water as Eala—oh, beautiful Eala, bright as a star and brilliant as a wish—moved to the front of the group and elegantly bent one leg to test the water.

No—she *stepped* onto the surface of the water. Impossibly, it held her weight. Her second foot followed the first, and she imperiously beckoned the other girls after her.

One by one, the swan maidens danced out across the lough. Their featherweight steps didn't even ripple the water beneath them, which stayed flat and glassy. As they walked, the red-tipped flowers braided into their hair shone brighter. Gowns shaped from daydreams materialized over their naked frames; kirtles of crackling red leaves and downy white frost, fragile pink mornings and golden sunrises. Gems cut from witch light ringed their wrists and traced their collarbones. I blinked, certain I was imagining it. But this was no illusion.

Somewhere near the middle of the lough, the girls began to descend. Impossibly—it was *all* impossible—they disappeared beneath the water, like an invisible staircase had opened up beneath them. One by one, their heads bobbed downward, until there was nothing left but moonlight and silence.

I lifted a quizzical eyebrow at Rogan. "I think you've been invited to another party, princeling."

The glance he gave me was almost corrosive. He strode out from between the trees without a word.

Whatever impossible path the maidens had taken, Rogan found. He sprinted across the water, and I didn't blame him—there was no way of knowing whether he might plunge into deep, frigid waters between one step and the next. But he, too, safely crossed the lough to disappear below the inky surface.

I exhaled, releasing a white cloud of traitorous envy. Now that Rogan and his exquisite intended were out of sight, I could focus on Mother's mission. I looked up at the fort looming dark on the star-drenched hill. The Gentry guard stalked to the front of my mind, as he had many times in the past four weeks. In my ultimate goal of getting close enough to the powerful tánaiste to steal his Treasure, the guard was my first obstacle. I doubted I'd be able to best him in combat. He'd been...formidable.

Movement near the lough stole my gaze and wavered my thoughts. One of the swan maidens—hadn't I counted twelve?—raced along the shore. She was still stark naked, save for a few bedraggled starflowers laddering her long dark hair. She pelted out onto the water without hesitation, her movements hectic as she followed the invisible path. Watching her, I almost had to smile—it was so obvious from her body language that she was late.

Too late.

Between one step and the next the path across the water simply ceased to exist, as I'd feared would happen to Rogan. The girl pitched forward, slapping face-first into the lough and disappearing beneath the black water. The splash was deafening in the quiet of the night, and I flinched. I strained my eyes toward the water, where an ever-expanding circle of silver pushed dislodged starflowers toward the shore. Surely the maiden could swim? I held my breath, counting my accelerating heartbeats.

The girl surfaced with a spray of water and a gurgled curse. She shook her slick head like a disgruntled seal and kicked haphazardly toward the beach, her movements even more frantic than they had been above water. The lough had to be freezing. Still, she seemed like a capable enough swimmer. My pulse slowed.

She was a stone's throw from the shore when movement broke the surface behind her.

A narrow furrow, frothing white. Moonlight glinting on a patina of scales.

Tension pulled me taut as the string of a bow. I opened my mouth, then shut it.

What did I think I was going to do—*warn* her? I wasn't even supposed to be here.

More movement beside her. A slender set of fins broke the surface, hung in the air, then slapped down with a sound like the crack of a whip.

The black water churned with chaos—a tumult of flicking fins and spangled scales and pale teeth. Webbed hands grasped the maiden's limbs and dragged her beneath the surface. My heart lurched to a stop. I held my breath, my eyes riveted on the turbulent water.

She surfaced with a gasp, kicking at the hands reaching for her legs and slithering tight over her torso. She fought herself free. But there were *more* of them—too many. And she was still too far from the shore. Those cold white hands were closing over her mouth and dragging at her hair and—

They were drowning her. And I was standing here doing *nothing.*

My fingers itched with the promise of a hundred quiet growing things. But how would that help a girl being drowned by aquatic Folk?

Morrigan be *damned.*

I pelted out from between the trees. My heavy boots dragged at my feet, but I didn't have time to unlace them. I shrugged off my fur-lined overcloak as I ran, then ripped off the softer woolen mantle beneath it. Frigid air stung my neck and face. The water was going to be worse. *Much* worse.

Fragments of ice at the water's edge gleamed silver, flashing a memory in my mind's eye.

I'd been twelve, and winter had arrived in Fódla with precarious and unusual cold. Cathair had dragged me out of bed before dawn and frog-marched me past Rath na Mara's palisade, out into the frost-webbed fields beyond. I'd begged him to tell me where we were going, but he'd shaken his head. The pond at the edge of the forest—where Rogan and I often swam—had been iced over. White lace embroidered its darkness and made strange shapes out of the leaves frozen below the surface. When I'd looked up at him in question, Cathair had waved me out onto the ice. I'd balked— the pond never froze solid. But he'd insisted. I'd inched out, the ice groaning at my weight.

Still the druid had waved me onward.

The ice had shattered without warning. Biting water closed over my head, and the world became darkness and panic. I'd gasped, inhaling frigid water before sinking like a stone.

Cathair had hauled me out by my cloak in the moment before I blacked out. And as I'd lain shivering and spewing pond water, he'd told me, "The Eleventh Gate led to Tír fo Thuinn—the Land Under the Sea. The towering waters were like ice, and those who could not swim in the cold drowned before we even met our foe." His face had been frozen, but his eyes had burned. "You must learn. You must learn to be strong, little witch, because the world is full of Folk who would exploit your every weakness."

So I'd learned. Cathair had made me plunge into the icy water again and again, until I no longer gave in to the gasp reflex. Until my muscles no longer seized up and made me sink. Until I could hold still long enough to remember which way was up—and which way was death.

After, I'd been in bed for two months with a bad bout of winter fever not even Cathair's potions could cure. But I'd learned how to be strong.

Now I took a deep breath, prayed I still remembered the druid's unpleasant lessons, and dived headfirst into the freezing lough.

Chapter Eleven

The frigid water tried to pummel the air out of my lungs. I clamped my mouth shut, and after a moment the instinct to gasp passed. My limbs twitched with cold as I cut through the frothing black water toward where the girl struggled against her attackers. She was still fighting, even as the creatures yanked her head viciously back and dragged her down by the hair.

This time, she didn't rise. A stream of pale bubbles popped quietly atop the settling water.

I kicked faster, slid one of the skeans from my belt, and dived.

Moonlight barely pierced the black surface of the lough, but the scales of the watery predators were iridescent, their slithering bodies casting a luminous trail. They were *fast*. Even hauling the unwilling body of the girl between them, the three—no, *four*—creatures were descending into the depths of the lough too quickly for me to follow. One of them looked up at me with a wide, eerie face ringed with fins, hair waving like pondweed.

Pondweed.

Inspiration struck, warming my sluggish blood. Instead of chasing after the Folk, I closed my eyes and sent my awareness sprinting past them. My Greenmark traveled where I couldn't. Through cold water, past floating blooms of algae. Into darkness—was it too dark? If sunlight did not reach this deep, nothing could grow...

There.

Embedded in the rich sludge of the lough floor was a submerged meadow of pondweed. Gentle fronds waved at me like friendly hands, edged in the barest sliver of moonlight. I poured my waning strength into my Greenmark, sending pulses of life into the cold, sleeping vegetation. The pondweed woke at my command, suddenly less gentle. And much less friendly.

In their haste to drown the maiden and avoid me, the watery Folk had descended nearly to the bottom of the lough. Their iridescent fins brushed through the tendrils of new growth billowing from the tips of the weeds. The plants wandered over their muscular limbs and silky tails. If an unexpected thorn scratched against their gleaming scales, they didn't notice.

Until it was too late.

I clenched my fists, turning the pondweed predatory. Soft weeds drew tight as nooses, wrapping around narrow waists and writhing fins. The fronds grew serrated edges, slashing skin and shredding the hands trying to unknot them. Vicious thorns sprouted, burrowing into tender flesh. Fear washed over the Folk like an invisible current. They began to struggle in earnest, fighting the animated pondweed as if their lives were at stake.

Which they were.

The swan maiden floated free of the predators' grasp, forgotten in their panic. Her form was barely visible in the depths, a point of stillness amid the thrash of pale bodies and green chaos. But she did not buoy to the surface, as she would if her lungs had air in them.

I propelled myself down, cutting through dark water on little more than a prayer. Somehow, I reached her. My hand closed around her wrist. If blood beat through her veins, I couldn't feel it. I wrapped my arms around her chest, taking her ungainly weight onto me. I kicked, even as fingers folded over my ankle. I still clutched my skean in one hand—I curled down and slashed blindly. The blade struck flesh. The hand retreated.

Blood mingled with water as I kicked with feeble limbs toward the surface.

The next few minutes passed in a blur. I was a strong swimmer, but it wasn't my strength carrying the two of us to shore. It was will alone that propelled me across half a lough in freezing temperatures, borne down by the impossible weight of a girl much taller than I. Will, and the belligerent, unrelenting hatred of failure.

I was made of weeds and dark water and unbreakable ice. I was not made to lose.

After what felt like an eternity, my feet struck ground. My boots slipped in the muck, but I dug them in. My legs were heavy as iron as I pushed through the shallows, dragging the girl's motionless form behind me. I flopped her as high as I was able onto the pebbled beach, but cold waves still slapped at her naked legs. My gasping breath was loud in the silence as I shoved sopping hair off her cold face. I pushed against her chest to force the water from her lungs, almost hard enough to pop her ribs. I pinched her nose and breathed into her clammy mouth. Pushed and breathed. Pushed and breathed.

If nothing else, the grim rhythm of the movement began to warm me up.

My strength was failing when the girl convulsed, choked, then turned to vomit a gush of black water onto the beach. Relief unspooled my clenched muscles, and I nearly collapsed. The girl hacked roughly for a few long minutes, working to expel the water from her lungs. Finally, the spasms eased. She inhaled a few deep, rattling breaths, then crossed her arms over her naked chest.

"What'd you have to go and do that for?" she rasped.

I gaped at her. "What, save your life?"

She got to her feet, wobbly and still shivering, although she was trying hard to look dignified. The girl was likely a few years younger than I. Extremely pretty, too, although her features surprised me. She didn't look like many people living in Fódla, not even the capital at Rath na Mara. I'd seen her kind of beauty only in the delegations sent from Mother's far-flung trade partners—rich amber skin, high sculpted cheekbones, wide tilting eyes the color of honey, hair like heavy silk.

But we weren't in Fódla. We were in Tír na nÓg.

"I didn't need you to save me," she was telling me, indignant.

I was almost too exhausted to be annoyed by this blatant piece of fiction. "What was that I interrupted, then? A fun midnight swim with friendly fish-Folk?"

She glared. "I had a plan."

"Oh, a *plan*." I angrily wrung out the wet hair clinging to my cheeks. "Let me guess—you were taking a little nap before putting it into action."

She opened her mouth, then closed it, staring at me. An uneven burst of recognition blurred over her face. She peered more closely at my features, and I cursed myself for a fool. I'd forgotten what I looked like—*whom* I looked like. And I'd forgotten I'd taken off my hooded cloak before diving into the lough.

"Who are you?" Confusion carved furrows into her pretty face. "You're—you're *her.*"

"No." The word punched out of me with such force I had to take a step backward to keep my balance. "No, I'm—"

I reeled another step backward and slammed into the unyielding frame of someone who was both exceedingly tall and blazingly, deliciously warm.

I froze.

"Go on." The low voice caressed my ears, dark as midnight. "Who *are* you?"

The subtle menace was unmistakable, and thorny fear bristled through my veins. Reflexively, I reached for my skeans, but my chilly fingers closed on nothing. I had lost the blades in the lough.

I looked sharply at the girl I'd just saved. If I expected to find my own fear reflected in her expression, I was disappointed. Instead, she looked... *relieved*. Albeit slightly worried.

When a blade kissed the soft skin below my jaw, I realized the worry wasn't for herself. It was for *me*.

"Tell me." The guard's voice took on an edge of command I found difficult to ignore. Or maybe that was just the steel at my throat. "Tell me who you are, colleen."

Colleen. The colloquial term—simply meaning *girl*—knocked me off-balance and distracted me from my impending death. In Fódla the term would have been considered deeply informal, almost rude. But in the Gentry guard's lilting burr it didn't sound like an insult. I struggled to imagine why he'd call me that, until I remembered what I'd said to him the last time I'd been in Tír na nÓg.

As far as I know, I'm just a girl. I'm just me.

All my life, I'd been called *little witch*. *Changeling*. And now this Folk warrior had the audacity to call me *girl*? It was... *hilarious*, actually. A snort of inappropriate laughter escaped me.

The Gentry guard made a noise deep in his throat. The swan maiden's eyes widened, and she gave me a tiny shake of her head. Although infinitesimal, the gesture spoke volumes.

Don't piss off the threatening guard currently holding a blade to your neck.

"If it's all the same to you," I said as mildly as possible, "I'd rather find somewhere to warm up so I don't catch winter fever. After, you know, diving into the freezing lough and heroically fighting off fish-Folk to save the life of your friend here."

The warrior shifted behind me, although his blade didn't waver. "Chandika, is this true?"

The girl—Chandika—pouted. "A few wayward murúcha sought to hold me hostage."

"You should have called for me," growled the guard. "It is my duty to protect you—*all* of you."

"And give them exactly what they wanted? I had things under control."

I followed the exchange with interest. Cathair had said Eala and the other girls were prisoners here. But I had seen them don gowns of silk and starlight and go swanning away through an uncanny portal. To a party, if Rogan was to be believed. And now this Gentry guard spoke not of keeping them prisoner... but of *protecting* them?

"I doubt that." The slightest hint of humor touched the guard's voice. "Why were you not with the others?"

"I was... late," admitted Chandika, shamefaced. "The path to the *feis* disappeared."

"Then you do owe this woman your life. Which means I, too, colleen, am in your debt."

The knife fell away from my neck. I exhaled and allowed myself to start plotting exactly how I was going to get out of this mess. A swift kick to his shins, a sharp elbow to his—

He gripped my shoulder with one large gauntleted hand, wrapped the other around my chin, and simply whipped me around to face him. There was no grace in the movement—only power. And then I was looking up at him.

We stood much, *much* closer than last time. And oh, Morrigan, he was *so*...

He was beauty and bane, magnificence and malice, delight and dread.

He towered over me, seemingly sculpted from moonlight and shadow. Beneath the sheen of his short black hair, his looks were just as arresting as last time—stark and exquisite, cheekbones sharp as steel. Only that plush mouth softened the severity of his angular features, his perfect lips parting slightly as his gaze fastened on my face. And his *eyes*—like new-forged metal, so silver they were nearly white. Or were they so dark they simply reflected light? I didn't know, but I wanted to keep looking until I found out.

I was so captivated by his eyes that I almost didn't notice the cascade of emotions burning across his features. At first, he radiated nothing but death and fury. Then, as he cataloged my stolen features, he frowned. A smolder of confusion—the space between us narrowing. His pupils blew wide, and savage hope scraped the bones of his face into jagged angles. He inhaled, sharp. His fingers tightened against my jaw.

I hadn't realized he still had his hand on me, so bewitched was I. I tried to wrench my chin out of his hand, but his grip was unyielding. He tilted my face up closer to his, and unexpectedly—impossibly— his eyes betrayed *recognition*. And not in the way Chandika had looked at me, as if seeing someone else's features on my face.

He *knew* me.

"It's you."

The Gentry guard's opaline eyes were still fixed on my face, flicking between my own mismatched eyes. The very wind thrummed with the force of his words. His black mantle jerked and thrashed behind him, although the night was still.

No—the whole beach was suddenly shivering and shuddering like a beast in its death throes. Beside me, Chandika dropped to her knees on the quaking stones.

Only then did it occur to me to be afraid.

Droplets of water stung my cold cheeks as water unspooled from the lough in dark ribbons. Trees at the edge of the forest screamed as their roots ripped free of the earth like teeth from decaying gums.

My heart came untethered from my rib cage. And I fell.

Up.

My feet left the ground. Dark water bloomed upward from the lough. Uprooted saplings hovered above the earth like dark skeletons. I opened my mouth to scream, but I couldn't make a sound above the thunder of rushing water, the screech of mangled wood, the shatter of falling pebbles. And standing at the center of it all was *him*, boots planted firmly on the earth, turbulent gaze fixed firmly on my face.

Abruptly, it ended. My knees smacked down onto the beach, sending fire lancing down my cold shins. Trees thudded into the earth. Water smashed down in a billow of ice-bright droplets. Pain creased my palm—I had fallen on one of my lost skeans. Blood squeezed between my fingers, but I didn't care. I curled my fist around the blade and looked up.

If I had truly seen hope in the guard's eyes before, it was gone. Now his eyes shone with nothing but danger. The tang of sharpened metal and unspilled blood filled the air. His hands fisted, the tendons contracting along arms etched in sharp black tattoos.

In my periphery, a shuddering Chandika climbed to her feet. The whites of her eyes glowed with terror.

Run, she mouthed, silent. And when she found her voice, she screamed it. "Run!"

For the second time in as many months, I left the fort at a dead sprint.

It's you.

The words chased me to the edge of Tír na nÓg. They hid beside me in the underbrush by the Willow Gate. They chattered my teeth and shivered my bones and transformed the freezing hours I waited for Rogan into something unbearable.

I couldn't banish the image of the Gentry guard's expression when he saw my face. He'd *recognized* me. He'd seen *me*. He'd *known* me. How, where, *why*? I didn't know.

But I'd swear it on Mother's golden torc—if I'd stayed another moment beside that lough, he would have killed me for it.

It's you.

By the time Rogan arrived at the gate with dawn at his back, I almost didn't register that he was alone yet again. For a second time, he'd failed to bring Eala back. But I couldn't question it— I had passed beyond shivering into a still, silent kind of trance. Rogan's confusion slipped into concern when he took in my bare arms, the wet hair pasting ice crystals to my cheeks, the crust of blood on my open palm. I tried to tell him I was fine, but my lips were too frozen to form words.

That was the only reason I didn't protest when he hurriedly wrapped me in his own fur-lined cloak, flung me bodily over his shoulder, and carried me through the gray-lit forest toward home.

Chapter Twelve

Ruis—Elder
Early Winter

As if I had summoned it with my careless words to the Gentry guard, winter fever caught me up and dragged me down. Coughing racked my whole body, and I shivered and sweated as days blurred into nights. Between Rogan and Corra, the fires were kept roaring, and I was plied with peppermint tea for my throat and willow bark for fever and ginger and honey for the infection. But in the end there was little to do except wait for the illness to run its course, and hope I came out whole on the other side.

Mostly, I slept. And dreamed scattered, throbbing dreams.

I dreamed of Eala, except I was she and she was me. And when I tried to gather the starflowers, my fingers bled and bled until my hands were stumps.

I dreamed of dark water and iridescent fins.

I dreamed of black hair, moonlit eyes, and a soft, wondering mouth. Instead of asking me who I was, he already knew me. He spoke my name, again and again, but no matter how loudly he shouted it, I couldn't hear him.

It's you.

My fever finally broke one week before the next full moon.

I jolted awake from a nightmare—flocks of black swans were falling from the sky, their broken bodies black as ink against white parchment. I shook off the dream with my sweat-drenched blankets. Wobbly but blissfully clearheaded, I climbed out of bed and swathed myself in a fresh quilt. But a chill squirmed through me when I saw pale feathers kissing the window glass.

I padded to the casement and looked down. This was no muzzy, macabre fever dream. Those weren't feathers. It was *snow.*

I fell back asleep in the twilight of dawn, lulled by the muffled whispers of snowflakes against glass, then woke late morning to a sea of white beneath a cornflower sky. Weak but ravenous, I pulled on clean breeches, swaddled my feet in all three pairs of socks I'd packed, and went out in search of provisions. The fort was bone chilled and silent as a tomb—the fire in the hall little more than embers in the grate.

"Rogan?" My voice echoed, querulous. "Corra?"

But not even Corra dared disturb the delicate hush of new snow—perhaps they'd gone to ground with all other small, annoying beasties. The image of the formless sprite snuggling tight in a rabbit's burrow had me smothering a giggle that quickly transformed into a coughing fit. But my lungs felt clearer, and the biting pain in the center of my chest was gone.

But where was Rogan? Not even he usually slept this late.

I tugged on the fort's broad doors.

"Chiardhubh mustn't go outside!" chided Corra, bursting sideways into the mask of a mournful, long-faced giant sloughing oak leaves from its skin. " 'Tis cold and snowy, and there are foul spirits about!"

So much for burrowing away with the bunnies.

"Fouler than you?" My sarcasm was ruined by another coughing spasm that doubled me over.

"She isn't well at all," remarked Corra to the stone pillars.

"I'm feeling much better," I insisted. "This is just lingering sniffles."

"Sniffles is sniffles until Death happens by," said Corra ominously before whizzing off into the bowels of the fort.

I frowned at that pleasant thought, then opened the doors anyway. Cold winter light cascaded through the gap. Drifted snow blocked the door, striped in sunlit shades of marigold and honey. I bent to brush my hand against it, gasping at the jolt of cold. Tiny crystals clung to my fingers, rapidly melting against the heat of my palm. A memory washed over me, of the first and only time I'd seen snow.

It had been some months after Eala was stolen and I was left in her place. Mother had not yet learned to love me—in the grief and anguish of losing a daughter, she ordered my nursemaid to keep me out of sight, to feed me, but to leave the windows open in case I exploded into a flock of birds. My nursemaid, Caitríona, was more interested in flirting with a smirking kitchen boy than minding me. So I wandered the halls and grounds of Rath na Mara like a tiny ghost, clad in little more than underthings.

There had been a snowstorm. Cold daggers stabbed down from dark branches. Stars gleamed through black trees. Pillows of white buried my legs to the thighs. And Rogan's warm hands, barely bigger than mine, enveloped my frigid fingers as he crouched beside me and brushed wings of white snow off my cold, bare shoulders.

It was the first time we met. I didn't remember why I'd gone outside or even what Rogan said to me when he found me. But after that night, we were inseparable. He gave me hand-tooled leather boots he'd outgrown and velvet cloaks he'd put holes in. He shared his portions with me at feasts so I didn't have to fight the hounds for scraps of meat. We slept curled together like puppies on his fine feather mattress.

Sudden sorrow burned my throat and pricked my eyes. Long before I'd fallen for him, before he'd chosen *her* over me, before we'd been thrown together in a strange place with an even stranger mission, we'd been... *friends*. Best friends. Things had gotten so complicated, so tense, so strained between us. But I missed him. I missed that boy who'd warmed my hands and brushed snow out of my hair and learned to love me even before Mother had. I missed my friend.

As if summoned by my thoughts, Rogan—now so tall and handsome and golden-haired—came thundering up the hill on his stallion. Finan was stark against the snow, his hooves launching a wake of white behind them. Rogan almost didn't see me standing there at the door to the fort, but when he did, his eyes narrowed to slits of blue sky. He flung himself down from his horse and came at me so fast I experienced a burst of irrational fear. He wrapped his arms around my waist and carried me back inside the dún like I weighed nothing. He kicked the huge oaken door shut behind us.

"What in Amergin's name are you doing outside?" he demanded, gruff. The cold had slapped hectic spots of red on his cheeks, and his eyes were bright in the dim hall. He held on to my waist even after setting me down, like he didn't think I could stand straight on my own. His fingertips were cold, but his palms were very, very warm. "You should be in bed."

"My fever broke," I told him. "I'm feeling much better."

"So you decided to get yourself sick again?"

He clasped my chilly hands between his large, calloused palms and gently rubbed them. The gesture was so similar to that snowy night twelve years ago that it made me dizzy. Did he remember? I doubted it. I pulled my hands free.

"Where were you?"

"I rode into Finn Coradh yesterday morning." He slung a heavy pack down from one shoulder. "You needed more medicine. I didn't expect the weather to turn so treacherous—I had to stay the night at the inn."

"An inn famed for its ale and its whores, if I remember correctly."

Hurt darkened his eyes. "Do you really think I'd bed a stranger when you were here, alone, fighting for your life with winter fever?"

I fought a spear of guilt. "What would I know of your bedding habits, princeling?"

"It was one of the worst nights of my life, Fia." He caught my arm. "I hated not being able to protect you when you were at your weakest."

His rough grip and soft words made me restless with confusion.

"I don't need you to protect me," I retorted.

"Are you sure?" he growled. "When you go and get yourself dripping wet and bleeding and frozen half to death on the coldest night of the year? If Tír na nÓg is too dangerous for you—"

"Then what?" I demanded. "You'll call off the mission? Leave Eala as an enchanted swan maiden forever? Betray your queen? Let the Folk win?"

"If it meant keeping you from harm?" His voice was taut with emotion. "Maybe."

I dared a glance at his face from beneath my eyelashes. The guttering torches on the walls caught the edges of his irises and gilded them gold. Our eyes collided with enough warmth to make me feel feverish again. I almost let myself bask in that heat. Then I remembered, as I always did—my face was *her* face, and she was the one he'd chosen.

Her bright hair, pale as moonlight and delicate as cobwebs. Her soft body, curving in its perfection. The heavy golden torc around her throat, marking her as noble, princess, banfhlaith. Not a changeling with a stolen face and a borrowed mother.

"Don't be ridiculous." I brushed past him toward the stairs. He shadowed my footsteps, then bounded past me, bracing his arm against the banister and blocking my path. He was close enough for me to see every fleck of blue in his green eyes. Smell his sharp, masculine scent, like sun-warmed skin and vetiver. I tried to push him out of my way, but I was still weak. His muscles were rigid under my palms.

"How do we make this work, changeling?" His voice held a note of desperation.

A wave of resentment and longing and frustration rose up in my throat, choking me.

I didn't want to do this now.

"Leave it alone, princeling," I bit out through clenched teeth.

"I won't. Before you got sick, you barely spoke to me for a month. But when I cared for you these past weeks, you leaned into me—like you accepted my care, wanted my affection. Now you recoil from me again." His eyes bored into mine. "What happened to us? We used to be so close. We used to be…we used to be friends. Of that much, at least, I'm certain."

The words were so close to my own thoughts that I had to bite back a flood of imprudent words. Words I wanted to scream at him. Words I couldn't—*wouldn't*—say to him.

Words like *I miss you.*

I love you.

But then his own words—still caustic enough after four and a half years to make me flinch—drowned them out.

I am a prince. And you—you are no one.

I would not show him where he'd broken me. I would not show him the cracks where I'd patched myself back together. And I would not show him how fragile those seams were, stitched together with little more than brittle threads of flagging resolve.

"Things change." I made my voice hard. "We're not children anymore."

"No. I suppose we're not." His gaze lost its warmth. "At least tell me what happened to you in Tír na nÓg."

I lifted my chin. "We've been over this."

"Twice now, I've found you frightened or injured at the Gate." His mouth tightened. "I'm just trying to help you."

"I don't need your help." I spat the words at him. "Do you need my help to rescue your princess?"

"Yes, in fact. I'd very much like your help." He noticed my eyes widen in surprise—his mouth curled in satisfaction. "What do you know of the bardaí?"

"The bardaí?" The word meant something like *guardians* or *wardens* in the ancient tongue. I thought immediately of the Gentry guard I'd faced twice in Tír na nÓg. And his words to me, spilling unbidden from his sensuous mouth. *It's you.* "Why do you ask?"

"I spoke to Eala last month."

The announcement shouldn't have fazed me—eventually, Rogan was going to interact with his future bride. Still, the words struck me like a punch to the chest, and I fought the urge to stagger back a step. Tendrils of longing crept over me, followed by a lash of envy, followed by...unbridled curiosity. Questions tangled over one another. Questions like *Is she as enchanting as she seems?* and *What is it like to love her?* But instead, I forced out a brusque "And?"

"And she had much to tell me. About Tír na nÓg and the people who rule there. About why she was stolen from the human realms. And how she may be rescued." His eyes flicked between mine, searching. "But there is much I don't understand. Cathair schooled you in the ways of the Folk, did he not?"

"Some." My hand tightened on the banister. "Tell me."

"Cathair told us the magic governing the Gates was weak." Rogan sat heavily on the top stair, planting his forearms on his knees. "Eala confirmed it. She said that a number of Folk objects had been destroyed in an uprising some years ago. Treasures, she called them."

Treasures. My pulse quickened, sending leaves of green and black to beat against the backs of my eyelids. "Destroyed? Why?"

"To set the magic free, I gather—so it could be used by all." He looked up at me, rubbed a hand against the nape of his neck. "But I thought all Folk were magical?"

"They are," I confirmed. "But theirs are small, innate magics. A leipreachán may craft an illusion of golden riches to tempt a greedy man. A darrig may glimpse a few days into the future. An aughisky takes the shape of a beautiful horse to drown its prey. The Treasures are capable of much larger magics." And if they'd been destroyed, then I'd been sent to steal something that no longer existed. "Who destroyed them? These bardaí you mentioned?"

Rogan nodded, looking supremely out of his element. "In the wake of the uprising, the dissident Gentry split Tír na nÓg into smaller territories—a domain for each Gate. They elected wardens—bardaí—to defend the Gates with the magic set free from the Treasures, and rule now as equals."

I digested this new information, so different from what Cathair had told me. If Eala spoke true, then the four noble Septs had been overthrown, their power ended. "Were *all* the Treasures destroyed?" If so, then my mission in Tír na nÓg was for naught.

"All but one. 'The sword is the key,' she said."

Again, my pulse jumped. Eala must mean the Sky-Sword—the very Treasure I'd been sent to retrieve. "The key to *what*?"

"Eala believes another war is brewing." Rogan stared at his clenched hands. "Although the bardaí hold the Gates for now, that will all change by Samhain next. The Gates will fall, and magic and mayhem will be unleashed on Fódla. Unless she can take control of this sword and free herself from her geas. Only then can the war be won and her captor defeated."

Cathair had said her captor was tánaiste of one of the Septs—but the Septs had allegedly been destroyed. "Who is her captor? One of these bardaí? And what does the sword have to do with breaking her geas?"

Rogan made a broad, bemused gesture. "I don't understand how it all fits together."

"Neither do I," I said honestly. But this new information had already taken root in my cramped mind, fighting for attention like hothouse flowers fighting for sunlight. I longed to solve this new puzzle, but as I churned it over, my fever-racked body protested. Standing up for an hour had taken its toll on my weakened muscles. I needed nourishment and rest before trying to solve any problems—mine or others'. I sighed. "I don't suppose you brought back any food from that famous inn of yours?"

"And ale too." The prospect of food and drink chased away Rogan's bewildered expression. "Do you want some?"

I pulled my shawl tighter over my shoulders, glancing down at the crooked table before the dying hearth, and nodded.

Breaking bread with Rogan didn't have to be a battle. As long as we were discussing matters of strategy instead of matters of the heart.

A morning of audacious sunshine melted enough of the snow for afternoon's cold snap to turn the world to ice and peril. I skated down the hill in my boots, falling three times and eventually resorting to scooting down the icy path to the greenhouse on my arse.

In the past week, I'd stayed in bed until lunchtime every day, my limbs heavy and my mind racing. But this decaying heap of a fort was wheedling its way into my bones—drafty hallways whispering my name and cracked earth begging for borrowed life from my fingertips.

I slid down the last few feet into the copse surrounding the grotto. Ice sheathed the trunks and weighed down the branches. Dense clouds loomed close, making me feel like I, too, was encased in a cold, lonely world.

I pushed open the rusted, creaking greenhouse door to see a mountain of supplies heaped on the long, pitted worktable. Trowels and spades and rakes and hoes. Loppers and trimmers and dibblers and dowels. A new-painted barrow with sturdy wooden wheels. Sacks upon sacks of good earth and better manure.

And seeds.

I held my breath as I ran my fingers over the brown packets tied in string. Vines. Roots. Shrubs. Vegetables. And flowers—oh, the flowers! Fieldspur and bell leaf and rabbit tail and silverknot. Their names were like fingerprints on my heart. I suddenly knew, in a way that had already started to hurt, this garden was going to be exquisite. And it would be *mine*.

A gust of cold wind tinged with woodsmoke made me think of Mother. Years ago, she'd caught me nursing seedlings in my rooms one winter evening, long after I should have been in bed. Her steps were heavy with ale, and she reeked of Cathair's musky incense. But her eyes sharpened on the tiny leaflets sprouting green gossamer between my fingertips. It was too early in the season for dovewort to bloom, and Mother knew it as well as I did.

"You prefer flowers to your own mother, a stór?" she'd accused, injury painting her tone. "For I cannot fathom why else you would hide them from me. In my own home. In the room I have provided for your safety. Beside the hearth I keep roaring for your warmth."

She'd reached down and plucked the flowers, one by one, tossing their ruined faces into the guttering flames of the fire. Then she'd lifted my chin, which was wet with traitorous tears.

"Flowers die so swiftly. Would you spend your time and energy on something so finite? They bloom to entice you, only to wilt and die quicker than it took them to grow. Do not waste yourself on something so fickle." Gently, she'd smoothed the hair back from my face. "Flowers cannot love you. Only I know how to love you. And nothing and no one will ever love you more than I."

Each moment I spent in this greenhouse pulsed with that same raw ache, like the earth was hungry for my care and attention, and I was the only one who could feed it. And perhaps it would never love me. But for the first time, I wondered whether Mother had been wrong.

Was it truly weakness to love something that could not love you back? Or might it actually be strength—to love something so selflessly that you did not care whether that love would ever be returned?

I pressed my thumb against the bracelet of nettles and hemlock to clear my head. None of that mattered. I'd simply made a bargain with Corra. One I was determined to get something out of.

A frenzied tapping at the clouded glass startled me. I cracked the door to let in a sharp-winged starling. It was one of Cathair's witch-birds—its shiny, well-preened plumage and intelligent eyes were unmistakable and reminded me too much of its master. I unlooped a length of parchment from its impatient leg. The message scrawled on it wasn't long.

The high queen wishes for news.

The message chilled me—as though by disagreeing with Mother, even in my thoughts, I'd summoned her disapproval. It had been two months—but what did I have to tell Mother about our progress? We had located Eala. But Rogan's revelations about the Gates and the bardaí and the Treasures had led us no closer to breaking her geas. And the only things I had to show for my forays into Tír na nÓg were a still-healing wound on my palm and the memory of that Gentry guard's expression when he saw me—the hope and fascination and violence wringing his striking features into a map I could not read, only dream about.

It's you.

There was no earthly way I was going to tell Mother about that.

"Corra!" I shouted, startling the starling. "Does our bargain allow for parchment and ink?"

I searched for the formless sprite in wood knots and smudged glass. When I completed my circle, I found a sheaf of fine paper stacked beside a stoppered jar of black ink. I scrawled out a quick note.

We've located the princess. As for the rest, tell the high queen these things take time.

I folded the note and grabbed for the starling's leg. But the witch-bird was having none of it—its razored beak attacked my fingers until I dropped the note with a hiss. I reacted before thinking— green light mottled my skin, smoothing away the hurt. I looked up, but the starling was gone, and the note with it. I touched the spot of blood where the wound had been, but the skin was already knitted back together.

Wonder dappled through my mind. I had never *healed* anything before. My Greenmark had only ever brought me death. And though I'd cursed the things I'd lost because of it, I'd always believed that to simply be the way of things. I was a weapon, and so, too, was the magic lurking in my Folk blood.

But a weapon could do only one thing. A weapon could only hurt, could only bleed, could only kill.

A weapon could not heal.

Again, I touched the place where the bird had pecked me. After all the things I'd destroyed, perhaps it was right that my power could heal as well as hurt. Nature demanded balance in all things—for every poison there was an antidote; for every wound, a salve. It made a strange kind of sense that my own magic obeyed the same innate rules.

I shook off the thought. I began to sort Corra's seeds into piles—spring blossoms and summer fruits and autumn vegetables. But as I stacked and sorted and planned, the idea of *balance* grew like its own subtle, stubborn weed inside me.

Chapter Thirteen

I was torn. Torn between following Rogan, his princess, and her retinue to whatever Folk revel they attended tonight, or stepping out beneath the staring moon, walking toward the fort glimmering like a dream atop the hill, and hoping *he* showed up.

I would eventually have to meet Eala. She had knowledge of the Treasures, information about her captor, and insights into breaking her geas. But facing my dazzling double—the princess who cast the light my shadow lived in—was still more terrifying than facing the Gentry guard who'd twice come close to killing me. Both prospects made my insides churn. But pursuing the Treasure was my priority. Mother would wish me to put that above all else.

Besides, the idea of watching Rogan woo the girl he'd always been meant to marry made me want to stab something.

So I hid beneath the trees as the swan maidens magically draped themselves in jewel-toned satins and luxurious furs and braided bright sprigs of berries into their hair. The night air was brisk, with a luminous clarity that made me think of giant fires, spiced breads, buckets of dark ale, and mistletoe over doorways. I wondered— were the Folk's winter revels anything like our human parties?

It didn't matter. This year, there'd be none of that for me. I waited for the girls to disappear, laughing and chattering into the night. Then I steeled myself to step out, beneath the staring moon, toward the sinister fortress.

I'd barely put one toe outside the wood when a hand squirreled into the crook of my elbow and yanked. I stumbled backward, falling on my arse in the snow. I yelped, although the wound was more to my ego than my backside. I glared up into the incredulous face of the girl I'd saved from the lough.

Chandika.

"Do you have a death wish?" She put both hands on her hips. "Or are you just stupid?"

"Excuse me?" I spluttered.

"Jumping into freezing lakes populated with killer murúcha? Tromping out into the open to get yourself slaughtered by the Gentry?" She narrowed her amber eyes at me. "You've already painted quite a picture of your personality. And I don't even know your name yet."

"Fia." I climbed to my feet and brushed snow off my backside. Then promptly remembered every story Cathair had told me about the Folk. "But don't even think about asking for my full name. I wouldn't trust anyone here with that."

She clearly found this funny; her grin revealed a lovely set of wide, even teeth. "Oh, that doesn't matter as much as they'd have you believe. Besides, I'm human—I couldn't use your name against you even if I wanted to. It's a pretty name, though. Mine's Chandika, although everyone calls me Chandi."

"Chandika," I repeated, rolling the syllables over my tongue. "Pardon my asking, but where are you from? You don't look like anyone I've ever met in Fódla."

"No idea," Chandi told me nonchalantly. "I was so little when I was taken. The name isn't even my real name—one of my sisters remembered it from a story and decided it suited me."

Her words woke a melancholy within me. I didn't remember where

I'd come from either. Not my name, my parents…who I'd been or how I'd lived. I'd been eight or so when I'd been abandoned to the queen's care—an entire childhood had been lost to me. "I'm sorry."

"Did you imagine it was a holiday being kidnapped into the realm of the Folk for twelve years? Transformed into a swan every day?" Her cheerfulness didn't match her dire words. "It's really not so bad. If I don't know who I am, I can be anybody. I like to pretend I'm the long-lost daughter of foreign royalty instead of the youngest, ugliest, and most annoying of twelve unrelated sisters."

"You're hardly ugly."

"But you agree I'm annoying." Chandi twinkled.

"Hard to tell." I shrugged, hiding a smile. "You do talk a lot. And you still haven't thanked me for saving your life in the lough. At great cost to my own health and well-being, I might add. That's pretty annoying."

She stuck out her tongue at me. "So which is it?"

She'd lost me. "What?"

"Are you stupid?" She made an expressive gesture at the snow-draped fort. "Or are you trying to get yourself killed?"

"It's…a long story." I decided to try Chandi's technique of abruptly changing the subject. "What are *you* doing here?"

"I live here."

I quirked an eyebrow. "I just saw eleven older, prettier, and less annoying girls go swanning into the woods wearing velvet and fur. You're wearing…*nothing*." Which was true. And disconcerting, even if her long black hair hid most of her pertinent bits. "Won't you get scolded for being late again?"

"For once, I'm actually not late." She was gleeful. "I've been sent to bring a guest."

"Who?" I asked, with a glance at the fort. "And to what?"

"You, of course," said Chandi. "You're coming with me to the Feis of the Nameless Day."

I crossed my arms even as curiosity flashed through me. "And why would I do that?"

"Because tonight, I promise to speak freely. And I suspect you need at least one person in this accursed place to tell you the truth."

Her promise was the only reason I followed Chandi down an unknown path into the breathing forest. At least, that was what I told myself as the chilly gray woods reached for me in the gloom, bare branches grasping the hem of my mantle.

"Ignore them." She scowled at the trees, who were suddenly and suspiciously motionless. "We're almost there."

I wasn't sure where *there* was until we stopped in front of a trio of ancient bone-armed ash trees. They lifted infinite hands toward the brittle sky, icicles hanging like diamonds from their branches. Nature had carved a large burl into the center of the largest ash. Chandi ducked in, waving me beside her. The pale gray wood arched into darkness above us, and I placed a shivering palm against the core of the old tree. I swore it touched me back.

Chandi pulled me back out into the forest.

Except we weren't where we'd been a moment ago. The sky glowed, the moon trapped behind layers of clouds. The forest here was spruce and fir, ruffled layers of deep green wearing gowns of pale silver. The snow-draped trees had all been decorated with small charms—ruby berries that looked succulent enough to taste, leaves hammered from shining gold, baubles of sparkling sapphire, tiny silver bells. A path lined with braziers wound silky between the trees, and in the distance the music of revelry wove between laughter and singing. Soft flakes of snow drifted down, hissing on the torches. Lanterns floated gently between the greenery. No— they were not lanterns at all, but tiny beings. Diamond-bright limbs, faces like starshine.

I ogled.

"Sheeries," Chandi told me, following my gaze. "They love this kind of party, the little show-offs."

One of the sheeries took offense at this and blew a haze of crystalline ice shards into Chandi's face.

"Sensitive too." She brushed snow out of her eyes. "Tell me what you want to wear."

"Hmm?" My attention was lost down the path, beyond the line of trees, where I saw golden firelight. Smelled woodsmoke and pine sap and spiced wine. Heard achingly familiar music. But when I hummed the melody below my breath, it came out atonal.

When I turned back to Chandi, she was holding out a few of the blood-tipped starflowers. Reality thundered down. "No, I—I can't."

"Not dressed like that, no."

"Not dressed like *anything*."

"If you like." Chandi raised an eyebrow. "Although some Folk will certainly stare."

"No, I mean—" I took a step back. "I'm not supposed to be here."

"Why not?" Chandi raised her other eyebrow. "He's already here, you know."

My heart became a fist hammering against my ribs. I didn't know which *he* she meant. I wasn't sure whom I *wanted* her to mean. "He *who*?"

"The human boy who keeps tromping around in the woods, following us to our revels. With the frilly hair and the beady eyes and the stupid, pretty mouth." Chandi's words reminded me, blindingly, of Corra. "I assume you know him?"

"He's nearly twenty-three." Amusement and affront braided through me. "And a prince. I don't think he's a boy anymore."

"I don't care how old he is." Chandi scoffed. "They're all boys until proven otherwise. Especially princes."

That, I couldn't argue with.

"So?" Chandi gestured at my worn fighting leathers. "What do you want to wear?"

I gave my head a helpless shake. "You decide."

"That is the correct answer." She tucked a few of the starflowers into my braids. "Close your eyes."

I obeyed stiffly. For a long moment, there was nothing but the kiss of snow against my face. Then—a subtle shift, as if all my clothes had become softer and heavier. I didn't wait for Chandi's permission to open my eyes.

The gown she'd bewitched me into was a thick blue velvet, falling in layers of midnight luster. I put my hands to my waist—a narrow bodice rose to a wide neckline edged in pale fur. A breeze touched my exposed collarbones and the tops of my breasts, and I shivered. I rubbed my hands up my arms, which were encased in tight sleeves. Swaths of dark gossamer glittering with tiny crystals fell away from the elbows and trailed from my shoulders, dragging like the night sky behind me.

My eyes were wide. "It's *beautiful*. How—"

Chandi had undergone her own transformation—a gown like liquid gold encased her, pouring itself along every one of her magnificent curves. A golden mask covered half her face, making her amber eyes glow. I lifted my hands to my own face—a velvety mask reached from the tops of my cheekbones to my hairline, obscuring my features. I was glad for it. Chandi tossed her hair, which fell in glossy black curls down her back.

"Balance." She twined her arm through my elbow and dragged me down the fire-fretted path toward the light and heat and music.

I thought she was warning me about the impractical shoes she'd shoved my feet into, which were exceedingly difficult to walk in. But she was answering my question.

"Balance," I repeated, the word curling a secret against the contours of my thoughts.

"Tír na nÓg follows the laws of nature," Chandi told me in a low tone. "Nature is not good or kind or clean. But it is fair. Day demands night. Summer demands winter. Life demands death."

My fingers itched with brambles, and the place where the starling had pecked me suddenly ached. "What does that have to do with conjuring gowns from thin air?"

"Everything. We—the swan maidens and I—aren't meant to be

here. We were taken against our will and have not been allowed to leave. We're powerless mortals in a place of great power and near-infinite life. Nature demanded a balance to that inequity. And so the flowers grant us magic."

My Greenmark pulsed within me. I'd always loathed it—my unwanted magic, my Folk stain. But to my knowledge, I was the only one in the human realm who possessed such innate magic. I had never imagined the opposite—never imagined what it must be like to live in a world of magic yet possess none.

"They give us some small measure of autonomy," Chandi continued. "But they demand their own kind of balance."

She unfurled her hand. It was lacerated with tiny bleeding cuts from where she'd held the flowers. Beneath the wounds were hundreds of older scars, little white stars crisscrossing her skin. The jarring sight made me reach reflexively for my own scarred and ragged wrist. But my bracelet of thorns and nettles had been magicked away with my fighting leathers.

"Nothing here is free, Fia. Power is pain, and pain is power. Everything must be in balance. If you remember nothing else I tell you tonight, remember that."

I shivered, and it wasn't from the cold. But before either of us could say more, we stepped beyond the tree into a spectacle of frost and starlight.

The clearing was a bowl carved out of the forest. A dusting of frost shimmered down between icicles sharp as fangs. Low braziers roared with flames, and high above, small mirrors strung between the branches caught the light and tossed it back like a thousand earthbound stars. And thronging the space . . . were *them*.

The Folk host was more dream than reality. They moved half-corporeal between the trees, their slender figures flickering like fireflies at dusk. They laughed and sang, and their revelry was the clamor of crystal bells, the heavy drift of snow, the wind through high trees.

I stepped forward.

Chandi caught my arm and pinched me, hard. The dart of pain rendered the Folk less strange and more real than a moment before. They were still the most beautiful beings I'd ever seen. But they ate with their hands and laughed with wine-stained mouths and shivered in the chilly wind.

Lower Folk thronged the revel. Red-capped leipreacháin gamboled between the stomping thighs of enormous Fomorians. Hairy gruagaigh with wide, wicked smiles teased moss-haired ghillies, holding flaming tapers too close to their birch-bark skin. But they were nothing compared to the Folk Gentry, with their kaleidoscope eyes and horns of spiraled glass and wings like streaming fire. They were dangerously, incandescently beautiful, and I struggled to tear my eyes from them.

"Welcome to the Feis of the Nameless Day," Chandi whispered in my ear. "Stay close to me, don't eat anything strange, and try not to get yourself killed."

I did as I was told, staying close by her side as we edged around the feis.

"Here." Chandi shoved a goblet of frothing pink liquid into my trembling hands.

Drinking strange things was not off-limits. Apparently. I stared at it askance. More than one Folk story started like this and ended much worse.

"Won't this make us stay in Tír na nÓg forever?"

"You're not strictly human, are you? You should be fine." She threw her own cup back with the relish of a thirsty sailor. "And I'm stuck here anyway. So drink up."

I took a small sip. The liquid caressed my throat, tasting like iced blackberries and borrowed joy. I loved it. When Chandi looked away, I poured it out.

I followed her along the edge of the clearing, staying within a few paces of the forest. She and I weren't the only ones masked, and we weren't the only ones keeping to the trees. Deeper in the dark forest, lithe bodies writhed against one another, languorous and lustful, even as more fearsome things seethed in shadow. I glimpsed a dearg due's long claws, slick with blood; the dark, dripping shapes of horses with glinting sharks' teeth; the flashing scales of a huge ollphéist coiling, sinuous, between snow-draped trees. I walked a little faster, heart accelerating.

"The Nameless Day separates one year from another," Chandi told me softly. "It marks the end of the Elder month and the start of the Birch month. It is a time to release that which no longer serves us; to welcome new beginnings. It is a time to bid farewell; it is a time to offer greetings. It is a time to remember the dark and to anticipate the light. But most of all, the Nameless Day is a time to make new friends."

Chandi's intonation changed on that last phrase, and the look in her eyes was suddenly intent, despite the intoxicating beverages she was steadily imbibing. A moment later, I was struck dumb by the sight of a girl turning toward me beside a roaring brazier.

It was Eala, regal and serene. She wore a crown of starflowers in her hair and a snow-shine gown sighing around her like pale feathers. The other ten swan maidens clustered nearby, looking at me with interest.

"Hello, Sister," Eala said. "It's time you and I have a conversation."

Chapter Fourteen

Eala smiled at me—a broad, gentle smile hiding secrets and laughter and trust. It was a sister's smile, meant to be returned. And despite the sudden breathless panic making a briar of my lungs—Eala, *Eala*, Morrigan help me, it was Eala—I couldn't help but smile back.

"Oh!" Her voice was also breathless. "Let me look at you."

She reached up to take off my mask. The unexpected touch startled me—but her fingers against my cheeks were cool and gentle. Her eyes—the same bright, pale blue as Mother's—studied me, eager and appraising. I was suddenly and fiendishly grateful for Chandi's daydream dress. I already felt rough, awkward, and dim before Eala's glittering beauty—it would have been so, *so* much worse to face her in dirty boots and worn leathers.

"You are quite lovely." Gently, she stroked my dark hair behind my ears and, taking hold of my cheeks, tilted my face toward the brazier's dancing light. "And the resemblance is indeed startling. Although not a perfect copy by any means."

She was right—this close, it was possible to see where our features diverged. Her blond eyebrows winged higher than mine—a

question mark to my constant scowl. Her nose turned up fetch-
ingly; her dimpled chin was softer than my stubborn jaw. I had no
mirror to compare us, but I'd seen my own face enough times to
know we looked our parts. Even gowned and jeweled, surrounded
by frosted fancies and starlight, it must be obvious—she was a
princess. And I was—

"My sister." The words surprised me. But the full-bodied embrace
she gave me a moment later shocked me. Her slender arms curved
around my neck, and her cheek pressed soft against mine. In that
moment, no sensation could have been more foreign to me. It was
pure comfort—worlds different from Mother's rare, brusque hugs
or Rogan's heavy male touches. It was *sisterly*, and the moment she
pulled back, I missed her closeness.

"You do know," I choked out around unfamiliar emotion clogging my throat. "You do know we're not really sisters?"

"We are." She swatted my words away like flies. "Raised by the
same mother, if not at the same time. We are bound in love."

I wasn't entirely sure what she meant by that, but I liked the
sound of it. And it occurred to me—with sudden, blinding clarity—
that contrary to Mother's words, I might be worthy of more love
than she had ever offered me. Mother had taken years to warm
to me, to accept the sharp thorns and dark leaves tangling in my
veins. Eala had loved me instantly.

"I would ask a favor of you, Sister." Her voice dropped, intimate. "In return, you may ask something of me."

"I'm happy to help you however I can." Her phrasing struck me
as odd yet familiar—although I couldn't place where I'd heard it.
"No reciprocity necessary."

"Oh!" She squeezed my hands. "And I will not be in your debt?"

"No." I frowned, unable to suss out why she was making such a
point of this. I stared at her more closely. In the glow of the brazier,
Eala's eyes were lambent, her pale hair gilded. When she smiled, I
swore her teeth looked just slightly too sharp.

The sudden thought shook me: She looked like one of *them*. But the unnerving realization was followed just as swiftly by a surge of heartrending sympathy. Why shouldn't she look like them? Behave like them? Speak like them? She had been stolen from her home as a child, cursed to live in the realm of her enemy for twelve long years. I knew better than most—survival was a volatile, capricious beast. So what if she seemed more Folk than human? Surely she had learned their ways in order to walk more easily among them, learned to mask her true self in order to be whatever they needed her to be.

Just as I had.

"Very well." She clasped my hands. "I hear you have made the acquaintance of our warden. What do you know of him?"

"Besides the fact that he keeps trying to kill me?" I shrugged. "Nothing."

Gently, Eala nudged me around the side of the brazier and pointed across the feis.

At the other edge of the clearing, on a raised and canopied dais bedecked in mistletoe and greenery, sat a handful of finely gowned Gentry. Their uncanny beauty set my teeth on edge, but I forced myself to study them. They did not look much alike, as the lords and ladies of Fódla looked alike. Mingling atop the dais, splashed with firelight and moonglow and snow shine, the Gentry were a study in wild contrasts. Skylit eyes matched with sunfire hair; cat-white skin with a flicking tail to match; night-dark complexions and diamond teeth; close-cropped raven hair above eyes like stars.

My gaze stuttered.

The Gentry guard wore the colors of a forest in winter: black bark and green moss and pearly frost. A burnished onyx torc gleamed around his neck. Shadows like black wings swathed his figure, twisting dark around him even as torchlight flared.

The twilight edge of confusion fell away before the cold dawn of realization.

As he sat atop the dais, surrounded by Folk Gentry and bedecked in finery, it was suddenly so obvious that I felt an utter fool. The

Gentry guard was no *guard*. He was the mysterious tánaiste who'd kidnapped and cursed Eala and the swan maidens. He was the heir to the Treasure Mother coveted. He was my enemy, my *mark*.

And Eala had brought me straight to him. He was sitting *right there*, drinking ruby liquid out of a delicate goblet shaped like a night-blooming flower.

I swept backward until the brazier hid me from the dais. Everything fell away—the otherworldly revelry and the exquisite gown and the sweet-sharp liquor still warming my throat. I felt as naked and exposed as if I wore moonbeams and naïveté. My hand flexed at my hip, but Chandi had disappeared my skeans along with my fighting leathers.

I should not have come here unarmed and unarmored. *Idiot*.

"Who is he?" I hissed. "And why have you brought me to him?"

"He is our oppressor." Eala's voice was soft as the snow sighing down around us. "And I beg your help in breaking the geas binding us to him."

Only the real fear glittering in her pale blue eyes convinced me. I relaxed slightly, although every one of my instincts screamed at me to turn my back on this place and never return.

Eala drew me once more around the brazier. One among the host had begun singing—a winding, wounding melody that threatened to latch on to my bones and steal my heart. I blocked it out, focusing on the princess's cool hand resting on my arm.

That, and *not* looking at the lord lounging like a coiled predator atop the dais. He sat slightly apart from the other Gentry, and his keen gaze methodically swept the feis.

"Twenty years ago, a human king begged Tír na nÓg for aid," Eala began softly. "It had been years since any diplomacy between mortals and Folk had been attempted, and the four great Septs were curious. They allowed the king to enter their realm."

I knew this story. This king was Rían Ó Mainnín. Mother's husband. Eala's father.

"But while the Septs deliberated, the king grew impatient. He attempted to steal one of the Treasures for himself. He almost succeeded. But he was caught as he tried to flee with his prize. In the resulting struggle, the Treasure of the Sept of Antlers was lost, the wildness of its elemental magic freed. The furious Septs retaliated swiftly, executing the king for his crime."

This was a new twist. I knew the anxious, pregnant queen had awaited her husband for long months, even as strange things happened throughout Fódla. Forest fires that were unquenchable but by tears. Tidal waves that devoured fishermen but spared their boats. Then King Rían's carcass simply appeared in the kitchen hearth of Rath na Mara. His clothes were kindling for the cook fire. His whitened bones had been fashioned into ladles. And his skull was a cauldron wet with bubbling blood. The horrific sight sent Eithne into early labor and solidified her hatred of the Folk.

But now I knew the reason for his death. He'd been executed because he'd tried to steal a *Treasure*. Creeping thorns of fear bit into my heart.

"Then Mother declared war upon the Folk and began attacking through the Gates," I supplied, through my cold, clenching throat.

Eala nodded. "But the destruction of one of the four Treasures upset the balance of magic in Tír na nÓg as it had existed for ages. Suddenly, wild magic could be accessed by any who chose it, and the Folk tasted what they could do—what *power* they could wield—when unfettered by the Septs' antiquated strictures."

Rogan had spoken of an uprising. I could guess what happened next.

"With their supremacy threatened, the three remaining Septs retreated to their strongholds and left their own people to die in the Gate War. Even as they suffered heavy losses from the human attacks, factions among the Gentry staged a coup against the Septs."

"And those factions took the Gates and named themselves bardaí." Disgust warred with fascination. "I entered Tír na nÓg through the Willow Gate . . . Where are we now?"

"The Elder Gate. Geata Ruish." Eala looked impressed by my knowledge. She tilted her head toward a silver-haired bantiarna who sat in a position of prominence atop the dais. She wore the thick, gleaming pelt of a white wolf like a cape, and the savage torc glittering at her throat looked fashioned from the long, sharp teeth of the same beast. Except...*was* it a cape? The white fur rippled as she moved, as if muscles slid beneath it. And that was no torc—the teeth were embedded in her skin, pointing outward in a terrifying gorget. "The lair of Almha, the Silver She-Wolf."

I suppressed a shiver. My eyes traveled unwillingly toward Eala's dark-haired captor. I was beginning to guess why he sat apart from all the other Gentry lords and ladies, why his eyes roved, predatory, over the Folk host. "The Septs were taken by surprise. Their scions were felled. And the once-powerful Treasures of the Septs were destroyed. All but one."

"Perhaps the Septs had foreseen their bloody end, for one of them had hidden its heir apparent until he could come of age," confirmed Eala. "He survived the cull and inherited the Treasure his family had guarded so jealously. But he was afraid. Afraid if the bardaí caught him, they would slay him and destroy his Treasure too. So he used the vast power of his inheritance to build a domain of his own, where he might safely reign, away from those who wished to destroy him. And he lured twelve human maidens into Tír na nÓg, binding them with geasa so they might not leave of their own free will."

"Why? What purpose did that serve?" *And why did he leave me in your place?* I barely stopped myself from asking.

Eala paused. "Do you know how Mother opened the Gates?"

"Blood spilled from the still-beating heart of one of the Folk," I answered automatically, before realizing it might not be the wisest thing to mention in the middle of a Folk feis.

"This deposed heir lords us over the Gate bardaí as insurance—as collateral." Eala bowed her head. "Because at any time, if he chose, he could use our hearts to wrest back control of the Gates."

"He would murder you—cut out your hearts—to regain control of the Gates?"

"For years, we have been most useful to him as a deterrent. But that could change at any time. His whims are fickle."

For a long moment, I was quiet. Thinking. "Why curse you as swans?"

"Irian's Treasure is the Sky-Sword. The magic he wields stems from the element of air. And before the slaughter, his dynasty was the Sept of Feathers."

Irian. I snuck a glance at the dais where he sat, wreathed in his wings of black shadow. His legs were thrown out in front of him, and his fingers loosely cupped his goblet. He almost smiled as the Folk dancing below the dais whirled faster and faster. Fury pierced me.

"Why don't they kill him now?" I asked, gesturing to the bardaí. "They have him outnumbered."

"Oh, they've tried." If my frank hostility shocked Eala, she didn't show it. "But the memories of the Folk run deep, and there are many who still secretly cling to the old ways—the old Septs. To confront him here, tonight, while he is protected by the laws of hospitality...It would be messy. The Silver She-Wolf would not want her sovereignty so publicly challenged."

"What would you have me do?" Frustration tightened my fingers into fists. "I have not yet heard your favor."

"As long as Irian wields the Sky-Sword, our hearts are not our own." Eala gestured at my gown, born of illusion. "The magic the white flowers afford us is so small compared to the power of the Treasures. But if we controlled the Sky-Sword, we could cut ourselves from his influence. We could undo the geas. Then, even if the bardaí succeed in opening the Gates at Samhain, we would be free. And powerful enough to win any war they might seek to bring to the human realms."

Her words chilled and elated me in equal measure. What were the chances the task Mother had set me—stealing the Treasure from its heir—would be the very thing needed to set Eala and her maidens free? It seemed improbable. Even so, the prospect sent hope to banish the dark clouds looming over my heart. If I was ruthless and clever, all this might be over in a few months. Mother would have her magic. Eala would be free. And Rogan—Rogan would have his lovely bride.

I tamped down the thought. "I'll take it from him."

"You are brave!" Eala gave me a new, appraising kind of look. "We will not be able to help you. He keeps us alive at his own convenience. We are not in his confidence."

I hesitated, wondering whether I should tell Eala of her—*our*—mother's plan. Mother and daughter were clearly of the same mind—surely there could be no harm in it? "The high queen also wishes to acquire the Treasure. As such, I have already given the matter some thought. It may take me a little time. But before long, the Sky-Sword will be ours, and you—*all* of you—will be free."

A ripple of surprise loosened Eala's features, followed by a slash of inexplicable ire. A moment later, her expression was calm and resolved.

"Then I leave the task on your capable shoulders." She hooked her arm in mine and leaned closer. "But as long as I am asking favors of you, I have one more to ask."

"All right."

"The prince." Her gaze shifted over my shoulder. "Tell me, Sister—what kind of man is he?"

I followed her gaze.

Rogan stood mere paces away, at the edge of the forest. For the briefest of moments, I didn't even recognize him—masked with evergreen and mistletoe, with his golden hair pulled back from his face and his mantle sparkling with snow, he was beautiful enough to pass as one of *them*. My heart catapulted into my throat when his blue-green gaze roamed toward me.

But he didn't recognize me. His eyes glided over me as if I were a stranger. Which, in this gown, I supposed I was. But I had recognized him within moments; he didn't spare me a second glance. He stared out across the Folk host. Looking for Eala, I supposed.

"Well?" prompted Eala.

I was staring. I turned back to my sister, whose lambent gaze was assessing on my face.

"He is—" I wetted my lips with my tongue and tried not to think about how much I loved him. "Rogan is kind, funny, and strong. He is also vain, privileged, and perhaps not always as loyal as he ought to be."

"I see." The firelight flashing on Eala's teeth made her mouth look bloody. "Well, one cannot expect too much. He *is* a prince, after all."

I grinned despite myself, to hear my own thoughts echoed aloud. "That he is."

Eala's pale eyes grew thoughtful. "Tell me, Sister—do you think I ought to make things easy on him?"

Her words killed my smile. I knew why Rogan was here—at this revel, among these uncanny Folk. It was to win Eala, to break the geas upon her and to bring her home as his prize and his bride for all Fódla to see. Clearly Eala knew that too. Yet she was asking me whether she should *let* him. Let him woo her, let him win her—or at least let him *think* he'd won her.

It was...calculated. It was almost cruel. Again, I wondered how over a decade living among the Folk might have tainted my sister. Whether they had stolen her not only in body, but also in soul—stripping away her brightness, her goodness, and leaving in its place wickedness and cunning.

It only strengthened my resolve. We had to find a way to break her geas and take her from this place.

"No need to make it easy." I tried for jovial but sounded wooden instead. "But he is here to rescue you. So there's no sense in making it too hard either."

Eala laughed. She reached over—we two were of a height—and brushed a faint, sisterly kiss against my cold cheek. And then she was gathering her maidens around her and slicing through the crowd. The Folk parted around her, and the gemstone gowns of the swan maidens were soon swallowed up by the feis.

I didn't follow her with my eyes. Instead, I looked at Rogan.

I saw the moment he noticed her. His expression became wondering. His mouth parted in adoration. His eyebrows lifted in awe.

Only then did I allow myself to look out across the feis.

At the center of the host, whirling amid the thunderous crush of bodies, Eala danced. Even amid the incandescence of the Folk, she glowed. In her pale gown, with hair like candle flame, she was a butterfly amid moths. She laughed as she spun from arm to arm, her merriness catching and spreading on the faces of those around her. She was *luminous*.

I had no right to envy her. She had never wronged me. She was my *sister*—it should be love for her cramping my chest, not jealousy. And yet—

I pressed my wrist, but my bracelet of thorns was gone.

I whirled away and nearly slammed into Chandi.

She hadn't gone down with Eala to dance. I fought to control my expression as I swallowed against a hitch in my throat. "Is there something you need?"

"I promised I would speak plain to you tonight. So you should know—Irian is incredibly dangerous." She inclined her head at the raven-haired tánaiste, whose feral eyes still roved the host. Revulsion rose hot in my chest. He was everything Mother and Cathair had taught me to despise about the Gentry. Self-assured. Selfish. Power hungry. And apparently, murderous. "I know Eala desperately wishes to return home. But you must be careful."

I looked back at her. "What are you saying?"

"There must be other ways to break our geas." She shook her head. "There's no reason for you to get yourself killed. The sword makes him nearly invincible. You should—you should leave Irian alone."

For a long, taut moment, her words smacked of betrayal. By

telling me this, she was defying Eala. But then I realized she was trying to *help* me. She was undermining her princess's command in order to warn me.

It was unnecessary. But I appreciated it nonetheless.

"Thank you." I briefly gripped her palm. "You've already wasted too much of the night with me—enjoy what remains of the party. I remember the way back."

Chandi hesitated. Then she nodded, helping herself to another frothing goblet of liquor before plunging into the mass of dancers, swirling toward where her sisters reveled.

I was nearly to the edge of the trees when a hand circled my wrist, tight enough to wring my bones. Fear catapulted into my throat, and I spun, grasping uselessly at my waist for knives that were no longer there. I looked up into the face of a strange Gentry man.

An eagle-sharp nose over curved lips. Tilted golden eyes beneath frowning brows. The glint of a copper torc from beneath the russet curls kissing his neck. I almost relaxed—he was handsome and smiling. But as he leaned closer, the moonlight warped and shifted over his face, bruising the hollows of his eyes and lengthening his teeth over his bottom lip. A sudden breeze threw his scent against my face; he smelled caustic, like carrion and burnt metal. The spell of his beauty dissolved, and I noticed the red fur rippling over his unnaturally swollen muscles; the sharp, pearly claws circling my arm.

I jerked back, but he squeezed me harder.

"Be still, kitling." His voice ground like gravel between the beguiling tatters of his glamour. "A lovely morsel like you should not wander the forest alone in the dark."

I forced myself to glare up at his rough-hewn face, his feral eyes, his hungry teeth. Uncertainty danced wild within me. Again, my free hand grasped at my hip as if I could will my skeans back into existence. "Is that a threat?"

"An opportunity." He gripped my chin in a painful grasp. His claws cut into my cheek; I felt blood trickle down the line of my jaw. Panic prickled up my spine and along my collarbones. "Perhaps even a bargain. I will keep you safe tonight—from anything that might harm you."

Funny, when he was the thing I needed safekeeping from. "And in return?"

"A kiss." He did not wait for assent before pressing his lips to mine. I jerked back, but his too-long canines caught on my lower lip and *tore*. Pain lashed over my face—my hand lifted unconsciously to my mouth, where two ragged cuts dripped blood down my chin.

Shock made me stupid.

"I'd rather die," I snarled.

The desire in his eyes turned deadly. Russet hackles lifted along his shoulders. "I am sure that can be arranged."

Terror shoved me from him. Right into someone else. I registered little more than deep blue silk enrobing the height and breadth of a man before he stepped in front of me, facing the predatory Gentry.

"She is not alone." His voice was cool and calming, faintly accented. I stared at the sleek mahogany hair spilling down the man's back, but I didn't recognize it. Or him. "She is with me."

"*Islander.*" The Gentry's voice was a snarl, but he gave way, stepping back half a pace. "Does your strumpet not know our ways?"

"The *lady* does. As do I, barda." The blue-robed man said this easily, but I suspected the last word was meant for me. Thorns of fear and fury tangled sharper within me—the fox-faced Gentry was one of the Gate bardaí? "And as her companion, the terms of your bargain extend to me. Is that not right?"

He reached forward, grasped the front of the barda's mantle, and dragged him forward for a kiss. Surprise and wrath flashed across the Gentry lord's face, and he shoved the blue-robed man away roughly.

"If I wanted you, islander, you would know it." The barda straightened his clothes, snarled under his breath, then paced briskly off.

"I am *sure* I would." The blue-robed man's murmur was sharp edged with sarcasm. He waited until the barda disappeared back into the revel before turning toward me. He studied me, and I him.

He, like the barda, was Folk Gentry. But that was where the similarities ended. Like me, his face was mostly hidden behind a mask—an intricate, sweeping design in blue and silver that made me think of waves upon the ocean. Beneath it, I glimpsed golden-brown cheekbones and a wide, wry mouth. His eyes were black.

"I daresay thanks are in order," he prompted.

"I did not ask for his advances." The encounter had left me bruised with fear, raw with pain. "Nor did I ask for your help in rebuffing them."

"Have it your way." His eyes were keen on mine. They were not black at all, but the deep, endless blue of an ocean at night. "But I did save your life. So I am nevertheless owed a boon."

Morrigan *damn* these scheming Folk. "What could you possibly want from me?"

Casually, he lifted a hand to my face. He wiped away blood with his thumb, then held it to the moonlight, where it gleamed emerald. Curiosity flashed in his fathomless eyes. He looked back at me, considering.

"The kiss the barda tried to steal." His smile was wide and winsome. "I wish for you to give it to me instead."

Wrath rose in me like a tide, sending thorns to spike my skin. Had I really escaped one predator only to fall into the claws of another? I clenched my fists, then decided the fastest way to escape this situation was to acquiesce to his dishonorable request. I puckered my bleeding lips and advanced on the blue-robed Gentry. But he waylaid me with a cool palm on my chest. My thorns ripped against his skin, vicious.

"Easy." His laughter was deep and unruffled, betraying no pain—even as his palms began to bleed. It stoked my ire even higher. "I wish to taste neither your gore nor your hostility. I will choose the time."

He wiped his hand—stained now with both my blood and his—on his robes, then walked away from me. A moment before he passed from earshot, I called after him, "Then I will simply avoid you!"

He paused and looked over his shoulder at me. The moonlight outlined his sleek profile in silver. "Try, Thorn Girl. You will find the magic of Tír na nÓg is not so easily fooled."

☙ ～❧

My feet flung me through the forest, my mind churning with fear and fury and slow-swelling resolve. But as my gown evanesced like a midnight strewn with dying stars, my scattered thoughts coalesced.

By the time I reached the Willow Gate, I was myself once more. My dark hair was braided tightly to my head. My collarbones and chest were protected by leather and steel. My hips hung heavy with my skeans.

But I was not the same as when I came here tonight. I had finally seen my enemies for who they were. The Folk Gentry were as terrible as I'd been told—most alike to humans in appearance, but most different in cunning and treachery. And if the others of his kind had cursed him for his wickedness, then the tánaiste who held Eala captive must be the worst of them all.

But he had not yet been punished.

That would be my job. And I was beginning to see how it would have to be done.

I knew little of this tánaiste—this heir of shadows. *Irian.* I knew only that he was a pariah, an outcast—alone but for a flock of swan maidens who despised him. And no one was meant to be alone for that long. Not even wicked Gentry heirs.

Chandi had told me to stay away from him. But that wasn't going to happen. For me to succeed at the task Mother—and now Eala—had set me, I was going to have to get close to him.

Then I would become the weapon I'd been forged to be. I would take his Treasure. And I would destroy him.

Part Two

The Shadow Heir

My heart is as black as the blackness of the sloe,
or as the black coal that is on the smith's forge;
or as the sole of a shoe left in white halls;
it was you put that darkness over my life.

—"Donal Og," translated by Lady Gregory

Chapter Fifteen

Beith—Birch
Winter

A re you daft, man?" I snapped. "Don't put it there!"

"Whatever happened to *princeling*?" griped Rogan. But he did as I said, dragging the massive sack of fertilizer toward the risers at the back of the greenhouse.

For a while after the Feis of the Nameless Day, Rogan had been nowhere to be seen. I'd tried not to care—I'd been busy. Corra had kept their end of the bargain—it was time I kept mine.

But in the past week, I'd spotted Rogan lurking at a safe distance, like a stray puppy hoping for scraps. He always had practice weapons with him—a claíomh or a bow or a staff—but the edge of his attention grated against mine.

I'd participated in enough pretense to know a sham when I saw one.

Finally, I'd put down my trowel, wiped my earth-streaked hands on my apron, and beckoned to him. He'd wandered over, looking surly—Rogan never could bear being alone for long. His hair was beginning to look unkempt, the stubble on his cheeks starting to wander into beard territory. He was also looking a little haggard, like he hadn't been getting enough sleep. Or had been eating too many meals that were mostly mead.

"Do you want to work?" I'd asked.

He'd nodded, a single jerk of his head.

"There will be no tossing of heavy objects willy-nilly," I'd needled. "You will not touch the plants. You will not break things. You will do as I say, nothing more and nothing less."

"And if I strike you three times, changeling, will you return to Tír na nÓg?" Rogan had grinned, an unexpected flash of mirth that instantly disarmed me.

But then I'd remembered how his face had transformed at the sight of *her* last month. He'd gazed at Eala like she was magic. Like she was music. Like she was *everything*. He'd never looked at me that way.

He was handsome, strong, and good. She was lovely, bright, and gentle. They were meant for each other. And I was trying to stop begrudging them their happy ending.

"Well?" I'd said, expressionless.

"Your terms are acceptable," he'd muttered, tense and formal, before stalking back toward the dún.

But he'd come down the next morning in old breeches and shirtsleeves. I'd given him a list of specific—and frankly difficult—tasks, which he'd completed without complaint and with annoyingly little effort. And so we'd worked together in uneasy near silence, braving slushy snowmelt and bracing frost to assemble the wreckage of glass and metal into something resembling a greenhouse.

❧

When I wasn't outside, I was roaming Dún Darragh's halls, searching for the library Corra had alluded to but was otherwise unwilling to discuss. Not that the infuriating sprite was particularly forthright about *anything*.

"Can't you give me a hint?" Yet another hallway had ended in a cobwebbed chute that looked like it led straight to Donn's dark realm, and I was annoyed. "This pile of rocks is a death trap."

"This *pile of rocks* boasts many nooks and crannies, a glorious maze," Corra responded archly. "With secrets and knowledge designed to amaze."

"You can't rhyme *maze* and *amaze*," I countered, kicking yet another omnipresent black feather into the shadows. "Just one teensy hint. Please? I'll pick you a bunch of my fresh-grown lavender."

Corra wavered. "In every row of posies, one flower does not fit. Ask me no more—that's it!"

One flower does not fit. I mulled the words over for days, examining every carven sigil that resembled a flower, every tapestry woven with a bouquet.

I almost passed by the sagging mantelpiece in a dust-choked antechamber without a second glance. But the light from my lantern caught on a curving edge and turned it marigold, and something soft as new lilies and yellow as spring whispered against my senses. The contours of the rosette carved along the mantel were as dusty as the rest of the room. I brushed it off, curious at first and then eager, as a row of little flowers appeared above the cold hearth. Full, delicate flowers that bloomed as I ran my fingers over them.

In the end, it was so obvious. The thirteenth rosette had fewer petals. *One flower does not fit.* I touched it, felt it give. Pushed until it clicked. The grate fell away, and the hearth opened onto a set of steps, curving up into darkness.

I stared, mouth parted, as surprise and elation and the barest edge of fear twined inside me. Part of me had never expected to actually *find* anything. Half the fun had been the promise of secrets long concealed, the notion that I might find something precious hidden away.

Without a second thought I ducked beneath the mantel and

climbed the staircase, coughing against ancient dust and the dense, brittle smell of old paper. Beyond, the alcove was little more than a cramped niche cut into stone; my dim lantern kissed all three walls and brushed golden wings against the ceiling. Unmarked books were crammed in rows of shelves and stacked on the single narrow table. Everything was so covered in dust that a statue standing in the corner looked veiled in ashes. Reverently, I touched the spine of one of the volumes. Then I sneezed violently.

"Corra!" I shouted to the air. "Can't you do something about all this dust?"

Corra obliged by picking up every mote of dust in the alcove and dumping it squarely on my head. I choked, blind and half-deaf as I tried to clear stinging particles out of my eyes and shake grit from my hair.

"You utter *menace*," I hacked, retching. "I'm going to flay you alive!"

"Catch us if you can!" sang Corra, ruffling my grime-streaked hair before fleeing the alcove.

But I was too intrigued to stay annoyed for long. Brushing my hands off as best I could, I lifted down one narrow volume, then another. Their brittle leather spines creaked as I pried them open. Loose, hurried handwriting filled the pages in ink that had faded to brown. I squinted at the words, struggling to make sense of them. It took me long minutes to realize they were written in the ancient tongue. These books—journals?—were truly *old*, from a time of legend, when living gods walked Fódla and humans commonly interacted with the Folk.

I was suddenly glad for all Cathair's dull, seemingly impractical lessons. I scanned the unfamiliar script, searching for some word, some phrase I understood.

—find her. I know—my love. Lost—Tír na nÓg.

It wasn't much—hardly a full sentence. But I thought immediately of the story Rogan had told me before we'd left Rath na Mara, of the man who was said to have built this place. The human warrior who'd become obsessed with a Gentry maiden he could not have. I'd thought it legend and nonsense.

But by Amergin's staff, what if it was all true? A smile crept onto my face. I had to tell Rogan—he'd never believe this.

I shoved one of the notebooks down my tunic, grabbed my lantern, and dashed out into Dún Darragh's echoing halls. It was late but not terribly so—Rogan would still be up. Halfway into a bottle of mead, most likely. But up.

I took the winding stairs to his tower room two at a time, ignoring the sweat prickling against the dust still caked along my neck. I was gasping by the time I reached the landing, but I barely paused before bounding through the door standing ajar to Rogan's chambers.

Only to find Rogan lounging, chest-deep in soapy water, in a huge copper bathtub across the room. For a stricken moment, I stared—at the candlelight pouring gold across his hair and chest, at the herb-scented steam ghosting heat into the room, at the surprise glossing his river-stone eyes. His fingers twitched, staccato on the metallic rim. His expression changed, a bemused grim sliding toward something more intent.

Gods, I *had* to learn how to knock.

"You're bathing." I stated the obvious. My breath still rushed in my lungs, although now I wondered whether it wasn't for a different reason. I angled my body toward the door. "I should—"

"Seriously consider joining me." His provocative words captured my shocked gaze. He leaned his head back against the tub and examined me from beneath his gilded eyelashes. Humor curled his lips. "You look like you could use it."

Of course—I was still covered head to toe in centuries-old dust. I cursed Corra and then doubly cursed myself for rushing here without changing. Without washing. *At all.*

"I was exploring," I said in a rush, still half-breathless. "Beyond the room with the tapestries, I found a stairway—a secret stairway—and beyond there was a kind of library, only it was all personal accounts—journals, I think—"

"Really, changeling." Rogan's sultry amusement sliced through my babble. "If you want to use it, I'm finished."

He stood without warning. Foamy water surged and sloshed around him, rushing down from the ends of his hair and sluicing along the hard contours of his torso. I looked away a moment too late—heat slapped my cheeks as I aimed my eyes toward the ceiling. Rogan's rough chuckle deepened my flush. Out of the corner of my eye, I saw him reach for a towel and wrap it low around his hips. Only then did I exhale, trying to cool the heat skeining through my veins.

But my relief was short-lived. He made no effort to dress further before coming toward me, his steps purposeful on the flagstones. He stopped at arm's length, far enough for propriety but close enough for me to count the beads of moisture studding his chest. Smell the sharp, spicy scent of his soap—vetiver and anise. Feel the damp heat rising off him like steam.

"Well?" he prompted.

My head was empty. "Well *what*?"

"What did you find, changeling?" He smiled slow. "Unless you really did come to share my bath."

I shoved the notebook at him. He perused it for a brief moment, then carelessly set it down. He stepped closer, lifting a hand toward my face. I must have flinched—he stilled, then slowly resumed the motion, dragging his thumb roughly along my cheekbone. He lifted the finger, inspecting the smear of gray dust he'd lifted from my face.

"You really are impressively filthy." He was close enough now for me to count the flecks of green in his eyes, to number the copper freckles dusting his nose, to name the desire softening his mouth. His face canted an inch to the side, and his eyes dropped to my lips.

"What are you doing?" I stepped back. He moved with me, closing the remaining distance between us. My back struck the closed door; I fumbled for the doorknob, but the metal slipped beneath my sweat-and-grime-streaked palms. "This isn't funny."

"Not funny at all." He touched my face again, sliding his thumb from my cheek down over my bottom lip. My chest hitched, sending my breath gusting over his knuckles. His other hand rose to cup the back of my neck, tilting my face up to his. Slowly—slowly enough I could have stopped him—he bent down and captured my mouth with his, sliding his tongue over the lip he'd just touched. I tasted his soap first. Then I tasted *him*. His warmth, his want, his willingness.

He pulled me against him. My hands came up instinctively, resting on his smooth, hard chest. A world of memories unfurled at his touch. Everything he and I had ever shared—every moment, every word, every desire. It was too much. It wasn't enough. He pulled me even closer.

Pinned between our bodies, my thistle bracelet bit into the soft, tender skin of my wrist. The prick of pain was enough to clear my head.

I broke off the kiss, tearing my mouth from his and shoving him bodily away. He staggered back, nearly stumbling on the wet floor. He lifted lust-dark eyes churning with confusion and asked, "Why *not*, changeling?"

I almost laughed. How many times had I asked myself that same question? Why couldn't he and I—princeling and changeling—be together? The answers were as endless as the questions. They tore through me now—hoping, hating, loving, longing. But there was only one I was willing to voice here tonight. The only one that wouldn't hurt me as much as it might hurt him.

"Because she is my *sister*." The words scorched my throat. "And you are promised to her."

Rogan didn't say anything, but a muscle jumped high in his cheek. He shook his head, then finally—*finally*—got dressed, hiding his heavy arms and chiseled chest behind a loose tunic. He pulled on a pair of breeches beneath the towel. And then he was in front of me again.

"How can she mean so much to you?" His eyes were hard. "You do not know her."

"I do know her, Rogan. I have known her all my life—she has always been everything I am not and can never be." I lifted my chin, conjuring her up like a luminous ghost between us. "And now that I have truly met her, she is as lovely and bright as I knew she would be. She is everything a princess ought to be. She is everything you've ever wanted."

"I'm well aware of what I should want." The hand he dragged through his damp hair tousled his curls. "But I don't want her, Fia. I want you."

"No." It wasn't a reply, but a rejection. My heart throbbed wild and weak with his words—*I want you*. They were far too little and far too late. And yet they grew inside me, eager as cramped saplings reaching ragged branches for a distant sun. "You are promised to her."

It was easier to say that than to show him the festered wounds he'd made, the badly patched heart he'd broken. It was easier than entertaining an impossibility I'd given up on over four years ago.

"I have made no promises." His voice came out ragged. "Not yet."

Cathair's voice slithered through the cracks of my resolve. *He will never choose you—you will never be more than an afterthought to him.*

"I will be no man's mistress," I spat. "I will be no one's whore."

"That is an ugly word." Hurt and fury tightened his voice. "You will always be more to me than that. My best and only friend. My first love. The girl I want to tell about my good days, the girl I want to tell about the bad. The person who knows me better than I know myself. What you are to me cannot be named."

"Then why—" The steel of his stirrup was still cold beneath my white knuckles. *I am a prince...and you are no one.* "It doesn't matter. I don't want this."

My fingers finally found purchase on the doorknob.

"What about what I want, Fia?" His voice hitched with longing.

"What *you* want?" I nailed certainty to my obdurate, damaged heart. "I stopped caring about what you want a long time ago, princeling."

I opened the door and made my escape. Rogan did not follow.

⁓

For the next three days, the only thing I allowed myself to think about was the Gentry tánaiste. *Irian.* I thought about him obsessively, tormentingly, hatefully. I thought about him until his cropped black hair extinguished the candlelit glow of golden curls, until his brutal silver gaze overwhelmed the alluring gleam of riverstone eyes, until the violence of his actions drowned out the irresolute words of a lustful prince.

In the end, I had something resembling a plan.

Stalk him, lie to him, ingratiate yourself with him, Cathair had told me. *You've grown into a pretty little thing—perhaps you could seduce him.*

I feared I was going to have to do all those things.

Chapter Sixteen

I crouched beneath the dún in Tír na nÓg, the field of starflowers sweeping up before me.

The moon was high. Rogan had already vanished with the swan maidens, without needing to be told. Chandi had trailed at the back of Eala's retinue, but though her eyes had searched for me, I'd hidden myself well. Her expectant smile had fallen in disappointment, sending regret glimmering through me.

I'd heard her warnings about the shadow heir. But I was going to have to disregard them. And I had no compelling way to explain that to her. I would see her again. But not tonight.

The first time I'd met whom I now knew to be the deposed tánaiste of the Sept of Feathers, I'd tried to pluck one of these starflowers. The second time, I'd saved one of his prisoners—or *wards*, depending on whom you asked—from drowning. It was no more than a theory, but perhaps he could sense when I interacted with his realm.

I supposed there was only one way to find out.

I reached for one of the starflowers and plucked it. A painful dark peppering of green-black blood burst along my forefinger. I hissed and dropped the blossom.

"They will do you no good," said a voice like midnight and peril. "They were not made for the likes of you."

I whirled, coming face-to-face with the tip of a long claíomh. The blade was hammered black and etched with a design I didn't recognize. It *thrummed*, sending exhilaration to crackle like lightning along my bones.

It had to be the Sky-Sword.

The heir stood a pace away, shadows roiling at his back. He held the blade loosely in his palm, like it weighed nothing and he might drop it at any moment. I knew neither of those things were true. Without the onyx torc and velvet tunic, he no longer looked like royalty. He was unlike any prince I'd ever met in Fódla. He carried himself with none of Rogan's casual entitlement. None of Connla's smirking condescension. He was hard as battle metal and distant as the night sky.

The human part of me didn't understand how something so beautiful could be so wicked.

The other part of me—the part of me crafted from the darkest parts of the forest—understood perfectly.

The blade flicked toward my face. I flinched, but the point of the claíomh glided above my hairline, pushing the hood of my mantle down from my head. Tonight, the sight of my features did not elicit the same reaction it had that night on the beach. His silver gaze jerked between my mismatched eyes, but his expression betrayed nothing.

"I know this face, if not the rest of you. Tell me how you came by it."

"I have borne it for as long as I can remember," I answered truthfully. "My lord."

The title startled him—a muscle in his jaw jumped.

"I am no one's lord. Least of all yours, colleen."

Colleen. Again, I almost laughed. That he should call me *girl*, when all my life I had wished to be nothing more and nothing less?

It was a name that pleased me about as well as *my lord* pleased him.

"I thought you were tánaiste of your Sept?"

"Your mistake, to think of me at all." The sudden edge to his voice sharpened the rest of him, banishing the clinging shadows. Details leapt out at me—the ragged border of his once-fine cloak, silver woven against black. The midnight sheen of his hair. The way the tattoos inked along his arms seemed to elongate, like wings poised for flight.

Sept of Feathers. Lingering fear and tortured hope braided up my spine when I remembered the power he'd wielded at the edge of the lough—the power contained within that midnight blade. I pressed my arm tight against my thigh so the thorn-and-thistle bracelet dug into my wrist. Then I lifted my hands in a gesture of peace, letting him see I had come here tonight unarmed.

Well, not *completely* unarmed. But he didn't need to know that.

"Perhaps we should exchange names," I said mildly. "We keep running into each other."

The noise he made deep in his throat set the hairs on the back of my neck to standing. "You wish to know my name?"

"I wish to know what to call you. Or what you wish to be called. It doesn't have to be your name. I could call you—" Morrigan, why not let him think me daft? It had worked well enough for Corra—I'd let my guard down with them completely. "Beefswaddle. Winkle-picker. Jelly Belly. Dizzy—"

"That is enough." His mouth worked. "*Jelly Belly?*"

"As you wish." I spared a glance at his abdomen, which even clothed and armored was visibly trim. "Not the one I would have chosen, personally."

"You are brave, colleen." The smile he gave me was feral. "I have eviscerated men for less."

I smiled back. "Good thing I am no man."

He tilted his head, as though considering whether my argument was sound. Finally: "You are still bleeding."

I followed his gaze to my hand, which was indeed still bleeding. My finger throbbed, but distantly—the wound was little more than a nick.

"Let me clean and bandage it for you." In his husky timbre, it sounded more like a threat than an offer of help. "It is the least I can do to thank you for saving Chandika's life two moons ago."

I almost scoffed—I was accustomed enough to bigger hurts to ignore such a small wound. And yet...

In the summer of last year, Mother had hosted a delegation from a kingdom across the channel. Throughout the week of organized feasts and tournaments and hunts, the foreign king had been consistently rude to the queen—talking down to her, explaining asinine facts to her, and implying she would have been better off passing the throne to a brother or male cousin after Rían's tragic death. Mother hadn't reacted to any of the insults, simpering and smiling at him like a girl of sixteen.

During the feast on the last night of his visit, the king had the audacity to recount a legend from Mother's own noble lineage—incorrectly, no less. Mother's gentle smile had never left her face, but I'd had enough. I'd risen from my chair, hot words scalding my throat. But Cathair had gripped my wrist and yanked me back into my seat.

"Why won't she stand up to him?" I'd hissed.

"She is a queen among kings. Nothing she does or says will keep her from being underestimated," he'd told me softly. "So she finds ways to let that serve her."

"I don't understand."

"He thinks her weak and stupid. Soft as marrow, and no threat to him whatsoever." Cathair had plucked a discarded boar rib from his plate and snapped it in half, then sucked the marrow from the bone. "In the autumn, he will move all his forces north to battle the Mac Loughlin clan, leaving his coastal settlements defenseless. Then our queen's fianna will strike. She will take his silver and his cattle and his eldest son as her fosterling. And then he will know—she is not marrow, but bone. And if he tries to bite down on her, he will break his teeth."

I'd been quiet, digesting this. Later that night, Mother had leaned over to me.

"To disarm a powerful man, do not let him see how strong you are. Let him see the weakness he expects of you. Then you may strike at him when he least expects, and he will never see you coming."

Then, the advice had made me indignant. Now, as I looked up at Irian, Mother's words seemed wise.

I made my face soft and lifted my injured hand up in front of me. The moonlight slid over the dark blood and turned it silver.

"Please." I made my voice plaintive. "It does hurt."

His face spasmed with an expression I didn't know him well enough to read. He stepped forward, clasped a hand on my shoulder, and bent the world around us.

Chapter Seventeen

The night air closed around me. Shadows beat against my skull and chest with great black wings. I opened my mouth to scream, but there was only the soundless weight of an endless sky.

I fell to my knees on smooth flagstones, my palms smacking down a moment later. My stomach heaved, and for a blistering moment I thought I might vomit all over Irian's boots. Which would likely be unproductive to my aim of seducing him. I clamped my mouth shut until the feeling passed, then glared up at him.

"What was that?"

"Apologies." He didn't look apologetic. He brushed the palm that had held my shoulder down the front of his leather breastplate, as if touching me disgusted him. "You will get used to it."

I clambered to my feet. "Not bloody likely—"

My words died in my throat when I finally looked around me. Somehow—in the spaces between midnight breaths and forgotten sighs—he'd brought me into the shadow fort. And it was... indescribable.

Like Dún Darragh on the other side of the Gate, the shadow fort was ancient and half-ruined. That was where the similarities ended.

The staircase ascending from the hall was shattered like the broken spine of some long-dead beast. The grasping roots of massive trees made eerie chandeliers, strung with broken glass and gemstones. An opalescent floor glowed the same color as the tánaiste's otherworldly eyes. Shadows wreathed the corners, thick with the ghosts of half-remembered faces.

I shuddered and forced my eyes to Irian. He knelt before a hearth and began stoking its flames. The light caught the edges of his striking face—smearing red on his cheeks and smudging charcoal beneath his eyes. He'd thrown off his outer mantle—the sleeveless tunic beneath it revealed the full extent of his tattoos, which stretched from his wrists to his biceps and disappeared beneath his clothes. I tried not to stare at the sculpted muscle sliding and bunching beneath them as he tossed wood onto the fire.

I had to keep reminding myself—his beauty was a deception.

I stood behind him, fidgeting, until he looked up at me. His eyes never failed to startle—pale as starlight and reflective as mirrors. "Sit down, colleen."

I fought the urge to obey. "That's not my name."

"I would imagine not." He moved a metal kettle onto the fire. "Does it displease you?"

"A little."

"I could call you something else. What would you prefer? *Beefswaddle?*"

I narrowed my eyes at him. His expression was a puzzle to me, and I couldn't tell if he was joking.

"You can call me Fia."

"Fia." In his rough lilt, my name sounded unrecognizable. His eyes slid over my face, but it was like he wasn't seeing me at all. Same as that night on the beach, something like hatred or hope or despair spasmed across his face before smoothing away. "It does not suit you."

I stilled. "Why do you say that?"

"Names are poetry." His gaze was too bright. "Yours fits your verse, but not your cadence. I suspect it did not grow with you, as it should have done."

The reaction caught me off guard, sending a delicate fear to dance along my spine. I had told him my name to soften him toward me. But what if I had given him something of myself I hadn't meant to give? Something *real*?

Chandi had said names did not matter in Tír na nÓg. But Cathair's tales told a different story. With my true name on his lips, Irian could command me to dance relentless reels until my feet were stumps. To count every grain of sand on an endless beach. To hang myself with a noose of my own hair.

"It didn't." I made my voice nonchalant despite the dread gripping my bones. "Mother—my *foster* mother—had the name picked out for another daughter. A—"

I stopped myself before I said *a real daughter*. It was true. Before the Gate War started—when Eithne and Rían happily dreamed of a large, sprawling family—Mother had selected the name Fia as the name she loved second, after Eala. Had she ever carried and borne a second daughter, she would have given the child my name.

No. Mother *had* had a second daughter. Me. We did not share blood, but we were—what had Eala said?—bound in love. I deserved this name. I deserved her love. Gods knew I had earned it.

"And you?" I sank to my knees. "You still haven't told me your name."

He was silent a moment too long.

"You may call me Irian." His teeth cut the name into something sharp, broken. "Did your foster mother not know your true nature?"

The reversal jolted me. As it was meant to. "I don't even know my true nature."

"So you implied." He tilted his head. "Surely she questioned the arrival of a strange Folk child in her home."

"She did. But in time, she grew to love her changeling daughter anyway."

The kettle whistled shrill, slicing the tension between us. Irian grabbed it from the fire and poured steaming water into a shallow bowl. A small box by the hearth held bandages and unguents. He hesitated so briefly I thought I must have imagined it. Then he reached for my injured hand.

If I thought his skin would be cold—like his eyes, like his face, like his demeanor—I was mistaken. His touch *burned*—so hot I gasped and nearly pulled my palm from his large grasp. I hissed through my teeth, even as the sensation of his skin on mine edged from pain toward pleasure.

I would've preferred his skin cold. It would have reminded me he was a monster, as wicked as he was beautiful. A vicious Gentry royal who wielded more power than anyone ought to. Who might murder innocent girls on a whim.

I made my voice silky. "Will I get used to that too?"

Irian's silver eyes held mine. He dipped a rag in the steaming water, squeezed it, and brought it to my fingers. Like his touch, the water was slightly too hot to be pleasant—discomfort spangled up my arm as he gently cleaned crusted blood from my hand. The cut burst open, and fresh blood spilled out. He pressed down with the cloth, applying steady pressure with a deftness I hadn't expected.

But I hadn't expected any of this. His willingness to help—and his competence in actually doing so—disarmed me. No one had ever bandaged a wound for me. I'd always had to care for myself. And even if my infirmity was a sham on my part, his gentleness seemed genuine—incongruous from someone as hard and guarded as he.

"While I'm pleased to offer you the opportunity to practice your field medicine," I said, armoring myself once more, "what am I really doing here?"

One side of Irian's mouth slid lazily upward, exposing a glittering canine.

"You intrigue me, colleen." His moonlit gaze lingered over

my face. "The practice of leaving Folk changelings in the human realms fell out of fashion a long time ago."

The thicket in my chest convulsed, digging sharp thorns into my heart. He'd stolen Eala—surely it had also been he who left me in her place? "I suppose it must be easier to steal human children and leave nothing in return."

I regretted the jibe even as it fell from my lips. I was here to win his favor, not disparage his transgressions. But his expression barely changed. If anything, his lazy half smile slid wider. "You truly have no memory of your origins?"

The brambles inside me tightened. His hot, calloused hands might be gentle on mine. But he was *remorseless*.

"No." Fury wrapped its vines around me. "But you know that, don't you?"

His smile disappeared. "How could I?"

"Was it not you who abandoned me—a friendless changeling with no memories—in the human realms to die?"

Fresh emotions flickered across Irian's face in quick succession—interest, anger, yearning. A split second later, his expression smoothed back to calm menace.

"I have done many unforgivable things, colleen. That is not one of them." Irian's voice was expressionless. "The bleeding has stopped."

Our hands were still clasped—his heat had suffused me, soothing my clenched muscles. I glanced down—my fingers looked delicate against his large, sword-calloused palm. Removing the stained rag, he deftly curled a clean length of bandage around my finger. He tucked the ends but didn't let go of my hand.

"I know why I invited you into my fortress." His head tilted. "I cannot fathom why you accepted."

Invited was a strong word. But unlike the heat of his skin and the intensity of his eyes, I was prepared for this. I inhaled, Cathair's oily voice sliding through my mind. *The best falsehoods, little witch, never stray far from the truth.*

"That night on the beach...you stared at me like I was a ghost. What did you see when you looked at me?"

For a long moment, Irian said nothing.

"A friend once told me our lives are like a great lake." His voice, when he finally spoke, was dark as purple hellebore. "Each moment in time is a stone tossed in the water. Our memories are the ripples, washing over us until at last they fade. The bigger the moment, the stronger the ripple."

I was losing patience with this conversation. "Am I supposed to be the lake or the stone in this incredible metaphor?"

"You are a ripple."

"So I remind you of someone."

"Very much so."

"Not Eala?"

He shook his head. "Your resemblance to Eala is striking but merely physical. Your resemblance to my friend is more... ephemeral."

Treacherous hope slammed against the inside of my chest. Somewhere, sometime, I must have had a real mother. Someone who birthed me, who nursed me, who sang me to sleep. Perhaps this woman he spoke of—

I *did* have a mother, I reminded myself. As real a mother to me as I was a daughter to her. A mother who'd raised a changeling girl whom others encouraged her to execute. Who'd given me love, strength, purpose.

Irian might not have been the one to swap me for Eala, but *someone* had. Either my birth mother had allowed me to be abandoned in the human realms...or she had discarded me herself.

Everyone knew the only thing waiting for a changeling in the human realms was death.

But all I needed was an opening—something to keep Irian talking, interacting with me. After what happened on the beach, I wasn't convinced that I was nothing more than a ripple in his memory. I remembered flying water, screaming trees, lofting pebbles.

It's you.

"There's more you're not telling me." I tilted my head, a mirror to him. "You recognized me. 'It's you,' you said. Tell me what you thought you saw."

"You may make demands of me, colleen, but I owe you no answers. Despite the familiarity of your appearance, you are no friend to me. You are a stranger. And strangers only ever enter my realm for one of two reasons. The first is to try and kill me. The second—" I didn't even see him draw his sword. The blade simply appeared in his hand, hammered black and sharp as sin. He held it out in front of him, the light from the fire dancing along its edge. "The second is to try and take *this* from me. So why have you come? Death? Or magic?"

I stared down at the blade, grasping for a new strategy even as dread hammered on my bones. I'd asked Eala whether the bardaí had ever tried to kill him. I hadn't thought to ask what happened to those who tried. "Would you believe me if I told you I wanted neither?"

"No." His lips curled away from his teeth. "So you will understand if I do not wish to share my secrets with you."

"Then I suppose we have no choice." I forced myself to meet his silver gaze with a level, unruffled stare. "We must endeavor to no longer be strangers."

"How do you propose we do that?"

"How do strangers ever become friends, except by sharing secrets?" I remembered what the blue-eyed Gentry stranger— whom I'd mercifully never seen again—had said to me on the Feis of the Nameless Day. "I saved Chandi's life. You owe me a boon."

"A boon I have just repaid," he said smoothly, "by bandaging your wound."

Fury spiked through me, tinged with betrayal. His gentleness— his willingness to help—had been nothing more than a ruse. "I never agreed—"

"A service was offered. A service was accepted." Irian's smile was a scythe. "You should be more careful, colleen—few things in the Folk realms are ever given freely."

I fought to calm my temper. "Then let me offer you a bargain."

"Surely you have been warned not to make bargains with the Folk." His smile grew even sharper. "I might steal your shadow. Devour your fondest memories. Keep you trapped in my fortress forever."

I laughed to mask the vines of fear creeping through me. "If you knew what a rude houseguest I am, you wouldn't go to such lengths to keep me."

"If I wanted you," he drawled, "I would go to any lengths to keep you."

My pulse jumped, pulling my eyes wide.

"Name the terms of your bargain." Irian's own gaze flashed with vicious amusement. "And perhaps I will agree."

"A story for a story." My words came out rushed, breathless. "You tell me what I wish to know, and I will tell you something in return."

"Very well." Some savage decision crossed Irian's face. "But I will choose the stories. Yours and mine both."

I frowned. "That doesn't seem fair—"

"Balance and fairness are two different things, colleen. Your stories are worth less to me than mine are to you. So I will choose."

"How do I know the story you tell will be of any use to me?" I knew plenty of stories. Folk legends hammered into me during Cathair's endless lessons. Stories of treachery and seduction, violence and vengeance, magic and mayhem. Stories with violent, tragic, unhappy endings. "The cat chased the dog—that's a story."

"By my troth, I promise that any story I tell will pertain to the matter you wish to know." He pressed a formal palm to his chest. "Will that do?"

I doubted I had room to argue. It wasn't much, but it kept me close to him, kept us interacting. Got me closer to the Treasure and closer to understanding what he'd meant that night on the beach. *It's you.* "It will do."

"Good." He still held the Sky-Sword loosely in one hand—he now whipped the blade toward me, too swift for me to dodge or block. I froze as its tip came to rest against my arm, sending a shock of energy zipping through me. I looked down. The sleeve of my mantle must have ridden up over my wrist as Irian bandaged my hand. The Sky-Sword now hummed against the raw, scarred skin beneath my bracelet of brambles, nettles, and hemlock.

"This." His eyes were molten metal. "I want you to tell me the story of this."

My bones were sticks. My heart, a rock. I stared at the bracelet, searching for words to explain. To explain what it was to me, how I used it. How the pain had become a friend, an ally, a constant companion. Cathair had schooled me in many things—poisons, blades, dead languages, seduction. But he'd never taught me how to be honest. I didn't know how to be vulnerable without baring something of myself I did *not* want to bare.

"There was once—in a time of long-lost battles and unknown pasts—a changeling girl," I began haltingly. Irian's attentiveness scorched me—I had to look away. "She was raised to be strong, hammered to be hard, and whetted to be sharp. But she had a weakness for green things, for she carried the forest in her blood."

My words died as I strongly reconsidered this regrettable bargain.

"Go on," Irian commanded.

I thought of Rogan choosing Eala and leaving like a ghost in the blue of dawn. Of the warm, humid flush of the royal greenhouses—damp earth and sweet scents and green leaves. Of Cathair pressing vials of poisons into my hands, instructing me to drink them, to pour them on my skin, to *become* them.

I'd fashioned the bracelet not long after that. Something to remind me that the things I loved—like hedgehogs and hothouse flowers and boys with river-stone eyes—could still hurt me. To remind me that love was more dangerous than hatred and always hurt more.

"She tried to keep those parts of herself separate," I continued in a rush. "But she could not. If a thing could grow, it could die. If a thing could heal, it could hurt. If a thing could be kind, it could be cruel. So she made the bracelet to remind herself."

"To remind herself what?"

"Pain is only useful if you're the one choosing to inflict it." It was my voice, but Cathair's words.

Irian made a noise deep in his throat. His blade jerked upward. The bracelet fell to the gleaming floor without a sound. He sheathed his black sword, then picked up the thorny bangle. I grabbed for the broken circle of bramble and nettles. But he jerked it out of my grasp, then threw it on the fire. It sparked, then was engulfed. Horror and relief and overwhelming sorrow throbbed through me in swift succession, each emotion more intense than the last. I fought tears as I forced myself not to rub my wrist where the bracelet had once rested.

I made my face expressionless before I looked up—I would not reveal to the tánaiste what he had taken from me.

"Your turn." My voice was rough.

Irian was silent for a long time. When he finally spoke, his voice had smoothed its edges.

"Stars fell from a black sky on the night Deirdre of the Sept of Antlers was born. Her family rejoiced, for her miraculous birth meant Deirdre was destined to inherit the Treasure of their clan. Danu—chieftain of the Sept—sent for a seer to bless the new tánaiste. But the seer brought grim news. 'This child will bring war to your lands and sorrow to your Sept,' he whispered. Still, Danu did not have the heart to kill the baby. So she hid her away behind high walls, hoping that in time, Deirdre would outgrow her terrible destiny."

Impatience grew inside me. I knew the Treasure of the Sept of Antlers had been destroyed—it was of little interest to me. "And did she?"

"For many years Deirdre laughed and danced and played in the walled garden. She grew from a babe to a girl to a woman. She was happy, although she had but one friend, almost like a brother. The tánaiste of another Sept—a little boy ten years her junior—who knew a secret way into her garden." Irian's moon-bright eyes fastened on mine. "And in all those years, Deirdre never set eyes upon a grown man. Perhaps that was why—when she came of age, rejoined her Sept, and inherited the Treasure of her dynasty—the young woman fell in love with the first man she saw."

A premonition of sorrow beat cold wings against the back of my neck. "Who was he?"

"He was the king of a distant land, and Deirdre loved him before she knew him. For his curling golden hair; for his long, strong limbs; and for the way he looked at her like she was something precious. She did not understand that he did not want *her*—he wanted her Treasure and all the power that came with it. When he lured her away, she happily abandoned her family and her Sept and her destiny. Or, perhaps, fulfilled it."

The man he was talking about was Rían Ó Mainnín, the high king of Fódla—of that I was certain. But this was not the story I knew—nor even the story Eala had told. "He betrayed her for her Treasure, even though she loved him?"

"Love is rarely anything but a prelude to tragedy, colleen." I wondered that I'd ever thought Irian's smile *lazy*. It was coiled and wild. Perilous. "Danu's heart was broken. She chased the king and her wayward heir across plain and over mountain. When at last she found them, she killed the young king where he stood. She was still splattered with his blood when she begged Deirdre to return home with her. But Deirdre had loved the king and could not bear her sorrow. She threw herself from a high cliff into the grasping forest. Where her body fell, exquisite flowers grew. Black as the night sky that wept on the night of her birth, and white as the stars that had fallen like tears."

Irian's voice faded off, to be replaced by the crackling of the fire.

"Surely that's not the end of the story."

"Of this story? Yes."

My fist clenched in my lap. I *hated* stories. Especially true ones—they never had happy endings. And if this version of the story was indeed true, then the high king of Fódla had seduced and kidnapped a Folk maiden who knew nothing of men, even as he broke his troth to his pregnant queen. His greed had destroyed them both, irrevocably broken the power of the Septs, and set the Gate War in motion. He was as much a monster as the Folk who slew him.

Sudden unease damped my fury. Was I any better? What was I doing here, if not seducing a tánaiste for his Treasure?

The only difference was Irian was no innocent doe in the forest. And so far, I wasn't doing a particularly good job of seducing him.

"Why have you told me this?" He'd promised me clarity and given me nothing. "What does this have to do with me?"

"I said my story would pertain to your question." Irian's plush mouth curved like a blade. "I never said I would tell you how."

He didn't give me the chance to ask him any more questions. He touched my shoulder, bending the world around me once again.

I fell to my knees at the base of the hill. When I was finished dry-heaving, I whipped my head around, but I was alone. The field of starflowers climbed to the distant fort, its otherworldly glow dimming as dawn approached. The only sign tonight hadn't been a dream—or a nightmare—was the spray of my own blood on one of the silvery flowers, and the neat little bandage adorning my ring finger.

⁓

As Rogan and I walked back to Dún Darragh in the gray light of dawn, Deirdre's story haunted me. But it wasn't the prophecy of her birth, or the alleged ruthlessness of the king, or even their calamitous deaths that needled me. It was Irian's callous words that echoed in my ears: *Love is rarely anything but a prelude to tragedy, colleen.*

As Dún Darragh loomed into view, I was startled by a crash in the underbrush. I glanced behind me. Where my footsteps had fallen, flowers had begun to grow. They were sharp and pale as glass. But growing between them were black flowers—dark as the bloom that had bitten me in the greenhouse.

"Something wrong, changeling?" Rogan asked from a few paces ahead.

His eyes were tired. I shook my head.

When I glanced back into the brightening wood, all the flowers—light and dark—had disappeared.

Chapter Eighteen

Luis—Rowan
Winter

As part of our bargain, Corra insisted Rogan and I celebrate Imbolc. One of the four high holy days of the year, Imbolc was traditionally celebrated with song and silence. I didn't know how we three—an invisible sprite I *wished* would be silent and a pair of brooding warriors who definitely couldn't sing—were supposed to celebrate.

I'd asked Rogan to split a graceful rowan trunk lengthwise—now it burned merrily in the hearth. Corra conjured candles from nowhere to drip from every available surface, encasing the hall in amber light and filling the air with the sweet scent of beeswax. I strung soft milky snowdrops over the mantel—the first of my winter flowers to blossom—as Corra rocketed along the ceiling and hollered an Imbolc song I'd mercifully never heard before.

Sun and star, the fire is lit
Around the hearth we all will sit
A branch for me, a branch for thee
Soon winter's chill will springtime be!

I covered my ears and glared at the ceiling. "Has anyone ever told you that you have a truly accursed singing voice?"

"Frequently, in fact," said Rogan from the top of the staircase. My gaze jolted toward him. "Although usually only when I've attempted to actually sing."

Corra blew raspberries as Rogan sauntered down the steps, swinging a jug of mead and trying to look like he hadn't already been drinking all afternoon.

"*Pfaugh!*" spat Corra from behind me. I jumped as a moon-faced gruagach carved onto the wall stretched its bandy legs. "He looks like hay."

"Hay?" I hissed out of the corner of my mouth. "That's the best you can come up with?"

"Yes, hay." Corra performed a saucy little dance. "After it's been eaten and swallowed and digested and—"

"Yes, *yes*." I turned my back on them. "Don't forget you're the one who insisted we have this stupid little ceremony. It wasn't my idea of fun."

"The villagers have yet again outdone themselves." Rogan gestured expansively, taking in the greenery, the candles, and the crackling fire. Corra cackled. I forcibly ignored them. "But remind me why we're doing this? I've never known you to be particularly religious."

I shot another surreptitious glare at Corra, who was gleefully picking their toenails on the wall. "Let's call it homesickness. Is there mead in that jug?"

There was. Rogan poured me a cupful, and for a long moment we drank in almost companionable silence. But I couldn't ignore how close to me he sat on the edge of the hearth—how his thigh bumped against mine when he leaned over me to pour himself another drink. I tried not to inhale, but his smell—like sun-warmed metal and spicy musk—invaded my senses with dogged familiarity. My fingers twitched toward my wrist, but of course my bracelet of brambles and nettles was gone.

"What do we do now?" He swirled his drink. "Swap stories or something?"

Morrigan, *anything* but that. Intrusive memories scorched me: deft bargains. Suggestive banter. Tragic tales.

I downed my drink.

"The prayer, the prayer!" squawked Corra, flitting across the hearth in the guise of a flock of seagulls.

I sighed. "Let's do an Imbolc prayer."

Rogan barely glanced at me as he poured us both more of the amber mead, but I dared a look at his face. His eyes looked glazed, bright spots of red standing out on his high cheekbones. He was already drunk. Disappointment thundered through me, unexpected and sour, limned with the barest edge of concern.

I forced myself to remember Rogan wasn't my problem. He wasn't my *anything*.

We bridged the space between us with our left arms. Rogan's fingers brushed my palm before circling around my wrist, and my pulse jumped. Rogan's eyes flicked to mine, shiny in the low light. For a moment, we sat like that, our hands clasped and our gazes colliding.

It was he who broke the silence, intoning the prayer traditionally said on the holiday.

"An echo of winter still lies on the earth," he said, and I joined him. "Make ready to welcome the seed of rebirth."

He jerked his hand out of mine and tossed back his glass of mead.

"Is that all?" he asked me.

"I—" I was almost too stunned to speak. "I guess so."

"Then I'll bid you good night."

He was halfway to the stairs before I couldn't take it anymore. Morrigan knew I had my reasons to keep my distance from him. But this was getting out of hand. Rogan hadn't slept; he hadn't shaved; he was drunk every day by noon. And much as I told myself I didn't care what he did with his free time, I had to admit I was *worried* about him.

"If you want to spend the night alone, spiraling to the bottom of a wine jug," I snapped, "be my guest."

His shoulders hunched. "You've made it very clear you have no interest in what I want, Fia."

The words would have sounded confrontational, except his voice cracked on my name, and cracked my rib cage open with it. Tangled roots squeezed my heart, unearthing feelings I'd meticulously kept at bay—sympathy, worry, guilt, desire.

"We may not see eye to eye on everything, princeling," I said softly. "But I'm still your friend."

It was what he needed to hear. He crossed the room. The jug fell from his fingers with a thunk as he dropped to his knees before me. He slid his hands around my waist and buried his head against my stomach. I froze, my snarl of emotions tangling into something sharp and complicated. Memories pummeled me—his tongue, sliding between lips that tasted like archive dust; his hands, lifting me against a crofter's cottage; his body, thrusting over mine in the gold-strewn fade of a long-gone twilight. Hesitantly, I rested my hand atop his blond head. He sighed against my stomach.

"I need you, Fia." The words were vehement, albeit muffled. "I've always needed you. And I can't—I can't do any of this without you."

"I'm right here."

"You're not." Rogan lifted his head, and his blue-green eyes on my face were wide, wretched, artless. The motion brought us close—too close. His hard torso pressed heavy between my legs; his warm palms circled my waist; his face rested inches below mine. "Not in the way I want you to be."

Lust and loathing quickened my pulse. "I told you, Rogan—"

"And I told you—you're so much more to me than any word can capture," he interrupted. "You remind me who I am and who I want to be. You have always seen the best in me, even when I have not seen it in myself."

My laugh was harsh. "So I am no more than a blank mirror to show you your finest self?"

"That's not—" Rogan's brow furrowed. "You're twisting my words."

"Surely Eala recognizes all your estimable qualities." I conjured her up, the radiant princess between us. "She is to be your wife, after all."

"She doesn't know me like you do. And I don't think she wants to." His eyes roved my face. "The few times we have interacted, she is a new woman every time. Cold, then hot. Coy, then cruel. She is beautiful as the moon and just as distant. She is making it very hard on me, changeling."

I stiffened. Eala's words from the Nameless Day echoed in my head: *Tell me, Sister—do you think I ought to make things easy on him?*

And I remembered my own petty response: *No need to make it easy.*

Guilt settled oily in my stomach, glossing over my resentment. I had wanted Rogan to taste a little of the heartache I'd glutted myself on—the heartache of having the person you wanted most in the world be always out of reach. But he was a prince—he had not been raised for disappointment or rejection the way I had.

"Come, princeling." I forced a smile and tried to ignore how close his lips were to mine. "What is it you're always telling me? 'The joy is in the thrill of a fight, not the promise of a kill.'"

"Not this time, changeling. Sometimes I wish—" He paused. I waited. "Sometimes I wish I didn't have to marry her."

It was the worst thing he could have said. Hurt bloomed inside me, fresh and sharp as that morning he left, over four years ago. Because he didn't have to marry Eala. Yes, he'd been betrothed to her as a child. But Mother had given him a choice. And he'd chosen her over me. Once, twice—a hundred times.

"No one's forcing you to do anything, princeling." My voice was hardwood pith. "This is your choice."

Rogan's broad shoulders bunched. "If there's one thing I've never had in this situation, Fia, it's a choice."

I extricated myself from him roughly. His arms fell from my waist, and my skin felt cold where his palms had been. I picked up the discarded jug of mead, taking a long swallow to banish the tight, hot words clogging my throat. But they refused to subside.

"But you did. You chose her over me, when I was standing right there." My voice sounded strangled to my own ears. "I gave you everything and would have given more. But you walked away from me. You *left* me."

"I chose—" A muscle jumped high on Rogan's cheek. "When did I choose?"

"After we—" I was suddenly trying not to cry. "After Mother found out what we'd done, and she summoned you. She made you decide which of her daughters you preferred. And you chose Eala."

Rogan's expression became ferocious. "Is *that* what she told you?"

"Was there more to tell?"

"That's *not what happened*." Suddenly, he was right in front of me. I reeled back a step, but he gripped my upper arms hard enough to leave marks. "The queen didn't summon me. I went to her of my own accord. I'd been in love with you for years, Fia, but until we—" He broke off. "I asked her to dissolve my betrothal to Eala, since the princess had been gone for so many years. I asked her to grant me your hand instead. I told her I knew what I hadn't before—that my love for you was returned. And do you know what she said to me?"

I shook my head, muddled and mute. My heart throbbed wild with his words: *I'd been in love with you for years.* I had to know the rest of his story, even if that was all it was—a *story*.

"She *laughed* at me. Then she told me you'd never be able to love me once I was reduced to nothing." The words were recited with the rhythm of repetition—as though he'd replayed them in his head so many times, they'd almost lost meaning. "If I wed you, she'd make sure my father disowned me, disinherited me, cast me out into the dirt."

"No." I tried to shake off his bruising grip. "She wouldn't—"

"She did." Agitation shuddered through him. "She also told me that without the protection of my betrothal to Eala, the peace between our kingdoms would be forfeit, and she'd see no reason not to march on Glenathney. Slaughter Bridei's cattle, burn our grain fields, then end the Mòr line with my brothers."

"That doesn't make any sense."

"I couldn't think of a way out." His voice was nearly toneless. "I was eighteen and powerless. The queen was right—if I stepped out of line, I would be disowned and disinherited. Never mind the money—you are worth more to me than gold. But my father is an old, sick man, and my half brothers have been badly raised. I am the crown prince of Bridei. I have a duty to my ancestors. To my *people*—and life is already hard for most of them. I couldn't bear to be the cause of more violence and sorrow. So I gave in. I thought if I returned home, I could bide my time until I was king. Then I'd have power. Then I could challenge the high queen. Then I could marry whomever I liked. I thought...I thought I had time."

My eyes burned. "You should have told me."

"I tried." Old agony striped his gaze. "I couldn't get near you—not with Cathair's witch-birds lurking everywhere I went. And then my father arrived and gave me the worst whipping of my life. I couldn't get out of bed for the three days before being forced to ride home."

I suddenly remembered Rogan's drawn white face the morning he'd left. I'd thought him cold and furious—but if he'd just been whipped, riding would have been torture. But that still didn't account for the cruel, crushing words he'd spoken to me. If it had truly been our parents forcing us apart—something I still couldn't bring myself to believe of Mother—then why had he said something so hurtful?

"If that's true, then why—" The question stuck in my throat like mud. "Why did you say it? Why did you say you were a prince, and I was nothing?"

"Nothing?" Confusion twisted over his face, followed by a brisk and brutal realization. "Donn's gates, Fia. *That's* what this is about?"

The brittle threads stitching together the shattered pieces of my heart began to fray. My eyes stung with unshed tears. "Never mind."

"I didn't say you were nothing." He caught my arm. "I said you were *no one*."

"*No one?*" Cutting open an old scar always hurt worse than the original wound. "That's better, then."

"*Listen to me.*" He grasped my chin, forced my eyes up to his. "Don't you remember that skipping rhyme from when we were young? *I asked all around, who broke the vase? No one, no one wants to show their face.*"

A sharp thorn of memory pierced me—something I hadn't thought about in years. Rogan and I sneaking into the scullery in the middle of the night, stealing Cook's fresh-baked bannocks and slathering them with jam. *No one, no one*, we'd giggled, stuffing our faces until we were crumb crusted and sticky.

No.

"We made a game of it for a while—don't you remember? Whenever we did anything naughty, we'd sing, 'No one, no one,' " Rogan breathed. "I needed the queen to think she'd won. I needed my father to think he'd beaten me into submission. And I needed you to know I was still fighting for you. I thought you understood."

"Why would you think that?" Misery clawed a cry out of my throat. "How was I supposed to know what you meant?"

"Because I wrote you. Every week, for nearly a year. I had to ride all the way down to Árd na Dare to hire a messenger so my father wouldn't catch on."

"I never got any letters," I whispered.

Something desperate welled in Rogan's eyes. "I stopped when—when you never wrote me back."

He stared at me, willing me to come to the conclusion on my

own—to absolve him of the responsibility of telling me something I didn't want to hear. But I twisted away from the understanding growing tall and sharp and despicable inside me.

"She wouldn't," I insisted, but even to me the words sounded feeble.

"Wouldn't she?"

Something broke inside me then, but it wasn't my heart. It was something else—something I'd believed would never break. It was strong as a queen and sharp as a blade and golden as a torc. It was something I'd believed I could trust above all else—something I had never dared to question.

"She wouldn't—I know she wouldn't." My voice cracked with anguish. "Why would she? Rogan, she loves me."

"Are you sure?" His voice held pity, understanding. "There was one last thing she said to me the day I asked for your hand. She told me I couldn't possibly know how to love something like you. She said you were made of poison nettle and steel—not something to be loved, but something to be wielded. A weapon, not a girl."

"I don't believe you," I whispered.

But I did—I *did*. I'd heard Mother's voice often enough to know her words. They had been slightly different—changed, I supposed, for my benefit—but close enough.

Only I know how to love someone like you. If she'd told me once, she'd told me a thousand times. *And no one will ever love you more than I do.*

For twelve years, those words had been a balm. But now they were a blade. A blade cutting me from her.

A knife appeared in Rogan's hand, echoing my thoughts. I reeled back in confusion, but Rogan ripped his mantle open at the neck and bent the blade to his own bare chest. The point cut a divot into the skin above his heart, just beside the cracked river-stone brooch.

"I swear it." A tiny droplet of blood squeezed around the blade. "If I've ever lied to you before, Fia, I'm sorry. But I swear it on my heart—I never chose Eala. Amergin help me, but I still can't. I still want you. I still—"

I broke away. I couldn't hear him say it, not after all these years. I flung myself toward the stairs, even as the room tipped around me, the floor twisting toward the ceiling and the walls closing in. And as I fled to my room, all the things I believed realigned themselves in grotesque new angles, until every facet of my life glared sharp and unfamiliar as a broken gem.

***

I shuddered and writhed in the embrace of my clammy sheets. Tears trailed cold down my cheeks and soaked the pillowcase, tasting of desire and resentment and wasted time.

I longed to go to Rogan. To tell him I still wanted him—still *loved* him. To savor the warmth of his skin on my fingertips. To linger on the taste of his lips—sweet as honey mead. To take him onto me and into me and pretend like the last four and a half years had never happened.

But the words Mother had said to Rogan beat against my skull, drowning out all else.

Not something to be loved, but something to be wielded. A weapon, not a girl.

My hand dropped to my wrist, tracing the puckered scar where my bracelet had been. Maybe Mother had said those words to Rogan. Maybe she had even wanted a warrior, a spy—an assassin— with my particular set of skills. But it was Cathair who had trained me in the ways of violence and venom. Mother could not have known about every sick lesson that man taught me, every torment and tribulation he used to forge me into something hard and strong and wicked. Mother knew I was more than steel sharpened to a killing edge. Mother *loved* me.

Only I know how to love you. And nothing and no one will ever love you more than I.

For the first time, I perceived a shadow lurking beneath those words—a tacit assumption that I was so difficult to love that only she was capable of the effort.

All these years, could that truly have been what she meant?

I refused to look at the notion head-on. Still, the ache of it bore steadily deeper—a creeping rot at the taproot of a tree I thought would never topple but was nevertheless beginning to decay.

❦

Sleet and ice gave way to the soft, slow patter of late winter showers.

A witch-bird arrived from Cathair, and though I glanced at the letter—war brewing between under-kings, a query for news, an exhortation for Rogan to write his father—I was too unsettled to respond to it. I crumpled it, threw it on the fire, and didn't bother telling Rogan about it. If he was avoiding his family, it was none of my business. He, like me, certainly had his reasons.

A few days before the next full moon, I awoke to a hooded mantle lying across the foot of my bed. Woven from a russet fabric pricked through with green, it was lovely and soft, with a velvety nap that caught on my calloused fingers. When I tried it on, it glided in rich folds to my knees. It whispered secrets of warm earth and sunlight on broad leaves and smoothed over a few of my jagged, creeping hurts.

"Corra!" I hid my smile.

"Chiardhubh?" Corra yelled back from somewhere in the rafters.

"I didn't ask for this!"

"Then throw it on the fire," a feral cat hissed from the wall, back arched. "We wouldn't want you to feel obligated to us for our many, many, many—"

"Corra."

"*Many* kindnesses."

I decided to keep the cloak, just to spite them. "We did make a deal for those supposed kindnesses."

"And the mistress has held up her end." The cat casually licked one sharp-clawed paw. "So far."

My smile widened. I *had* kept up my end of the bargain—the greenhouse was no longer just a gap-toothed collection of metal and glass. Bulbs had begun to peek green shoots from dark earth, promising spring blooms. And I was beginning to enjoy the work— in a way I hadn't since those long-ago days in the royal green-houses. *Work is love*, the gardeners used to say. *We do the work to show nature we care.*

And I did care. I cared in a way that made me think perhaps I could be more than venom and death. More than a weapon.

A weapon could only destroy. A weapon could not grow. A weapon could not care. And a weapon certainly couldn't love.

Chapter Nineteen

Y ou really don't have anything to say to me?"

I slid my eyes over to Rogan, who looked miserable beneath the dripping hood of his woolen mantle. It was hard to tell if the full moon had risen—thick banks of clouds made a dull gray bowl of the night sky. I gnawed my lip and trained my eyes toward the Willow Gate.

"What would you like me to say?" The argument we'd had last week—and the revelations that followed—had already torn me to pieces. The places where I'd patched myself back together still felt raw. But much as I ached, I knew in the root-tangled cavern of my heart that nothing had changed. The obstacles standing between us were the same as they'd always been.

"Something. Anything." Frustration etched his face. "I told you I wanted to wed you, Fia. It's the kind of thing that deserves a response."

"Wan*ted*. Past tense." I forced my voice to remain neutral. "Unless you're planning to break off your engagement to Eala now?"

"I *can't*." Resentment harshened his voice. "My duty is to my people. I wish I could leave that to my brothers. Brighid knows my father's wife would gladly see her eldest, Cillian, as king. She already seeks to secure him a royal match from Usdiae. If she does, he could produce an heir before me. Then Father will give him Bridei. But Cillian is idle and dissolute—he'll gladly sell off our best farmland to Fannon if it means his choice of Connla's prize stallions. And Bridei will not survive another bad king. I must be the one to dig us out of penury—for my people, if for no one else."

"I don't blame you for leaving, Rogan—not now that I understand why you had to." Tiny raindrops needled my face and frizzed my hair. "But nothing has changed. If we give in to this—if we follow our foolish hearts—it could be the ruin of thousands. And for what? Childhood infatuation? We're too grown to believe that will have the ending we want it to."

"Fia—"

"A princess is still trapped in Tír na nÓg," I interrupted, blunt. "A geas still has to be broken." Silently, I added, *A Gentry tánaiste still holds a Treasure I mean to steal.* "You will return to Fódla with a bride and an inheritance and a throne. And I…"

I paused. Mother had said I would return as an honored warrior in her fiann, a respected member of her court. After what Rogan told me at Imbolc, those words had begun to ring hollow. But Mother's love was still more sure than Rogan's was—even if her love was a poisoned, imperfect thing. I couldn't turn my back on my one chance to be accepted, to carve out an ending for myself that was wholly my own. Stealing the Sky-Sword, freeing Eala, and returning both to Fódla was still the straightest path toward that resolution.

"You and I…we were never more than an impossible story," I said. "A story we told ourselves so many times, we both started to believe it."

"Plenty of impossible stories have happy endings, changeling."

"But this isn't a story." I finally looked at him. In the dim pale moonlight, Rogan's eyes shone like brittle glass. I almost wavered.

But I set my jaw. "You were right four years ago. You *are* a prince. I *am* no one. We were never meant for each other."

I turned back to the Gate. But not before I saw Rogan's eyes shatter.

❧ ～❧

It wasn't raining in Tír na nÓg. Instead, a bank of choking fog settled over the forest, sifting eerily between the trees. As we walked toward the shadow fort, figures seemed to trail us in the mist. Voices called, just out of earshot. Damp hands reached for the hood of my new mantle.

My vigilance skittered toward high alert. My ears strained for the slightest sound; my hands hovered over the weapons at my belt; my nerves sang with danger.

At last, the forest thinned. The sound of lapping water penetrated the fog. The field of starflowers breathed silver through the gray. I couldn't see the fort at all.

"Be careful, Rogan." The fog swallowed my words. "Wherever you go tonight, do not tarry. In this fog, it will be hard to tell time and be easy to get lost."

His eyes—dark gray in the mist—lingered on my face. Then, with a jerk of his head, he disappeared.

I stared up at where I knew the fort to be. Night after night—restless in my bed despite working my body to exhaustion in the greenhouse—I'd pondered my last encounter with Irian. His words looped relentlessly in my mind as I sought for deeper meaning in the story he'd told. I'd combed my memories of his predator's grace for any sign of weakness, any chinks in his armor he might unwittingly have revealed. But every night, as dawn sighed into my room, I had nothing but broken nightmares and unanswered questions to show for it.

The shadowy tánaiste was still a dreadful mystery to me. And I was afraid—yes, *afraid*—of putting myself under his spell once more. I didn't trust myself not to fall for his illusion of gentility, of refined eloquence.

It's you.

"What're you doing down here?"

I jumped so high my feet left the ground. I spun to see Chandi lurking beside me in the undergrowth. As usual, the taller girl was wearing nothing but her own thick black hair. The swirling fog didn't flatter her honeyed skin and amber eyes—in fact, the gray miasma lent her a corpse-like pallor that did nothing to calm my vaulting nerves.

"Morrigan, don't sneak up on me like that!" Instinct had put a pair of blades in my hands—I carefully sheathed them. "I could have killed you."

"Jumpy tonight?"

"I don't like this fog."

"It's called féth fíada." Chandi fluttered her fingers ominously. "A magical mist said to bring invisibility to whoever casts it. They say it only appears when wicked deeds are afoot."

A chill kissed my spine. "You're not helping."

"Tír na nÓg just has strange weather." She rolled her eyes. "Anyway, I need to ask a favor. You know that...*lummox* you seem to be friends with?"

I quelled a laugh. I had a feeling Chandi and Corra would be fast friends. "Rogan?"

"Yes, the hulking boy." She gave her head an expressive wiggle. "Tell him to stop being so moody."

"Pardon?"

"He's ruining the fun with his sad skulking." Her nose scrunched. "Eala doesn't like it. Full moons are for dancing, drinking, and kissing things with pretty lips. Tell him to stop brooding."

I had no intention of telling him any such thing. Imbolc leapt to the front of my mind. Rogan's head pillowed on my lap. His arms around my waist. The look in his river-stone eyes when he said, *She is making it very hard on me, changeling.*

I opened my mouth to suggest Chandi instead tell Eala to stop toying with Rogan, but a cluster of sounds at the edge of the lough stole my attention.

A rattling sigh like something heavy being dragged over stone. A sick thud like flesh being struck. A high-pitched keening like a wail of pain.

And the skittering clang of metal.

Battle.

I took off in one elastic motion, years of training taking over my body before my mind had time to catch up. My first thought was for Rogan—out here in this bewitched fog, an encounter with armed, vicious Folk could be deadly. But a moment later, all thoughts—including ones of Rogan—flew out of my mind.

In the past few years, I'd encountered more than a few Folk monsters. Most of them, I'd slain. With blades or arrows or even— once or twice—my bare hands. I'd grappled with pincers and talons. My skin had been scored by fangs and horns. I had stared into slitted pupils and bulging ommatidia and flanged antennae.

I had never encountered anything like *this*. The stench reached me first—carrion and filth wafting strong enough to make my eyes water. And then I saw...*it*. An ollphéist—a Folk wyrm. But it was *massive*—so huge I couldn't see all of it at once. It wove in and out of the fog, flashing features that didn't belong together. A long, muscular tail, coiling like a serpent. A heavy-jawed maw snapping with oversized fangs. Slashing paws ringed with talons. Staring eyes glowing yellow as lamps. And oil-slick scales—overlapping like head-to-tail chain mail.

I reeled back from the nightmare of scales and flesh and slavering fangs. Even in Tír na nÓg, the thing was unnatural. *Wrong.*

And around the ollphéist's lunging form darted a figure. I caught only glimpses—a whirling dark cloak, an impression of height and grace. And an ink-black sword slicing through the mist and dripping with ichor.

Irian.

And that high keening sound, like bells ringing? It was the *sword* that was singing.

A gasp of fear startled me out of my stupor. Chandi had caught up with me and stood gaping at my shoulder, pale with terror.

I rounded on her. "Go get help!"

She nodded, wide-eyed. Then disappeared without a word into the swirling murk.

Morrigan damn this uncanny fog.

I crept closer to the fray. Miraculously, Irian was holding his own against the monstrous ollphéist. I'd assumed he was combat trained, but seeing him in motion was...*magnificent.* He moved with the grace of a dancer and the precision of a predator. There was no separation between his body and his blade, as if he, too, were hammered from hard metal. But as the monster lunged at him, again and again, spiraling around him in ever-tightening loops of serpentine flesh, even he began to flag.

My warrior's heart screamed at me to join him, to lend my blades to his battle. But my strategist's mind urged me to wait. After all, my purpose here in Tír na nÓg was to *take* Irian's Treasure—for Mother, for Eala—then destroy its heir. I could risk life and limb to save him, only to later outwit and assassinate him. Or...I could pry the Sky-Sword out of his already cold, dead hands once this ravening monster inevitably killed him.

But then I'd never know what he'd meant that night on the beach. What he'd seen in my face that had driven him to upend the lough, nearly uproot the forest.

It's you.

The ollphéist pounced on Irian. Its claws met his blade with a wailing clang that juddered in my ears. Irian tried to disengage, but the monster clamped down, wedging the blade between its talons. Its tail whipped around. The armored flesh connected with Irian's leg, hard. The tánaiste made no sound as his leg gave way, but he dropped to his knees on the pebbled beach. The wyrm wrested the sword out of his hands, discarded it like trash. Pounced on Irian. He ducked, rolled to one side. But the monster had size, strength, and brutal stamina on its side. Its claws were lightning as it slashed out.

A wound opened Irian's back, scoring his flesh from shoulder to hip and shredding his armor. This time, he roared in pain. Beneath his mantle, blood gushed out, silver in the fog. He lunged forward, reaching for his ichor-striped sword, but the ollphéist flicked it out of his reach with one deft claw.

Resolve hardened my limbs. This was a massacre. If—*when*—I killed Irian, it would be swift and justified. Revenge for the pain he'd caused and the lives he'd destroyed. His execution was meant to be my triumph.

But standing idly by as he was torn limb from limb by a monster ten times his size? That didn't feel like victory.

I unsheathed my knives and launched myself at the wyrm.

I struck the ollphéist's thick, writhing tail and had to scrabble for purchase. I'd expected the wyrm's scales to be slimy, but they were slick—the overlapping scutes smooth as glass. I gripped with my knees and sliced with my blades, but the scales were better than armor—my skeans glanced right off. The wyrm's stench of rot and death slapped me in the face, and I gagged.

Cursing, I pushed myself to stand on the monster's tail, which was thick as a felled tree. Fighting for balance, I took three dancing steps, then flung myself upward onto its heaving back, aiming my blades directly down. The impact was bone jarring. Like before, one of my skeans simply skittered off, wrenching my wrist as I clung to it. But the other stuck, lodging deep in the wyrm's flesh. I swung sideways, the full weight of my body hanging from my grip on the narrow dagger.

The ollphéist lofted its head and screamed at the sky, its tail thrashing wildly. I tried to swing myself back up onto the crest of its spine but had no leverage. I squinted up at where my sweaty palm was beginning to slip from my dagger. And realized I'd been going about this the wrong way.

The blade had lodged between two scales, in the tender flesh below. Fresh adrenaline pulsed into my flagging muscles. I didn't need to destroy the armor—I simply had to find the chinks. Hoisting myself upward, I reached with the other dagger, aiming for the nearest gap between two glistening scales. The blade sank into flesh. Again, the monster howled and shuddered beneath me, wheeling as it tried to shake me off.

I grinned, even as sweat sheened on my skin and my legs swung wildly beneath me.

Tonight was finally getting interesting.

I climbed the monster like a wall, slamming my daggers into its flesh and kicking up for my next hold. It wasn't easy going—I'd never climbed a wall this angry. But although I had succeeded in diverting the wyrm's attention, I wasn't sure it was much help to Irian. He was badly injured. Out of the corner of my eye, I saw him try to climb to his feet, but the leg the monster had struck hung limp, and he crumpled back to the ground. His entire left side was stained with silvery blood. More of the liquid pooled on the ground beneath him.

He was bleeding out. If I still wanted to ferret out his secrets, then murder him myself...I was running out of time.

Panting, I hauled myself onto the ollphéist's skull. It reared up and whipped its head back and forth, but I braced myself with my daggers. Then I swung, aiming for the monster's only visible weakness—its glowing yellow eyes.

My dagger burst the outer membrane like a bubble. Heavy, burning ooze gushed out. The wyrm's iris rolled wild and excruciatingly close as it howled havoc at the sky. I tried to shove the dagger deeper—I had to pierce its brain to kill it—but the fluid was too thick. The monster clawed at its face, leaving purple score marks on its own scales and narrowly missing me.

"Colleen!"

Somehow, Irian had made it to his feet. In the fog, his eyes glowed like twin moons. He held up his ichor-striped blade.

"Catch."

He flung the Sky-Sword. It sliced through the mist, dark as the wing of a great black bird. And I—painfully aware I was risking a finger, if not a whole hand—reached up to catch it.

The hilt of the Treasure struck my palm. Power sizzled through my whole body, scalding in its intensity. It was nothing like the creeping, bristling sensation of my Greenmark. This—this was like being struck by lightning. Energy sizzled along my bones. A high wind buffeted my hair. Pure, unfettered *magic* sang along my skin, nearly overwhelming me. My eyes fluttered shut.

Images flashed behind my eyelids—black cliffs, silver skies, bones of metal holding a dying world together at the seams...

I snapped my eyes open, clinging to the shreds of my resolve. I raised the blade high. And sliced it down into the monster's staring eye.

Chapter Twenty

The black metal sliced through vitreous liquid, pierced bone, and drove deep into the creature's brain. I didn't so much hear the monster's death-scream as *feel* it, reverberating upward through my arm until my whole body resounded with it. The ollphéist swayed, bucked its head. For a breathless moment, I hung weightless in the air. Then the wyrm collapsed beneath me, and I fell with it.

I grasped for the sword, my dagger, *anything* to hold on to. But my hands were slippery with ichor. I dropped, slammed hard against armored scales, and bounced off. My training curled me into a loose ball before I hit the ground, but the impact still jarred me to my bones. I tumbled over the pebbled strand, rolled to a stop. My vision blurred.

I forced myself to my feet.

The ollphéist coiled in its death throes, the Sky-Sword like a shard of night piercing its eye. Irian was also struggling, clearly racked with pain as he collapsed back onto the ground. The earth and air—the very shadows—rumbled. Wind howled, and pebbles bounced ominously on the beach. I threw myself down beside him, skidding on shale.

"Stop moving." Morrigan, there was so much *blood*—if that was even what you called the bright liquid pumping out of his wounds. I jerked my new mantle over my head—sorry, Corra—and balled it up against Irian's back. It did little to stanch the flow—within moments, the russet cloth was bathed in silver.

Irian looked moments from death. His marble skin was gray as the fog, and the black tattoos climbing over his arms and chest looked like they might strangle him.

My hands stilled as the thought once more caressed me: Would it be so awful to just...step back?

I hadn't wanted to watch him mangled to death by a monster. But this? This would be easy. I wouldn't have to slit his throat or plunge a blade into his heart. His eyes would close. His body would still. And I could take the Sky-Sword and Eala and Rogan and *run*. Back to Fódla. Back—

Beneath me, the earth grumbled another warning. The trees at the edge of the forest shook. A flare of memory seared me—another night on this same beach, when I'd saved Chandi from drowning. Water falling upward, stones flying sharp as arrows, roots ripping free from the earth.

Sudden dread crept close. If Irian died...what happened to *this* place?

"I am...fine." Irian's voice was barely audible. His head lolled onto his shoulder. He cracked one silver eye open. "Need to... fort."

"You don't look fine." I quirked an eyebrow at him. "And if you need to get to the fort, can't you just—"

I wiggled my fingers. When he looked at me blankly, I mimed putting my hands on my knees and vomiting into the grass. Astonishingly, this seemed to amuse him. It was the first time I'd seen him smile fully—his lush lips parted to reveal straight, gleaming teeth. The expression turned my heart to glass and threatened to shatter it. Even moments from death, he was so obnoxiously *beautiful*.

"Too weak."

"And too heavy." I pressed my sodden cloak tighter against his wounds. "So me carrying you is also out of the question."

He slumped against me. The beach quivered, black waves slapping higher. His skin radiated fever through the shreds of his ruined armor. His breath ratcheted against my throat. My fingers flexed, although I wasn't sure whether I wanted to hold him tighter or end him right then and there.

Fortunately for him, I'd left both my blades somewhere on the steaming corpse behind us. And I wasn't in the mood to kill any more monsters tonight.

"Stay with me." I took great pleasure in slapping him awake. "Irian, you're dying."

"Sword...will not let me." His low tone held a surety I didn't share.

Interesting. But unhelpful.

"Unless your sword is going to start scooping up your blood and putting it back inside your body, we're going to need a backup plan."

An idea grew swift and sudden inside me. The Sky-Sword might be the most powerful magic here tonight, but it wasn't the *only* magic. That day in the greenhouse, when the starling pecked me— I'd healed myself with my Greenmark. It had been a small cut— much smaller than this gaping wound.

I might not be able to save him. But maybe I could delay the inevitable.

And that gave me leverage.

"I think I can heal you."

His voice was rough with pain. "Then what are you waiting for?"

"You were the one who told me nothing in Tír na nÓg came free." I almost felt guilty dangling his own life in front of him like bait. Almost. "I want another story."

Surprise and an obscure kind of admiration winged his gaze.

"Ruthlessness becomes you, colleen." His head lolled. He didn't call my bluff. "I agree to the same bargain as before."

It was good enough.

I ripped my sodden mantle from Irian's back and placed my hand there instead. I glanced down at his ashen face lying limp on my shoulder, his sweat-slicked hair pasted to his temples.

He might be my enemy. But he was also a fighter. A fellow warrior. Watching him fight that wyrm had been like watching flames dancing silver along the edge of a blade. I wasn't sure I'd truly have been able to stand and watch as he bled to death in front of me. Part of me was glad I wouldn't have to find out.

"This is going to hurt."

I spread my hand over the wounds, silver liquid pooling over my fingers. The gouges left by the wyrm's claws were deep; shards of white bone pricked through layers of muscle, fascia, skin. I almost lost my nerve. I wished—not for the first time—for my bracelet of thorns and nettles. It would have helped me focus. Instead, I thought of my work in the greenhouse. Dead seeds being coaxed back to life. Dirt and scrub tempted toward loamy lushness. Flower buds unfurling.

Here in Tír na nÓg, I barely had to imagine it before it became real. The forest was so close—so vital. All I had to do was reach out, and my Greenmark was *there*. Waiting.

Brambles tangled out of my fingertips, delving sharp into the ragged skin of the cuts. Irian's eyes flew wide as hundreds of piercing needles dug into his flesh. At the edge of the forest, roots shifted and trees screamed.

"Go on, then." I didn't want him to rip this place apart before I patched him back together. "Tell me your story."

"*Now?*"

"Are you busy with something else?"

"Besides dying?" He jerked as another line of brambles cut into his skin.

I made my brambles stop twining together, leaving the edges of Irian's wound open. The muscles of his neck corded in tension, and his hand tightened into a huge fist next to my thigh. Pebbles chattered like teeth.

"Once—in a place at the edge of nowhere, where cliffs reared tall as giants above a dark sea, and selkies rode foam pale as white horses—there was a boy." Irian squeezed his eyes shut as the brambles tightened once more. "He was—*thought* he was—a boy like any other, wandering the moors and exploring the cliffs. When the sun was high, he would scrabble down layers of shale to the stony beach below his cottage, hunting for spooning cockles, clams, and winkles—"

I bid damp green moss to grow into the gaps between the brambles, stanching the flow of blood. Irian gritted his teeth but kept talking through the pain.

"One day, he discovered a high stone wall he had never seen before. He wished to know what it hid, so he found a way inside. There he found Deirdre. Though she was many years older than he, the two became friends. She sang him songs and told him stories. That summer, he spent every day in her garden, and when night came, he hated going back to his mother's drafty cottage."

"He loved Deirdre." I packed the wound with fresh yarrow for clotting. Calendula for healing. Poppy for pain.

"Like an ocean admires the sky." Irian bared his teeth. "Like a brother loves a sister."

I sat back and inspected my work. There was still blood—*too* much blood. But Irian was alive. His back was a mess of thorns and flowers, but he was alive.

"What happened to him?" I looked up.

Irian was already gazing at me, his opal eyes vivid with pain, shock, and something unreadable. His sweat-slick head was inches from mine. He radiated fever. Beneath us, the earth had stilled.

"The same thing that happens to all boys." His voice was hoarse. "He grew up. He traded winkles for war, songs for steel. He learned to kill. And then he learned to like it."

I waited for him to go on. He didn't.

"That's it?" I asked, incredulous.

"It is."

"Your stories are terrible."

"Why?" A glimmer of his earlier smile played across his lips. "Because they do not have happy endings?"

I shook my head and moved to stand up. But Irian's hand—still braced beside my thigh—shot out and closed around my wrist. His grip was metal hot from the forge. He twisted my palm upward.

"Your turn." He tilted his head toward my hand, which was stained with dark earth and silver blood and scarlet flower petals. "I want the story of your gift."

Gift. I closed the hand into a fist. "Your tale bought your life. I owe you nothing."

I rose, jerking my hand out of his. He winced and exhaled, reaching around himself to prod the edges of my botanical bandage. Satisfied it was holding the rest of his blood inside his body, he levered himself to his feet. He swayed. I wondered whether it was from blood loss or from the narcotics tingeing his bloodstream. He looked down at his mantle and leather armor, which were held together by nothing more than bloody shreds, then tore the rest of the raiment apart with his hands, exposing himself to the waist.

I tried not to stare. And failed miserably.

Even covered in monster ichor and shaking with blood loss, Irian was magnificent. He was perfectly proportioned—tall and lean, yet broad through the shoulders and narrow at the waist. His muscles might have been carved from marble, they were so defined. Only the angular black markings laddering his arms and hugging his back marred his perfection. And even they were savagely beautiful. I wondered what they'd feel like beneath my fingertips, my hands on his shoulders with his flaming skin licking against my own, his weight pressing above me—

I forced myself to look away, to clench my fists, to *breathe.* Irian might not be fanged or taloned or covered in scales. But he was as much a monster as the corpse behind me.

"My sword." Sudden worry racked his already pained expression. "I cannot lose my sword."

I followed his eyes. Twenty paces behind us, the ollphéist had begun to *liquefy*, its bulk spreading outward as its scales separated. What had once been flesh and bone oozed between the cracks, bubbling and steaming. The odor of rot and death intensified, making me clap my hands over my nose and mouth. Irian moved—or tried to move—toward the corpse, but he swayed like a tree in a high wind. His eyes rolled back in his head. I caught his elbow.

"You're in no state."

"To do what?"

"To do *anything*. I'll fetch it."

I thought he wasn't going to listen to me. But then he seemed overcome by the sudden urge to sit down on the ground and put his head in his hands.

Definitely the poppies.

I stomped off toward the corpse, cursing. I wasn't thrilled by the idea of fishing around in a decaying monster for mislaid weaponry but saw no other option. Besides, both my knives were somewhere in there too.

By the time I'd retrieved the Sky-Sword—my skeans were sadly lost to the mush—I was covered to the knee in monster goo and stank like carrion. I trudged back toward Irian, hoping he was still alive enough to thank me for the trouble. I was a dozen paces from him when I realized—

I was holding the Sky-Sword. The Treasure I'd been sent to retrieve. The weapon Mother and Fódla needed. The means by which Eala's geas might be broken.

My steps faltered.

I hefted the weapon. The hilt was silver and bone, finely etched with a pattern of feathers that closely matched the tattoos laddering Irian's arms. But the blade—the blade was forged of a material I had no name for, a metal black as starless night skies. In the wake of battle the blade was silent. But at my touch, impressions blew over me like a high wind—starlight and sunrise and cirrus clouds painted against the dawn. Lightning crackled against my palm, so different from the slow, steady throb of my own magic that I almost dropped the blade.

Irian was gravely injured. I just had to *take* it. He wouldn't be able to chase me, let alone catch me.

I just had to *run*.

So why did my feet feel like stones?

My eyes flicked to Irian, half-collapsed on the strand. He was watching me closely, despite the pain glazing his silver eyes. He cocked his head, a tiny motion that never failed to ice my blood. I tensed, shifting the blade into guard position.

Movement by the edge of the forest startled me. Swan maidens spilled from between the trees, dressed in silver and white. They glowed through the prowling mist like fallen stars as they hastened toward me and Irian. Eala led them, elegant and exquisite in her shining gown. She held out her hands as she approached, like she wanted to embrace me. But she was reaching for the Sky-Sword.

Some instinct pushed me back from her. She paused.

"Brava, Sister!" She laughed, a sound like quicksilver. "You've done it. You've taken the Treasure. And so speedily!"

My gaze slashed back to Irian. If he was shocked by Eala's revelation, he barely showed it. The bloodstained plane of his jaw merely tightened perilously. "It was not as difficult as anticipated."

"That is good news." Again, she lifted her hands, palms up— almost a supplication. "May I hold it?"

"Colleen." Irian's eyes slid liquid along the blade in my hands; his voice knelled with warning. "That is not a good idea."

My hand tightened on the Sky-Sword's hilt. Indecision burgeoned within me.

"Come, Sister." Eala's pale blue eyes glittered. "We discussed this, did we not? The Treasure lends us power we otherwise do not have. With it, we stand as his equals. At long last, we will be able to break the geas upon us—to unbind us from his Sept."

"Even if you were able to use it—which you are not—you could not break the geas." Irian's husky voice carried little inflection.

"Do you think I have not tried? But I did not bind you with its magic."

"He's lying." Eala's gaze never left my face, but Irian's words stole mine.

"What do you mean?" I demanded. "Why can't we use it?"

"*She* cannot." His voice dropped even lower. "The Treasures... were not forged for human hands."

His words sent another shiver of energy sizzling up my forearm, speeding my green-dark pulse. The implications swept through me like a gale: if humans could not wield Treasures, then Mother's plans were for nothing. As were Eala's. And as for me—

"She is not human?" Eala's shrewd words echoed my own racing thoughts.

"Apparently not."

"It doesn't matter." Eala turned back to me. "It is still a weapon. Kill him for us, Sister, and perhaps that will be the thing that sets us free."

"My death will not set you free." Irian's voice was unwaveringly composed, even as his limbs visibly sagged beneath him. "Had the geas bound you to my Sept as I intended, my death might have released it—for with my death my Sept ends forever. But I did not bind you to my Sept. I bound you to *me*."

"I fail to see the difference."

Irian's eyes were jagged, but his voice was even. "If I die, you die. All of you."

His words rippled shock through the swan maidens, followed swiftly by a wave of visceral fear. A jumble of denials and protests and recriminations wafted angrily through the fog.

Eala's eyes widened, her brows winging upward. But her surprise swiftly flattened toward frustration, then outright fury. She slashed out an imperious palm, and her maidens fell silent.

"He is *lying*," Eala said sharply. "Why wouldn't he have told us this before? It is a manipulation—a falsehood to save his own skin. The Sky-Sword is still the most powerful magic left in Tír na nÓg.

Between the two of us, Sister, we will find a way to break the geas."
She beckoned to me. "Let us take it and go."

"Perhaps I am lying to save my own life. Perhaps I am not."
Irian's head lolled. His eyes were stars against the shadows writhing at his back. "But are you truly willing to take the risk? If you
take the Sky-Sword now, I will die. And imminently."

That, at least, I was inclined to believe. But everything else
seemed suddenly less certain. If Irian was lying, then Eala was
right—with the sword, perhaps we could still find a way to break
their geas. Whatever Folk blood lurked in my veins allowed me to
wield it—I would return to Fódla with the magic the realm needed.
Without his powerful Treasure, Irian would no longer be a threat
to anyone.

But if he was telling the truth—

"*Fia,*" Irian said.

It was that—my name on his lips—that decided me. For though I
searched his dark, husky tone for any hint of Folk command, of false
maneuvering, of manipulation, I found only an appeal. An appeal to
my deepest, most authentic self—the shaded forest in my veins, the
green leaves around my heart. It was only my name, and yet—

I flipped my grip on the Sky-Sword. And slowly handed it to the
man to whom it belonged.

Irian closed his fist around the hilt. A crackle of power sparked
lightning through the fog, and a gust of carrion-scented wind lifted
the hair off my neck. Then he exhaled and collapsed sideways
onto the beach.

My pulse throbbed. I took a step toward him. But Chandi and
the other swan maidens were already there, surrounding the dying
tánaiste in a cluster.

All but one of them.

"Oh, Sister." Reproach suffused Eala's face, harsh on her gentle
features. "I fear you have chosen him over me in our time of need."

"But I haven't." Her words took me aback—they struck me as
something Mother would say. "Surely you understand—the stakes

are too high. If any part of what he said was true, then your life—
all your lives—are forfeit. I could not risk it."

"Then it should have been our decision—all of ours." She lifted
her delicate chin, a bitter kind of helplessness in her eyes. "You
made it yours. I hope you do not live to regret that."

"Rogan and I are here to save you, Eala—not consign you to
death." I gripped one of her hands. It was limp and white in my
gore-streaked palm, and after a moment, I released it. "We will
find another way to break your geas."

She said no more as she moved to rejoin her maidens. As a
group, they had gotten Irian to his feet. I followed them with my
eyes until the mist swallowed them up. One by one, their shining
gowns disappeared, like stars burning out.

In the moment before they disappeared, a pair of opalescent
eyes stared back at me through the fog. And I hoped to all the gods
that I'd made the right choice.

❧

I could not find my way to the Gate. The dense, eerie fog swirled
in treacherous circles, confusing my footsteps. I passed one sturdy
rowan tree, only to pass it again moments later. I paused, helplessness breeding uncertainty in my mind.

"Fia!" The voice sifted through the pale gloom. "Changeling!"

I hurtled toward the sound, then nearly collided with Rogan—
he was closer than I'd expected. We must have passed mere feet
from each other in the fog. Beyond him, I sighted the tenuous outline of the willow tree, the hard line of the bridge.

"Thank the gods," I breathed, gripping his arms in relief.

"What in Donn's black gates happened to you?" Worry and
horror racked Rogan's face. I was still covered in gore, bruises, and
Irian's silver blood. I must have looked a mess.

"Long story," I said. "We need to get back to Roslea before this
enchanted fog keeps us here forever. Ready?"

We passed through the Gate quickly. Beyond, the forest still dripped with lingering moisture but was blessedly free of mist.

Rogan's hand on my elbow spun me to face him. "Now tell me what happened."

I hesitated. I didn't think I could keep my mission a secret any longer—at least, not where it intersected with Eala's fate. And perhaps it was selfish, but I didn't want Irian's revelations to reach Rogan's ears through Eala's mouth. Better I tell him and be done with it.

"I...had the chance to deal a mortal blow to the Gentry tánaiste who cursed Eala and the other maidens." The words tasted ragged on my tongue—they weren't completely true. "But he said such an act would only doom them. Their geas is bound to his life—if he dies, they die."

Rogan absorbed this.

"So I let him live. I didn't know what else to do. But Eala—she's angry with me. She thinks he's lying."

"The Folk are treacherous," Rogan said slowly. "Perhaps he was lying. Perhaps he was telling the truth. Either way, you did the right thing."

Relief sighed through me—a warm wind unraveling cold fog. "I thought you might side with Eala."

"You did the only thing you could with the information you had." He reached out, gripped my palm. It was the first time we'd touched since Imbolc, and my frayed pulse accelerated. "You fought for her. Prioritized her life—no matter the cost. If she doesn't see that, she's blind."

He didn't let go of my gore-streaked hand until the fort loomed up before us in the dawn. And his words were the only thing that let me fall asleep that morning, lending me some small measure of comfort.

Chapter Twenty-One

Nion—Ash
Late Winter

Inside the tiered grotto surrounding the greenhouse, the world had cracked open, letting light inside. Winter branches were furred with new leaves. Crocuses in red and purple lolled their heads. The air smelled of moss and fresh beginnings.

The earth was still too cold to transplant most of my seedlings from the greenhouse, so I busied myself with clearing years' worth of old leaves and stubborn weeds from the beds. And when the icy rains chased me inside, I cleaned—sweeping cobwebs from the rafters and dust from the corners and ash from the chimney. I found more of the lustrous black feathers. Careful with my fingertips, I tossed them out the window or burned them in the grate.

And when that was done, I ensconced myself in the secret alcove I'd discovered, painstakingly decoding the ancient journals. Time and linguistic shifts had rendered the looping, ornate script nearly unintelligible. But I forged ahead, laboring over incoherent translations by torchlight until my head hammered.

More than once, I almost caved and wrote to Cathair for help.

Another letter had come via starling—it would have been so easy to ask. But now I'd set my mind to the task, I belligerently refused to fail. The druid had taught me the ancient tongue for a reason—proof I was more than a blunt object designed only to hurt.

Slowly, a narrative began to take tenuous shape. There had been a man, the ancient warrior who'd written the journals and built this fort. There had also been a Gentry maiden, although it was unclear whether they'd known each other well before being separated across realms. He referred to her only as *mo chroí—my heart.*

But mostly, he was obsessed with Folk bindings. *Geasa droma draíochta,* he called them—inviolable magical imperatives. Plenty of human tales spoke of geasa, but these curses he referenced seemed infinitely more powerful. Some of these bindings survived death itself, forcing dead spirits to linger in life. Some followed their subjects into Donn's dark realms. And that made me think—inevitably—of Irian and Eala.

I leaned back in my chair, massaging a cramp from my hand and staring at nothing.

My death will not set you free, Irian had said. *If I die, you die. All of you.*

I still didn't know whether I'd made the right decision in giving the Sky-Sword to the shadow heir. But I had to believe it was a good thing I hadn't let the Gentry tánaiste bleed out on that beach. I understood why Eala was so keen to break her geas. But if Irian had truly bound her and the other swan maidens with one of these inviolable geasa...then their lives might all be twined so tightly, not even death could separate them.

Rogan and I were going to have to start thinking more creatively.

⁊ ～ ౨

"Fia, I swear on Amergin's soft, sweet lily-white knees!" This inventive round of cursing startled me as Rogan burst into the greenhouse. "How do other men stand it?"

I set down a tray of seedlings, careful not to crush their delicate stems. "Stand *what?*"

"The beard!" He practically clawed at his face, which was covered in a scraggly mess of uneven blond and brown hairs. I supposed it could be referred to as a beard—if I was feeling extremely generous. "It itches. I can't stand it."

I didn't know why he was growing the damned thing out in the first place. It looked worse than his uncombed hair. Irritatingly, he was still the most handsome man I'd ever met.

Well. The most handsome *human* man.

"Shave it off, then."

He fidgeted. With a rush of amusement, I realized—he was embarrassed about something. Borderline *bashful*.

Rogan Mòr didn't get embarrassed.

"Brighid's forge, Rogan." I brushed earth from my palms. "Do you not know how to shave your own face?"

"I always had—" He twitched with discomfort. "I've always had attendants to do it."

"You're twenty-two years old, Rogan."

He looked at me, then away, squinting at the sun peering out from behind a bank of downy cloud. "Twenty-three, actually."

"Rogan." I stood straighter. "I forgot your birthday, didn't I?"

"It doesn't matter." He shrugged, but the gesture had a plaintive quality to it.

It did matter. When we were children, we'd promised never to forget each other's birthdays. Rogan's father had never celebrated his first son, as the wintry day of Rogan's birth had also been the day his first wife had died. He'd never forgiven Rogan for the death of his greatest love. And I—I'd never known when my birthday was, or if I even had one. Cathair liked to say things like me weren't born—just made. And Mother cared little for frivolities like birthday parties. So Rogan and I had picked a day in early summer, when the lilacs were blooming, and celebrated it privately.

Princeling and changeling. Before everything had gotten so complicated.

"I'm sorry." The soft promise of springtime made me pliant. I crossed to him and wrapped my arms around his broad chest. He stiffened in surprise before returning the gesture, looping his muscular arms around me. His scent—like sun-warmed metal and spiced wine—made me think, suddenly, of home. When I looked up at him, his eyes were the bright blue-green of the ocean below Rath na Mara. "I'll make it up to you. Shave your beard. Trim your hair."

"Do you know how?"

"Do you care?"

"Not really." His low laugh stirred something warm in my belly. "If you mess it up, you're the only one who has to look at me."

We both knew that wasn't true. But maybe we could pretend it was.

I pulled back. "Did you even pack a razor?"

"Yes. But I can't vouch for its sharpness."

"I'll take what I can get." I grabbed his hand and pulled him behind me, beneath the garlands of budding trees. "It's either a dull razor or a pair of rusty gardening shears."

"Either way," he laughed, "I'm in need of pruning."

* * *

The great hall was sullen after the roaring brightness of the day. I trailed Rogan as he made for the stairs.

"You go ahead," I told him. "I'll be right up."

I waited until he'd disappeared up the stairs before scanning the shadowed ceiling.

"Corra?" I called. "Are you there?"

None of the carvings moved, but I was growing accustomed to the faintly perturbed weight of Corra's attention.

"Fetch supplies to Rogan's tower for me, won't you?" I told

them. "Hot water. Towels. A whetstone or leather too, if you please."

For a long moment, the only answer was silence. I crossed my arms and frowned. Finally, a snub-nosed fish swished to life on the wall, blowing irritated bubbles.

"For the cream-faced, puke-livered knave?"

"Do you mean the strong, handsome prince?" I smiled sweetly. "Who does, in fact, have a name?"

Corra slapped their tail in warning. "He'll leave."

I rolled my eyes. "In half a year, beastie, we'll both be leaving. And it's entirely up to you whether we miss you when we go."

It wasn't my best manipulation. But it must have been enough. When I crested the coiling stairway to Rogan's tower room, I found a ewer of steaming water, a pile of fluffy towels, a strip of raw leather, and a bar of sweet-smelling soap. I grinned, then frowned.

If Corra had harvested my freshly grown lemon balm without asking, there'd be hell to pay.

I carried the supplies into Rogan's tower room. His chambers were almost as dark as the first time I'd been up here, that gray day months ago. Afternoon sunshine poked feeble hands through a single window, sending only the weakest of shadows scuttling to the corners. I wrinkled my nose at the faint odor of soured wine and unwashed man clothes. Dirty glasses lined the windowsills, and the covers on the bed were hopelessly rumpled.

I lifted an incredulous eyebrow. "I see the chambermaids have been shirking their duties."

Rogan looked down, red coloring his neck. "I suppose so."

"Hmm." I set down Corra's supplies on the table and marched toward the window. I examined a dirty tumbler. Dried wine clung to the chipped rim. I stared at it a moment longer, then tossed it out of the opening. Far below, glass shattered on stone.

"What—" Shock loosened Rogan's expression. "I was using that!"

I laughed and pushed the rest of the glasses out the window. I

spun, staring around the gloomy tower room. Lines of light prickled at intervals along the walls—more windows. I strode to the
nearest one, found the edge of the drape, and yanked. Yellow light
spilled in, through glass smeared with grime and time. I reached
for another, but large, unyielding arms caught me around the waist
and pulled me against a hard torso.

"What do you think you're doing?" Rogan growled into my ear.

There was an edge to his playful words. My awareness sharpened toward our bodies molded together—my rear flush against
his hips, my shoulder blades conforming to his muscular chest. His
hands shifted minutely across my front, one palm splaying warm
over my navel.

Warm, not scorching.

I inhaled at the thought of Irian, sudden and intrusive in this
very human space. With my next breath, I pushed the thought
away, twisting in Rogan's arms to face him. Only now, I was
pressed painfully—*deliciously*—against his chest. His rough hands
slid against my neck, making me look up at him.

"Haven't you ever heard of spring cleaning?" I grinned, trying
to break the tension rising between us.

Rogan didn't smile. His river-stone gaze collided with mine. His
hand tightened against my back, his fingers crushing the fabric of
my kirtle. Sudden warmth burned through my veins and pooled in
my belly. Rogan shifted his hips against me, the beginnings of his
arousal pushing through our clothes.

I jerked away, pulse racing. Bands of afternoon sunlight sliced
through the windows I'd wrenched open. Outside poured in, smelling of fresh grass and tree pollen. I wasn't sure what had compelled
me to rip those curtains down, but in that moment I was grateful
for the full force of the sunlight, if only to clear my spinning head.

Rogan stepped back and adjusted his trousers. I turned at the
same time, fussing over the towels and soap to hide my flaming
cheeks. A razor lay half-open on the table, and I gave it a few
experimental swipes on the strip of leather. It was, indeed, dull. I

set to sharpening it. Rogan dragged a chair in front of the window and sat down.

"You do know how to shave a man," Rogan asked over the rhythmic strop of steel on leather as I sharpened the razor. He was trying to act normal—but his voice rasped uneven. "Don't you?"

"Nervous?" The metal began to gleam.

"Yes, now, a bit." He waited. I let him sweat. "Honestly, changeling, do you know how?"

"If I wanted to slit your throat, princeling, I'd have done it a long time ago." I tested the edge of the razor against my thumb. It was sharp enough. I reached for one of the soft warm towels, meaning to wrap it around Rogan's shoulders. "Your mantle will get wet."

With his back to me, he misunderstood my words. He sat straighter in his chair, then pulled his mantle over his head. Sunlight bathed the sculpted planes of his chest in jessamine and honeycomb. A constellation of freckles kissed his shoulders, bunching with muscle as he threw the garment on the floor. Scars etched his thick arms and rippling back, souvenirs of reckless blades and cruel fathers. Some, I'd given him. Some were new. Others, I remembered tracing with my fingertips as sunset bled toward night.

My fingers twitched against the towel, hanging limp from my hands.

"Changeling?"

I dropped the towel, hurrying to pick up the ewer and soap. Water slopped all over the floor.

"Tilt your head toward me." I hoped he couldn't hear the catch in my voice.

He did as I asked. I poured warm water over the top of his head. Rivulets streamed down his hairline and pooled in the hollow of his throat. I rubbed the sweet-smelling soap into a lather between my hands. Taking a deep breath, I worked the foam through his hair and beard.

I started on the hair first, combing through the mess, then trimming the ends. Clumps of dark gold fell to my feet. A sudden image of close-cropped raven hair above moonlit eyes floated into my mind's eye, and I was briefly tempted to cut it far shorter than would be fashionable. But Rogan would never forgive me if I chopped off his golden curls. I might not forgive myself.

Then I moved to his face, bracing one hand on his chin and tilting his head against my chest. The dampness of his hair soaked the fabric of my bodice and sent a restless chill zipping over my skin.

Short strokes—*scritch, scritch, scritch.* As I carefully swiped the razor along the stubble-rough planes of his face, I was painfully aware of my stomach pressing against his arm. His lips parting at my touch. His golden eyelashes fluttering shut as he exhaled a sigh of pleasure.

Finally, it was done. I poured the last of the lukewarm water over Rogan's head, washing away lather in a stream of gray foam. In the moment before I handed him a towel, I schooled my expression.

Rogan briskly scrubbed the cloth over his head and face, then turned to face me.

Sunlight sculpted half of his face from golden stone and threw the rest of him into shadow. I was staring—Rogan's mouth quirked, and he lifted a hand to gingerly pat his head.

"What? Have I been overpruned?"

I blinked. "No, I just—"

I circled the chair to face him in full sunlight. It wasn't that I'd forgotten what he looked like without the beard. It wasn't even that he looked more handsome clean-shaven—although he did—or that he looked so much older than when we were children, with his hard cheekbones and wry mouth. It was that in the simplest way possible—with water, soap, and razor—I'd changed him. With the sun streaming in on him, he seemed newly made, clean edged.

His eyes caressed my face, lingering on the curve of my lips. He took a step toward me. I took a step back, suddenly remembering the last time I'd been in his room.

"You never said—" His voice was low. "You never said how you learned to shave a man."

He took another step. My spine struck the edge of the window-sill. I swallowed.

"Fionn liked to be clean-shaven."

"Fionn?" It was less a name than a curse. "Who's that?"

"The blacksmith's apprentice."

"And what," he growled, "was my little changeling doing shaving the blacksmith's boy?"

Bitter memories slowed the blood thrumming too fast in my veins. In the year after Rogan left, Fionn had been one of the many toxic substances I had taken into my body. Like the poisons Cathair had fed me, he had changed me. Polluted me. Hardened me. I still remembered the way his face had twisted with shame and disgust when his friends found out we were sleeping together.

Love a cailleach like her? He'd laughed at their taunts. *I just like that she lets me do anything I please to her.*

I steadied myself against the sill.

"He liked me to shave him, in the mornings after I spent the night in his bed." I forced myself to maintain eye contact, even as Rogan's gaze darkened. "I think it made him feel powerful, to have me serve him."

"You are the foster daughter of a queen." He took one last step toward me. Barely an inch of sunlight separated us. My heart beat a wild pattern in my chest, and I tasted violets in the back of my throat. Rogan's bare chest rose and fell with the pulse of my heart. Beneath the scent of soap, he smelled like sunlight on grass, warm as the memory of a long-lost summer's day. "You were not made for blacksmiths."

"Oh?" I kept my voice light. "What was I made for, then? Not princes."

"Why not?"

His words stirred up old pains, old desires. I forced my tone to remain flippant. "What can a prince do for me that a blacksmith cannot?"

The words sounded less a joke than a *challenge*. The outrage in Rogan's eyes blurred toward something more provocative. His pupils blew wide with want, and the hands that had been clenched at his sides reached out to circle my waist, to jerk my hips flush against his. An aching flare of heat painted my spine in marigold and rose. His face lowered toward mine. My eyes dropped to his parted lips.

"Many, *many* things, changeling."

His hands smoothed down my waist, over the curve of my rear. He lifted me up onto the windowsill like I weighed nothing. The chill of the stone through my frock shocked me, and I gasped. Rogan caught the sound with his lips, sliding his mouth over mine and dragging his tongue across my teeth.

I froze. Self-loathing pulsed through me, warring with the desire now burning an unquenchable path toward my core.

I shouldn't still want this. I shouldn't still want *him*.

Perhaps his confessions at Imbolc had softened me toward him. But regardless of anything that had come before, he was still Eala's betrothed. Once we broke her geas and returned her to Rath na Mara, they would be wed. Which left me with a choice—to have nothing of him...or to give up the last piece of my pride to have *something* of him.

To be his mistress. His whore. His shadow.

But in this moment—with his hands on my hips and his mouth on mine—I didn't want to think about that choice. In this moment, I wanted what I wanted.

I rocked forward, arching my back as I slid my arms around Rogan's neck and opened my mouth under his. His lips were somehow both hard and very, very soft. I closed my eyes, cupping his clean-shaven face and reveling in the movement of his mouth on mine. My fingernails traced the line of his jaw to the top of his spine and tangled in his damp golden hair. His shoulders flexed beneath my hands, and he groaned, digging his fingertips into my hip bones and dragging me to the edge of the windowsill. I molded myself against him—my breasts against his chest, my stomach against his firm torso, my core against the hard line of his belt. The buckle bit into the tender skin of my inner thigh, and I shifted to relieve the pressure.

Rogan's palm flexed tighter on my rear, and when he pulled me back against him, I felt his hard arousal. Fire unfurled within me. I trailed a finger down the sculpted planes of his stomach and reached for the waistband of his breeches, wanting to touch him. To feel his length and weight. To make him burn, the way I burned.

Breaking the kiss, he caught my hand at the wrist and pushed it behind me. His eyes—bruised dark with lust—stayed fixed on mine as he found the hem of my kirtle and dragged it up over my knees. I shivered at the sensation of sunlight on my bare skin. His fingertips grazed my ankle, then traveled upward, skating up the inside of my calf, skimming along my knee, gliding against the soft skin of my thigh. His hand lingered at the edge of my undergarment. Then he pushed the flimsy fabric aside to caress me between my legs.

I sucked in a breath, leaned back on one arm, and rocked against his touch. He slipped one finger inside my wetness, then another, even as his thumb drew teasing circles that stoked the bonfire burning away my self-control. Vines of heat writhed toward my center, throbbing and wild. My hands flexed on the windowsill—runnels of moss jeweled with phlox spilled unbidden from my fingertips. My breath quickened as I danced along the edge of the seething, aching sensation growing inside me. And finally, there was nothing to do but surrender to it.

The world splintered into shards of gold and green. I fractured with it, breathing Rogan's name in a helpless moan. He caught the sound with his lips, kissing me fiercely as I came apart at the seams. I shuddered against him, but even as the wildness between my thighs calmed, it wasn't enough. I'd had him—*all* of him—before, and I wanted it now. Wanted his velvet thickness between my palms, wanted his length sheathed inside me. Wanted to rise with him toward the next peak and fall with him as we crested together.

I grappled for the buckle of his belt. He gripped my hips, fingers digging almost painfully into my skin. His mouth dropped from my lips to my neck. He dragged his teeth down my throat, over my collarbone, and nipped lightly at the skin above my breast. Then paused.

Uncertainty blew dark clouds over the blue sky of his gaze. I followed his eyes. Behind me, moss had climbed halfway up the window casement. Tiny white flowers studded the green, shining like diamonds. Motes of glittering dust scented the air with a delicate, earthy perfume.

I turned toward Rogan, fumbling for some explanation about why I'd lost control over my Greenmark. But my eyes caught instead on the far wall, illuminated suddenly by the lowering sun. Stark outlines—scorched patterns twisting dark against chipped plaster—seized my gaze.

My heated blood cooled to dark sludge.

I instantly recognized the drawings as scenes from Tír na nÓg. Cold, jagged branches. Ethereal castles. Leering faces with mouths full of hawthorn leaves and acorns for eyes.

And *her*.

It wasn't hard to recognize the face, because it was my face. Almost.

Eala was everywhere—sketched small, in corners, with painstaking detail. Large, in savage sweeps of charcoal. Each drawing was a desperate prayer, an unspoken wish, a choking need. Those imperious brows lifted over pale eyes. That even, elegant smile. The delicate, dimpled chin. The—

"Changeling?" Rogan's hands trembled at my waist. I flinched and pushed him away. Hurt pooled in his eyes, followed a moment later by dawning comprehension when he followed my gaze to the wall. He whipped his head back to me a second later, and his gaze was urgent, pleading. "It's not what you think."

I barely heard him. The swell of confusion and distress I'd felt when I first saw the drawings was swept away by a vicious wave of shame. Behind me, the moss began to dry out, crumbling to a fine dust that scattered on the breeze. I lowered my eyes, slid off the windowsill, and straightened my clothes with shaking fingers.

Morrigan, I was *so stupid*.

"Fia—" Rogan tried to catch me as I crossed the room. I shook him off. "Let me explain."

The plea in his voice stopped me at the door. Impulses warred within me—the need to escape with some shred of my dignity still intact; the desire to hear some wild, compelling explanation that would make all of this hurt less. His large, rough palm folded over my hand, arrested on the doorknob.

"It's how I process things." His voice was rutted with regret. "It's easier than talking. It's a hell of a lot easier than writing. It's been that way ever since we were children. You know that—you've always known that."

Perhaps I did. Rogan used to hoard sheaves of parchment beneath his bed—the only one of his possessions he had never shared freely with me. But he had guarded those drawings jealously, showing me only a few chosen pieces from time to time. Mostly, I remembered the castoffs—the prancing horses with ill-shaped hooves, the disproportionate serving girls, the rude little doodles meant to elicit a laugh. They had been nothing like these disturbed dreamscapes, these raw, remarkable portraits.

"Just tell me this." I forced myself to look up at him. "Were you thinking of her when you were touching me?"

"*No.*" He spat the word as if it cut his mouth. "How many times must I tell you, changeling? I think only of you."

Tears burned behind my eyes. "And yet she is the one on your wall. And she is still the one you will wed."

Chapter Twenty-Two

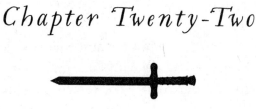

Three nights later, Rogan and I waited by the Gate. The evening unfurled around us, lily soft and violet edged. No sound disturbed the silence but the distant, trembling lament of a restless bird. The world felt poised—balanced in these last moments of twilight.

I'd never wanted anything as much as I wanted the moon to rise.

"Fia." Rogan's voice desecrated the hush. "We need to talk about—"

"No." I hunched on a mossy stone that had once been an aughisky's rump. "We really don't."

For a long, fraught moment, he was silent. Then:

"The day I broke Eala's doll was also the day I learned I was to marry her." He looked down at his palms. "Can you imagine? I was a little boy. I liked hitting rocks with sticks and terrorizing ant colonies and pinching my little brother when his mother wasn't watching. But that day, I was lashed for something I hadn't done, then informed I must someday wed the tiny terror who framed me for it. I knew I was a prince—I knew things were expected of me. But that?" His hands flexed into fists. "I had nightmares for months. Dreams where she chased me through the halls of Rath na Mara. Dreams where she was the one who whipped me, while wearing that broken doll's grinning face. Dreams where I sat on my father's throne, and she stood behind it, giggling and hissing with all that fair hair floating around her like clouds.

"I was glad when she was taken by the Folk." His voice shook with old malice. "There was keening in the halls of Glenathney, I remember—mourning for a stolen princess. But I secretly rejoiced. I thought I was free. Not long after, I met you, and—."

My gaze flew up to him, but he kept his eyes lowered.

"I've always known my duty, changeling. That doesn't mean I've ever had a choice in it." He finally looked up at me. His eyes were the color of the darkening horizon. "I won't have a choice when I finally take Eala to my marriage bed. And I won't have a choice when it's your face I see—your body I imagine—for the rest of my life."

Resentment and sympathy and lingering heat tangled inside me. "It doesn't change anything, princeling. And you've always known that too."

When the moon finally rose, we crossed the Willow Gate in miserable, weighted silence.

❧

Tír na nÓg was coming alive. The forest sang as we hiked to the fort, swarming with bright green leaves and strange flower buds. Moonlight polished the lough to a high shine, but there was no sign of the swan maidens. Rogan made off through the trees without looking back at me, as though he knew exactly where to find them.

I exhaled, following him with my eyes until he disappeared. I had my own business to attend to tonight. Irian's revelations—if true—had put a decided kink in my plot to steal his Treasure and then destroy him. Somehow, I needed to ascertain if he was telling the truth.

The shadows between the trees coalesced like falling feathers. Irian stepped onto the path.

I faltered back, fighting to calm my racing pulse. I searched for silver eyes amid the curling shadows he wore like wings. Slowly, he came into focus: tall, lean frame; soft mouth and hard jaw; black sword and coiled alertness.

"You're not dead," I observed. "Or actively dying."

"Oh, I am." Irian looked relentlessly composed—his gaze harsh and dangerous. It was a look I hadn't seen him wear in months, and it sent a tendril of alarm to wind around my bones. "Just very, very slowly."

In the month since I'd seen him last, I'd convinced myself that saving his life from that ollphéist, then returning the Sky-Sword to him instead of giving it to Eala must have earned me his trust. I saw now that might not be the case. It occurred to me in a rush of dismay that instead of stealing a Treasure and freeing a princess, I might have lost both my knives, ruined Corra's new cloak, alienated my closest kin besides Mother, *and* lost what little confidence I'd earned from the Gentry heir. All in one fell swoop.

"I daresay thanks are in order." I smiled wide, ignoring his disdain. Perhaps, with some willful ignorance and a touch of guile, our connection could still be salvaged. "Or is disembowelment by ollphéist not usually a terminal condition?"

"You do have my gratitude, colleen." He gave me a terse, tense bow. "For my life, I owe you a boon. But you also tried to take that which is most precious to me, after telling me you did not covet it. You may ask anything of me, and I will be honor bound to give it to you. But once my debt to you is paid, I cannot promise I will not kill you for once more trespassing on my lands without invitation."

I wasn't surprised by the creeping fear his words elicited. I *was* surprised by the sharp burst of disappointment that accompanied it—as though his harsh words stole something from me I hadn't even known to miss. Irian was my enemy, and we had interacted only a handful of times. Yet some renegade part of me had already started looking forward to the full moons purely because I would get to see him. I hardly dared admit it to myself, but I *enjoyed* the cutting rhythms of our banter. The beguiling thrill of his stark, striking beauty. The unnatural heat of his skin when he touched me.

Perhaps it was merely the challenge of an opponent more dangerous and deceitful than any I had faced before. Or perhaps it was more than that.

Here—in Tír na nÓg, in Irian's presence—I could be more myself than I ever could in Fódla. My conniving nature inspired respect instead of contempt; my magic inspired admiration instead of disquiet. And perhaps I was deceiving myself, but I suspected he secretly enjoyed our encounters as much as I did.

My mission hadn't changed—nor had my enemy. I had every intention of setting Eala free and returning home with a Treasure. But was it possible to achieve more by truly gaining Irian's trust than by attempting to seduce or outwit him?

"You won't kill me."

His smile was feral, his lips curling up from his glittering teeth. "Whyever not?"

"Because the thrill is in the joy of the hunt, not the promise of a kill." I lifted my chin to hide my dread. "And I think you have been alone too long to let me go so quickly. Not when things are just getting interesting."

"You are bold, colleen." He tilted his head, a hawk with prey in sight. The danger in his voice was limned with delight. "By that logic, the moment you bore me, I am free to slit your throat."

"Then I shall endeavor never to bore you." I plunged forward before I changed my mind. "For saving your life, this is the boon I would ask you: that you and I become friends."

"*Friends.*" He mouthed the word as if it was foreign to him. "I am not sure that is possible."

I kept my tone light. "Are we forever doomed to be enemies?"

"Those are not the only two options." His eyes darkened to

iron. His smile was a knife. "I warned you, colleen—if I decide I want you, I will go to extraordinary lengths to keep you."

I flushed hot. His words burned intrusive thoughts behind my eyes: how his scorching palms might feel on my naked skin, how his marble torso might feel pressed above me. I shivered, but it wasn't from cold.

"And I warned you, tánaiste—I don't scare easily." I leveled him with a stare. "It's one of the things that makes me so diverting."

"Then friends we shall strive to be," he drawled. "But friendship cannot be one-sided."

"Then let our old bargain stand. And I will go first." I inhaled, making a show of dropping all pretense. I had a few secrets I intended to keep, but he didn't need to know that. "Once—in a time of lingering hostilities and stolen children—a changeling was left in the care of the high queen of Fódla, who raised the girl as her daughter in place of the princess that had been stolen. When a forgotten Gate to Tír na nÓg was discovered, she sent the changeling to rescue her sister from her geas. The changeling thought stealing your Treasure would achieve that goal. But your revelations last month precluded that option. And now the changeling needs to understand the swan maidens' curse. She needs to understand why your death buys theirs."

If he was surprised by my candor, he didn't show it. "I should be furious that you wish to free my wards."

"But you aren't." I eyed the inky sword belted at his waist. "Last month you said you yourself have tried to break the geas. Surely you wouldn't mind if I did it for you?"

My words blunted his edge. His expression lost its brooding distance, its cruel flirtatious smile. He hesitated, then stepped to the edge of the forest and looked out into the night. "Walk with me."

I frowned. "Where?"

He pointed into the distance. Behind the fort, barren moorlands sloped up toward hills bathed in shifting pennants of moonlight and shadow. "This story requires I show you something. *Friend.*"

I followed him along the edge of the lough toward the fort, where the land veered sharply upward through patches of thorny gorse. Sheets of black stone sliced up through the green sod. Hummocks of purple foliage tangled around my boots. Irian set a quick pace, his steps solid and sure on the twisting, uneven ground. I matched it as best I could, stealing glances at his powerful stride, the easy swing of his broad shoulders. My gaze dropped to the black sword belted at his waist.

If the Sky-Sword could heal lethal wounds in a month, imagine what it could do for the starving. For the ill. For the victims of raids and wars. Only, Irian had said it was not made to be wielded by human hands.

But I was not fully human. Imagine me—the little changeling witch—ending up as Fódla's salvation.

Exertion soon stole my grim fantasies away as I turned my focus toward not twisting an ankle on the rough terrain.

Irian finally stopped, bracing one leg on a stony outcropping as wind ruffled his short dark hair and sent his shadows swirling. We'd climbed high. Below us, the vale spread out, a tapestry in black and silver.

"Colleen." The sound of my unwanted nickname on his lips warmed the pit of my stomach. I found I didn't hate it as much as I once had. I told myself that was why, when he held out his hand, I gripped it without hesitation. He pulled me to the top of the ridge beside him. The palm he placed on my shoulder burned through my clothing. "Do you see it?"

He pointed beyond the line of stony hills. A ribbon of silver water unspooled toward an expanse of sea, edged in great cliffs. And perched above that sea was...a *city*? It was hard to see in the shifting moonlight, but I glimpsed a curtain wall, white stone sparkling with crenellations of gold. Towering parapets rose sharply upward, pinnacles glinting above winding streets and coiling roofs. But windows gaped. The gates were open. In the harbor, skeletons of ships canted broken masts toward dark water.

Even from here, I could tell the city was empty.

Then I saw why. Behind the city, what I'd thought was a looming black mountain was a...*wrongness*. Skeins of shadow and movement tore at the edges of things, warping and twisting them. Veins of darkness scattered light like black prisms. Despair clung everywhere like a dead hand. I inhaled sharply, and a gust of wind brought the distant scents of rot and death to my nostrils.

They were the same smells that had clung to the fox-faced barda who'd assaulted me. And the noxious, overgrown ollphéist that had attacked Irian.

"What is this place?" I stepped closer to him.

"The city is called Murias, and it has been abandoned for over twelve years."

"Why?"

"Once—in the time of gods and legends—Amergin and his kin wrested Fódla from the Fair Folk." This close, I smelled Irian's scent of cool wind and black metal—a stark contrast to the carrion wafting from the distant city. Yet his shadows wreathed wild around him, the same shape and color as the ugly, warping darkness far below.

"Fódla was rich in many things. Good soil, plentiful game, generous weather. But most of all, it was wealthy with wild magic. The seas seethed with it; the trees breathed it; the birds sang with it; the hearths crackled with it. Amergin's people sought to claim that power out of greed, for their gain. Fearful of the mortals' intemperance, the Folk searched for a way to protect the magic. The first chieftains wrought potent geasa, binding that wild, unfettered magic to powerful Treasures forged by the legendary smith-king Gavida. They built themselves a home—a place they called Tír na nÓg, Land of Eternal Youth, guarded by twelve indomitable Gates held fast by the magic of the mighty Treasures."

Cathair had told me the same story. Only, in his version it had been the Fair Folk greedily stealing magic from noble Amergin. "And then?"

His mouth curled. "If I told you they all lived happily ever after, would you believe me?"

"No."

His silver eyes caught on mine, searing me. "For some years, the Folk did live in peace, sequestered away from the violence of humans. The Treasures were tithed from tánaiste to tánaiste, and the Gates stood strong. The Septs' sovereignty over wild magic was not always tolerated, but even the discontented Gentry thought the Septs' hegemony unassailable. Until Deirdre of the Sept of Antlers died of a broken heart, and her Treasure was lost to the forest."

My breath hitched.

"The balance of magic irrevocably shifted. Without its Treasure, the Sept of Antlers fell into disarray. The human queen attacked soon after. The Folk armies struggled to hold the Gates, until the bravest and shrewdest among the Gentry dared to draw upon the raw wild magic loosed from Deirdre's Treasure. And it was unlike any power they'd wielded before. It was pure and potent—unfettered by rules or strictures. With it, they could rout armies and boil oceans, crack the skies and rain fire on their enemies. The tide turned in the human queen's war.

"But there was a reason the first chieftains had forged the Treasures. Not even the Gentry were meant to channel wild magic in the way they now channeled it. All magic demands balance. And the cost of this magic was high. It warped and devoured, consuming minds and tainting even the purest intentions. It transformed all those who used it—slowly but irrevocably."

Irian's forearms flexed, and the black feathers inked along his skin lengthened. A wrongness I barely had a name for slithered through me.

"All those who tasted such power yearned for more. And Deirdre's death had shown the dissident Gentry something they had not known before—Treasures could be destroyed, their heirs killed. If all four Treasures were destroyed, they reasoned, then all that wild, elemental magic would be set free, and with it, they could do anything. The Gates would be broken. They could retaliate against the human queen. They could rule over both realms as gods."

"So they rose up." I knew this part. "Why didn't the Septs strike back, if the Treasures were still the most powerful magic in Tír na nÓg?"

"The Treasures are always weakest just before they are tithed to new heirs. That was when the dissidents struck." With moonlight in his hair and shadows flaring out behind him like great wings, Irian was remote and uncanny. "And they did not just *rise up*, colleen. The wild magic had warped them beyond mercy—they *butchered* us. They slaughtered the living tánaistí and destroyed two more Treasures, but they didn't stop there. They massacred whole lineages—wedded couples taken by surprise in their marriage beds, children torn screaming from the arms of their dead and bloodied mothers."

Pity and disgust brought bile to my mouth. Eala had made it sound as if the Septs deserved their fate. But this—this sounded like carnage.

"Only Nuada's heir escaped," Irian continued after a beat. "She flew from Gorias—stronghold of the Sept of Feathers—with the Sky-Sword. And on the Ember Moon, she tithed the last remaining Treasure to the last remaining tánaiste, even though he had not yet come of age."

"You."

"Yes." Shadows dimmed the silver of his eyes, and I recognized something in his expression that I'd seen a thousand times in the mirror: self-loathing. "I was raised in seclusion. I knew little of my inheritance. I was not prepared for the power of the Sky-Sword. Nor was I prepared for the tide of wild magic hammering against the last Treasure—the magic unleashed when the others were destroyed. And I was not prepared for the dissident Gentry themselves, hunting me along the cliffs of Tír fo Thuinn. Through the flowering fields of Ildathach."

Unexpected sympathy pierced me. I understood what it felt like to be forced onto a path you hadn't chosen. To be forged into a weapon sharper than you wanted to be. To feel your destiny like a weight pushing you toward doom. And if this all happened over twelve years ago, he would have been only—what? Thirteen? But guessing his age was like trying to guess the age of a diamond or a moonbeam. He existed beyond sundry things like months or years.

"That's why you wanted to take the Gates. To deter the Gentry from killing you and destroying the sword?"

His sculpted jaw hardened. "Pardon?"

"Isn't that why you stole Eala and the other human daughters? To sacrifice them for mastery over the Gates?"

"Someone has been telling you stories, colleen." His voice rang with barely tempered violence. "I stole the twelve maidens, yes. But not from the human realms. I stole them from the power-hungry Gentry themselves."

The earth shuddered beneath my feet. "What?"

"They—the self-proclaimed bardaí of the Gates—would have slaughtered them, as they slaughtered my family." He exhaled roughly. "With the Sky-Sword still intact, the bardaí could not open the Gates. Only the Treasures have such power. So they sent lower Folk spies through the old folkways—fairy rings and quicken trees—to kidnap human children. One for each Gate. Girls whose hearts they could bleed for magic."

I considered this. "So you stole Eala and the others from the bardaí to *protect* them?"

"Is that so hard to believe? They were just children, and I was barely older." His jaw set. "Exhausted and tormented, I made an impetuous, reckless decision. I used the power of the Sky-Sword to build a haven and a secret Gate—one I controlled. I spirited the twelve maidens away from the bardaí. And I bound them to my Sept. Or so I intended. I always meant to set them free when the time was right. To send them home through the Willow Gate once the danger was past." For a moment, he was silent. "But I over-reached. I did not know where the power of my Treasure ended and the seething mass of wild magic began. I paid a price for my inexperience, and so too did the maidens."

"The geas was wrought with the corrupted wild magic." The puzzle pieces slotted together. "That's why they're cursed as swans—the magic took the link to your Sept too far."

Irian gave his head a sharp cut of affirmation. "And why I am . . . bound in shadow."

"And why you can't undo it."

"I have tried. But the wild magic is dangerously unpredictable. I fear I would only make things worse." He glanced at me, and a ferocious hope crossed his face—same as that night on the beach, when I'd saved Chandi. Like he wanted something he shouldn't want or wished for something that could never come true. "I truly believed I was protecting them. Protecting the barrier between our worlds. Protecting *myself*. But all I did was curse twelve maidens as swans and curse myself to live alone. Until I inevitably have to die."

"Until you *inevitably have to die*?" I jerked back, my boots sliding on loose shale.

Irian caught me before I fell, his hand like a firebrand on my forearm. He pulled me flush against him and stared down into my eyes.

"Every twelve years, beneath the Ember Moon, the Septs' heirs apparent tithed their Treasures to new tánaistí. The lineages were vast; the potential heirs, manifold. From the many that showed promise, the magic chose its one vessel. In this way, the magic was renewed, and the Treasures returned to their full strength." He inhaled. "When I created the Thirteenth Gate, I bought myself a thirteenth year. But it has been over twelve years since the last tithing. The Sky-Sword is dying—the weakest it has ever been. If it is not tithed to a new heir this coming Samhain, all wild magic will go free. The Gates will fall to the bardaí, who will glut themselves on power. Both human and Folk realms will burn."

Tithe. He kept saying that word—*tithe*. "What is the tithe?"

"It is as it has always been—the life of the heir." Irian's eyes were metal. "My life."

For a moment, the only sounds were the sighing of the wind over the moors and the distant thrum of a city held captive by corrupt magic.

Thoughts and emotions blew through me like dried leaves in a gale. Irian's eyes were locked on my face.

"So you must die to renew the Treasure. And if you die, Eala and the other girls die too."

He nodded.

"There must be another way. To separate them from you. Or... or to separate you from the Sky-Sword."

"The only way to separate me from the Sky-Sword is death." His smile was grim. "And the outcome is the same. If I die before I tithe the Sky-Sword to a new tánaiste, the last of the wild magic goes free. And the Gates will fall to the bardaí, who will unleash wicked magic upon the human realms."

What had Irian said to me the night he'd brought me to his fortress? *Strangers only ever enter my realm for one of two reasons. The first is to try and kill me. The second is to try and take the sword.*

The murúcha in the lough, who had tried to kidnap a swan maiden under a tánaiste's protection. That vengeful ollphéist stinking of rot and vengeance, unleashed upon a warrior a fraction of its size.

"They're still coming after you."

"The bardaí are determined to finish what they started." His jaw was set. "There was a time when the Treasures were sacrosanct. The heirs, holy. No one would have dared raise so much as a finger against me. But that time is past. Many Folk wish to see the human realms under the dominion of Tír na nÓg—to rekindle a war that has gone cold."

"And me?" The rising wind stole the words from my lips. It all came back to this—the way he'd looked at me that night on the beach. *It's you.* "How do I fit into this?"

Irian's plush mouth softened. He lifted one large hand to cup my cheek. Like a flower turning toward the sun, I found myself grow-ing accustomed to his searing touch.

"The first time I saw your face, I thought you were a hallucina-tion conjured up by the magic I have misused. A creature born of balance, sent to destroy me at last. A punishment for my arrogance. My selfishness. The violence I have caused. And for a moment, I thought—" He paused. His thumb skated along my jawline, and the look in his eyes verged on wonder. "I thought I might not mind oblivion, if you were the one to deliver it."

Heat rushed to my face. I jerked back, and his hand fell away. Echoes of his burning touch mingled with the blood staining my cheeks.

"I asked you a question. One you did not answer." My tongue felt like glue in my mouth, but I was unwilling to let him distract me. "Who am I, in all this?"

"I will tell you, *friend*." He tilted his head. "In return for the story you still owe me."

For a moment, I didn't know what he was talking about. Then I remembered—last month, after I'd patched his wound, he'd asked about my Greenmark. About my so-called *gift*.

"I owe you nothing." I crossed my arms and glanced at the hori-zon, which was lightening toward gray. "I told you—your story last month bought your life."

"A boon I have now repaid with the promise of more stories." His smile was coiled, lazy. "Is our new friendship no more than a ruse for you to get your way, at the expense of my own desires?"

My hands dropped instinctively to my belt, but of course my knives were lost. I'd asked Corra for new ones, but they'd been wobbly and unbalanced. I supposed formless sprites had limits to their capabilities.

Besides, what was I planning to do? *Stab* Irian for asking me personal questions?

I took a deep breath.

"Once—in a time of oak leaves and early frost—there was a

changeling girl. She did not know her name or her place. All she knew was the trees rustled their boughs for her when she stepped into the forest. The fallen leaves chased her down the path. The late blooms waved as she passed. But she spent too long in the woods. Night fell, and her nursemaid came looking for her."

I remembered Caitríona's frantic cries for me. Not that she'd been worried about *me*. She'd just been worried she'd be whipped for losing me.

"At last, the nursemaid found her charge. But the changeling didn't want to go home, where she'd be scolded and sent to bed without supper. She wanted to stay in the forest." My voice caught like wet leaves in my throat. Caitríona had been a careless girl and an unfeeling caretaker. But she hadn't deserved what I'd done to her. "The nursemaid caught her around the waist and prepared to drag her back. The changeling transformed the nursemaid's legs into saplings and her hair into vines and her face into a flower. In the dark of the night, the changeling was sorry for what she had done, and wished it away. But the sun rose and the maid remained a tree. And that was how the changeling learned that she had a *gift* no other human had."

After a beat, Irian said, "Your endings are not sunshine and roses either, colleen."

"Just following your lead." I tamped the hateful, painful memories down, never to be dredged up again. "May I go home now?"

"You may. But I wonder whether it is truly your home."

He put his hand on my shoulder. Space bent around me—the night sky swallowing me up and spitting me out. My knees hit dirt. I doubled over in leaf-strewn loam and fought nausea. When I finally looked up through watering eyes, Irian was nowhere in sight.

❧

Dawn flushed lilac across an azure sky. Birds warbled awake, adulating the day with a riot of song. I gazed up at the shadows of the leafy canopy, churning with questions as I trudged back to the fort beside an exhausted Rogan.

Tonight felt like a dream. Revealing, confusing, heartbreaking, unexpected.

My enemy—my friend?—was dying. And all things being equal, I wasn't sure I wanted him to.

If Irian died before the Treasure could be renewed, Eala and her swan sisters would die. Control of the Gates would fall to the bardaí. Fódla would not survive the onslaught they would bring, and everyone I cared about would die in the attack.

And if Irian tithed his life to renew the Treasure, Eala and her swan sisters would also die.

Either way, his death meant my failure. Even if I brought Fódla the Sky-Sword, Mother would never forgive me for the death of her true daughter.

I had to find a way to do all things. To renew the Sky-Sword to its full power without risking Irian's life. To break Eala's geas so she might go home. To bring magic to Mother without exposing Fódla to a war no one would win.

Irian would help me. Of that, I had no doubt. After all, his time was running out. And I was his only ally.

My face still tingled where his thumb had grazed it.

I might not mind oblivion, if you were the one to deliver it.

Perhaps I would deliver him oblivion. Or perhaps I would deliver him salvation. He didn't matter. It only mattered that I save my kingdom, my queen, my sister . . . and perhaps even myself.

Chapter Twenty-Three

Fearn—Alder
Early Spring

Changeling."

The voice was far away, filtered through obsolete phrases and aching lines of poetry.

Spring had arrived with ephemeral glory. But despite the new colors pricking bright against the backdrop of brown and green—new threads in a threadbare tapestry—I barely spent any time in the gardens. The old alcove with its trove of books had swallowed me whole.

While I was still no master of the ancient tongue, my translations of the warrior's books steadily became easier the longer I spent in the archive. Part personal account, part philosophical treatise, part magical grimoire, his prodigious writings were scattered, strange, and deeply sad. His longing unfurled from each page, boundless and bittersweet. But at times, his focus on Folk lore and magical bindings veered into the obsessive. The more I read, the more I tasted his thirst for knowledge in the back of my own throat, querulous and unquenchable.

"Changeling," said the voice, louder.

I continued frowning down at the obscure translation I was fixated on. *Our hearts were made for breaking; that magic made for mending. I gcothromaíocht*, the bygone warrior had written. But the last phrase stumped me. It meant something like *in counterpoise*, but in this context . . .

"Fia," Rogan said.

The sound of my name finally captured my attention.

The prince looked utterly out of place in my little library— his broad shoulders filled the spaces between the shelves, and his golden head nearly brushed the ceiling.

"What are you doing here?" I asked stupidly.

"Looking for you, of course." My lantern glinted in his gemstone eyes. "You've been avoiding me."

I scowled at him.

"If you keep making that face," he warned, "it might get stuck. It's almost dark, you know. You've spent all day up here."

"Shite, really?" I cursed and stood up, sliding my half-finished translation between the pages. "I was supposed to weed today."

"I did it." Rogan held out a hand. "Come with me. There's something I want to show you."

"What? And where?"

Rogan grinned, a sharp dazzle of humor meant to disarm me. "It's a surprise."

"You know I hate surprises."

"Only when other people surprise you." His smile widened. "You love it when *I* surprise you."

"I especially *hate* when you surprise me," I argued. "Your surprises are usually ill timed and frequently painful. Like my sixteenth birthday, when you strewed roses all around my bed in the middle of the night, except you didn't take off any of the thorns, and when I woke up to pee, I cut up my bare feet."

His smile slipped. I tried not to feel guilty.

"Your choice. But hurry, or else we'll miss it."

I crossed my arms. Rogan shrugged, then walked out of the alcove. I cursed his receding back, then ducked down the hidden stairs after him.

Rogan didn't speak as we meandered through the dún and stepped out into a perfect spring evening. I paused, shading my eyes against the last rays of day striping the estate in shades of chrysanthemum and forget-me-not. I felt fleeting guilt for neglecting my garden; grudging gratitude for Rogan's interruption; cooling calm as my feet on the earth chased away my cerebral agitation.

I kicked off my shoes, flexed my bare feet in the sun-warmed grass, and followed Rogan toward the forest. He paused beneath the long shadows, peering into the green silence between the trees.

"What are you looking for?" I asked, cautious. These woods were too close to Roslea—to Tír na nÓg—for me to trust them completely. "I don't have my knives."

"This isn't something you can fight, changeling." He chuckled. "We're just early."

I stepped next to him and followed his gaze. "Early for *what*?"

He quirked one golden eyebrow at me. "Has anyone ever told you you're an extremely impatient person?"

"I consider it a virtue."

"You would." He sank down on the grass, tilting his head to catch the last of the sunlight. "And patience? Is that an equal virtue?"

"Depends." The balmy afternoon showed no signs of cooling as evening approached, so I shucked off my outer mantle as I sat beside him. I didn't miss the way his eyes grazed my suddenly bare shoulders, the curve of my breasts beneath my shift.

"On what?"

"Whether the thing you're waiting for is worth the wait."

"How do you know whether it's worth it, before you have it?" His eyes lifted to mine, suddenly intent. A whisper of intuition told me we'd passed beyond banter into something more serious. I suddenly wondered whether he really had anything to show me down here, at the edge of the forest.

"Rogan," I said, not ungently. "What are you talking about?"

"You know—" He paused, brushing golden hair off his brow. "You know how unhappy I've been. How hard this has been for me."

"Hard?" I laughed. "Yes, I imagine following a charming princess to a series of exquisite Folk revels—flirting with her and wooing her—must be hard indeed."

"Don't do that, Fia." He caught my hand, and his pulse throbbed quick against my skin. "Don't make a joke of this."

I looked away.

"Eala doesn't want to come home." His voice had an edge to it. "She's been raised *there*. With *them*. The nights she regains her human form, she spends with the Folk. She knows their ways, attends their revels, sings their songs. Has done since she was eight years old. She barely remembers her mother the queen, let alone a forgotten childhood in the human realms."

My eyebrows lifted. Eala had been so eager to steal the Sky-Sword—to cut away her geas so she could return to Fódla. Why would Rogan say the opposite? Either he was lying to me, or Eala was lying to him. But I bit my tongue and let him speak.

"You know I do not relish the idea of marrying her." Bitterness splintered his voice. "I know she does not relish the idea of marrying me. She is sweet-faced yet sour-tongued. She will dance with me, then spurn me. Flirt with me, then insult me."

A thorn of residual guilt tore at me. I had been the one to encourage Eala to toy with Rogan. But I had never meant for her to *torment* him. At least, not to this extent.

"But I've turned it over in my head a thousand times, change-ling. I can't find a way out."

I met his gaze in surprise. "A way...*out*?"

"I don't want to do this anymore." His eyes were the same color as the river-stone winking from his collar. "I don't want to go *there*. I don't want to chase after *her*. I don't want to playact the hero when I feel like a failure and a liar."

"What *do* you want?"

"You."

The directness of his answer stole my breath. We'd danced around this for so long. A twilight of dread and desire made a muddle of my thoughts.

"Changeling, you've had it so wrong." He brushed the back of his hand against my cheek. I hated myself for it, but I leaned into his touch. "You accused me of thinking of her when I was with you. But it's the other way around. All I can think about—with her, without her; day, night—is *you*."

I wanted to eat his words like honey. I wanted to savor every warm, tempting promise.

"But if you want to protect your people, there is no way out," I whispered.

"If there is, I cannot see it." He clasped my chin, sword-calloused fingers rough against my cheeks. The sensation made me think, abruptly, of Irian—as though his scalding fingers had left imprints on my skin from the last time he'd touched me. "At first, I thought to run away. We could sail abroad, to my cousins in Caerafwyn. But it would be mere months before the queen discovered what we'd done. Before she hunted us down."

"She would kill us both. Me for betraying her. You for defying her."

"And even if she was merciful, there is too much at stake." His hands fell to his sides. "I cannot abandon Bridei to my brothers. They would malt our best grain for the distillery, then drink and gamble and whore their way to empty coffers and fallow fields." His words were bitter. "No—Bridei will not survive another bad king. But for me to rule, I must marry Eala."

"What would you have me do with these words, Rogan? They mean nothing." My voice came out hoarse. "We are right where we started. The princeling and the changeling, always together and yet fundamentally apart."

"We were *torn* apart." Rogan caught my hand again, threading his fingers through mine. His eyes matched the sky dimming to cobalt behind him. "But look at what we've done to this green-house, Fia. This whole garden. Seeded with new growth. Reforged. Mended. Couldn't that be us? We are not so broken that we cannot be put whole with care and work and time."

"How?" His words were a balm against my thorny heart, but I fought the urge to melt into his arms. "When she is still your betrothed?"

"Surely there is a way."

It took me a moment to realize what he was suggesting.

"How many times must I say it?" I willed my heart hard as stone. "I am no one's whore."

"Then let me be no one." He shook his head, pulled my stiff body closer. He brought his lips to my ear and whispered a snatch of a rhyme against my hair. "*I asked all around, who broke the vase? No one, no one wants to show their face.*"

I closed my eyes as that silly, childish rhyme conjured up a gauntlet of memories. They chased me, teased me, bruised me. The silence between us cut its teeth on my desire and drank my hesitation like liquor.

Rogan was never meant for me. He wasn't the man I would wed, would bear children to, would grow old with. But that wasn't what he was asking me for. He was asking for part of me—and he was offering only part of himself in return.

Morrigan help me, but I had wanted him for so long. And maybe I could have him. If not forever, then...for now. Eala's geas was not yet broken. He was still mine. For a little while longer.

It was wicked to want such a thing. But I'd asked for so little for so long, and been given even less. Didn't I deserve this one small thing?

"*I thought I heard a giggle, a whisper in the hall.*" I murmured the next verse of the nursery rhyme. I slid my hands around his neck and pulled him toward me. I tilted my head, parting my lips. Dusk blurred around us, turning the air blue and gold and shy with desire. "*But no one, no one was ever there at all.*"

At the edge of the trees, a flicker of metallic light caught my eye. I startled, whipping my head around. My eyes dredged the shadows, searching for—what? The glitter of bloodstained flowers, the sweep of a black cloak, the rattle and claw of a distorted monster. But this wasn't Tír na nÓg. The night here was softer, as was the light I'd seen. It flashed, then disappeared. Another glimmer appeared a few feet away. Then another.

"There." Rogan's laughter was soft. "I knew it would be worth the wait."

He stood, offering his large, warm palm to lift me to my feet. He pulled me toward the edge of the forest until we were adrift in a sea of shadow and glow.

Fireflies danced in profusion, pirouetting through the twilight like captured stars. They paid us no mind, swirling heedlessly in our wake. A bright snatch of music snagged my hearing—strange amid the silence of sunset. I twisted to see a bright light drifting over my ear. Cupping my palm around the tiny body, I carried it close. Golden light splashed my face as the melody rose. It was an ancient song, soft and strange. I exhaled and released the firefly to drift away.

Rogan reached for another, cupping it in his palm the same way. We bowed our heads together. A melancholy melody rose up, like an elegy for a broken heart.

"It's too early for fireflies," I whispered.

"These are no fireflies, changeling." Wonder and wariness colored his voice.

No—they were the songs lilting in the moments before I fell asleep—the lullabies from *before*. They were the songs moss sang to stones, the songs trees sang to seedlings, the songs earth sang to sky. They were the songs of my green heart unbound.

I reached for another. But Rogan caught my lifted hand with his calloused fingers. "Do you remember the night by the pond?"

My pulse vaulted as he uncurled my fingers and brushed his lips against the palm of my hand. "How could I forget?"

Rogan's eyes—pools of indigo shot through with golden stars and leaves of green—grazed mine, heavy with a question. A question with an impossible answer. I hesitated for one last breathless moment.

"One night, Rogan," I murmured. "One night to let this flame between us burn itself out."

"One night." His lips brushed mine. "To be no one?"

"To be no one," I whispered into the dusk.

I parted my lips, sliding my mouth over his and slipping my tongue between his teeth. He tasted like woodsmoke and want. In an instant, the kiss lost its gentleness. Rogan's hands dragged up my bare arms, gripping my shoulders as he drew me hard against him. Our mouths met with a clash of tongues and lips and wet heat, speaking a language only our bodies understood.

I rose up onto my toes, molding my hips and stomach to his front, where already his desire was rising. His groan was a low rumble of pleasure that vibrated deliciously through my chest. His hands dropped from my arms to my waist and then lower, smoothing over the curve of my rear. He cupped my thighs and lifted me against him.

My shift rode up over my legs as I wrapped them around his waist, hooking my calves in the small of his back. The night air grew cool against my bare skin, but I didn't care—Rogan's muscled torso radiated warmth against the inside of my thighs, even with his shirt in the way. I looped my arms around his neck and bent my face toward his, my hair making a dark curtain around us. But another dark breeze kissed a chill down my back and raised gooseflesh along my arms. I hesitated.

"It's getting dark." My voice came out husky. "We should get back to the fort—"

"No." Rogan's pupils were blown wide, dark as the sky fading around us. "It's too far. And I've wanted this for too long."

In one smooth motion—without setting me down—he unbuckled the mantle from his shoulder. His river-stone brooch fell in a blur of blue-green. Rogan flicked the fabric open with one hand. It snapped like a sail before billowing down to the grass. Swiftly, gently, Rogan laid me down on the cloth, then knelt above me to take off his tunic. I rose up onto my elbows, watching hungrily as he ripped the fabric over his head, his golden waves settling onto the freckled ridge of muscle connecting his collarbones to his shoulders. The hard planes of his stomach flexed as he leaned over me, sliding one of his knees between my thighs. The heat building in my core gave a throb of need. I skimmed my fingers down the range of his torso, reaching for the waistband of his breeches, where the bulge of his arousal pressed. But he caught my hands and lifted them, pinning them roughly above my head. I inhaled, biting my lip as my hips bucked up against him.

"You've waited more than four years to have me inside you again." His low voice held an edge of provocative humor. "You can't wait a few more minutes?"

I tilted my chin, bringing my lips toward his ear. "Will it be worth the wait?"

"Oh, changeling." His smile was shameless. "I'll make sure of that."

My heartbeat accelerated. Rogan released my wrists, dragging his hands down over my arms. He found the straps of my shift, sliding them down over my humming skin as he exposed me to the waist. His gaze grew heavy-lidded as he took in the sight of me—his eyes roving over my face, my throat, my modest breasts. Gently, he slid his hand against the soft curve above my ribs. I shivered and arched my spine, pushing the fullness of my breast into his palm. He leaned down to capture my hard nipple in his mouth, laving his tongue over the sensitive skin until I threw my head back and moaned from the aching promise rising inside me.

Where the world had made me hard, Rogan made me feel suddenly soft.

The rest of my dress fell away beneath his grasping hands. His breath hitched when his touch roamed lower and pushed aside my underthings. Maintaining eye contact, he slipped his hand between my legs. I gasped as his fingers slid against my slick warmth, moving in slow, deliberate circles. Heat twined insistent in my core, and I rocked against his hand, urging him on. But he just smiled, gliding his fingers in teasing caresses. I whimpered from the yearning ache building inside me. He leaned down to catch the sound in his mouth, sucking on my lower lip as I quickened beneath his touch. My fingers flexed in the grass.

I wanted more. I dragged him toward me. This time, when I reached for the waistband of his trousers, he let me. I tried to be deft on the laces, but after a moment, Rogan reached down and unlaced them for me. His erection sprang free, and I took his smooth length in my palm. My fingers curved around it and Rogan groaned at my touch. His head fell back and his lips parted as I caressed him. His hardness swelled in my hand and he jerked as I stroked him faster, the muscles of his stomach tensing.

"Enough." He pushed me onto the cloak, kissed me rough. His lips were as swollen as mine felt. He settled himself between my open thighs. "Enough waiting, changeling?"

"Yes, princeling." Anticipation made my smile slow. "Enough waiting."

He sheathed himself inside me in one long, slow stroke. I moaned, heat and tightness building my pleasure to a fever pitch. My fingers flexed in the grass. He moved deeper, burying himself to the hilt until all I could feel was him. His length, his weight above me, his mouth on the skin of my throat. Roots snaked from my touch, sliding in the earth beneath me.

Rogan rocked against me, slow at first but building speed as we rediscovered the rhythms of each other's pleasure. His hands pulled shivering touches up my waist, over my nipples, against the column of my trembling throat. His thumb grazed my bottom lip in the moment before he dragged his mouth over mine.

"Definitely worth the wait," he murmured against my skin.

Everything inside me tautened, like a strung bow. The arrow

loosed, singing through me as I unraveled at the seams. I arched my back and came apart, crying out as I writhed against him. I dug my nails deep in the grass, and violets burst from the ground below me, pushing against the edge of Rogan's cloak and tangling like a corona around my head.

Rogan registered the surge of purple flowers and heart-shaped leaves. He hesitated, his movements slowing as unease slid behind his eyes. But then he buried his head against my shoulder and followed me over the edge, thrusting deeper and faster until his whole body hardened. He groaned as he spilled himself inside me, slumping over on top of me.

For a long moment, we lay together, sweat-slicked and panting. Then I slid out from under him, sitting up in darkness. Night had fallen—silver stars shone down instead of golden fireflies. The newborn violets lifted curious faces toward me. A breeze kissed my cooling flesh, and I pulled the tatters of my ruined shift to cover my nakedness. It would have been so easy to lie there—beneath the stars, twined in flowers—and forget the rest of the world. But nothing—not even finally giving in to what I had wanted for so long—could quiet my rattling mind.

"Changeling?" Rogan reached for me, his hand a bracelet around my wrist. "What's wrong?"

Sudden doubt slicked over me. "We shouldn't have."

He surged up behind me, looping one heavy arm across my chest and pulling me against him. His muscular torso was warm against my back, a contrast to the chill raising the hair on my arms and peaking my bare nipples. "Yes, we should have."

I let him pull me down beside him. I pillowed my head on his bicep as he pulled the hem of his mantle over us both. But as his breathing settled into the deep, even rhythm of sleep and the waning moon sailed above us, the forest rustled. Briefly, it sounded like someone's voice.

I might not mind oblivion, if you were the one to deliver it.

Beneath the stars, twined in flowers—I scrunched my eyes shut and tried to sleep.

I awoke to the full-throated chorus of birdsong.

Dewdrops trembled on my eyelashes, and I blinked heavy eyes against the wash of dawn light. For a long moment, I didn't remember where I was. I rolled onto my elbow, glancing around in half panic. The sky was the color of a new lily. Mist shrouded the trunks of trees and swept a haze across my garden.

Rogan stirred beside me. And I remembered. The weight of his large hand splayed over my stomach sent a throb of heat pulsing through me. His face was pillowed on one hand, his golden hair trailing in the grass. In the pale light he looked deceptively innocent, his mouth pouting like it hadn't kissed me hard enough to bruise. His eyelashes were bronze against his cheeks. He cracked one eye open, brilliant as an ocean after a storm.

"Changeling?"

I pushed hair off my face. "Yes?"

"Go back to sleep."

"I would." I grimaced at the sky. "But the birds are yelling."

He closed the eye. "So yell back."

But his awareness shifted as he, too, remembered what had passed between us last night. Tangled together beneath his cloak, a mess of limbs and warm skin, it was hard to forget. His hand flexed against my stomach, then trailed up to cup my breast. His mouth found my throat. And when he shifted his weight above me, he was already aroused.

"Is it still tonight?" His voice was rough with sleepy desire.

"If it's not...?" I laughed, throaty. "No one, no one will tell."

We slid together in the hush of mist and morning. Drowsy, at first, then more intent. He pushed inside me slowly, and his eyes on my face were steady, his touch intimate. I threw my head back and let him drive me toward climax.

But as the sun crowned the trees in gold, I kept a close hold on my errant Greenmark. And no more uninvited flowers joined the violets crowding vibrant around my head.

A week of rain gave way to steady warmth and riotous wildflowers. Brookweed and buttercup, wild thyme and gentian. The flowers filled the air with perfume and painted the fields with frenzy.

The well-tended gardens suddenly grew weeds. The archive gathered dust. Because Rogan and I were busy with each other. One night became two. Then three. Then a week. After so long apart, we spent every waking moment together, glutting ourselves on each other's company. And bodies.

We half napped in the grass as bees drifted around us, filling the air with an indolent hive hum. My gaze lingered on Rogan's mouth, and I tasted all our stolen kisses in a rush of heat against the back of my throat.

We discovered a trove of ancient sketches hidden in another forgotten vault, and when a few of them crumbled to dust at our touch, I cried. And he laughed at me crying, which made me laugh too. And then punch him in the arm. Hard.

And we shared a hundred kisses. Slow, intent kisses in the shade of towering pines; hasty, dusty kisses sandwiched between gales of laughter; cool, quiet kisses between dreams as we drowsed in bed.

Two weeks passed quickly. Not quickly enough.

The night before the full moon, we built a fire beneath the stars and reminisced about our childhoods while passing a flask of whiskey between us. Later, we climbed the vertiginous stairs to Rogan's tower room and made love by drifting moonlight.

But when I gasped, fisting my hands in the sheets and sending tiny pink blossoms netting across his mattress, Rogan's face shifted.

"I wish you wouldn't do that," he muttered at me in the dark.

I moved my hands. The blossoms crumbled into dusty smears of brown pollen.

And just like that, with a handful of words, Rogan reminded me who I was. *What* I was. Too other—too Folk—for his liking. For his love. For his forever.

The night of the full moon—without discussion or fanfare—we changed into our fighting leathers and dingy tunics. And as we traipsed in silence to the Willow Gate, I knew, as I'd known from the start, that the story we'd been telling ourselves was coming to an end. And in real life, stories didn't end in grand climaxes or tragic denouements. They simply faded—dim beneath the dust of duty, dark in the afterglow of burned-out lust.

Chapter Twenty-Four

Tír na nÓg was wild with blooming.

Knots of candy-colored petals burst open as we passed. Hook-leaved ferns waved in shades of blue. Flowering vines prickled with thorns white as teeth. Golden-edged fronds with spots like liquid eyes watched us walk by. I shivered with the delicious promise of unfolding, unfurling, unbinding. I surreptitiously ran my fingers through the garlands of colors and smiled when my fingers came away stained with the shades of spring. Heady chrysanthemum, bold magenta, ambitious blue.

Rogan—who was celebrating the first properly warm evening of spring by wearing a close-fitting sleeveless mantle that hugged his powerful torso and showed off every one of his sculpted arm muscles—peeled off near the lough to follow the elegant gaggle of flower-clad maidens sweeping toward their monthly revel. After spending nearly every moment—waking and sleeping—in his company for the past two weeks, I felt his departure keenly. I tried to name the emotions whirling inside me. But they were restless as the spring breeze tangling in my hair—jealousy giving way to relief, coiling toward guilt.

I forced myself to turn toward the fortress. Although I'd barely looked at the archives these past weeks, I wanted to ask Irian his insights on that phrase I'd come across—*i gcothromaíocht. Counterpoise.* But as I moved between the trees, I found nothing of the tall Gentry heir.

Instead, I found Eala.

She waited, framed by the branches of a frothing dogwood. The glow of the moon outlined her slender frame in silver. Shining flowers glittered in her hair, but she was not yet gowned. When she saw me, she stepped toward me, smiling that broad, gentle smile. Her sister's smile. The one that spoke of shared secrets and hidden laughter.

I smiled back, although more tentatively. The last time I had seen her, Eala had been angry with me for returning the Sky-Sword to Irian. At the time, I'd thought I didn't deserve her pique. But in the months since, I had shared secrets with her captor and begun to sympathize with his plight. I had also shared a bed—and many not-beds—with the man who would one day be her husband. Contrition and shame chilled me despite the warmth of the air. I steeled myself for whatever censure she might decide to lay on my head.

"Sister." She took my hands. "I missed you last month."

"I'm sorry." I wasn't sure which of my many sins I was apologizing for. "I didn't think you'd want to see me. I assumed you were angry with me."

"Not angry, no." Her voice was breezy. "Surprised, perhaps. But only that you were quick to trust a stranger over me. I suppose I expected you to be more...dutiful to the bonds of kinship."

She said it pleasantly, but I wasn't entirely sure she meant it as a compliment. "I'm not sure what you mean."

"I speak of our mother, of course." Confusion must have registered on my face, because Eala's own expression gentled. She held out a slender white palm to me. "Come, Sister—shall we walk together? I have been longing for a moment alone with you."

I nodded and she linked her arm through mine, leading me through the effervescent forest.

"Do you know how old I was when Mother first betrothed me for personal gain?" Eala leaned close, her voice confidential—intimate. "I hadn't even been born yet. She sold her unborn daughter—not even knowing she'd be a girl—to a man. And not just one. Publicly, she gave me to a small princeling whose still-grieving father wanted to wage war against the world, but not the Folk. My future maidenhead bought his fianna—the first armies to die beyond the Gates."

Disgust rose up in me, instinctive. But such were the ways of royalty. "You are a princess. These things are common."

"That does not make them good." Eala's tone remained conversational. "Privately, Mother gave me away again. Not to one under-king. To *all* of them. To their sons if they had them. To them if they didn't. Before I had even been named, I had been sold several times over."

Mother could be mercenary—she was a war queen infamous for her ruthlessness. But Eala's accusations bordered on the barbaric.

"Mother mourned you deeply when you were taken," I said carefully. "And always spoke of you with great affection. I know she loves you."

"Even loving parents make tools of their children." Eala laughed, rueful. "Shovels to bury their pasts. Chisels to chip away at their ambitions. And weapons sharp enough to carve out revenge."

A tendril of alarm tangled up my spine. "Why are you telling me this?"

"Because I see she has made a weapon of you, as she did me. Although I wonder whether I haven't been more rigorously forged."

The space behind my eyelids burst green and black with rushing blood. I thought of the words Rogan told me Mother had said over four years ago.

She said you were made of poison nettle and forged steel—not something to be loved, but something to be wielded. A weapon, not a girl.

Much as I'd tried to explain them away, those cruel words had wormed themselves deep into my mind, infecting me with bitterness. But I wasn't sure I was ready to admit that out loud.

"If anyone made me into a weapon," I said slowly, "it was Cathair. And he only did it because he had to. To keep me safe from the Folk. To keep *Fódla* safe from the Folk."

"Cathair? Mother's fawning, ingratiating druid?" Eala laughed, high and bright. "Then she was cleverer with you than she was with me. She thought of a way to pass along the blame for her exploitation. I always knew exactly who to hate."

Another hot flush sent forest shadows pulsing through my veins. I bit down on the inside of my cheek, allowing the pain to ground me.

"If I am a weapon," I said tightly, "then I am both sword and swordsman. I've been taught to trust my instincts and react as new facts present themselves. No one makes my decisions but me."

"Is that your way of apologizing for returning the Treasure to our dark-hearted captor?"

"I had every intention of giving you the Sky-Sword that night. Until I found out Irian's death bought yours as well."

"So he says."

"Until I know it to be a lie, I will operate as if it were truth. The stakes are too high to do otherwise."

"Very well, Sister." She paused. Her smile turned coy. "Tell me, though—how long have you and Rogan been in love with each other?"

Surprise and guilt numbed my limbs. "What?"

"So you *are* in love." Her smile broadened. "I saw the way you looked at him on the Nameless Day. And he has a thoughtless habit of talking about you—*thinking* about you—whenever we're together. You are exceptionally pretty, so I understand why Rogan finds you difficult to resist. I confess, however, that it's beginning to annoy me."

"Eala, forgive me." I barely heard the compliment—if it even was a compliment. "He and I have been friends since childhood, but I never—"

"Oh, Sister! For this, I don't want your apologies." She let out a glittering laugh. "I want you to sleep with him."

The numbness climbed my neck. A cascade of fresh and frantic memories clawed at my mind. Rogan and I, sprawled in the grass, stretched out on his bed, splayed on the table. "You want *what?*"

"Let me rephrase." Her icy eyes grew thoughtful. "I realize that in this little love triangle, I am the interloper. Prior to a few months ago, I had only ever met Rogan once. I was four. He was a towheaded little bully who took my favorite doll and tore her head off. I have barely thought of him since." Her casual recounting of the anecdote that tormented Rogan shocked me. "But you—you know him intimately. You have shared his trust and his love and—I daresay—his bed. I am envious of that closeness. He may be my betrothed. But he still belongs to you."

My throat was tight. My skin, tighter. I suddenly wanted to be anywhere else.

"If you want him," she continued, "you should have him. Allow your shared attraction to progress. Let the infatuation run its course."

Infatuation? "I would hardly call twelve years of camaraderie and intimacy an *infatuation*," I snapped.

"Again, I misspeak. Too many years living among the Folk, I fear." She ducked her head, chastened. "I simply mean our fates are already sealed. I was always going to wed Rogan. He was always going to wed me. But we have not yet broken my geas—I am not yet free. And I would not—could not—begrudge him a few months with you. If that was what you both chose."

Confessions and self-recriminations tangled against my lips. I ought to tell her what had happened, how we had already given in to our shared lust. It was the right thing to do—I owed my sister that honesty, at least. But instead of any of that, I heard myself ask, "How can you be sure he won't fall more in love with me?"

"Perhaps he will." She gave me an assessing look, making me suddenly aware of my worn armor, garden-dirt fingernails, and messy braids. "But people desire most what they think they cannot have. Forbid a child from playing with a toy, and they will want to play with nothing else. Give it to them, and they will soon tire of it and move on to other pursuits."

I wasn't sure what offended me more—Eala likening me to a toy Rogan would soon grow tired of playing with...or the creeping apprehension that her assessment was correct.

"Rogan isn't a child. He's a grown man. A prince. And—as you pointed out—your future husband."

"Princes are good for many things. Fidelity is not one of them." Eala's smile was indefatigable. "As his wife, I will require Rogan's love, fealty, and protection. But I don't need his fidelity."

There was a callousness to her words that reminded me, suddenly and blindingly, of Mother. "An interesting perspective, if one my own self-worth won't allow me to share."

Eala's smile finally faded, and I hid a burst of cold satisfaction. But she wasn't finished. "One last thing."

"What?"

"I know Irian can be charming when he wishes to be. But I have known him for twelve years. You must trust me when I say he is violent, arrogant, and selfish. He has no thought but for his own objectives. He is not to be trusted."

Her words were eerily close to what Chandi had told me at the Feis of the Nameless Day. Eala's comments about Rogan had strung sharp lines of tension along my bones, but I forced myself to release them now. She might be my sister, *bound in love*, but we were still practically strangers. We had not had time to learn the other's experiences and perspectives, quirks and triggers. It was natural that we would find ways to offend each other, simply by speaking our minds. Our relationship was a work in progress. But we still had the same goals—we still wanted the same outcomes in all this. I unclenched my fists and raised my hands, a gesture of supplication.

"Then it is good I do not trust him," I assured her. "But he knows things—about Tír na nÓg, about magic, about your geas. I understand why you hate him. But he wrought your geas—I fear we will need him to undo it."

"He is a blade sheathed in silk, Fia. You will not know you have cut yourself until you are already bleeding."

"I am well versed in the way of blades, Sister." A note of pleading crept into my voice. "I realize you do not know me well. But you must trust that I have your best interests at heart. That everything I do, I do for you—for Fódla."

"Then do it *with* me." She stepped forward, gripped my outstretched hands. "Together, we can discover a magic equal to the Treasure. A magic that will set me and my maidens free. I want you by my side—as my ally, my friend, my *sister*. Imagine what we could accomplish with our minds set to the same problem. Imagine the power—the *magic*—we two could wield, in a world that has always wanted us powerless."

Her words made my pulse jump—twin vines of green and black rushing bold and brilliant through my veins. The first was exhilaration—the feverish, instinctive thrill of wielding powerful magic that others could not. The second was dread—for I knew, better than most, what the cost of that magic was. All too often, I had found, the price was death.

"I know more of power than I would wish on anyone, Eala," I murmured. "And I would think you'd had enough magic to last you a lifetime."

"Magic being done *to* me," she said, vehement. "Against my will, without my consent. But I am so tired of being powerless—tired of being a coin to barter or a tool to wield or a heart to trade. I want to stand on equal footing with Irian—with the bardaí. With Mother. With all the grasping, power-hungry princes and kings of Fódla. Come, Fia—tell me you're with me."

Indecision tangled within me. Part of me wanted nothing more than to acquiesce to her—to let her passion guide me, command me. But all my life, I had let others lead me. Mother, Cathair, even

Rogan—I had let them tell me how to behave, what to believe, whom to trust. But it suddenly occurred to me—if I was truly as brave and competent and valued as they assured me I was...wasn't I capable of making those decisions on my own?

"I do stand with you. But I must do this my way," I told her, as gently as possible. Between my discoveries in the archives and Irian's admissions, I was close to getting answers about her geas. I just needed her to trust me to do it on my own. "Tell me you understand that."

Eala released my hands. Her expression shifted, some brightness extinguishing in her pale blue eyes.

"I think I do understand." She gave me a suddenly assessing glance, as if I were a horse at auction whose value she could not quite calculate. "Let it not be said that I didn't warn you to stay away from the heir of the Sept of Feathers. I would hate to see a girl as softhearted as you outwitted by a man as heartless as he."

Eala turned on her heel. Her shining hair swept out in a moonlit train behind her as the forest swallowed her up.

Something snapped inside me, releasing all my pent-up emotions—guilt, shock, disappointment, indecision. I whirled around and slammed my fist into the nearest tree. The bark splintered around my hand, long vertical cracks running the length of the trunk. Lichen sprouted from the fissures, followed a moment later by tiny blue flowers. Pain slivered up my arm, but when I lifted my hand, my skin was unblemished.

"As far as sparring partners go, trees have never been my favorite."

I spun toward the voice. Irian stood where Eala had been moments before, his wings of shadow stark against the blooming trees. The moment he saw my face, all humor drained from his expression, replaced with terrible, towering menace. In three long strides, he closed the distance between us. Momentary fear throbbed thunder through my veins, until I realized—his fury was not for me.

"You are upset." Irian slid a palm beneath my chin, tilting up my face. His touch sent sparks flaring along my skin, and I suppressed a shiver. He wiped a traitorous tear, thumb sliding feather-light against my cheek despite his vengeful expression. "What did she say to you?"

"How long were you there?" I jerked my chin out of his grasp, swiped at my cheeks.

His hands fell to his sides. "I do not make a habit of eavesdropping."

"That doesn't mean you didn't hear what she said."

"I heard her exhortation to stay away from me. That is all." A shadow slid across his opal eyes. "But I doubt that was what prompted you to assault a tree."

"It wasn't."

"Then tell me what troubles you."

I couldn't look at him. Everything Eala had told me twined into an impenetrable knot inside me. Eala . . . Rogan . . . Irian . . . me. What a strange little square we four made. The prince, the princess. The changeling, the monster. But much as I tried to disentangle our stories, they only twisted tighter.

My sister's ambitions for power had surprised me—I suddenly had to wonder exactly who she was. Irian, on the other hand— I did know exactly who he was. He was Folk Gentry. He was tánaiste of the Sept of Feathers. He was powerful, merciless, and likely self-serving. And he was still the key to everything. He held the Sky-Sword, the means of my kingdom's salvation. His lineage held the Gate bardaí at bay. He held the geas binding the maidens as swans—and potentially the knowledge to unbind them, if only I could wring it out of him.

"Only this." Making my expression serious, I lifted my gaze to his. "If I am to stay away from you, then who will protect you from all the ravening monsters trying to make a meal of your innards?"

He tilted his head. "I *am* quite a delicacy."

I dragged my gaze down his lean, sculpted figure. "I suspect you'd be rather gamey."

His lip curled up. "Taste me and find out."

I flushed, the sound of those suggestive words in his rough voice flooding me with heat.

"No need, tánaiste. I already know you to be an acquired taste."

"And how could you know that?" His smile slid wider. "Unless you have already begun to acquire it?"

I opened my mouth to reply but found I'd run out of clever responses. Irian's eyes on my face were molten—the same heat radiating from the palm he lifted to my face. He brushed a strand of hair off my cheek, curled it behind my ear. His hand slid against the nape of my neck. He bent toward me.

"Perhaps you *should* stay away from me, colleen." His lips brushed my cheek, soft as a feather. His breath tasted like petrichor. "If not for your sake...then for mine."

"I would." My voice came out reedy. "But we made a bargain. *Friend.*"

He released me. And, with a lingering smile, stepped away. "Go on, then. What is your story?"

"Once—in a time of living gods and limitless possibility—a mortal warrior fell in love with a Gentry princess." I fought the urge to touch my cheek, where Irian's kiss still burned. "When he could not follow her into Tír na nÓg, he went mad. He built an isolated fortress and became obsessed with the Folk, with magic, with bindings and releasing. He wrote and wrote and wrote, searching for a way to be reunited with his ladylove. And the principle he kept returning to was i gcothromaíocht. Counterpoise." I exhaled. "Tell me you know what it means?"

"That is not a story, colleen." Irian cocked his dark head, the gesture endlessly intimidating. "It is a question."

I scowled. "Do you know what it means or not?"

"I do." His true smile never failed to dazzle me. "I may also know the ending to the story you just began."

I stood straighter. "You do? Tell me."

"I will tell you..." His silver eyes grazed my face. "For a kiss."

Shock and heat flamed through me, followed by swift, icy fury when I remembered the Feis of the Nameless Day. The fox-faced barda, his claws pricking my skin as his fangs tore my lips. And the sleek blue-eyed Gentry who ostensibly saved me... only to demand the same price.

"Why do your people insist on bartering kisses like coins?" I lifted my chin. "Kisses should only ever be given when they have been earned."

"I could never hope to earn your kiss." His canines flashed. "I could only ever hope to steal one."

"Kisses may only be stolen under the most perfect of circumstances." Tension and temptation thrilled through me. "Solemn vows. Shared secrets. Superb sunrises."

"In that case... my story will be better told elsewhere. Meet me here next month, and I will reciprocate my half of the bargain." He started to turn away, then paused. "And, colleen?"

"Tánaiste?"

His smile was sharp. "Come dressed for a party."

He melted into the trees before I could argue. I returned to the Gate to wait for Rogan, but Irian's words shoved against me, like hothouse flowers against clouded glass.

I may also know the ending to the story you just began.

For the first time, I had not even left Tír na nÓg before I longed to return to it.

Chapter Twenty-Five

Saille—Willow
Spring

I had every intention of ending things with Rogan. But spring-time and Eala's dubious requests and Irian's perilous flirtations had wakened something restless inside me. My blood sang songs of damp earth and sweet flowers and endless skies, and I couldn't sleep. So when Rogan crawled into my small bed in the middle of the night, bare-chested and warm-bodied and hungry-eyed, I was slow to push him away.

"Princeling," I whispered, even as his fingers found the hem of my nightclothes and his face nuzzled my throat. "We really shouldn't—"

"Just one kiss, changeling." He brushed my lips with his, send-ing flares of desire tangling toward my core. "Just let me taste you."

And I let him, knowing full well it wouldn't be just one kiss. When his fingertips dragged up my spine and he shifted his weight on top of me, I experienced the briefest respite from the thoughts and worries multiplying inside me. I lost myself to the easy gratifi-cation of a *now* I knew couldn't last long.

It didn't. As soon as Rogan and I rolled apart, spent and sweaty, the thoughts returned with a vengeance. After a fruitless stretch of willing myself to sleep, I left him—snoring gently in my garret bedroom—to pace Dún Darragh's midnight halls and grapple with the maelstrom brewing inside me.

The crumbling corridors swallowed my footfalls. Lit braziers limned cracked columns and sway-backed archways in flickering gold, transforming them to a forest at sunset. A few stray ink-black feathers swirled off into the shadows as I passed the mantelpiece carved in rosettes. I slowed, then kept walking, down a narrow clerestory lined with staring eye-shaped windows, until I reached a long hall draped with tapestries. I'd glimpsed this place during one of my prior explorations but had not taken the time to properly regard it.

The ancient weavings were choked with centuries of dust. Gently, I shook them until particles drifted to the floor like snow. Exquisite threadwork shone out—bold, delicate, striking, eerie.

Trees of glass embracing pale sleeping maidens. An ancient oak, branches hanging low enough to clasp its own twisting roots. Doomed men wearing shackles of bone. Girls with skin like jewels, weaving flower garlands.

Eala. Yearning, adoring blossoms choked beneath bitter leaves when I remembered her silken voice and flaxen hair and hungry, contradictory words. She had inveighed against Mother's mercenary actions, the ambitions of princes, the hegemony of the bardaí. And yet she herself had expressed a desire for power, for *magic*. Her reasons were not groundless—I sympathized with feeling powerless; a tool wielded in a conflict you did not start. But she had tried to use those reasons as a weapon against me—as a way to control *me*. And despite my affinity toward my bright, brilliant sister...that had made me uneasy.

As had her words about Mother, which scratched me like nettles.

She thought of a way to pass along the blame for her exploitation. I always knew exactly who to hate.

An ancient memory surfaced. I'd been nine when Cathair began my specialized training—less than a year after I'd accidentally returned Caitríona to the forest. Only a handful of months after Mother had finally showed an interest in me, beckoning me to her table to eat tidbits from her plate and pet her favorite hound.

I hated Cathair's workshop. The grimoires on the shelves radiated an energy that set my teeth on edge. The jars on his worktables were filled with wet, grim objects—the hand of a dead man, a stillborn Folk fetus, a seven-headed wyrm. And on that particular day, there'd been a metal pail on the cold, dank floors. A pail squirming with live rats. Rats Cathair meant me to murder with my Greenmark.

"They're naught but vermin." He lifted one up by its thick, bald tail and let it dangle in the dim light. It squeaked, revealing long teeth. "Cook will reward you with cake for ridding her kitchen of pests."

But I didn't want cake. Not if it meant exterminating a bucket full of rats. I shook my head, hoping the druid would give up and let me go play outside with Rogan.

But Cathair dropped the rat in my lap. The panicked thing scrabbled up the front of my dress, scratched its way up my neck, and burrowed into my hair. I screamed, grabbing for it. It writhed in my hand, thrashing around to bite my thumb. I flung it instinctively. It smacked against the stone wall with a sick thump, then dropped lifeless to the ground.

"See?" Cathair's smile had been calculating. "That wasn't so hard, was it?"

I dashed over to the animal, gathering its broken body into my palms as my green-dark blood stained its pelt.

"You're horrid!" I shouted at him, tears prickling. "Why would you make me do that?"

"You are soft, little witch. And this world is hard. You must learn how to be strong."

But why did compassion make me soft? I searched for some

argument, some reason to make him leave me alone. But I could think of only one.

I wouldn't fully understand his relationship with Mother until years later, but I knew the queen commanded him. She could stop this. Surely she would, if she only knew about it.

"I'll tell the queen." Hot tears squeezed from my eyes. Where they fell on the rat's limp corpse, moss sprouted, growing thick over its fur. "Last week she told me to call her Mother. She—she *loves* me. I'll tell her you made me do this. And she'll make you stop."

Cathair had stared at the rat in my hands as its tail transformed into a coiling vine bright with multicolored flowers. Then he'd crossed to the door and flung it open.

"Go on, then." The sunlight filtering down the cramped, narrow stairs had looked like salvation. "Go to your *mother*. Tell her of your great concern for vermin. Tell her of my wickedness. Cry in her lap. See how much she loves you then."

For years, I'd thought that a manipulation. A callous challenge meant to exploit the insecurity of a child who'd only just gained a mother. But for the first time, I wondered whether he'd meant it. Whether he'd truly wanted me to go to her, if only to show me what I really was to her. Not a beloved daughter, but a project. A tool being honed. A weapon being forged.

Even loving parents make tools of their children.

Forcibly, I shook out the next tapestry. It depicted a king upon a throne, a shining crown upon his brow. But above him hung a huge carven sword, pointing down. My next worry unfurled.

Rogan. Rogan, who I still loved. Rogan, who had as much as admitted he loved me. Rogan, who was still betrothed to my sister, the woman who suggested I sleep with him. By making such a request of me, Eala had proven how little she cared about Rogan's heart. Or mine. Or even, perhaps, her own.

As his wife, I will require Rogan's love, fealty, and protection. But I don't need his fidelity.

No—Eala did not respect Rogan. She did not honor him. And she certainly didn't love him. But that did not make what I was doing with him any more right.

I shook out the last tapestry. The weaving depicted a man and a woman locked in a passionate embrace between trees of silver and gold. He had hair like midnight; she wore a gown of flames. Above them, stars fell from a blushing dawn.

Perhaps you should *stay away from me, colleen. If not for your sake…then for mine.*

Irian. The feelings I'd thought were repulsion were beginning to transform into fascination. Temptation heated my blood when I thought about his searing palms, his silver eyes, his magnetic voice. Eala and Chandi had both told me he was a monster. He himself had more or less said the same, confirming everything I'd already suspected. He was warped by wild magic, feral after more than a decade alone, utterly *wicked*.

So why couldn't I stop thinking about him?

I looked again at the tapestry. On second glance, the picture was more sinister. For though the couple's lips were locked, each held a ready dagger to the other's back.

I stepped away, disquiet dark as hellebore unfurling in my chest. And with it rose a vine of climbing bittersweet. I knew what I must do.

But decisions made at midnight were best left until daybreak. So I left the tapestries to their secrets and continued wandering Dún Darragh's labyrinthine halls like a dream. An illusion conjured from green-gold daydreams. Something with a seed for a soul, a memory for a face, and woodland whispers for a heart.

❧

I woke the morning of Bealtaine to the scents of warm grass. The windows were flung open, letting in a bouquet of sunlight and fresh air. Wildflowers graced a hundred mismatched jars set on every open space in my room. Cornflower and phlox, daisy and wallflower, wild carrot and milkweed.

"Corra?" I asked the sweet-smelling air. No reply came, but I sensed the edges of a sly grin flitting around the room.

I turned to my bed and met with another surprise. Laid across the coverlet was a row of new frocks, in shapes and colors wondrous as the gowns the swan maidens wore in Tír na nÓg. I gathered the soft pretty dresses up, one by one. A breezy frock made from overlapping petals of blue iris. A slender shift iridescent as a moth's white wing. A dress golden as sunset, trimmed in translucent leaves edging from ocher to plum. And my favorite—an emerald-green gown with dainty lace whispering along the sleeves and the long, narrow train.

"Corra?" I said again—because there was no doubt who had done this. Had they somehow known about Irian's odd request last full moon? *Come dressed for a party.* "Corra, these are—"

I searched for words. Excessive? Impractical? Unbelievable?

"Corra, they're magic. Thank you."

And finally the formless fiend relinquished their modesty and came careening into view, bursting amid the wildflowers in a flurry of petals and pollen. A grand sunflower nodded merrily.

"Dresses impresses!" Corra screeched at the top of their voice. "Dresses impresses, much worse it could be: dresses depresses, we sadly would be!"

I feigned an eye roll as the sprite hurtled loudly around my room, ruffling my hair. But a smile curled the corner of my mouth, even as the prospect of my own heartache grew heavy in my chest.

I changed into the frock Corra had conjured from evergreen dreams. The delicate lace whispered secrets against my bare skin. I let my dark hair fall unbound down my back and plucked a few flowers from Corra's bouquets. Primrose, hawthorn, and marigold were sacred on Bealtaine. They stained my fingertips as I braided them into my hair.

My garden was adorned in spring's bright ribbons and baubles.

The greenhouse was no longer broken and battered, choked and strangled. Now its clear glass panes reflected blue skies dotted with clouds and the rustling foliage of trees in full flower. Vines burst with a flourish of blossoms—musk roses and eglantine. Plump new fruits peered between waxy leaves.

I stepped to the burbling spring at the center of the grotto and tossed a few blossoms onto the pool, whispering:

The Bealtaine fire sends flames to the sun,
The promise of summer warmth to come.
Hazel branch and hawthorn flower
I offer for Brighid's bower.

"Chiardhubh!" Corra trilled, spinning rivulets of water to swallow up the flowers. "It's time! Twigs, branches, and prickers, a bough of black briar. Snap, crackle, and flicker, we want that bonfire!"

I smiled past the pit yawning in my stomach. "You little firebug."

Last week, I'd spent the better part of an afternoon dragging all the detritus of the gardens out into the open, piling fallen branches and dry underbrush and weeds into a huge heap on the lawn sloping up to the dún. Now I bent with my flint and steel, striking golden sparks to smolder in the kindling.

Whump!

I jumped back as blue flames burst from the heart of the bonfire, gathering edges of yellow and orange as they tore through the dried twigs. I stepped another long pace away from the blaze, careful with the ends of my hair and the hem of my dress.

"Corra!" I accused. "I still think that's cheating."

A fiendish, gleeful face grinned from the flames. "What works, chiardhubh, works!"

The bonfire roared, black smoke spooling upward as afternoon striped the long green grass with gold. And I waited—waited for the moment I had been dreading since the last full moon.

The moment was a long time coming. And yet it came too quickly.

"Changeling." Rogan's low voice drifted through the roar and crackle of the fire.

"Princeling," I whispered.

For a long moment, we stared at each other across the flames. He was the first to move, rounding the fire toward me.

"I was waiting for you in the dún." My appearance startled him. A whisper of suspicion rocked him away from me, as if he thought my enchanted dress might bewitch him too. But he recovered himself. Stepped closer. "You should have told me you'd already started."

"Do you remember the first Bealtaine after I became a woman?" I asked softly. I'd been fourteen, and it had been the first holy day when I'd be allowed to leap over the bonfire, hand in hand with a man, if I so chose. Rogan had teased me mercilessly, pointing out various young men in the fiann and extolling their dubious virtues. Secretly, of course, I'd wished he'd be the one to choose me. "You sang me an old song and swore up and down it was true."

"I remember." He grinned. "*The fair maid who, the first of May, goes to the fields at the break of day, and washes in dew from the hawthorn tree, will be irresistible to he who holds her heart.* I'm fairly certain I made it up."

"I know you did." I couldn't muster a smile to meet his. "How you howled with laughter when I tried to sneak into the fortress at dawn, utterly drenched in hawthorn dew and reeking of the cow manure I stepped in on my way back from the fields. And in the end, you were able to resist me quite well."

Rogan's own smile slipped, regret ghosting over his face. "For a while, at least."

"But you see," I continued haltingly. "I have always been at your mercy, in a way that you never were at mine."

He reached for me. "Fia—"

"Let me finish." I held up a hand to keep him at bay. If he got too close—if I let myself touch him—I wasn't sure I'd be able to do this. "I loved you from the moment you brushed snow from my shoulders and warmed my hands in your own. And that love only grew with everything you shared with me—everything from your outgrown boots to your spare coins to your precious secrets. But much as I wished it, my love for you could not transform me into any of the things I wanted to be. Rich. Beloved. Royal. *Human.* I was such a poor fit for you, in every possible way, that any story I told myself that ended with us together necessitated my change." The old hurts needled at me like nettles, but for once I didn't repress the pain. I let it boil to the surface in snatches of resentment and regret. "That didn't stop me, of course—for years I told myself those stories, endlessly. Stories where I was a princess in disguise. A lost heiress. Made lovely enough by Bealtaine dew to attract your attention. But if love demands alteration to exist, is it even love at all?"

Ever since we were children, I'd been able to read Rogan's moods like a book—from his spirited jags of energy to his petulant sulks to his occasional fits of introspection. I'd mapped the way his eyes changed color to suit his temper—aquamarine for surprise, emerald for desire, azure for fury. I knew every expression, every lift of the mouth and narrowing of the eyes. And I'd seen this look on his face only once before.

It was that cursed day over four years ago. The day he'd mounted his tall black stallion and ridden away with his father's fianna. The day he'd said goodbye to me.

This time, it was me saying goodbye to him.

"It doesn't have to be that way, Fia." He closed the space between us in one long stride. He reached out and twisted a dark curl of my hair around his forefinger. "We can make this work—"

"How?" The word abraded my throat. "By sacrificing our dignity? You making a mockery of your marriage vows, while I hide in the shadows as your whore? Should I keep hiding my magic, too, to make you comfortable? Should I keep pretending to be someone else, in the hopes that you will someday forget that I am no one?"

High on his cheek, a muscle jumped. "What are you saying?"

"You know." I swallowed my ire, made my voice gentle. "It was only supposed to be one night. It's time we let go, Rogan."

He leaned down toward me, lifting my chin. I let him kiss me, one last time. We lingered on each other's lips as all the secret things he and I had shared this spring—this *lifetime*—slid against our tongues and clashed between our teeth.

Honeyed echoes of *before*. Hiding from Cook's wooden spoon after she learned we'd put frogs in the stew. Hiding from the hunt, by the brook deep in the forest. Hiding from training, beside the pond, as fireflies flickered to life in the dusk. Heated memories of *now*—desire mingling with the creeping feeling that we didn't fit together as well as we thought. And finally, secret hopes for *then*— for an impossible future that had all but vanished. *Then* tasted the most bitter on my tongue, and I pulled away from Rogan first.

"Fia." His voice broke on my name, and I nearly broke with it. "I will never be able to let you go. You will always have a piece of my heart."

And you will always have a piece of mine, I wanted to say. I wanted to scream it, to write it in the sky, carve it in stone. Because the truth was, part of me would love part of him for as long as I lived. He was my oldest friend, my dearest companion, my first love. But I was starting to understand—he wasn't going to be my last.

"A piece is not enough." My whole body hummed with regret. "I was made of earth and sky and endless waters. I was made to be loved fully, or not at all."

Grief grooved his handsome face. "What am I supposed to do without you?"

"You will always have me, Rogan." I gripped his biceps, firm. "I will always be your friend, your ally. Yours and your lady wife's, too, once she is freed from Tír na nÓg."

His face shifted, confusion and then resentment birthing shadows in his eyes. "So this is about Eala."

"She needs you, Rogan. In the same way I once needed you."

Doubt weighted his gaze. "I mean it, Rogan. She, too, is struggling to get past her difficult beginnings. She needs your strength, your safety, your optimism, in the same way I once did. She needs someone to stand beside her who is steadfast and loyal. Someone who is willing to love her for all that she is, instead of leveraging her for power or status or gold. It may be the thing that saves her. So you have to try."

"To love her?" His words were flat. "I don't know if I can."

"You won't know," I said gently, "until you try. And I know you have not tried."

"Because I still believed in us." His eyes searched my face. "Brighid help me, I still do."

"We were only ever a story we told ourselves, Rogan. The worst kind of story—a story without an ending." I cupped my hands briefly against his face, memorizing the rasp of his stubble against my palm, the planes of his cheekbones beneath my fingertips. "We were never meant for each other."

Turning away from him was the hardest thing I'd ever done. And yet, somehow, it was easier than I'd expected.

Chapter Twenty-Six

I found Irian pacing at the edge of the wood. I'd vowed to maintain my composure around him, but with the spring breeze in my hair and warm air on my arms, the sight of him sent tendrils of restless green to quicken my pulse. My outfit didn't help—Corra's moth-wing gown whispered silky against my skin, pale as cobwebs and delicate as yearning. I clutched my fists in the cascade of white and green gossamer trailing from my waist, even as I sent tiny green vines laddering my bodice and twisting over my collarbones.

It wasn't the fighting leathers and breeches I was used to. But tonight I needed a different kind of armor.

"Irian," I said.

He turned. He, too, was elaborately dressed—his black mantle embroidered in forest green and trimmed in silver. He wore what looked like ceremonial regalia—dark leather armor intricately embossed with silver. The same onyx torc he'd worn at the Feis of the Nameless Day circled his neck, and the Sky-Sword hung sheathed from his waist. But it was not his formal attire that arrested me. It was his perfect *face*. Wonder and want softened his plush mouth and softened the rest of him with it—the harsh angle of his brows easing, the hard line of his jaw blunting. His gaze brushed the floating hem, of my airy dress before grazing up the length of my legs, the curve of my hips, the swell of my breasts, my flower-studded shoulders. Shadows bled away from his face, leaving his eyes incandescent.

Irian was always vexingly handsome. Tonight, the sight of him stole my breath.

"Fia, you look—" He closed the gap between us with a stride, his palm finding mine in the dark. I jolted at the unexpected touch, then froze as he lifted my hand. He bowed over it, poised and formal, before brushing a swift, scalding kiss over my knuckles. "*Exquisite.*"

My tangled veins sparked, sending blood to paint my skin with warmth. "So. What's the occasion?"

He straightened, eyes glittering with a light that might have been anticipation...or trepidation. "A Gentry wedding."

"A *wedding*?" When he'd told me to dress for a party, I'd expected another Folk feis—beguiling, alluring, but a known quantity. A wedding was something else entirely, and I couldn't help but think— fleetingly, fiercely—of *them*. If Rogan and I were successful in breaking Eala's geas, soon enough it would be their turn to wed. And although everything I'd told Rogan on Bealtaine was true, it didn't mean I liked the thought of witnessing their nuptials. Not when just weeks ago, it had been his hands on my waist. His lips on my lips. His—

Confusion and unease and the afterglow of lust burned through me in quick succession. I forced the thoughts away.

"I wasn't invited."

Irian lush mouth quirked. "Neither was I."

"Then why?" I narrowed my eyes at him. "The other Gentry despise you—seek to destroy you. Why would you want to intrude uninvited upon one of their weddings?"

His head tilted dangerously. "I wish to...make a point."

"Exactly how sharp is this point?" I folded my arms over my chest. "Am I likely to get cut?"

"The geas of hospitality is strict," Irian promised. "You will come to no harm."

"But you promised to answer my question from last month." I set my jaw. "You promised to tell me the ending to my story."

"And so I will. After we arrive."

I wavered. "Fine. But don't try and make me dance."

"I doubt I could *make* you do anything, colleen." Reaching behind me, Irian plucked a green tendril trailing from a nearby tree. He twisted the flowering vine over his fingers and held it up between us. "Perhaps you will do the honors?"

I frowned, not understanding.

"It is best if your...extraordinary features remain a mystery to all but me."

I remembered the velvet mask Chandi had conjured for me on the Nameless Day. I plucked the vine from his hand and forced a mocking smile.

"Am I really so loathly that you need to hide my face from your friends?"

"They are not my friends." His expression darkened, the shadows at his back coiling tight against his shoulders. "And know that you are lovely, colleen. Bewitchingly so. Try not to blame me for wanting to keep that beauty all to myself."

I drank down his words like a parched person might swallow water, even as I lifted the vine toward my face. I bade the tendrils to lengthen and twist, creeping around my eyes and sliding against my scalp. The vine had tiny thorns that prickled my skin, but I welcomed the sensation—it cleared my head. Flowers burst along my cheekbones and coiled in my hair like a crown.

"How do I look?"

Something like regret passed behind Irian's eyes. "You look like one of us."

If Irian hadn't bent space and whisked us somewhere else in an instant, I might have known where we were. But from the moment our feet touched down on the bright runnels of moss flooring the forest, the only thing that mattered was how exquisite everything was.

The wedding bower was festooned in a thousand milk-white anemones, illuminated by delicate pink and yellow lanterns. Magnificent piles of food towered on vast banquet tables. Vernal bouquets bloomed in every color imaginable—peonies and dahlias and lilacs. A colossal, unimaginably ancient tree wore gossamer garlands of eglantine and woodbine that tumbled down to trail along the ground. Exuberant sheeries winked around us like captive stars.

But Irian's arrival was met with a silence that trickled through the Folk wedding like acid. Guests and revelers ceased their merriment. Conversation halted. Drinks were set down. The fluting music jangled to an awkward stop. Even behind my mask, I could read the expressions that met our arrival—bewilderment, alarm, outright malice.

Fear threaded down my spine. I longed for my knives.

Irian didn't move. Even here among the elegance and grace of the assembled Gentry, he was tall and devastatingly handsome. He wielded his height and beauty like a weapon. His jaw was sharp as a blade, his shoulders thrown back as if he were marching into battle. Slowly, he held out an arm to me. I gently placed the tips of my fingers upon it. Even through the dark leather of his vambraces, his skin radiated heat.

He stepped forward, and I followed.

Guests fell away before us like sheaves of wheat. Although most of the attention was reserved for Irian—revering and reviling in equal measures—many glances were directed at me. I tried not to wither beneath their regard, lifting my chin like I belonged here.

No one knew I was not of the Folk. How would they know? I didn't even know.

Finally, the gauntlet came to an end. The music resumed with a jaunty reel that sounded like hummingbirds and honey days. Folk

returned to their conversation and their drinking and their dancing. Beside me, Irian dropped his arm. His shoulders relaxed.

"You weren't lying when you said you weren't invited." I tried
for levity and failed.

"No." He slid a glance over his shoulder. Despite his claims
about the rules of hospitality, his vigilance bordered on violence.
"But I should have been."

I shot a nervous glance toward the wedding bower. "You're
not planning to claim their firstborn child or place a geas on their
descendants, are you?"

For the first time since we'd arrived, Irian looked directly at me.
He wore no mask, and his face was frozen into hard, meticulous
lines. He looked as deadly as the first night I'd seen him, and I
suddenly questioned the wisdom of my decision to come to a Folk
wedding on the arm of a dangerous Gentry tánaiste who was a
pariah among his own people. Fear laid cold fingers on my neck.

But then Irian's sensuous mouth curled into a sharp smile.

"Maybe. But only if the wine is unforgivably bad."

꧁ ꧂

The revel whirled around the colossal old tree festooned in lights
and flowers. Irian led me toward it. Its boughs—thick as the trunks
of smaller trees—arched low over our heads, nearly brushing the
ground beneath the weight of millennia. I gazed in awe toward its
canopy, but its branches laddered too high for me to see. I placed my
palm against its mighty trunk. Beside me, at the same time, Irian mirrored my gesture. Impossibly, the tree began *singing*. Music welled up
inside me, as wide and deep and endless as the eons between stars.

Irian lifted his hand and I reluctantly did the same, dragging
myself back to reality. For a moment, my handprint lingered green
upon its brindled bark.

"We call it the Heartwood." Irian's voice was close to my ear.
"Legends say this tree has stood here since the dawn of time and

will stand here at its dusk. All magic is said to pass through its roots and branches. The Flaming Shield was carved from its wood. It is holy to us."

I believed it.

"Many of our ceremonies are performed beneath it. Naming days. Coronations. Weddings. Tithes."

"Here?" My attention sharpened. "Why?"

"Because of the principle you mentioned last month—i gcothro-maíocht." Irian's eyes narrowed to glittering crescents. "My education had barely begun when the bardaí slaughtered my Sept and drove me from my fosterage at Emain Ablach. But this, I remember. It is the principle of balance that governs all magic. It means for whatever power is taken, something must be given."

It was the same thing Chandi had told me at the Feis of the Nameless Day.

"Yet it is more complex than that," Irian continued. "You translated the phrase to mean *in counterpoise*. That is part of it—the cost of magic is usually equal and opposite. Light demands darkness. Heat demands cold."

"What is the other part?"

"The balancing is eternal, but it is not immutable." His gaze slid over my face. "Neither the magic nor its cost is ever fixed. That is why the swans transform back to maidens by night. Why the Treasures must be renewed beneath the Heartwood every twelve years—the original tithe paid again and again. And it is why the price of using the wild magic is so high. Why it warps all it touches."

"Because endless growth without dormancy isn't natural," I guessed. Nature did not thrive in constancy. Everything had its cycle—that truth was engraved on my bones.

Irian nodded. "Gavida forged the Treasures the way he did for a reason. Freed from the natural cycle of regeneration—of rebirth—the power they once contained now violates the most basic principles of magic."

"Wild magic is like summer without winter. Day without night."

An involuntary shiver cascaded down my spine, and I thought sharply of Pinecone crumbling to dust. Of Eimar devoured by the hungry forest. "Life without death."

"Indeed." The flash of his smile did not quite hide bleakness. "But come. Let us leave such grim talk for later. This is a wedding, after all. And the vows will soon begin."

Irian took my hand. Curving upward against the side of the tree was a carven set of narrow steps inlaid with mica and opals. Together, we climbed.

Above, the broad boughs were wide enough to walk on. Hollows carved from the tree's natural bolls boasted pillows of moss and cushions of dandelions. Around us, Folk began settling in the tree or on the grassy sward facing the wedding bower. Irian lifted me down into one of the hollows, behind a garland of milky flowers. The only way to sit comfortably was to lounge, and it brought me uncomfortably close to Irian's long, well-muscled body. I leaned over the lip of the hollow, trying to ignore the press of his shoulder against my shoulder, the way his hand came to rest against the slope of my back, igniting fire along my spine.

Before the heat climbed to my face and gave me away, music swelled from below and the ceremony began. The bride was gowned in green and crowned in white flowers that shone like diamonds in her scarlet hair. The bridegroom wore russet and gold, autumn-warm against his brown skin. They made a stunning couple as they came together beneath the bower.

"This wedding is unusual for the Gentry." I turned toward Irian's low voice. The motion only brought me closer to him—my hip jutting against his thigh, my face angling up to his. He wasn't looking at the happy couple below us. He was looking at me. "It is a love match."

I swallowed. "Do your people not marry for love?"

"Marriage is usually a practical connection. It unites dynasties and breeds strong children. Love is—" He broke off, considered his words. "We Fair Folk tend to be careful with our hearts."

Below, the bride and groom clasped hands. A ribbon of white was looped around their wrists, then a ribbon of green. Purposeful words drifted across the glen toward us, recited in the ancient tongue. Irian intuited I wasn't fluent—he leaned even closer, whispering a translation. The words in juxtaposition—unfamiliar yet familiar, communal yet intimate—clamored secrets against my ribs and conjured promises in my veins.

Blood of my blood
And bone of my bone,
I shall not permit thee
To wander alone.
Give me your heart
And let it be known
That then, now, and after
You are my home.

I shivered. "Do the vows have a meaning?"

"They say there was once a Gentry lady so beautiful none could withstand her charms." Irian's hand flexed minutely against my back. "Against all odds, she fell in love with a handsome mortal warrior. But she could not trust the human loved her for anything but her looks. So she requested he spill his own blood upon the earth to prove his devotion. This he did, gladly. But she was not satisfied. She asked for one of his bones as a token. He happily cut off his little finger and strung it upon a necklace for her to wear at her throat. But still she was not satisfied. She demanded he give her his heart. He willingly tore his still-beating heart from his chest and placed it in her hands. And as he lay dying on the ground, the lady finally knew that he had loved her true."

Leaning my weight on one elbow, I faced Irian fully. The motion rocked me even closer to him—the bodice of my gown flush against his ceremonial armor. His hand rested at the dip of my waist. Shadows brushed my cheeks and collarbones. Our faces were inches apart.

"Was that the ending you promised me?" My voice came out disconsolate. "Did my warrior truly reunite with his ladylove, only to die at her feet?"

"Perhaps. Perhaps not." Irian's low laugh vibrated along my skin. "It is but a story, colleen. One that has been told for hundreds of years among my people. And a story, once told, exists beyond the truth of the thing that inspired it. Perhaps it did not happen the way it is told. Or perhaps *your warrior* was happy to die for love. Who are we to say?"

His twisted words still thrilled through me. "Is that why you are so careful with your hearts? Because the things—people—you love can be a weapon used against you?"

"A heart is powerful magic." Irian's eyes pierced me. "Love can create or destroy. It can be a beginning...or it can be an ending."

I fought for something clever to say, but his closeness consumed me. My gaze dropped to his deliciously full mouth, lips parted in veiled amusement. His hand tensed at my waist. My breath hitched. He leaned down—

The expectant hush below exploded into raucous noise. I startled away from Irian and looked down at the couple, who—now wedded—were locked in a passionate embrace. The assembled Gentry clapped and cheered and sang. By the long banquet tables, oaken casks of mead were tapped with ashen spigots, and tables were piled with cool fruit and hot meat and bread slathered with sweet honey.

Beside me, Irian rose easily. He held out a hand to help me up, but I scrambled up on my own. The hand fell.

"Come, colleen." If I had glimpsed any gentleness in him moments before, it was gone now—replaced by a brutal kind of determination that made me nervous. "It is time I made my point."

Chapter Twenty-Seven

We descended from the Heartwood, then stepped onto the grassy sward where the Folk host had begun to revel in earnest. As before, guests blatantly avoided Irian, stepping out of his path and giving him as wide a berth as possible. Within a matter of moments, a path had cleared between us and the newly married couple merrily accepting well-wishers beneath the wedding bower.

Irian hammered out the softness of his mouth to metal and malice, gathered his shadows around him like armor. Without even glancing down, he held out his arm for me. I accepted, even as tension climbed my spine and clutched at my throat. I considered trying to voice some dissuasion or diversion from the dire intrigue he seemingly had planned. But whatever point Irian intended to make, I was already wrapped up in it. It was too late for me to walk away.

He prowled forward, a blight of shadow among the pastel flowers and sparkling lanterns and brightly clad Gentry. Silence and strain heralded his arrival to the bride and her groom, who looked up from the throng offering them gifts and congratulations. Alarm swirled their gazes—a brisk tempest of hurried conversation passed between them and their wedding party. A young fénnid with scarlet hair who strongly resembled the bride reached for the ceremonial weapon belted at his waist; a golden-skinned, hawk-nosed Gentry who could only be the groom's father swiftly forestalled him with a broad arm across his chest. After a moment, the groom stepped forward, angling himself slightly in front of his new wife, whose lovely face was suddenly troubled.

"I wish I could say we are well met, tánaiste." The groom's voice was carefully flat, his tone just shy of unfriendly. "But I cannot fathom how you have come to be here tonight, on the occasion of my wedding."

"The *how* is rather boring." Irian's stance was easy; his voice, hard. "The *why* may prove to be more interesting."

The bride's eyes glittered. Her hand convulsed against the bodice of her gown.

"Why have you come?" She hurled the words at Irian. "We have no quarrel with you."

"Is that so?" Irian's attention traveled past the groom, to the older Gentry lord. "And you, Dualtach? Lord barda of the Ivy Gate? Did you have no quarrel with the chieftain of the Sept of Feathers—my grandfather and your oath-sworn liege—when you slaughtered him in his bed? Did you have no quarrel with my cousins when you spiked their heads on the cliffs above Gorias? Did you have no quarrel with me when you hunted me like prey across the plains of Mag Mell?"

Above his aquiline nose, the Gentry's yellow eyes grew thunderous. A carrion-scented breeze rippled through the brown-and-gold hair pushed back from his face. No, not hair at all, but burnished *feathers*. Beside him, the bride's brother once more moved to unsheathe his blade. Again, Dualtach waylaid him with an arm I now saw ended in brutally sharp talons. My fingertips tightened on Irian's vambraces, thorns nettling at my fingertips.

Irian might have been made of stone.

"The geas of hospitality protects me and mine," growled the

hawk-eyed barda. "Speak your piece, tánaiste. Then begone. You will enact no vengeance here tonight."

"Vengeance?" Irian's smile was cruel. "I wish no vengeance. Rather, I wish to offer the happy couple a blessing. As is my right."

His words conjured a gale of whispers and murmurs among the assembled Gentry. The bride's eyes flew wider, and she clutched harder at the arm of her new husband.

"No!" Her voice was strangled. "We want no blessing from you. Iarlaith—!"

The groom glanced helplessly at his wife, then over his shoulder at his father, who gave his plumed head a swift jerk. A flash of condemnation crossed the groom's face in the moment before he returned his gaze to us.

"It is indeed his right, my love—he is still heir apparent of the Sept of Feathers. It is as it has always been." His words were fallow, final. "Speak your blessing, tánaiste. Then leave us be."

"I bless you to love one another wholly—and only." Irian's voice was assiduously even, yet a strain of magic sang between his words. A prelude for lost things, an elegy for an aching eternity. "No parent nor sibling nor friend shall you ever love. Not even your children shall ever know your love. You shall only know love for each other—through this life and the next, your souls irrevocably bound. Forever."

The bride cried out wordlessly. Again, she brought her hands to the front of her bodice, and I finally noticed the pleasantly convex shape of her stomach beneath her bridal finery. Horror pulsed through me as she fell to her knees beside her new husband, who sank down to gather her against him. As she began to keen, the rest of their family and friends surrounded them, reaching comforting arms toward the newly wedded—and newly cursed—couple.

Irian cut a sharp, sardonic bow, turned on his heel, and walked away. My feet carried me after him—numbly, dumbly. I glanced over my shoulder at the sorrowful scene, shocked anew by the mayhem Irian had wrought with just a few carefully chosen words.

He had certainly made his point.

By the deserted end of one long banqueting table, beneath the shadow of a lantern-strung oak, I dug in my heels and wrenched my arm from his. Irian paused, then turned. His face was a careful mask of hard, guarded lines, and I swore I sensed his tattoos sharpen and lengthen beneath his black leather vambraces.

"Colleen?" he said evenly.

"You told me you *weren't* planning on cursing their descendants."

"I did not." From the feasting table, he idly picked up an abandoned goblet filled with glittering ruby liquid. He swirled it, then tossed it back in one long swallow. "Besides, the wine really is terrible."

"*Irian*," I snarled.

At the sound of his name, his gaze sliced down to mine, viciously bright and slick with challenge. Like he was *daring* me to chastise him—to scold or berate him for what he had just done. I suddenly wondered *why* he had brought me with him tonight. Why had he made me a party to his vengeance? Made me witness to his mercilessness, his cruelty? His *inhumanity*?

Eala's words from last month crept through me—words Irian had claimed he hadn't overheard.

I would hate to see a girl as softhearted as you outwitted by a man as heartless as he.

I understood. This was a test. Irian was showing me exactly who he was—who everyone knew him to be. Who he himself had told me he was. Perhaps he meant to frighten me. Perhaps he meant to drive me away. Or perhaps—with his peculiar Folk logic—he was being honest with me, as brutally as he knew how.

I sheathed the blade of my righteous anger and made my voice as smooth as his.

"That seemed *particularly* unkind."

"What have I ever done to relay the impression that I am kind?" His mouth curved sardonically. "Please tell me, so I may refrain from doing it again in the future."

"You stole Eala and the other maidens from the bardaí—you

went to great lengths to protect them. You've even tried to break their geas." I searched his eyes for some flicker of contrition or remorse. I found nothing. "You can't be *all* bad."

"Do not mistake good deeds for goodness, colleen." His voice held grim amusement. "I am not a good man. More to the point—I am exactly what *they* made me. Do not feel sympathy for them. They are merely reaping what they have sown."

"But you did not punish those who hurt you." I gestured in the direction of the wedding bower. "You punished their children, cursed their children's children."

"Was I not a child, punished for a parent's sin?" He was calm, callous. "Would my own children, should I have ever sired them, not suffered for being mine? No—they would be just like me. Friendless and feared. Their legacy ground to dust. Their extended families long dead, butchered without cause. What is that, if not a curse?"

I had no ready response.

"Whatever human morality has been hammered into you, colleen...it does not obtain in Tír na nÓg." At last, some measure of compassion warmed his cold gaze. But it was not for the couple he had just cursed. It was for *me*. "Liberate yourself from ideas of heroes and villains, good and evil, right and wrong. Here, we are all villains. Here, there is no judge or jury to decide whether good prevails or perishes; whether evil thrives or dies. There is only balance—in all its infinite permutations."

"And vengeance? Curses?" I whispered, struck sorrowful by the bleakness of his worldview. "Are they balance?"

"How could they be anything but?" He lifted his hand to my face, brushed a scorching thumb against my chin. "Besides, colleen—how can you know what I gave them is not truly a blessing? There are few things more oppressive than a parent's love, as uncompromising as a parent's expectations. Perhaps I have simply set them all free. Perhaps their child will be as wild and wicked as I, and his parents will be grateful they do not need to love him. And perhaps he will be grateful he does not need to be loved."

"You may be wild and wicked, tánaiste." I fought to keep my voice level despite his touch thrilling fire through my veins. "But not even you can be grateful for not being loved."

Irian's hand glided along my jaw to cup my nape, tilting my face up to his. His touch was hot, intimate. But his eyes on my face were searching—winged with distant regret.

"No. Perhaps I am not." He cocked his head, but for once the gesture seemed less threat than invitation. "Dance with me, colleen."

I laughed to hide the confusion sparking against my skin. "You promised you wouldn't ask."

"I said no such thing." That coiled, perilous smile. "Must I beg?"

I tossed my hair. "As tempting as that sounds, I don't dance. Not with anyone."

"But I am dying. May I not demand that which I desire?"

"You're *going* to die. That's different. We're all *going* to die."

"Yes, but I know when."

I rolled my eyes. "Lucky you."

"It is lucky." The intensity in his words sobered me. Silhouetted against the lanterns bobbing between the boughs, his hair was darker than the night sky; his eyes, brighter than the moon. "I know exactly how much time I have left. And I know exactly how I want to spend it."

That was hard to argue with. I swallowed, then held up a finger. "One dance."

He tilted his head. "One dance."

He pulled me back toward the Heartwood, where revelers moved in graceful whirls and spirals on the grassy sward. The music was smooth, sultry—the unearthly instruments singing eldritch through the night. Irian's fingers twined with mine.

A couple spun in front of us, locked in a tender embrace. A sharp burst of familiarity stole my gaze and arrested my pulse. The woman had ice-blond hair knotted in flowering braids down her back. A mane of golden curls spilled over the man's makeshift mask. And his eyes—trained adoringly on his dance partner—were a dark blue-green. The color of river stones.

My eyes latched on to Rogan and Eala, spinning and dipping a few paces in front of us. A thorn of envy pierced my heart. They were... *perfect* together. They matched in a way that he and I never could—never *would*.

Rogan bent to whisper something in Eala's ear. She threw back her head, laughing merrily. He took the opportunity to sweep a tender, sensual kiss against the pale column of her elegant throat.

That hadn't taken long. The thorn withered, growing brittle as it crumbled to dust. I'd been the one to ask Rogan to try harder to fall in love with Eala—I knew that. But I hadn't expected it to happen *instantaneously*. Or to witness it.

I'd promised myself one night of passion with him. A close to a chapter that should never have opened. An end to a story that was veering toward tragedy. But one night had become many—what I had meant to be a farewell had become less a culmination than a complication. And although I'd said goodbye to him... well.

But if Rogan could move on so easily, then there was no reason for me to mourn him. To mourn *us*. There was no reason I shouldn't—

"Colleen?" Irian stepped in front of me, his broad shoulders blocking my view. "What troubles you?"

"Nothing," I said.

"You are a terrible liar." He followed my gaze to Rogan and Eala. A moment of confusion faded behind a sudden blaze of realization. "*Him*."

"No." I didn't know what I was dismissing. Because for so long, it *was* him. "I—"

"You love him." Irian's voice cut through my stuttered denials. "The human prince has your heart."

"No," I said again. "Maybe once, but not now. I—" The organ in question lurched as Irian's words finally registered. "You know about Rogan?"

"Of course I do." Slight derision curled Irian's lip. "His dirty boots tread my demesne; his coaxing words whisper through my trees; his vulgar scent carries on my winds. He is here to break Eala's geas and set the swan maidens free."

My pulse resumed, pumping fear through my veins. "He's only trying—"

"He is welcome to try. I rejoice his efforts. I bear him no ill will." Irian's voice was black metal and broken magic. "But he does not deserve you."

I stared at him. "Why do you say that?"

"Because you love him, yet he is wooing *her*." Shadows unfurled like wings at his back and made a night sky for his moonlit eyes. "If I had your heart, I would not be dancing with another."

A surge of emotion streaked through me—I tasted wet earth and bitter leaves in the back of my throat. I reached out and gripped Irian's arms.

"Show me."

For a long moment, Irian stood motionless. Then his hand on my wrist flicked out, sending me swirling out into the revel. My gown blossomed pale around my knees, and the world blurred into smears of color and light. The music had changed again—drums throbbing like a heartbeat beneath a secretive melody. Swaying figures slid away from us, but I barely noticed anyone but Irian. Beneath the force of his gaze, all my nights with Rogan faded to nothing.

Irian caught me against him, twining my fingers in his as he slid one powerful arm around my waist. If I worried our heights would make dancing difficult, I was wrong. We fit together well. *Too* well. An intoxicating thrill skated along my bones as we began to move—a swaying dip, the world tilting on its axis. We glided across the grass, our steps quiet and sure beneath the hypnotic beat.

The revel melted away, until I was alone with him, caught between the arching branches and the night sky and the trembling light of a thousand lanterns. Irian's eyes did not leave my face, and

I shivered beneath his gaze. I wondered how I'd ever thought his silver eyes cold. They were liquid with heat, igniting my blood. His palms burned my skin. His face tilted down toward mine.

I didn't see the gleaming blade slashing toward my throat until it was too late.

Chapter Twenty-Eight

I rian's shadows moved before I could, shoving me backward.
I stumbled. Fell.

The long silver claíomh sailed through the space I'd been standing, its tip embedding in the soil by my feet. Screaming rent the air.

I wondered if it was me.

The red-haired Gentry warrior wrenched the sword back up, swung it again. This time, Irian lunged forward and blocked it with his shoulder, the sharpened metal skidding off his ceremonial armor. He caught the next strike between his crossed gauntlets. He twisted his arms, hauling the blade out of the attacker's grip and flinging it away. The sword disappeared into the crowd of wedding guests, who scattered like leaves in a high wind.

The Sky-Sword appeared in Irian's hands so swiftly I never saw him draw it. With smooth, deliberate control he drove it through the Gentry warrior's throat. The bride's brother choked, coughed, grappled at the shard of midnight splitting him in two. Irian twisted the blade, slashed sideways. The young man's head lolled off his neck. His mangled body dropped to the ground. Blood spurted out, staining the delicate moss black.

Instinct overcame shock, and I pushed myself to my feet. The
guests had all dispelled, and the figures who replaced them were
not there to dance. Blades rang from scabbards and glinted in the
scattered light of shuddering lanterns. Many of these warriors also
had scarlet hair; a few sported glaring yellow eyes and aquiline
noses.

Ah. Another point being made.

"You flout the geas of hospitality? You attack the tánaiste of the
Sept of Feathers at a wedding beneath the Heartwood?" Distaste
contorted Irian's face. "Far have you fallen from the dignity of your
ancestors."

The fénnidi who moved toward him were grim.

"Not as far as you," snarled one as he hefted his weapon.

Below us, the earth shuddered. Discarded bouquets scudded
across the ground, driven by a wind that struck my nostrils with the
faint odor of rot. Irian flexed his arms, and beneath his onyx torc,
tattoos lengthened and sharpened, black as his shadows. Thunder grumbled above the canopy of the Heartwood, and tendrils
of lightning crackled along the length of the Sky-Sword. Briefly,
Irian glanced at me. His eyes no longer shone like moonlight—they
flashed like steel. His expression warped—regret chasing anger
and humiliation across his face—before it settled into feral, violent
lines.

"Chandika," he said in the moment before the men surrounded
him. "Take her and *go*."

Cool, slender fingers closed around my arms and dragged me
away. If I'd had a moment longer to think—if I hadn't still been
in shock from the attack and surprised by Chandi's sudden
presence—I would have fought harder to stay. As it was, I tried to
wrench my arms out of her grasp, craning my neck to look back
over my shoulder. But I didn't have my knives or my armor, and
I was dressed in a stupid gown that caught around my legs and
threatened to trip me. Surely I could still do something, *help* in
some way—

"Stop fighting me!" Chandi dragged me into the waiting forest. Flowers and leaves showered down around us as we fled, and between the trees, faces stared with hollow eyes. Silver branches pulsed with molten veins. A creature with a face like the shifting shadows on a forest path thrust bright antlers into the dim.

Behind us, steel rang against steel. And one of the swords was singing.

"I can help him," I protested.

"You can't." Chandi slowed, finally looked at me. She, too, wore wedding finery—an exquisite lilac gown that made her eyes glow like suns. "You would only get in his way."

"I know how to fight—"

"He would be trying to protect you, instead of himself." Chandi's voice was flat. "Don't forget—if he dies, we die too. We need to get to the Willow Gate."

Chandi set a brisk pace, threading a path known only to her. We passed pale-skinned ash trees crowned in silver. Waterfalls that sounded like the laughter of children. Gold-veined crystals the size of houses jutting out of the earth. We scrambled down a rocky escarpment that ate pieces of our gowns and skinned one of my calves. Worry pounded through me all the while.

Finally, we passed some invisible boundary and Chandi stopped abruptly, the line of her shoulders relaxing briefly before she rounded on me.

"What were you doing parading around with him like that?" Her amber eyes were ablaze. "I warned you not to get too close to him."

I set my jaw. "And I appreciated the warning."

"But you chose to ignore it."

"I chose—" I rubbed a hand over my forehead. My leg hurt, and I needed to get out of this dress. I didn't have to explain myself to her. "I chose to use the information to my advantage."

Chandi's voice rose. "What advantage?"

"I need him, all right?" I hissed.

"For *what*? You're here to break the geas on us, not fraternize—"

"That's not why I'm here," I interrupted, and Chandi fell silent. "Rogan or I *will* find a way to break the geas cursing you as swans. But that's not why I'm spending time with Irian."

"The Sky-Sword." Understanding swept over her face, followed by betrayal. "For yourself. That's why you wouldn't give it to Eala."

"Not for myself." I motioned for her to keep her voice down. "For the *queen*. For *Fódla*. To feed her people, to vanquish the plague, to defeat the sea raiders."

"So you're hoping if you tryst with him, Irian will *give* you the damned thing? Because that's never going to happen."

"I'm trying to figure out how to *take* the *damned thing* without sacrificing all your lives and Fódla's future in the process." I blew out a breath. "The Sky-Sword must be renewed at Samhain, otherwise its wild magic will go free, the Gates will fall to the mercy of the bardaí, and chaos will reign in both realms. Irian plans to sacrifice his life to ensure that never happens. But if he dies, *you* die. And I can't let *that* happen."

"Fine. But unless you think swapping saliva with a Gentry heir is going to break our geas, then I still have no idea what you're doing getting so close to him."

The sound of heavy footfalls turned both our heads. A towering dark-haired figure appeared from nowhere, stumbled on a root, then sagged against a tree.

Irian's mantle was torn, his armor badly damaged. Blood drenched him, and at least some of it was his—silver rivulets dripped down his mantle and spattered the sharp angle of his cheek. I hitched up my skirts and ran toward him.

"Irian," I breathed. "Are you hurt? Did you—"

He barely looked at me. His gaze focused over my shoulder. "Chandika?"

"Yes?"

"A moment alone, please."

She hesitated. I gave her a small nod. I was fairly certain she rolled her eyes at me before withdrawing into the forest.

"What happened back there?" I demanded. "Did the bride's family...?"

"Know this, colleen—it was never my intention for this night to end in violence." He coughed, doubled over. His arm snaked around his ribs. "Another time, I might have let them live. But they tried to hurt *you*. So I killed them all."

He closed the distance between us and caught me around the waist. I suddenly remembered everything I knew about him. Things I had told myself to remember but had begun to forget. Things he had told me in his own words.

Here, we are all villains.

He was wild and wicked. Dangerous. I should be terrified of him. And the shrinking human part of me was.

But the other part of me? The part made from thorns and venom and bad omens?

That part of me thrilled at his words, his closeness, his touch. That part of me never wanted him to let me go.

With a push, he pinned me against a tree. My bare back rasped against the rough bark, and I gasped. He pressed closer, until his knee nudged between my thighs, his shredded breastplate dug into my bodice, and his broad shoulders blocked my view. The only place I could look was up.

Irian's eyes were nailed to my face. Even blood-spattered and exhausted, shuddering with pain and adrenaline, he was magnificent.

"Once—in a time of sunlit mornings and barefoot afternoons—there was a boy." He spoke swiftly, intently. "He was not always careful where he played. One day, in the wood, he stepped upon a thorn. Though small, it drove deep beneath his skin—too deep to remove without pain. So the boy ignored it, hoping it would come out on its own. It did not. Instead, his skin grew around the thorn. Every step the boy took, he felt the agony as that thorn dug deeper and deeper into his flesh. Soon, the wound festered. A healer was finally called. The healer had to carve into the boy's skin with a knife, clean the wound with burning salt water, and cauterize it with fire and steel. The scar left behind was jagged and unsightly. If the boy had but plucked out that tiny thorn when it first pierced him, all that pain could have been avoided."

I tried to piece together the meaning behind his words. But I could barely think beyond the weight of his gaze, the heat of his proximity. "What are you saying?"

"That prince does not deserve you. He is a thorn beneath your skin. Cut him out of your heart. Then cauterize the wound."

Irian leaned down. Hesitated for barely a second. Then slid his bloody hand beneath my chin, lifted my face toward his, and captured my lips with his mouth. He kissed me slowly, then ferociously. Bruisingly. He tasted like cold metal and ice water, night at the edge of dawn. His hand on my jaw trembled, and the forest around us vibrated with it.

Before I had a chance to kiss him back, it was over. He stepped away, clutching his ribs where silvery blood seeped through his mantle. I lifted a hand to my scorched lips.

"Apologies, colleen." A ghost of a smile spasmed over his face. "There were vows. One or two secrets. But I could not quite manage the sunrise."

Irian disappeared into the night without another word.

Chapter Twenty-Nine

Huath—Hawthorn
Late Spring

Fledgling summer took flight—buoyant gold-blue afternoons strung one after the other like jewels on a necklace. And I—I was bewitched, bewildered, delirious.

I forced myself to train. I ran hard intervals around the lough, then spun through my forms and variations with the set of newly forged skeans that'd finally arrived from Finn Coradh. I worked long hours in the garden, catching up on the weeding I'd neglected. I pruned overzealous lilacs. I seeded late summer crops. I thinned the fruit trees for autumn's harvest. And when the lengthening days finally faded toward night, I repaired to the archive, meandering through the ancient cares and worries of someone long dead, in order to avoid my own.

After the Treasures of the Folk, wrote the ancient warrior in his looping, runaway script, *a heart is the most powerful magic in Tír na nÓg.*

Yet no matter how hard I worked—how exhausted I made myself—my dreams tangled with visions.

A colossal tree singing songs I almost recognized.

A deadly sword slicing down.

A searing kiss stolen beneath melting trees.

Waking was little better. No matter how much I controlled my body, my thoughts wouldn't stop spiraling, always to the same place.

Irian.

The way he'd spoken to me after bestowing his dubious blessing—candid, callous, cruel. *I am not a good man.* The way he'd danced with me—as if I were less a girl than a goddess. The way he'd kissed me—feral, intense, tender. Temptation painted shades of honeysuckle and poppy on my skin.

Morrigan, how I *wanted* him. I shouldn't. But I did.

But he wasn't the only thing troubling me. Irian's words beneath the Heartwood had lashed my thoughts into tortured patterns I struggled to untangle.

"Corra?" I called, sitting back in my chair. It was past midnight—torches guttered in their sconces. I knew I should go to bed, but a theory was coiling between my ears—one I wanted to voice before it lost its gleam. "Are you there?"

Corra coalesced into a carven otter, who flicked its rounded ears. "Dark sky, what hour is nigh?"

"A bargain, fiend." I leaned over, reaching into a drawer for something I'd been tinkering with over the past few weeks. "I have something for you. I'll give it to you . . . in return for one completely honest answer to any question I ask."

"What is it?" Corra's otter wriggled its stocky webbed legs. "Riches? Treasure?"

"Not quite." I smoothed my fingers over a rough collection of sticks held together by bits of twine and ribbon, then set it on the desk. Woodworking had never been my strong suit, but I'd done my best to build a little manikin—a strange little figure twice the length of my palm, cobbled together from straw and sticks, with little beads for eyes and a dried red berry for a mouth. "If you ever need to speak with me, and there are no carven walls or tree knots nearby . . . perhaps this will do instead."

On the wall, the otter froze. The tiny manikin shivered to life, scattering bits of straw and thread over my lap. Corra gave their uneven limbs an experimental shake, then turned gleaming eyes to mine.

"Wicked mistress," giggled Corra, their red-berry mouth twisting with mirth. "We've not had a body in a very long time. Ask your question, and we promise to answer truthfully."

I knew the ways of the Folk—a truthful answer did not necessitate a complete one. Corra would find a way to evade any question as direct as *What are you?* or *Who wrote the journals left here?* I rolled phrases over my tongue, searching for the right one.

"When we came here, you asked us to rebuild the greenhouse, renew the gardens, celebrate the high holy days. Why?"

"The cycle of life, the ebb and the flow." The little manikin clicked their knobby knees and peered up at me. "The magic of nature—you reap what you sow. You give; we take: a seed to plant, a pie to bake."

"So my work in the garden regenerates your magic." Corra's answer confirmed my suspicions—even here, the principle of balance was at play. But it also sparked a thousand other questions. "But what is that magic? *Why* are you here?"

"One question, chiardhubh!" The little manikin pranced off, gleeful.

I cursed. That manikin had taken me weeks. I should have bargained for more questions.

⁂

I saw Rogan from time to time. We still lived together, after all. Whenever our paths crossed, he was extremely polite, exceedingly helpful, and extraordinarily detached.

If I missed him, I refused to admit it to anyone. Least of all myself.

He is a thorn beneath your skin. Cut him out of your heart. Then cauterize the wound.

Chapter Thirty

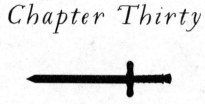

The moment I crossed into Tír na nÓg, apprehension and desire and a traitorous shiver of shyness raced through me. I sucked in a deep breath of balmy night air, waiting for Rogan to wend through the trees after Eala before I willed my rooted feet to move.

My struggle didn't last long. Irian appeared, wraithlike, between the trees, his tall, shadowy figure blocking the path a pace in front of me. I jerked back a step, fighting to calm my suddenly pounding heart.

"You startled me," I gasped.

"I know." Moonlight struck his eyes, transforming them into chips of opal. "After the events of last month, I thought you might try to avoid me."

I lifted my chin. "Do you think me so easily frightened?"

"I hoped you would not be." The expectant slant of his smile unsteadied me. He held out a hand. "Join me."

My pulse sped. "We're not crashing another wedding, are we?"

"That does seem unwise." His smile widened. "I have no nefarious designs, colleen. I promise you that."

I believed him. I grasped his large, hot palm and let him lead me into the wood.

Irian didn't speak as we threaded through the trees. I kept my eyes on the supple movement of his back and tried not to notice how the fabric of his dark mantle stretched tight over the broad lines of his shoulders. Or how he slid glances at me, as though I was something precious he was afraid to lose. Emotions raced through me, as fleeting and insubstantial as the flimsy clouds veiling the moon.

Curiosity. Hazy confusions of alarm and appeal. Furtive tendrils of desire. And the creeping knowledge that the reasons I'd been sent to Tír na nÓg were beginning to fade behind the veil of my own selfish wants.

Abruptly, Irian halted and put a finger to his lips. His eyes were intent across a clearing in the wood. He slid into a crouch beside a leafing ash and beckoned me close. I sidled up to the trunk. His palm wrapped around my forearm, tugging me down beside him in the brush—close enough that our thighs pressed up against each other. I tensed and dared a sidelong glance at him. But he wasn't looking at me—his gaze was trained across the narrow glade.

"What is it?" I whispered.

"There." He pointed between shifting patterns of moonlight.

"I don't see anything."

Carefully, Irian moved behind me, lowering his head next to mine and wrapping his arm around my shoulder. I tried to breathe normally as the solid muscles of his chest pressed against my back, seeping heat through our clothing. His sharp scent—like ice-chased water and cold steel—washed over me. I tried to focus—focus on anything but the rough brush of his jaw against mine, the tickle of his short hair against my cheek, the thunder of his heartbeat between my shoulder blades.

He pointed once more. "Do you see them now?"

I gazed across the glade, letting the calmness of the nocturnal forest wash over me. My breathing ebbed in time to the flow of nature, slowing my leaping pulse and cooling my skin.

I saw the doe first. She was poised and lovely, with depthless eyes and a constellation of white dots scattered across her brow.

She knelt beneath a spreading oak, her forelegs tucked beneath her. She wasn't alone.

Her tiny fawn was brand new. Spindly legs tipped in dainty hooves sprawled on the leaves as she struggled to stand. Bright white spots ran in uneven lines down the curve of her chestnut back; her coat was still dark and damp from her mother's vigorous washing. Her bright fluff of a tail twitched and flicked as she wobbled, finding balance in her new world.

Time slowed as the pair danced through the ancient choreography of new life. I sensed the rhythm of their bonding, the joining of two creatures in a shared closeness. Until the fawn was old enough to fend for herself, she would rely on her mother for everything— from food to shelter to protection from predators. And the doe— she would give her child everything. Her milk. Her love. Her life, if it meant protecting her fawn's.

A fist of sorrow gripped me. Had I ever had this? Had I ever been held, nurtured—*loved*—in the way only a mother could love her child? Or had I been *made*, as Cathair had always told me? *Other*—outside the infinite circle of birth and death.

The queen loved me—I knew that. But I suddenly—achingly— wished I'd had *this*. To be held by a mother like life held us all— loose in the palm of its hand, nurturing yet unyielding.

Eventually, the deer snuggled down into the long grasses, folding long legs beneath them. I reeled my attention back in to find myself kneeling in the underbrush, captured in the hot circle of Irian's arms. His breath was soft and deep. The midnight hum of nature had lulled us both.

But when I shifted my gaze toward his, I found he wasn't watching the deer—his quicksilver eyes were trained on my face. He lifted a hand to brush an errant strand of sable hair off my cheek. We were close enough for me to feel the brush of his writhing shadows, count the lashes lying like ink along his high marble cheekbones.

"This has made you sad, colleen." His voice hummed. "Why?"

The intrusive question dispelled my meditative state. I stood so fast I knocked my head against a branch. Leaves fluttered down as I stared at him, wondering whether this was some new game—some calculated seduction to follow on the heels of the kiss he'd stolen last month. Irian looked taken aback by my reaction; his thumb skated unconsciously over the hilt of the Sky-Sword belted at his waist.

"Apologies, colleen." His jaw tightened. "I only thought you might like to see the newborn fawn."

"I've seen fawns before, Irian." My words came out blunted, harsh. "They are easily born and easily slain."

"Yes." A muscle jumped high on his cheek. "And yet precious nonetheless, if only because they remind us of our own fleeting mortality."

If the words were meant to disarm me, they served their purpose. I kept forgetting—Irian was *dying*.

Cathair had told me the Folk lived long, ageless lives—yet because of the Treasure he'd inherited, Irian's natural life span had been cut short. I wondered—perhaps for the first time—whether my own Folk blood granted me some unforeseen longevity. I shook away the thought—the question of my own mortality meant nothing to the thousands of Fódlan citizens dying of plague, of war, of famine.

"As compelling as your existential dread may be," I snapped, "we had a bargain. Do you have a story for me, tánaiste? Or has your usefulness run out?"

"I see my efforts at subtlety are lost on you." Irian stood briskly. "I have two stories for you, colleen. One of magic, and one of desire. I will only ask one story from you in return. But I decide what I want to know. Are we agreed?"

I experienced a burst of regret for my harsh words, and a flash of anger toward his. But I held his gaze and said, simply, "Agreed."

"Once—in a time of falling stars and terrible prophecies—an heir was born to the Sept of Antlers." I frowned—he had already told me Deirdre's story. But I didn't interrupt as he continued.

"Hidden in her garden, she discovered a secret about herself—a secret she guarded jealously, if only because there was no one to tell it to. The secret of her anam cló—her soul form."

"Her *what*?"

"Her animal avatar." Irian's eyes glittered. "Among the lineages of the Septs, shape-shifting was considered a mark of power. Prestige. Those rare few who possessed an anam cló were revered for their ability." He paused, as if considering his next words. "The little boy who frequented Deirdre's garden was never supposed to see her transform. But he witnessed his friend change, and he saw what form her anam cló took."

Caught between moonlight and shadow, Irian was a study in contrasts—dark shadows, bright eyes; black hair, marble skin. I could not decipher his expression.

"What was it?"

"It was a doe."

Surprise jerked my gaze back toward the deer and her fawn. But the dainty animals were invisible amid the undergrowth. "You told me Deirdre died."

"She fell from a great height in her sorrow. The wild magic was released from her lost Treasure. Death was assumed, but no body was ever found." Carefully, he stepped closer, looming over me. "If you have been paying attention, then you have surely guessed that Deirdre is who you remind me of. That night on the beach— she was who I thought you were, the first time I saw your face. The color of your hair, the timbre of your voice, the substance of your magic. Perhaps, if she somehow survived her fall, you might be—"

"What? Her...daughter?" The notion shocked a laugh out of me. But Irian wasn't joking, and his expression sobered me. "And my father?"

"The only man she ever gave herself to. The human king who stole her heart and set in motion two decades of misery for both the Folk and human realms."

That, I couldn't laugh at. His words struck me squarely between the shoulder blades, cowing me. I reached out to steady myself against a tree, only to find Irian's huge hands bracing my weight against his.

"It is only a theory, colleen." His low voice gentled me. "But you are the right age. A child born to both worlds has not been recorded in living memory, but you—you seem neither fully Folk nor fully human. Perhaps you have some memories…?"

"None." The word gasped out of my tight lungs. Moments ago, Irian's words had seemed absurd and impossible. But now the notion squeezed my chest with hard, dark roots, seeking the softest parts of me with devious little fingers. Deirdre of the Sept of Antlers, my mother? Rían Ó Mainnín, my father?

Eala, my *true* sister. Bound in blood, not just in love. Sired by the same father, raised by the same mother.

But the rest of it made no sense. If Deirdre had not died, then why had the wild magic of her Treasure been freed? Unless she destroyed the Heart of the Forest herself. And if she had been pregnant by the high king and lived long enough to birth me, then how and where had she raised me? And why—oh, *why*—would she have abandoned me in the human realm, where I would more likely be killed than kept, burned than be loved?

"It's impossible." My voice came out bare edged and brusque.

Irian's candescent eyes burned. "Colleen—"

"I understand why you'd want to believe your friend still lives." My words were sharp enough to cut. Anger welled inside me—at him, for planting this idea in my mind, and at myself, for letting it take root in my heart. "But this is a cruel tale to tell. People do not return from the dead. Tragedies do not have silver linings. And I have never been a princess in disguise."

Irian tilted his head. "I have upset you again."

"No." My denial was swift. I schooled my features—I didn't want him to see how much this had indeed affected me. "I simply know when a story doesn't have a happy ending."

He showed his teeth in what might have been a smile—or a snarl. "Then I fear you will dislike my next tale."

Although the night was balmy and still, Irian's shadows twisted and churned behind him. Again, his thumb skated over the hilt of his sword—the only unconscious gesture I'd ever seen him make.

"I have disliked all your tales, tánaiste. That hasn't stopped you before."

"Very well." His eyes glittered with unfamiliar wariness. "Once—in a time of war and mayhem and dying magic—there was a boy. He was young, arrogant, violent, and selfish. He took things that did not belong to him, built things he should not have built, made decisions that were not his to make. Because of what he did, he was doomed to be alone. But neither age nor loneliness improved him—they only made him worse."

He slid a hand under my chin, lifting my face up toward his. Heat sang from his fingertips into my suddenly sparking veins.

"I am still arrogant, colleen. I stole a kiss from you last month— I believe you liked it, as I liked it. I believe you desire me, as I desire you. And in the few months I have left of my worthless life, I am arrogant enough to believe I could make you happy. If not in love, then at least in lust."

I flushed, praying the moonlight bleached the stain from my face. My eyes slid helplessly to his lips. Last month, he'd tasted like spilled blood and desperate desire. I wondered what he tasted like tonight.

"I am also still violent." The blade of his jaw sharpened. "I am tempted to kill that prince of yours, simply for ever daring to hurt you. So the story I would ask of you tonight is this—why should I not?"

My tongue grew hot and heavy in my mouth. Conflicting emotions raveled me raw—desire and disquiet and the faintest feather of fear.

"Once—in a time of small hands and feet and huge, loud grown-ups—there was a changeling girl." It was a story I'd told myself a thousand times, with a thousand different endings. It was shockingly easy to tell it to Irian. "She had just one friend in all the world—a little prince with whom she shared everything. Her meals, her small bed, her deepest secrets. But as they grew, so too did the changeling and the princeling change. The love they shared as friends became something more. They fought it, for they were never meant for each other. Later, they stopped fighting. But still, they were not meant for each other. They parted. But not without hurt."

I searched Irian's face for understanding. "Yes, the prince hurt the changeling. But she hurt him too." I remembered his story from last month. "They left painful pieces of themselves embedded like thorns beneath each other's skin. We have cut the pieces out. We have cauterized the wounds left behind. But...the scars remain."

"I am also still selfish, colleen. *Very* selfish." Irian's palm slid down my throat to rest over where my heart beat erratically. "When you give yourself to me, I want all of you. I am not willing to share."

My green-dark pulse throbbed. I tried to think of something to say, but thorny vines of indecision twined up my spine and silenced my words. Eala's warnings echoed through me: *I would hate to see a girl as softhearted as you outwitted by a man as heartless as he.* Perhaps this *was* a calculated seduction—nothing more than a predator's illusion of candor designed to disarm. Why else would Irian pursue me? There was nothing to be gained by making love to me—I had no riches, no crown. His magic dwarfed my own.

Another voice inside me whispered a treacherous alternative, an alternative Irian himself had denied: He couldn't be *all* bad. After all, he was admitting his flaws to me—*his feelings*. He was confessing that he wanted me. The thorny vines climbing my spine grew tiny buds of perilous desire.

A burst of daring made me sweep my hands up his chest, rigid beneath my seeking palms. I grazed my fingertips over his shoulders to tangle in the soft black hair at the nape of his neck. He made a noise deep in his throat and curved his palms around my waist. I tilted my face to his, registering the faint surprise making diamonds of his eyes.

He had not been sure I would return his feelings.

"Another story without a happy ending, tánaiste?" I said.

"Perhaps the unhappiest ending of all." He bent, brushing a simmering kiss against my mouth. He tasted like caged lightning and cold nights, and my skin throbbed where he touched me. "But that does not matter so much now, with the story only just begun."

The buds inside me blossomed, dark and lovely, their heady perfume as intoxicating as Irian's searing kisses. And I no longer noticed their thorns scratching a resigned warning against my thrumming skin.

Chapter Thirty-One

Duir—Oak
Early Summer

Rain drenched Dún Darragh and churned the lough to froth. I was grateful for the rotten weather. Golden summer was all languid temptation—long days and endless warmth creating the illusion of unlimited time. But the looming clouds reminded me that this season—like all others—was transient. I knew it would pass more quickly than I expected. Samhain was but a bare handful of months away, and I was no closer to breaking Eala's geas, finding magic for Fódla, or saving Irian from his doom.

I blamed *him* for that. He was too captivating—and I, too susceptible to his charms. I constantly reminded myself of all the reasons I couldn't—*mustn't*—pursue our shared attraction, but every argument grew flimsier by the day.

He was wicked. I'd met humans far more violent, arrogant, and selfish than he.

He was a monster. If magic made a monster, then I was one too.

He'd likely be dead by Samhain. I was no stranger to death. And I found I was not one to begrudge him the desire to live fully, if only for a few more months.

And maybe he'd been right—maybe I was still bleeding where I'd cut Rogan from my heart. But I'd begun to wonder whether Irian's scorching kisses might be the very thing to cauterize the wound.

That, and smoothing over the jagged edges lingering between me and Rogan. Part of cutting him out of my heart had to be forgiving him for the choices he was always going to make.

❧ ⁓ ❧

"Princeling."

Rogan jolted at the sound of my voice. He was training bare-chested in the dún's echoing great hall—rain lashed at the windows and hammered at the door. And yet the trousers hanging low around his hips displayed the golden, sweat-slick topography of someone who was no stranger to sunshine. He stopped moving through his sequences, sheathed his claíomh. His hands flexed, then fell loose at his sides.

"Changeling."

"I have something for you." I laid a leather-bound notebook stuffed with folded pieces of parchment on the table. "Well. For Eala."

"What is it?" Wariness darkened his eyes. "Folk spells?"

"It's no grimoire—there are no spells or incantations. But it does speak of magic and how power is bound up in the natural balance of growth and rebirth. It speaks of binding and unbinding." I tapped the cracked leather, still unsure whether I was willing to give away any of the ancient warrior's precious words, even to free my sister. But I had to put what I'd learned to use—otherwise I had truly wasted my time. "And it speaks of the power of a heart given in love. The kind of magic that might be accessed even by a cursed human, trapped amongst the Folk."

Rogan was staring at me like I'd lost what precious little sanity I had left. I patted the book once more.

"It's all in there. Just give it to Eala—perhaps she will find use for it."

"I will." He looked down at the book. Hesitated. "Are we still friends, changeling?"

"Always." My breath caught on a splinter of sorrow. I smiled past it. "As promised."

"Then as a friend, let me extend you a warning." Rogan's eyes were still lowered; on the table, his suntanned hand curled into a fist. "Stay away from the Gentry tánaiste who holds the swans captive. He is too dangerous to...dally with."

The thorn in my chest grew into a thicket, scratching my ribs with acrimony. Those were Eala's words—I knew they were. Yet they bothered me even more coming from Rogan than they had coming from my sister. I had never been Rogan's peer in the eyes of the world, but between us we had always stood as equals. I could beat him in a fight, drink him under the table, match him easily in wit. How dare he patronize me, as if I did not know my own mind?

"Is that a warning?" My voice was cold. "Or a command?"

His gaze jerked up to mine, bitter blue and jealous green. "If it was the latter, would you obey?"

"You are in no position to command me," I snapped. "You are neither my brother nor my father. You will never be my husband. And you are not yet my king."

"You're right—I am none of those things." His eyes flashed with resentment. "But if a heart given in love is indeed powerful magic, then I beg you, Fia—guard yours. I understand how bewitching Tír na nÓg can be. Especially for...someone like you. But you do not belong there. You do not belong with *him*."

"Stop." His words sharpened my resentment to a knife's edge. *Someone like you.* There it was—the truth at the heart of everything. No matter how much I'd changed myself to be loved, I would never be anything more than a changeling—not even to Rogan. Once, I would have lashed myself into a frenzy trying to prove how human I was—how little my Folk blood mattered.

But I wasn't human. And my Folk blood *did* matter.

Tír na nÓg was bewitching. But no longer in a way that felt dangerous—in a way that felt familiar, like a long-forgotten dream painted in sweeps of fading color. Not home, perhaps—but neither was Fódla. Perhaps I was born of two worlds. Maybe I didn't belong anywhere. But that meant I was free to claim either. Or neither. Or both.

Regardless, the choice was mine—and mine alone.

"I appreciate the warning, princeling." I forced icy calm into my tone. "But I will hear no more of it. Give that book to your princess. Give *her* your love, your attention, your concern. I am perfectly capable of looking after myself."

Chapter Thirty-Two

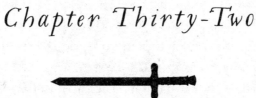

The storms had ended by the full moon, but Tír na nÓg echoed with their memory—heavy branches fallen over the path, trunks darkened with moisture, beads of water sliding down the veins of leaves. The brook beneath the willow was swollen and white capped.

The moment I split away from Rogan, I began to run. I hurtled through the night, then skidded to a stop in the wet loam when the path to the lough was blocked by a group of girls. The swan maidens stood together in a loose semicircle, clad in rippling, sparkling gowns. I scanned their faces—Chandi was the only one I knew by name. I counted as I kicked mud off my boots.

Eleven.

Eala wasn't with them. I exhaled, disappointment and traitorous relief twisting through me.

"You're in a hurry," remarked Chandi. "What's the rush?"

Making up for lost time, I wanted to say. Instead, I shrugged and tried to push past them. But the girls surrounded me in a giggling mass, pulling off my damp mantle and unbraiding my hair and even bending down to unlace my boots.

"Hey!" I protested. "What are you doing?"

"You've been spending too much time with *him*." Chandi nodded at the shadowy fortress. She lifted clusters of starflowers to braid against my scalp. "We claim you tonight."

"But—"

"Girls only." Chandi stepped back. My clothing shifted—wool and leather transforming into smooth fabric and stiff boning.

The kirtle Chandi imagined up for me was the most revealing gown I'd worn yet in Tír na nÓg. The slick, sultry fabric clung to my every contour, leaving my arms and most of my bosom bare. Black boning nipped in at a narrow waist and twined up around my torso like bare branches. My legs flashed white below a sheer emerald skirt.

"No." I squeezed my eyes shut and wished vainly for my own clothes. "Absolutely not."

"Please?" One of the other swan maidens pouted. She wore a blood-red dress slit to the thigh and heavy kohl around her eyes. "It'll be fun."

"We have so much to show you," said another—a honey blonde with dimples. Her coin-bright gown glittered like serpents' scales when she moved.

"The first full moon after Midsummer is when the Folk celebrate the Feis of the Wild Hunt." Chandi braided more stinging flowers against my scalp and lowered her voice. "There is something I would show you."

"What?" I breathed.

"Magic." Her eyes were serious. "Magic we humans cannot touch."

I stopped fighting her prickling fingers. "Why?"

"Just come with us. It might prove useful in breaking our geas."

I wasn't convinced. "The last Folk revel I attended nearly ended with my head on the ground."

"That only happened because the Folk didn't know who you were—only who you were with." Chandi's amber eyes regained their mischievous light. "This time, everyone will know better than to try and harm you."

"I don't understand."

The swan girls shared an unreadable look. One of the maidens in the back stepped forward and handed me a looking glass. The moon caught its edge and limned it in silver. I looked at my own reflection.

Chandi hadn't just created me a gown—she'd created me a crown to match. Black branches and sheer green silk reared up from my hairline in an eerie botanical tiara. Real vines tangled with the fabric, reaching long, wicked thorns down the side of my face. Starflowers glittered like diamonds. I looked fearsome and beautiful and...regal.

I didn't look like me. And not only because you couldn't see my dark hair.

I understood. Tonight, they didn't want me to be myself. They wanted me to be *her*.

Rancor tangled with temptation in my stomach. How many times had I wondered what Eala's life must be like? Valued, protected, admired? Surrounded by sisters, friends, suitors? Dancing the night away at a Folk revel?

I was suddenly and ravenously curious.

"My eyes are different," I pointed out, with a touch of disappointment.

The girls all laughed.

"Trust us," said the one with flaming copper hair and a gown like midnight. "In that dress, no one will be looking at your eyes."

"And where is Eala tonight?" It was the last excuse I could muster. "That I may go to the feis in her place?"

Again, the maidens glanced at each other.

"She's with him. Your prince." A meaningful smile wreathed Chandi's face. "Alone."

A fleeting prick of envy faded swiftly before an unfamiliar blossom of...peace. I glanced behind me, as if Rogan's presence lingered at my shoulder. But of course he wasn't there, and I was glad for it.

I was glad for *him*. Brighid knew he deserved a happy ending as much as anyone.

"Let's go," I said.

❧ ～～❧

I'd only glimpsed Murias—the abandoned Folk city—from afar. But it wasn't hard to recognize. Glittering white walls reared up, crowned in delicate parapets. Elegant buildings etched fantastical shapes against the night sky. Streets like necklaces of gold draped between airy, flowering trees. But up close, a taint crept on vile feet through the once-glorious city.

The flowers on the trees were veined with shadow. Festering vines cracked stone and crumbled mortar. Skeleton birds flitted above the broken roofs of towering monuments. And beneath it all was an awful *sound*, juddering along my bones and rooting behind my teeth.

Twenty paces ahead, the swan maidens paused to see why I'd stopped in the middle of the street.

"Come on!" Chandi called.

Sick hesitation rooted me to the spot.

"Can't you—" They were all staring at me. "Can't you hear that?"

"The music?" The red-haired maiden in the black dress laughed. "Brace yourself—it'll be even louder once we get there."

I opened my mouth to protest, but the girls practically carried me forward into the revel.

Colored lights blossomed behind shattered walls. Music pounded strangely as we entered a huge, dark space that must once have been a great hall. But instead of pillars, four contorted oak trees lofted toward the sky, glowing lanterns tangling in their unseasonably bare branches. Folk thronged the space, gyrating to the throbbing music, which was almost loud enough to cover the incessant hum of the distorted wild magic.

And across the marble and granite walls, painted in moving color, illusions of monsters and marvels danced as well.

"The Feis of the Wild Hunt." Chandi had to shout in my ear to be heard. "A long time ago, the Wild Hunt blazed across the sky on the night of the summer solstice, hunting giants, beasts, monsters, and humans who had displeased them. But when the Treasures were forged, the Wild Hunt's power was stolen. So now the Hunt lives only in the memories and dreams of the Folk."

All around me, visions of violence seethed.

Hawks with human eyes and men with wolfish teeth and frightened deer bleeding red upon the grass.

Hounds with white pelts and flaming eyes, pursuing brittle-legged creatures of bone. I could almost hear their unearthly baying: it was a bronze-edged bell of primordial fear, and it raised the hairs at the nape of my neck.

"This?" I gasped. "This was what the world was like before the Treasures were forged?"

"So they say."

The base of my skull throbbed in time to the music. My throat was dry. I tried to look somewhere other than the shifting, echoing images, but they were everywhere.

Sympathy softened Chandi's eyes. She waved the other swan maidens away, and they happily submitted to the churn of strange bodies surrounding us.

"This wasn't what I wanted to show you. Come."

It was a relief to leave the noise and chaotic visions behind. Chandi led me around the side of the building. What once had been a small park or garden had been utterly reclaimed by nature. But— like everything else in this accursed city—it had grown *wrong*. The leaves on the trees were more shadow than shape. A small stream was clogged with blooms of fluorescent algae. A gust of wind blew the scent of decay down from the hills, and the distortion billowed closer. My blood thrummed with its sick vibration.

I stopped. "I don't want to go any closer."

"To what?"

"The...corruption?" I didn't have another name for it. "Morrigan, can't you feel it?"

Chandi frowned, but not at me. She hesitated for a split second, then schooled her features. "Only a little farther."

She bent beside the polluted stream. In the darkness, I hadn't seen the swath of flowers cutting across the path. But now rotted fluorescence sheened their petals, and I saw they were the same shape as the starflowers the maidens plucked each full moon. But these weren't white. They were black.

"Remember what I told you on the Nameless Day?" Even Chandi's eyes glowed wrong this close to the distortion—filaments of green and black discoloring her amber irises. "Like nature, Tír na nÓg demands balance. Everything here has its duality. When we came here, the white flowers began to grow. They protect, create, imagine. These black flowers—they are the balance. They cut, destroy, remember."

I shook my head. "Why are you showing me this?"

"When we were young, we discovered something about the white flowers. When we swallowed them, we were able to see into the future. A glorious, extraordinary, wonderful future. But we soon realized it was no more than an illusion. Beautiful but false." She considered her words. "We...learned that the dark flowers have an equal but opposite effect. When ingested, they too elicit visions."

Something cold wormed down my neck. "True visions?"

"Forgotten memories. Unknown futures." She rubbed a palm down the front of her dress. "If Irian is truly determined to die at Samhain, then we are all running out of time. The geas must be broken, lest we all die with him. Eala believes—we *all* believe—these flowers might hold the answer."

I stared at the uncanny blossoms, struggling to think clearly over the slick throb of the wild magic. "Then why haven't you used them?"

"These flowers...are not for us." Her expression shifted. "But you are not like us. Our fate is in your hands, Fia."

I hesitated. The night was warm—cloyingly so—but my arms prickled with gooseflesh. I knew I should not flirt with magic beyond my ken. There was no way of knowing what I might be risking—what price I might be required to pay, what terrible consequence I might risk.

But what might I also gain? Further insight into the swans' geas would solve at least once piece of my puzzle. Eala, home to Mother. Rogan, out of Tír na nÓg. Irian, freed from at least one of his burdens.

I plucked one of the midnight flowers. And before I could change my mind, I bit down on the blossom, crushing it between my teeth.

Its petals cut my tongue—blood burst metallic in my mouth. A hiss of pain escaped me, even as Corra's irreverent voice tiptoed through my mind.

The magic of nature—you reap what you sow.

A moment later, I tasted the flower—a flavor sweet as kissed lips and dark as heartache. I tried to swallow it, but my throat convulsed. I gagged and spat the mangled blossom onto the ground.

I glanced at Chandi, but she was gone. Nonplussed, I stood, looking around the small park for her tall frame. She wasn't the only thing that was gone—the distortion no longer blotted out the sky. Stars glittered in a velvet sky. The leaves on the trees were green as emeralds. Colorful birds sang a kaleidoscope of midnight songs.

Behind me, Murias glowed like mother-of-pearl in the moonlight. Delicate towers laddered toward the stars. Greenery clung to walls and archways, flourishing in the breeze. The air was filled with the scents of flowers and fresh water.

Movement at the edge of the park caught my attention. A tall figure loped toward me. His golden hair spilled over his shoulders. What was he doing here? I thought—

"Rogan!" I called. He didn't hear me. I lifted my skirts and ran after him. I reached for his shoulder.

It wasn't Rogan. This man was of slighter build. His hair was a few shades too blond. And his face—his face was handsome but haunted. His mouth was taut with pain and indecision. His eyes—warm brown, like fresh-turned earth—looked exhausted. I didn't know him. And yet the golden torc around his neck sent a spark of familiarity pulsing through me.

"Who are you?" I asked.

Fresh anguish skated across his face. "You don't know me?"

He turned away from me in distress, back the way he'd come.

"Wait!" I lunged after him, but he moved between the suddenly lofting trees more quickly than I could follow. When he reappeared, he was not who I thought he was.

The figure was towering. Their naked thighs were corded with muscle. Burnished fur cascaded along the tops of their shoulders and dug grooves between the golden muscles of their torso. Around them, the forest stretched and grew. Human alarm raised the hairs along my arms, but the green-glowing heart of me was soothed by the dimming closeness of the wood. I lifted my gaze to the figure's face but saw only the dappled shadows of a forest path. Above them, antlers reached pointed tips toward a sky embossed with silver.

They beckoned claw-tipped fingers toward me. Behind them, I glimpsed a clearing glazed with starlight. A chime of clear music called to me—a lullaby from an unremembered infancy.

I knew—suddenly, perfectly—that if I followed them into the keening night, they would lead me home.

I followed.

Notes rang out beneath my feet as I ran. The ancient trees twisted arms to guide me—branches wrought in silver, with arteries of gold. The figure's antlers struck the boughs when they passed, the sound like the distant baying of hounds or the throb of a lover's heart or the lament of a dying man. The leaves falling in their wake were glass, shattering where they fell. Shards of pain prickled my calves. I dashed onward, though my steps were now marked in blood.

"Colleen!"

The sound jangled in my ears. That was not my name.

Up ahead, many Folk were gathered to greet me. And there were humans too—people I'd known, or seen from afar. They smiled as I approached.

"My lady," they cried. "Lady!"

And they spoke my true name. A name that sounded like being lost . . . and then found.

"Fia!"

The word was a briar, piercing me.

"Fia!"

Whose name *was* it? I turned.

A monster lunged at me in the languid moonlight. A nightmare— the afterbirth of midnight and magic, conjured against the silver forest.

I recoiled.

The monster roared. Its black-edged bulk was a blight on existence. Huge black wings beat around my face. I dropped to my knees and covered my head with my arms. Still it reached for me, pulling me against the wringing crush of its mangled bones. I struggled. But it was strong—too strong. It wrestled me still, pinning me against the throbbing earth.

Voices filtered through my panic, but they were very, very distant.

"You never should have—" The male voice was distorted. Furious. "Why did you not summon me sooner?"

"I'm sorry." Female. Anguished. "I didn't think—"

"No. You did not."

But then they both sifted away. Leaving me to drift on visions of silver and green toward a forest made of wishes. Toward a crowd of smiling people who knew me.

Who *loved* me.

Chapter Thirty-Three

Waking was like resurrection. I clawed my way toward heat and light from somewhere dark and deep. I forced my eyes open, although they ached. All of me ached. Dim light filtered beneath my eyelashes. And I was hot.

Savagely hot.

Someone had stripped me down to my underthings. Every inch of my bare flesh was molded against another body. A body slick with sweat and corded in lean muscle, with skin that seared against mine. Tattooed arms were looped protectively around my chest.

I tensed, fighting for clarity. My mind still echoed with unrelenting delusions; the edges of my vision pulsated with melting flames and laughing shadows. The air scintillated with steam that took on the shapes of nightmares.

"Are you awake?" Irian's voice was an inch from my ear. His cheek rasped against mine, igniting my raw nerve endings. I shuddered.

"I think so." Talking hurt—there were cuts in my mouth. My thoughts wove in and out of each other, fractured threads and clashing colors. Was any of this real? "Why is it so *hot*?"

"The best way to process the drug is to sweat out the toxins."

I tried to lift my head, but it was a boulder lashed with vines. *"Drug?"*

"Drug." His anger rumbled against my back. "Chandi did not tell you the whole truth about those flowers. They are born of wild magic."

"The black ones?"

"And the white ones."

I struggled to organize my memories. "Chandi told me they bloomed to balance the powerlessness of the swans."

"That may be a convenient lie. Both the white and the black flowers began to appear after Deirdre's Treasure was lost. They cluster where wild magic distorts the landscape—the abandoned cities, my fortress. Perhaps they have more innocent origins. I fear they do not."

"Chandi told me they would show me...memories. Secrets. Lost truths."

"Sometimes they do. Some among the Folk ingest the black flowers for their hallucinogenic visions, which are often truth couched in delirium. But when humans ingest them—" He trailed off.

"Tell me."

"They leave humans...open to suggestion."

Even in the steamy air, a chill shivered through me. "How open?"

"During the War, the Folk used them to turn human troops against their own brethren. They overcome loyalty, love, allegiance. Only a will like iron can withstand them."

"But I'm not fully human."

"Neither are you fully Folk, colleen. Because you were—" Again, he hesitated.

A shudder racked me, and I curled forward. Sweat-damp hair clung to my forehead. "Say it, Irian."

"The distortion." Horror whetted his voice to a dark blade. "You were heading straight for it."

I remembered now. It was like recalling a dream long after

waking—images and feelings stitched together like scraps of cloth ripped from a blanket.

The figure with the antlers.

The beguiling forest.

The crowd of family and friends and admirers.

Home.

A tear slid down my cheek and splashed onto the arm supporting my neck. Irian's bicep contracted. He pulled me closer.

"So it wasn't real?" Pain made my whisper hoarse.

"Does it have to be real?" His voice held infinite gentleness. "To be true?"

Another tear squeezed beneath my eyelashes and mingled with the beads of sweat clinging to my face. I wanted it to be real. I was glad it wasn't.

"It is over now." Irian smoothed my tangled hair from my face. "Sleep, colleen. By dawn, it will have been nothing more than a dream."

I surrendered to sleep.

❧ ～❧

A thick ruff of black feathers smothered me, prickling my back and neck like thousands of tiny needles. I struggled, summoning a scream, but I couldn't breathe, couldn't speak, couldn't make a sound. The monster wouldn't let me go, sheathing me in giant black wings. I was too hot. I drowned in the muffling dark.

❧ ～❧

Panic jolted me out of sleep. I sucked in a breath, shaking off the vestiges of the nightmare. It had been so real. But there was no Folk revel, no beckoning forest. No winged monster. There was only a man, lying with his chest against my back, arms looped loosely around my neck and waist.

Dismay crept through me. After I'd tried so hard to cut him out of my heart, had I really fallen back in bed with Rogan?

I twisted in the man's arms. He wasn't Rogan. Black tattoos slid sharp over sculpted arms. His hair was short and dark. His jaw was a blade. His mouth was soft. His eyes were closed, but I knew they were silver.

Pleasure warmed me before cooling to confusion. I stilled. What was I doing with Irian? Jumbled memories licked at me like flames. Had I danced with him somewhere? Had he kissed me beneath trees dripping with spring blossoms? Had we—

No. That, I would have remembered. But I didn't know why else I would be in his bed, nearly naked, dozing in the circle of his arms.

It occurred to me—this was another dream. Like the revel, the forest, the monster. A *better* dream.

Irian stirred, curling in closer to me. His face was an inch from mine. His eyelashes fluttered over chips of opal. His lips parted.

It seemed like an invitation. I saw no reason not to take it—after all, this wasn't real. I tilted my chin and kissed him, sliding my tongue over his lower lip before taking it into my mouth. He tasted like cold wind and new-forged metal. I swept my hands over his chiseled shoulders and buried my fingertips in his hair. It was short and soft and damp with sweat. Heat burned through me. I deepened the kiss, swirling my tongue over his teeth and pressing my barely covered breasts against his hot, bare chest.

He groaned against my mouth. The hand resting over my waist tightened, nudging my hips closer to his. Then every inch of his body stiffened. His arms became marble. His torso flexed, hard muscle rippling against my stomach. His thighs went rigid as his knees bent. He jerked his hips and the beginnings of his arousal away from me.

"No." His lips unfastened from mine. "*No*."

I pouted. My dreams didn't usually reject me. I reached for him again.

But he caught my wrists in his huge hands and pinned them across my chest.

"No," he said again. "Not like this."

I frowned—I didn't know what he meant. But it didn't matter much anymore. I rolled over and slid into unconsciousness.

✦

I woke in the dream-glow of dawn. Remnants of the flower's toxin still coursed through my veins—apparitions lurked at the edges of my shivering vision. The ordeal had left me with skin like sand and bones like glass. But the warmth on the horizon quickened my pulse.

"I need to get back to the Gate," I croaked.

Silently, Irian helped me dress, then bent space to deposit me beside the Willow Gate.

Tír na nÓg by dawn was exquisite. As the sun rose, riotous colors burst from impossible flowers. Trees with honeycomb leaves reflected prisms of light. The birds' aubade was like bells tolling across still water.

"Irian—" I turned toward him. But there was nothing but retreating shadows and a few stray black feathers catching the air and slicing it into shards of red and gold.

He was gone. And I was late.

After the glory of Tír na nÓg, Roslea felt devoid of color or life. I fell forward onto the loam, choking against the lingering aftereffects of the black flower—nausea, dizziness, creeping hopelessness.

"Changeling!"

Rogan dropped to his knees before me and, before I could react, gathered me against him. He was solid—almost too solid. He crushed me in the circle of his arms until I thought my bones might break.

"I was so worried," Rogan was saying in my ear, low and fierce. "I waited at the Gate until nearly sunrise before crossing over. I didn't know whether something had happened to you or whether you crossed over early and went home without me—"

"Thank you for waiting." My voice came out hoarse and listless.

Rogan pushed me to arm's length, taking in my bedraggled appearance. But instead of concern, his eyes narrowed with something like suspicion. He caught my chin, tilting my face up to the light.

"You've been kissing someone."

I jerked my face out of his hand, climbed crookedly to my feet. "I haven't."

"You have." He also stood. "I know what it looks like. I've seen it enough."

His palms gripped my arms, too hard. My frazzled nerve endings sparked. Green rippled along my skin.

"Let go of me, Rogan."

"It was *him*, wasn't it?"

"You don't get to be jealous." Spiny thorns burst from my biceps and shoulders.

Rogan jerked his hands away, hissing as droplets of red pooled on his palms and fingertips. "I'm *not*. I'm concerned. I warned you, Fia—he's dangerous."

"I think I am a better judge of who among the Folk is dangerous—and who is not."

"Changeling—"

"You don't get to tell me who I can or cannot spend my time with," I snapped. "Focus on yourself—focus on your princess, like you did last night."

He stared at me. "What?"

"I know you finally got to spend the whole night with Eala. *Alone*." I hadn't meant for it to sound so venomous. But I was finished with him trying to keep me for himself, even as he pursued another. "Well done, princeling."

"Who told you that?"

"It doesn't matter." I smoothed my hands over my arms. The thorns were still there, sharp and stinging. I pressed my palms against them, letting the pain ground me to this world. "Yes, Rogan—I kissed someone. Did you not kiss Eala?"

His lips pressed together. "That's different."

"Why?" My resentment spiked. "Because you still expect me to be your mistress? Because you want a queen at your side and a whore in your bed?"

"Because I care about you. I refuse to let you get hurt."

"When are you going to get it through your thick head, princeling?" I turned my back on him in the lofting dawn. "I don't need you to protect me."

Chapter Thirty-Four

Tinne—Holly
Summer

A wave of feverish heat smoldered through Dún Darragh, rippling along the tops of trees and hazing the horizon. The greenhouse was unbearably muggy, and even the perpetually drafty fort was oppressively hot. I tossed and turned as the midnight hours slogged toward dawn.

A tapping sound roused me from fitful, hard-earned sleep. I cranked my eyes open.

A bird perched haughtily on the sill, jabbing its beak at the glass. With its silver-black plumage, the starling was unmistakable. One of Cathair's witch-birds. I pushed a surge of panic away as I opened the window. It had been months since Cathair had written me. Probably because I'd simply stopped responding to his letters.

The starling hopped onto the bed, lifted a talon, and shot me a long-suffering glance. I uncurled a scrap of parchment from its leg. Cathair's spiky handwriting stared up at me.

A wet summer promises a poor harvest. Disease surges in the south, fomenting unrest among the under-kings. Are we to expect a returning banfhlaith and a Folk Treasure before Samhain? Or will the little witch scuttle back in shame and failure to the realm that spawned her?

My fingers itched. I crumpled the message, then hurled it at the witch-bird, who fluffed indignant feathers.

"I don't owe him a response," I snarled at it. "I don't owe him anything."

The starling cocked its head, trilled a mocking note, then took off into the sunrise.

❦

Lughnasa dawned hot and hazy, washing indistinct colors against a cornflower sky.

"Chiardhubh!" A chubby brass doorknob spat out a mouthful of leaves and berries as I trotted down into the great hall. The doors stood slightly ajar, splashing shades of lily and rose across the flagstones. "We must celebrate!"

"What are we celebrating?" I put my hands on my hips. "A spare moment of peace and quiet, I hope."

"She's grumpy," remarked another brass head to its twin. "Do you think the mattress in her bed is lumpy?"

"We think it's that hulking Porridge Face," suggested the first head primly. "His head is bumpy. His legs are stumpy. His—"

"All right, all right!" I bit my tongue. "How would Your Unbodilyness like to celebrate Lughnasa?"

"A bonfire, of course!"

Lughnasa always seemed too hot for a bonfire, but Corra was right. All the high holy days called for fire. At Rath na Mara, they'd be building a pyre atop the tor. Cook would have butchered a bull and spent all week preparing dishes from the early harvest, and the younger lads in Mother's fianna would all be boasting about their wrestling prowess.

Besides, building a bonfire sounded better than stewing here, my mind spinning in circles.

"Where's the highest hill?"

"Depends on what you mean by 'high,'" said the right head.

"If you turn the lough inside out, it's a mountain," agreed the left unhelpfully.

I threw my arms up. "I'll point myself up and stop when I start going down."

The morning blurred, sultry with heat. I shaded my eyes and peered up at the moor looming gray and purple above the emerald fields. It looked more than high enough for a proper Lughnasa fire.

"Chiardhubh!" A tiny voice interrupted my thoughts. "We want to come!"

Corra pranced behind me in the guise of the little manikin I'd made them, toy legs whirling. They'd made a few improvements to the body—hands fashioned from pink claw flowers, luminescent eyes cut from a dead butterfly's wing. They wore a petal for a shirt and a cobweb for a hat and a little black mantle crafted from—

My heart jolted. Corra had sewn together a few of the night-black feathers that strewed the dún, wearing them like a cloak that reminded me of—

I tasted blood and heat and ice-chased metal. I *wasn't* going to think about him.

I bent, offering Corra my hand. "I'll carry you. I just need to gather some firewood."

Corra perked, grabbing my thumb and hauling themself up onto my shoulder. "You won't need wood."

"Why not?"

Corra wiggled wilted pink fingers. "You'll see."

"Hold on tight, then. We're climbing."

Corra curled soft velvet hands in the shell of my ear and began to sing at a bloodcurdling volume. I winced but managed not to protest as I climbed the sunlit moor.

A massive pyre already flared from the peak of the hill. Sparks attacked the sky, red as slaughter against a field of blue. Stripped to the waist, golden muscles flushed with heat and exertion, Rogan tossed a huge log onto the blaze. Sweat-damped hair clung to his neck.

"Porridge Face is here?" I glared at the manikin sitting pert on my shoulder. "You knew."

"We know everything!" Corra launched themself to the ground, landing neatly on twig legs and sprinting toward the bonfire. Moments later, I spotted the manikin lying prone in the grass while an unearthly mouth howled in the fire. I took a deep breath, feeling mulish, then stalked toward where Rogan toiled.

"Rogan." He didn't hear me over the roar of the fire. I touched his shoulder.

He flinched, muscles bunching beneath my palm as he whirled on me. For an instant, his gaze was midnight with something like regret. Then his eyes paled to azure. He barked a laugh and threw his arm around my shoulder in a rough, affable embrace.

"Changeling." His breath ruffled my hair. He let me go. "You surprised me."

"And you me. What are you doing up here?"

"You've wanted to celebrate every high holy day since we got here." He shrugged, bending to heave another log onto the eager bonfire. "I assumed today would be no different."

I stared at him. After our last interaction, I'd been sure I wouldn't see Rogan again until the next full moon. "I'm touched."

"Besides, I couldn't sleep." Rogan shielded his eyes against the sun, which was roaring toward noon, then glanced toward the shadow of a craggy rock. "I thought we'd make a day of it."

Frowning, I followed his gaze. Tucked beneath the crag were a rumpled blanket and a basket overflowing with bread and food and a jug of what was likely liquor.

"Mead?" I teased lightly. "In this heat?"

Something akin to displeasure slithered across Rogan's face. But he hid it, bending to uncork the bottle. He sloshed a measure of amber liquid into a cup. He shoved it at me.

"Yes, mead. I'm in the mood to get blisteringly, blazingly drunk, changeling." His mouth quirked. "Want to join me?"

We picnicked in the shade, heather-scented wind coiling in our ears and blowing smoke in our eyes. There were bilberries from the garden and tart blackberries from the hedge, fresh bread from the oven and cool cheese from the cellar. All courtesy of Corra, who was ignoring us in favor of tormenting a family of chipmunks nesting in the rocks.

The cool honeyed taste of the mead was hard to resist, and I drank it more quickly than I should have. A buzz climbed my spine and filled my forehead. But not even tipsiness could blot out the weight of my spiraling thoughts.

"Are you going to tell me why we're getting blisteringly, blazingly drunk in the middle of the afternoon?" I sloshed more of the tempting mead into my cup and tried not to slur my words. The sun had climbed over its zenith, the fire now mostly embers.

For a long moment, Rogan was silent, lying on his back to gaze at the sky. Finally, he rolled up onto an elbow.

"First, I need to apologize to you for the other morning, changeling. I have no right to command you. I have no right to do many things." He slid a forefinger over the rim of his cup. "These past few months have...not brought out the best in me."

"Apology accepted." His candor cooled the heat building behind my eyes. "And second?"

This time, his silence lasted even longer. He sat upright, grasped the jug of mead, and rolled it restively between his palms. "She was angry with me the other night."

"Who?" My thoughts churned slow. "Eala?"

He nodded.

"Why? What did you do to offend her?"

"You," he said.

My hand jerked, sloshing golden liquid over my fingers. The mead suddenly tasted sour in my mouth.

That wasn't right. Eala had explicitly encouraged my dalliance with Rogan.

"But she—" I stopped myself a breath too late. I couldn't tell Rogan that Eala had practically commanded me to bed him. He was already skeptical of her motivations—if I told him this, it would destroy what little faith he had left in their betrothal. But what if I'd already betrayed his confidence by keeping the information to myself? I took a deep pull from my glass, then held it out to be refilled. I didn't know what else to do.

"How did she find out?" I asked.

"I don't know." He scrubbed golden curls off his face. "She said she couldn't trust me. She said my love for her was dishonest. But...can any love really be honest?"

The smoky wind stole the breath from my mouth. I licked my lips, but that only made them drier. "What does that mean?"

"Three months ago, you told me that if love demanded change in order to exist, it wasn't love at all." Rogan unclasped the cracked river-stone brooch from his shoulder and passed it from palm to palm. "But I have never known a love so unconditional. My father's love demands I perform the role of golden heir. Eala's love demands I tolerate her fickle games, her schemes and manipulations. And—" He looked abruptly away, swallowing words that nevertheless made a battlefield of his face.

I'd never heard Rogan talk like this. Unsteadily, I set down my glass and wished I'd had the forethought to remain sober. "What *is* honest, then? If not love?"

He looked at me. "Death."

"Rogan." Shock spiked blood to my already flushed cheeks. "Rogan, that's—"

"Bleak? Miserable? Grim?" His eyes on mine looked more blue than green. "Do you disagree, changeling? I've seen what your Greenmark can do."

He wasn't wrong. If there was anything my Greenmark had taught me, it was that death was nothing more than life's backward glance. A glimpse of golden light down a dimming pathway ringed with trees. But it hurt to hear *him* say it—as if he, too, saw me as nothing more than a weapon in the dark, a poisoned blade designed only to cut.

"That's not death, princeling." I fastened the certainty to my heart with soft braids of flax and curling fronds of blossoming clematis. "It's transformation. A different kind of life, maybe. But not death."

"Fine—life *and* death are simple," he rasped. "Love is not. I have never known a love that did not twist, did not curdle, did not poison. Life hurts. Death levels. But love—love destroys."

It was the most cynical thing I'd ever heard him say. My heart thundered hollow between my ribs. "Isn't that a little dramatic?"

"Maybe." He stood. The wind caught his golden hair and flung it against the sky. "What do I know? According to you, I don't even deserve a happy ending."

Pain writhed through me. Had I said that? "Rogan—"

"Never mind." His eyes went flat. "I'm going to stoke the fire."

My head felt heavy. I lay back. Closed my eyes against rising tears.

I must have drowsed. I hallucinated hands like flowers and silver deer and falling stars.

When I woke up, afternoon had trundled into evening. The heat and the haze and the smoke had transformed into great glowering clouds hanging low over the moor. And I—I was alone.

Chapter Thirty-Five

If I expected respite from the heat in Tír na nÓg, I was sorely disappointed. After a sticky hike through Roslea, I was a sweaty mess. I loitered at the edge of the forest, trying to decide whether a swift plunge into the flat, still lough would improve things...or make everything worse.

"What is wrong?"

Irian's husky voice came from behind me, and I spun. He looked effortlessly cool and relentlessly composed. I dropped the wad of hair I'd piled on top of my head, and stopped fanning my sweaty neck.

"Nothing's wrong."

"You have been standing here staring at the lough. For half an hour."

He'd been watching me? I prayed for a breeze to cool the flushing rising up my neck. "I'm hot."

He waited for me to finish. "And?"

"I've always hated the heat, ever since I was a girl." My curls were sticking to my neck again. I gave up on looking calm and collected, and piled my hair back on top of my head. "Not that I particularly enjoy ice or snow, but you can always bundle up on cold days. The heat's more oppressive. There's only so much clothing you can take off before you're naked. And then you're still hot and unfit to be seen in public besides."

"I confess, I thought perhaps you were starting to get used to the heat. Maybe even enjoy it." Irian stepped closer, his presence like a magnet drawing me toward him. His moonlit eyes had lost their distance and menace. "But if it makes you take your clothes off, I will not complain."

"I will complain," I said, smiling sweetly, "if you use my hatred of the heat to try and get me to take my clothes off."

Irian's lips lifted in a lazy grin. His eyes dropped to my mouth and then my throat and the swath of skin below where I'd tried to yank my collar wider. His palm slid over my shoulder and rested against my collarbone. He nudged his fingers beneath the fabric and slid it sideways, exposing my shoulder. My pulse jumped at his touch, then stuttered when I remembered how he'd rejected me last month.

"In three short months, tánaiste, you die. And the swan maidens with you." I made my voice arch. "You have told me many tales, but none of any real use. Why should I let you distract me when there is so much at stake?"

"I am indeed doomed." He did not move his hand from my collarbone as his eyes returned to my face. "Riddle me this, colleen: How might a dead man feel alive, with so little time left? If you can tell me that much, then perhaps I will part with more of my tale."

"That is an unreasonable demand." The heat of his touch was nothing like the sluggish, sweltering heat of the night. It sparked lightning through my veins and put a storm in my belly. "But I suppose either a remembrance of times past...or a felicitous hope for an impossible future."

A thought ignited behind Irian's eyes. "That is very good, colleen."

Space bent around us, wringing my organs into contorted shapes before bending me backward and spitting me out. I hunched over on the top of a rise behind the fort, gagging. I twisted to glare up at Irian.

"You need to warn me before you do that!"

He smirked. "And ruin the surprise?"

"I hate surprises."

"You hate the heat; you hate surprises." He arched one sculpted eyebrow. "For someone so small, you possess a shockingly large capacity for hate."

Annoyance buoyed me to standing. "For someone so large, you possess a shockingly small—"

I bit off the rude words before they could cross my lips. But Irian's half smile blossomed into something fully fledged and utterly lovely. His perfect teeth were a scythe in the night.

"Please." Humor crackled along the edge of his voice. "Do go on. A shockingly small . . . ?"

Heat touched my cheeks. I looked away, making a show of inspecting our surroundings. Rocky outcroppings sheared down into a ravine choked with ferns and bushes. "Where are you taking me?"

Irian ducked behind a twisting alder and dropped a foot in height. "Down."

I squinted. Narrow stone steps—cracked with ancient roots and slanted with time—laddered precariously down into the dim, moonlit forest.

I crossed my arms. "If you want to murder me for insulting your manhood, there are easier ways than pushing me off a cliff."

"I cannot think of any." Irian cocked his head. "Do I have to carry you down, colleen?"

A challenge. Stubborn, I picked my way behind him as he loped gracefully down the stairs. I was moments from refusing to take one more step when the trees stopped suffocating each other. Trunks spaced out and branches roofed higher. Far above, the rocky edge of the ravine cut against the sky.

A star-bright mountain stream laughed down the cliff face and carved out a deep pool in a broad clearing. Moonlight speared down, slicing the misty spray into silver prisms. Translucent shallows deepened to midnight near the center of the pond. Glittering flowers spangled sloping banks. A rush-lined stream looped away into the forest.

Irian was already at the water's edge. He shucked off his boots in a few jerks, then stepped out of his clothes. My eyes followed the surge of his shoulders to the crisp taper of his waist. Crests of muscle carved grooves down the sides of his hips, toward—

I jerked my gaze back to his face. He was watching me, his mouth curved into something that wasn't quite a smile. I inhaled, tasting the hot thick air and savoring each of its flavors: the refreshing froth of mountain water, the sharp tang of unspoken words, the heady perfume of simmering desire.

Irian plunged into the pool. The water opened up and swallowed him without a splash. He dived, deep enough for his form to be a star of white against the dark. Deep enough that I caught my own breath and held it with him.

He surfaced at last, heaving silver ripples onto the bank. He flicked his hair, flinging clear water out in a crystalline gyre. When he looked at me, his eyes were moonlight on deep water.

"Are you coming in, colleen?" He smiled that coiled, perilous smile—the one that melted my bones. "Or are you...lily-livered?"

"Lily-livered?" I choked.

"Yellow-bellied? Milksop?" His teeth gleamed. "Coward?"

I laughed, stepping close enough for the pool to lap greedily at my boots. "I've been called many things in my life. But never *coward*."

"Is that so?"

"It is." I toed off my boots, unlaced my trousers, and waded in wearing only my shift. The mountain chill was bracing against my heat-flushed skin. A thrill stitched my bones. "Just ask all the brave men I've bested in battle."

I launched myself at Irian without warning. My hand caught his shoulder; my knees smacked his chest. Then water closed over our heads, shattering the world into ruffled shards of black and silver.

Effervescing moonlight. Opalescent eyes. Sideways trees.

We grappled in an exuberant frenzy. My arms found his neck, dragging him backward as he sputtered and flailed. He lurched sideways, his mass pulling me down. I curled hands around his head and churned above him, then plunged his face beneath the surface. He caught me around the waist, dragging me underwater with him.

For a long moment, all was still in the buoyant embrace of dark water. Shafts of moonlight painted a silent susurrus against the pool floor, illuminating blooms of algae and mollusks curled tight among greening fronds.

We surfaced. I clutched his shoulders, laughing and choking and blinking cascades of water out of my eyes. I pushed a sodden length of dark hair off my face, and then all I saw was him.

I swallowed, suddenly aware of how close we were. My legs were latched so tightly around his waist that his hip bones dug into my thighs. My saturated shift clung to the contours of my body, a chilly sliver between my skin and his radiant heat.

"So which is this?" My voice sounded breathless. "Nostalgia? Or optimism?"

His eyes were molten. "Both, I think."

"And is it working?" My chest rose and fell in time to his heart drumming madly between my breasts. "Does the doomed man feel alive?"

"Almost." He dragged his hand along the column of my throat, tipped my chin up toward his. "But not quite."

His lips parted. A frisson of anticipation sparked in my veins, followed by creeping doubt.

"You pushed me away," I murmured, my mouth an inch from his. "After the Wild Hunt. You said you didn't want me."

"No." His eyes went iron dark. "What I said was 'Not like this.' You were high. You did not know what you were doing. I was not sure you would even remember. And when—" His throat worked. "When you and I join, colleen, I would have you remember it. *All* of it."

His words sent heat unfurling along my spine. *When.* Not *if.*

I shifted my weight, hooking my heel in the small of his back and molding myself to the hard planes of his torso. The movement brought my rear fully into his hands. He made a noise low in his throat, and his calloused palms flexed against my skin. I pressed my breasts against his chest and looped my arms around his neck, trailing my fingertips through the soft hair at his nape.

"If not like that," I whispered, "then maybe like this?"

I pressed my wet lips to his. The kiss tasted of indescribable things—of sleepless nights and hidden desires. My hesitation, ragged but lingering. His want, hard and bright. And cleaving between them, a vining tendril of something keen and clear. Something unnameable thrilling against the back of my throat and leaving me breathless.

Irian pushed us through the water until he found firm footing at the edge of the pool. Water rushed down from my legs, making me feel heavy in his arms. Hot, humid air kissed my skin, nearly as shocking as the water's chill. Irian's hands rose from my rear to my waist as he set me onto my feet. He found the hem of my sopping shift, sliding the clinging fabric over my head. The garment slapped down into the grass. He pulled me against him, his skin licking flame-hot against mine. When his growing arousal brushed my stomach, I inhaled sharply.

So that was why he'd been so entertained by my jibe at the top of the hill. It was because I'd been hilariously—*hugely*—off base.

I bit my lip. Smiled. "Like this?"

I reached down, slipping my hand along the velvet length of him and curling my fingers around his girth. He went rock hard in my palm. He groaned, stomach flexing. He dragged his mouth along my neck, nipping the tender skin below my ear and sending pleasure arrowing sharp toward my center. I stroked him slowly, purposefully. His breath ratcheted in his chest, and his pulse throbbed, uneven against my touch.

"If you keep doing that, colleen," he said roughly, "there will not be much to remember."

He pulled away, pushed me gently back against the mossy bank of the stream. Flowers crushed beneath me, filling the air with a sweet, bold scent. Water droplets clung to my eyelashes, fracturing the world into a kaleidoscope.

Irian folded himself beside me. His hungry gaze drank me in, sweeping down my reclining form. One restless hand followed, sketching my outline in searing lines—a touch against the side of my throat, a thumb gliding along the line of my collarbone, a palm skimming the curve of my breast. He splayed one large hand over my stomach, then slid it lower, sending spirals of heat coiling toward my center.

I arched myself toward him and recaptured his mouth. He made that sound in his throat again and drew me closer, fitting me against him as I hooked a leg over his. He moved his lips from mine, dragging his teeth against my jaw before sliding his tongue over the tender skin of my throat. I twined my arms around his neck, closing my eyes as I explored the shifting planes of his back, tracing the sharp lines of his tattoos by touch alone; the skin lightly puckered beneath my seeking fingertips. He shuddered, forearms flexing as he trailed his mouth lower. He kissed the outside of my breast, then slid his tongue over my nipple, stroking it to an aching peak.

"Yes." He murmured against my skin. "Like this."

I sighed, burying my hands in his silken hair as he explored lower. He trailed his mouth between my breasts, along the ridges of my ribs, down the soft, taut skin of my stomach. His hand flexed lower, moving slowly—deliciously—against the warmth between my thighs. He nipped my hip bone, making me hiss from the blurring of pleasure and pain. Anticipation intensified the ache building inside me.

Around us, bluebells unfurled from the mossy bank, glittering like sapphires in the moonlight. I tensed.

"Sorry," I whispered, hoping I hadn't ruined the moment.

Irian smiled against my skin. Slid his mouth lower. When he spoke, his breath sent shivers up my body. "Colleen, never apologize for who you are."

I rocked my hips up to meet him. His tongue glided hot and wet over my sex, and I nearly came undone. My hands convulsed in his hair. He stilled, then slowly resumed, laving me with short, deliberate strokes that pushed me toward the edge yet didn't force me over. My breath hitched, and I gazed toward the starry sky as he devoured me.

I should have closed my eyes instead. Glimmering, shimmering lights came wafting down from the trees, bright as moonlight and tiny as fireflies. Again I tensed, my body hardening. Irian stilled. He lifted his head from between my legs and followed my gaze.

"Sheeries." His voice was rough with want. His scalding fingers curled around my thigh. "Ignore them. They are harmless."

But sudden uncertainty tangled in my chest and cooled my blood. Echoes of lost things bubbled up inside me—memories of another night, another pond. Flickering lights in another sky. Another man.

And with them came Rogan's bitter, brutal words from Lughnasa: *Life hurts. Death levels. But love—love destroys.*

And on the heels of those words, totally unbidden, Cathair's voice slithered into my thoughts. *You were made of bloodroot and mountain laurel. You were made to destroy.*

I looked down. Irian was watching me. His eyes still blurred with twilight desire, but now they held an echo of my disquiet. "What is it?"

"It's…*me.*" My voice was almost inaudible.

Irian's eyes clouded, dark as a summer storm. He slid his frame back up over mine, propping himself on his forearms as he traced the lines of my face with taut, troubled eyes. The heat between us cooled as the promise of our joining faded. But this was a new kind of closeness—the weight of his body, the weight of his gaze. Heavy not with suspicion or wariness, but with concern. And acceptance—for whatever I might say.

"And what," he murmured, "could possibly be the matter with you?"

"I was raised to be a weapon." I gathered my thoughts like nettles, hoping not to get stung. "What if I am truly nothing more than rocks and bones and stinging things—a blade wrapped in brambles? My love has only ever destroyed."

"Do you truly believe that, colleen?"

"Part of me does." I prodded the edges of the long-festered wounds inside me. "My whole life, I have been treated as nothing more than a collection of sharp edges—a dark, wicked thing made to hurt. And there is truth in it—I am those things. I am hard as the earth. Sharp as a thorn. Ruthless as winter." I waited for his eyes to shutter, for his mouth to twist in disdain. But he just watched me, absorbing my words with an attentiveness I'd never known before. "But the earth is gentle to the seeds she holds in her palm. Thorns protect the fruit swelling inside the thicket. Winter promises new growth in due time. I am all these things too. But I don't know whether the love balances the hurt. Whether the life balances the death."

"You are all those things and more." His voice was rough, fervent. "You are dangerous and intoxicating. You are sharp thorns and bright flowers. You are darkness and the starlight shining within it. You are whatever you wish yourself to be. Do not let anyone tell you what you are or what you are not."

My throat swelled with emotion. I breathed a laugh. "Not even you?"

"Especially not me." He pressed his forehead to mine. I let my eyes fall closed as I breathed him in—cool nights and endless skies. When I rested my hand on the planes of his chest, his heartbeat throbbed against my fingertips. "When you give me your heart, colleen, I want all of it. I want all of you. If you are sharp with broken thorns, let them cut me. If you churn with dark shadows, let them engulf me. And if your love only destroys, let it destroy me. I am already a doomed man."

His lips found mine in a careful, precarious kiss—as if I were the only thing tethering him to this world. His desire lingered, sweet as cool honey and deep as a mountain spring. My own blood quickened once more, a summertime flush of marigold and lilac.

But Irian pulled away from me and slowly rose to his feet. He held out a hand to help me up. We dressed in comfortable silence. If I thought he'd be sullen or angry in the wake of my hesitation during our lovemaking, I was wrong. There was no perceived rejection—no need to be comforted when I was the one hurting.

He was not what I'd been taught to expect from a love mate.

"I am willing to wait for you—for *all* of you." His mouth was soft, bruised. But his gaze was winged with distant dread. "But I fear we are beginning to run out of time."

We didn't talk as we made the hot trek up the crumbling stairs toward the shadow fort. But Irian held my hand and didn't let me go until I returned to the forest beyond the lough.

Part Three

The Black Swan

Seven stars in the still water,
And seven in the sky;
Seven sins on the King's daughter,
Deep in her soul to lie.

—"The Dole of the King's Daughter" by Oscar Wilde

Chapter Thirty-Six

As I hiked back toward the Gate, I grappled with disconcerting hope.

I hadn't meant for things to go so far with Irian. Not just physically—I understood how body, mind, and heart did not always desire the same things. But I hadn't expected the way our fragile emotions had begun to bind us together, delicate as gossamer.

The way his words had transformed from flirtatious banter to naked honesty within a breath as he reassured me instead of punishing me for the sudden wash of emotions that ended our tryst.

The way his scalding touch sought not to take his own pleasure but to learn the rhythms of mine.

The way he'd stopped looking at me like someone he'd lost, and started looking at me like someone he'd found.

We'd gotten too close. And yet... not close enough.

When you give me your heart, colleen, I want all of it. I want all of you.

Anticipation fluttered honeysuckle against my spine. And I allowed myself to wonder what it would be like to *stay*.

Here. In Tír na nÓg.

With *him*. With what time he had left.

And with *myself*. With all the parts of myself I'd spent my life hating. I'd been raised to loathe my wicked heart and wild eyes, my warped magic, which turned hedgehogs to dirt and nursemaids to trees. To believe that the only love I deserved was half-hearted and wholly conditional—predicated on the rejection of every characteristic that made me unique.

But what if all that had been a betrayal—a betrayal enacted upon me by all the people who said they loved me, but merely wanted to keep me docile, obedient, dutiful?

For nearly thirteen years, I had shunned and despised the realm that had spawned me. Despised my blood—my very body. My *self*. And for the first time in my life, I wondered what it might be like to step inside the parts of myself I did not understand, and explore them for exactly what they were.

Arching oaks and heaving earth...moss embroidered over cracked stones. Shadows and light. Sharpness and softness. Living and dying.

Movement beside the bridge caught my eye.

It wasn't Rogan. It was Eala. And beside her was Chandi.

"Hello, Sister," said Eala. "We come to make amends. And to give you one last warning."

I shook my head stupidly, my far-flung thoughts struggling to catch up to her words. "Amends?"

Eala smiled her trademark sister's smile at me. "Chandika?"

"I'm...so sorry." Chandi stepped forward. Her amber eyes flicked to mine and then down to the dirt. "I should not have encouraged you to eat those flowers. I knew you were part human—I knew the flowers might steal your will. I hoped—*wished*—your Folk blood was stronger, so that you might foresee a way to break our geas. But I should not have taken the risk. I understand if you're angry with me."

"I *am* angry." But I wasn't angry only at Chandi. I had a sneaking suspicion it hadn't been her idea to make me dine on

black starflowers. At least, not wholly. Of the two women standing before me, I knew which of them dictated and which of them
obeyed. Eala's contradictory behavior had shaken my belief in
her—I didn't understand why she would have encouraged me to
sleep with Rogan, only to spurn him for the same thing. What
had he said? *Eala's love demands I tolerate her fickle games, her
schemes and manipulations.* I wanted to believe the best of my sister. But the evidence against her had begun to stack.

I slid my eyes from Chandi to the princess, who stood cool and
unruffled despite the smothering heat. "No apology from you?"

Her eyes widened. "Whatever for?"

"You had nothing to do with what happened last month?"

"How could I?" Her voice held a note of injury. "I wasn't even
there."

"That doesn't mean it wasn't your idea."

"Sister." Her expression grew grave. "From the moment you
came to Tír na nÓg, I have had nothing but your best interests at
heart. Did I not seek you out to tell you truths no one else would?
Did I not free you from the constraints of your conscience when I
cleared the way for you to pursue Rogan? Have I not warned you
against allying yourself with those who would do you harm?"

Eala had done all those things. But had she done them for my
sake... or for hers? "So?"

"So why would I suddenly throw you to the wolves? Risk your
life and sanity for—" She glared at Chandi. "For some half-baked,
harebrained scheme to trifle with magics we don't understand and
could never hope to control?"

Again, Chandi's eyes flicked to me before fastening on the
ground in obvious remorse. I stared between the two women, trying to read the subtext flying between them, but it was no use.

"I forgive you," I finally said. "Although I will not quickly forget."

"Understandable," Eala said.

"Dawn approaches. If you still have a warning, deliver it
quickly."

"I do. *We* do." The way Eala bared her teeth was not quite a smile. "Despite my prior warnings, you seem to have formed an attachment to Irian."

I gritted my teeth. "What of it?"

"Has it occurred to you that he is seducing you?"

"Has it occurred to you that I am seducing him?"

"Oh, I doubt that." Eala's face took on its now-familiar appraising cast, as if I were an oily oyster at market. "He is tánaiste of the Sept of Feathers. Bred to wield immense power. Born to a merciless lineage. His first language is treachery. He has outwitted you."

Disquiet kissed my neck, a chill to spite the heat.

"Perhaps he kept you at arm's length at first," Eala continued. "Perhaps even pretended to scorn you. But slowly, he would have warmed to you. Allowed his hardened exterior to soften. Shared anecdotes about his supposedly traumatic childhood. They would, of course, be fabricated. But they would serve their purpose of making him seem sympathetic."

A shadow of doubt winged down to roost above my heart. I'd been the one to establish the dynamic between Irian and me— I'd been the one to strike the bargain for more stories. But now all Irian's tales about himself blurred against my mind's eye. The boy on the cliffs. The boy with the thorn in his foot. The boy who learned to kill. I had believed them to be true. But of course I had no way to verify them...

"Perhaps he is simply not all bad."

Eala's smile held the barest edge of pity. "Once you had begun to see him in a more genial light, he would have really dug his talons in. Perhaps he told you he did not steal me and my sisters to murder us, but to protect us. Perhaps he contrived a scenario where he would have been in danger, and you would have felt compelled to rescue him. A scenario where you witnessed his exquisite warrior's grace but also his vulnerability. Beset by enemies on all sides yet poised and uncomplaining. Tragically doomed to a fate he did not choose. Resigned yet stoic. An attractive set of qualities designed to soften a violent nature, an arrogant self-regard, and a selfish and unflagging hunger for power."

My stomach churned. I didn't want to believe a word out of Eala's pretty mouth. But her words were so similar to Irian's own that another thread of doubt stitched cold over the notches of my spine.

The boy was young, arrogant, violent, and selfish. Neither age nor loneliness improved him—they only made him worse.

I sliced my gaze toward Chandi, but she kept her amber eyes resolutely fixed on the forest floor.

Whatever Eala saw on my face made her keep talking. "And when he saw you were beginning to feel more favorably toward him, he would have begun the real seduction. The heated touches, the lingering glances, the private smiles. A hesitant kiss, perhaps. And finally, he would tell you he desired you. Desired your love. Desired your heart."

"You can't possibly know—" The world blurred. Green nettled through my veins. "Have you been watching us?"

"I didn't have to." Grim satisfaction hardened on Eala's face. "You aren't the first to be targeted by his insidious schemes. Simply the latest."

"I don't understand. He's a pariah among the Folk; he's been *alone*—"

"Alone, with *us*." Eala gave the final word weight. "I wasn't the first either. I suppose he targeted Niamh first since she was the eldest, although that didn't matter much. We were all just children. Children who had been stolen and bewitched and had no parents or friends. Only each other. And *him*. I suppose it's lucky I had the experience to see through his ploys. I was already accustomed to being manipulated by someone who should have loved me. Unlike you, I always knew exactly who to hate."

She was talking about Mother again.

"Suppose Irian is manipulating me." I forced my voice to stay even. "Tell me why."

"The same reason he manipulated us. The same reason he stole us, bound us, cursed us." She reached out and tapped my breastbone. "He desires this."

I suddenly remembered the ancient warrior's journals and the translation I had given Eala. *After the Treasures of the Folk, a heart is the most powerful magic in Tír na nÓg.*

Irian wanted my *heart*?

"If he is so vicious and treacherous, why doesn't he simply take it?" My pulse throbbed green and black. "He should have no compunctions killing a nameless changeling."

"He doesn't want just your heart. He wants your *willing* heart."

"What's the difference?"

"Did you not read the journal you gave me?" Her eyes were bright, and she spoke with the rhythm of recitation. "A heart can open a locked gate, break stone, or heal a festered wound."

Although it had struck me as an abstraction when I read it, I recalled the passage. I finished it now. "And a heart given willingly in love can destroy that same gate. Move a mountain. Or save a doomed life."

Eala looked sorry for what she was about to say. "And whose doomed life might *your* willing heart buy?"

Realization struck me like a blow to the chest.

The tithing of the Sky-Sword. Eala was suggesting that Irian wanted my heart—given willingly in love—to keep the magic from destroying him.

He wanted to trade my life for his own.

Briars burst around my wrists, biting me with thorns. I hid my hands behind my back and blinked against burning eyes. Mortification and denial sent alternating waves of heat and cold crashing over me.

"No." The word came out hoarse. "He wouldn't."

Eala sighed. She lowered her eyes, then reached out to grip Chandi's palm. For a moment, the other girl's arm was boneless in hers. Then Chandi squeezed back.

"I was the latest. The last." Chandi's voice was hollow. Wooden. When she lifted her eyes to mine, they burned like coals. "You know I'm the youngest of us. So young, I don't remember a time before I came here. The others had parents, childhoods, *memories*. I was barely four—maybe younger. I had nothing. Nothing but them, and *him*. And yet he would manipulate me, seduce me, try and steal—"

She broke off, then buried her head against Eala's slender shoulder. Eala slid her arms around the taller girl and murmured something softly into Chandi's ear. When Eala turned to me, her gaze was fierce.

"We do not tell you this to hurt you. As you see, it hurts us more than it does you. We are only trying to help."

Her words crept through me like black rot.

Morrigan, but I'd been so stupid. Mother and Cathair had taught me the Folk were treacherous—unfeeling predators hiding behind exquisite masks. Everyone had warned me of Irian's heartlessness. I myself had witnessed the depths of his callousness at the Folk wedding. And still, I had fallen for the trap. For the brutal and bewitching beauty of someone—some*thing*—that did not love me. *Could not* love me. And I'd almost given myself to him. Not just in body. But in *heart*.

When you give me your heart, colleen, I want all of it. I want all of you.

I closed my eyes against the drowning, deceitful memories. Then I lifted my gaze to Eala. "What should I do?"

"With the translations you gave me, I believe I can break the geas binding me—*us*—to Irian." Her renewed smile was hard for me to read. "If the Sky-Sword truly cannot be wielded by human hands, then it is no use to us. Take it from the tánaiste, Sister. Hide it, damage it, destroy it—I care not. Only make it so it cannot be tithed anew. Then the last of the wild magic will be released, and the Gates will crack open. And we will be free. We will *all* be free. To pass between realms. To heal Fódla. To conquer the bardaí, and all Tír na nÓg, should we so choose."

Images from the Feis of the Wild Hunt flooded my head, raising doubt in their wake. Fell, feral voices baying at the night. Wind-whipped moors. Gruesome revels. Bloody armies.

"If wild magic goes free as in ancient times," I said slowly, "won't we be consigning not one, but *two* worlds to violence and chaos?"

"No, Sister." Eala's tone was clipped. "We will be returning what was stolen from us long ago. Magic. Humans will once more be able to wield the power that has so long been denied us by the Folk. And we will finally stand as their equals." She glanced up at the pinking sky, bruised with distant thunderheads. "Think on it, Sister."

Eala took Chandi's hand. But in the moment before the pair disappeared into the forest, Chandi paused. She glanced over her shoulder and met my eyes.

Before I could decode her expression, both girls were gone. A few minutes later, Rogan came crashing through the trees, his expression as tempestuous as the storm massing on the horizon.

We didn't talk. Halfway to the dún, a cool downdraft cut through the forest. The underbrush whispered. The trees turned the silver undersides of their leaves skyward. Lightning split the clouds. Fat raindrops splatted down, gathering intensity until the whole world became water.

The heat wave was over.

Chapter Thirty-Seven

Coll—Hazel
Late Summer

Dún Darragh echoed with unspoken thoughts and muddled feelings, and I was restless and bored and weary. Yet again, I'd drunk too much and eaten too little, and now the torchlit carvings on the walls writhed at the corners of my vision.

I snatched the half-empty bottle from the table, barely stumbling as I slipped out into the warm blue night. A waxing moon draped lengths of sheer silk across the world. I staggered into the trees.

I knew where I was going, although I wasn't sure *why* I was going. There was nothing for me there. Nothing for me anywhere.

But I was trying not to think about that.

The uncanny stones of the bridge by the willow glowed as if sun-touched, casting eerie shadows on the trees. Movement flashed on the other side of the stream—lofting antlers, muscular limbs, a face like a forest path. But then I saw it was someone else.

He stood on the arch of the bridge. He was like moonlight pooling between the trees, or rippled starlight on black water. He was—

Abruptly, I wondered when I'd stopped hating the inhuman smoothness of his marked skin. Hating the way he stood so still, like he encompassed a universe beyond himself. Hating the way he looked at me like he *knew* me.

"It's you," I murmured. "The one whose sword sings my name."

"What name?"

But I couldn't remember. "What is yours?"

"I was made of storm-rattled cliffs and star-hollow sky and the shadows beneath the moon. My name is—"

But the word he spoke was torn out of his mouth by the wind.

"What is your name?" he asked again, more intently.

"I was made of rot and moss and endless things," I told him. "But I don't know who I am."

Displeasure made his face grotesque. His limbs warped and twisted, the black feathers along his arms lengthening. He rushed toward me, even as he grew into something monstrous and malformed. My feet were too slow. He caught me, sweeping me up in great black wings.

"How can I have your heart?" His scream shattered the sky. "If you do not even know your own name?"

⌖

I bolted upright in bed, my pulse hammering in my chest. The nightmare clung to me like tatters of shadow. I jerked out of my clammy bedsheets and flung myself toward the open window. Cool night air dried the sweat on my neck, and I leaned my forehead against the stones of the casement.

The night was clear; the moon, a sliver shy of full. For three weeks I'd grappled with all the things I knew—or thought I knew. And now the full moon was two nights away, and I was running out of time.

We were all running out of time.

I had to make a decision. I had to *do* something. Even if it was the wrong thing.

I could continue to follow my heart—my wild, wicked heart. My heart, which was steeped in so much Folk magic I could no longer trust it. My heart, which told me to abandon Fódla—my family, my training, my loyalties—and put all my faith in the darkest parts of myself. The quiet, mossy corners that whispered secrets of home; the throbbing, root-tangled depths that sang acclamations of love.

Or I could follow my common sense. My calm, calculating warrior's mind, sharpened by years of training and whetted on poison and vengeance. My shrewd practicality, honed by a mother who raised me despite my Folk origins. My stubborn strength, ground into me by a man who saw my potential despite my small size and innate softness. My sound judgment, which told me my sister had no reason to deceive me.

Irian had every reason to deceive me. To seduce me—inebriating me on his treacherous beauty and sating me on carefully prepared stories. To steal the very thing I had fought so hard to make my own.

After the Treasures of the Folk, a heart is the most powerful magic in Tír na nÓg.

I clenched a fist prickling with tiny stinging spines. I remembered Irian's story at the Folk wedding—the origin of the wedding vows. A Gentry princess with greedy demands. And a foolish, lovelorn warrior, bleeding to death in the dirt because he thought he had to prove his love for it to mean something. And I remembered the first story Irian had ever told me—the story of Deirdre, the maybe mother I never knew, and the dastardly king who seduced her for her power. What had Irian's words been, when I complained about the ruinous ending?

Love is rarely anything but a prelude to tragedy, colleen.

Maybe, in his duplicitous Folk way, Irian had never really lied to me at all.

An inaudible laugh escaped me. In a way, Irian and I were perfect sides of the same coin. I, too, was arrogant—to believe I could seduce and outwit a Gentry lord on my first real mission. Selfish, to think I deserved an ending happier than the one already written for me.

And was I violent? Oh, yes.

Maybe Mother had been right: Only she knew how to love something like me. Maybe Cathair had been right: I was never made to love. Maybe Rogan had been right: Love only destroyed.

If they'd all been right and I'd been wrong...then maybe Eala, too, was right.

A breeze ruffled my hair, smelling of early frost and the first feather of dawn. I closed the shutters.

Summer was nearly over. It was time to remember who I was— what I was made for. I was loyal to Fódla. I was loyal to Mother. I was loyal to Eala, even if I did not agree with all her choices.

I was forged to be a weapon—raised to be strong, hammered to be hard, and whetted to be sharp. And weapons didn't think. Weapons didn't complain. Weapons didn't love. They cut where they were aimed.

I would take the Sky-Sword. I would destroy its heir. I would set Eala free and deliver Rogan his bride. And then...I didn't know. I didn't think it mattered.

After all, this was never my story. And once I had played my dark part, it would go on without me.

Chapter Thirty-Eight

I sent Rogan into Tír na nÓg ahead of me. I told myself it wasn't reluctance that slowed my steps—it wasn't indecision ratcheting the breath in my lungs. It was the anticipation of violence, the joy of the fight.

The promise of a kill.

I paused at the edge of the trees to steady myself. Then I closed my eyes and relinquished control over my Greenmark, letting the midnight magic of the forest creep over me. My rough breeches and fighting leathers melted away. Other sensations took the place of my clothes—the soft press of flower petals, the light rasp of long grasses, the velvety sweep of dark moss.

I opened my eyes. The slender, silky gown was like the glory of late summer. Golden as gorse flowers, it wafted like dandelion, plucked through with rosy streaks of aster and edged in the velvet black of a sunflower's eye. I pressed my hands against the front, relieved to discover I'd successfully kept my skeans—albeit hidden cleverly down the bodice.

Before I had the chance to reconsider my plan, *he* was there.

I felt him before I saw him—a storm on the horizon, a distant rumble of thunder.

He strode between the trees like a dark-edged wraith. His hair was black as a raven's wing. It had grown longer since I'd first met him—kissing his brow and curling around his ears. The ink-dark feathers embossing his bare, muscular arms pulsed in time to my racing heart. His eyes were silver as stars. For the space of a breath, I was once more bewitched by him.

He smiled. I tried to tell myself it was a smile like steel whispering against a bare throat.

But it wasn't. It was a single bar of moonlight breaking from behind a cloud, and it tasted like hope. That smile nearly broke my resolve.

I fisted my hands in the fabric of my gown and forced myself to remember every manipulation and deception. Every false story, every duplicitous touch. He had seduced me, groomed me, primed me to die.

And I—I had stalked him, plotted against him, cataloged his weaknesses.

Whatever stories I'd tried to tell myself, the truth was he and I had always been at war.

So I smiled back at the man I meant to destroy.

He stopped in front of me. I scanned his figure, forcing myself not to admire, but to inventory. His light but coiled stance. His restless gaze, which roved from my face in flickers of silver, constantly scanning the undergrowth for danger. The way his left hand floated higher than his right, never straying more than an inch from the Sky-Sword's hilt. To someone else, it might not mean anything. But I'd seen him fight, and I knew he was ambidextrous. Discounting the bare second between the speed of a left-handed draw and a right might mean death to a lesser warrior.

I lifted my eyes to his face. And regretted it.

His face was like music, like magic. More beautiful to me now than the first time I'd seen him. Now I knew the slight quirk to his eyebrows that meant he wanted to ask me a question, the way he tilted his head to look down at me from his superior height, the way that sensuous mouth felt pressed against my own—

I bit the inside of my mouth hard enough to taste blood.

"There you are, colleen." His voice was stretched tight with anticipation. "I have missed you."

Lies. All lies.

"And I you." My voice came out breathless, but that could only be to my advantage. Let him think me prey already caught.

I stood on my tiptoes and lifted my arms, curling them around his neck. I tilted my face toward his, drew him down to me, and kissed him. Fiercely. Hungrily. I dragged my teeth over his lips. I skimmed my hands down the front of his light tunic, trailing my fingertips over the ridges of hard muscles as I searched for more weapons hidden beneath his clothes.

He pulled me flush against him, my hips against his hips. Traitorous heat sparkled through me, like summer sun on rustling green leaves. I inhaled and reached for his belt, gripping the leather with my clammy fingers and preparing to push it through the silver buckle.

Irian lifted his mouth from mine. With a perilous, meticulous kind of self-control, he pushed me away.

"What are you doing?" His eyes simmered with desire, and his mouth was bruised by my vigorous kisses. But some intuition or insight swept across his expression, and his gaze sharpened on my face. "Something is wrong. You are shaking."

Shite. I clenched my fists, cursing him for his predator's instinct. It didn't help that I was out of practice at this kind of thing.

You were never very skilled at seduction in the first place, little witch. A cruel little voice that sounded a lot like Cathair whispered inside me. *Remember Connla?*

But it was too late to doubt myself now.

"I'm—" I stepped closer to him. I slid one of my hands—which were, indeed, shaking like leaves—up the front of his tunic. I lifted my eyes toward his face, making them wide and lambent. "I'm a little nervous."

He held himself stock-still. "Why?"

Again, I stood on my tiptoes. The top of my head barely cleared his shoulders. I tilted my chin, the skin of my cheek against the faint rasp of his jaw, and whispered into his ear.

"We started something last month." I brushed my lips against his neck. He shuddered. "I intend to finish it."

Irian's hands trailed up my arms, sweeping over my collarbones to cup my chin. The pupils of his eyes were blown dark with desire, obscuring the silver irises. Even so, his gaze raked my face, searching my expression for—what? I didn't know.

Whatever it was, he must have found it. Because he gathered me into his arms.

Space bent, churned, collapsed.

I fell to my knees on cool flagstones. For once, I didn't feel like I was going to hurl my dinner. Probably because I already felt nauseated about what I was doing.

No. I was made of sharp metal and dark deeds and black magic. I was made for *this*.

Irian's hand rested in the small of my back as he guided me to my feet. We had returned to his room—the tower room at the top of the dún. The same room Rogan had chosen for himself, in another world. A burst of vertigo made me dizzy, and I stumbled against Irian. He steadied me, then cupped my cheeks between his hot palms.

"Colleen." His voice was rough with want. "You are everything I never knew to hope for. I didn't think I had anywhere left to fall. And yet—I've already fallen."

For a moment, my resolve left me, and I was nothing but the lost changeling girl who'd waited all her life to be chosen. To be loved.

My eyes trembled shut. I fought for clarity, for purpose.

My senses came flooding back. My stomach churned. How dare he try to manipulate me with those words? And so easily. An icy, unsettling fervor settled over me, patching the shards of my resolve. I welcomed the coldness. It chased away the uneasy heat pulsing through my core and making my limbs weak. It reminded me who I was—and who I wasn't.

I silenced Irian with a searing kiss, fumbling for the fastenings down the front of his tunic, then simply ripping the fabric. The cloth tore, sending buttons bouncing into the corners and exposing his tattooed torso. His breath hitched as I reached out to touch him, his perfect expanse of musculature flexing beneath my hands. He let me trail my fingers down to the line of soft hair rising above the waist of his breeches before he caught my hand in his.

"Why the rush?"

"Why wait?" I purred, reaching out with my free hand to press against the front of his trousers. "Last time, I let my thoughts get in the way. Tonight, I mean only to act."

Beneath my stroking fingers, his arousal strained against the fabric. He leaned into my touch, resting his forehead against mine as he buried his hands in my hair. I nudged him two steps backward. His calves struck the edge of his low bed, and he abruptly sat. I pushed him onto his back and climbed on top of him. My gown sighed around us as I pinned him with my thighs. I raked my hands up his chest and bent to kiss his neck. He inhaled as his eyes fluttered closed.

I hesitated. His easy surrender to my advances was disarming. Briefly, I regretted that I could not abandon myself to this moment in the same way.

Swallowing my guilt, I struck.

There wasn't much for me to work with up here in this tower of pale stone. But I had anticipated that. His bedsheets were linen, and within seconds they disintegrated into the flax they'd been woven from. Long, fibrous stalks whipped around Irian's arms and tangled in his hair, sprouting tiny lavender flowers. My gown of gold and black—crafted from the magic of the forest below for this purpose—fell apart around me. Tough, thorny gorse grew swiftly over Irian's legs, pinning him down. Purple aster twined between his fingers, cuffing them to one another. Dark moss anchored everything else to the suddenly rotting mattress below. Within moments, Irian was entombed in greenery and flowers, and I was in my underclothes, crouched atop him with one of my skeans flush against his throat. The other was pointed below his belt.

Instead of fighting against his floral prison, Irian froze. Emotion winged across his face and beat his shadows into stiff, stark blots of darkness on the bed behind him. I recognized shock, followed swiftly by rage. But instead of descending toward all-consuming violence, his expression settled into... *hurt*. Surprise rustled to life inside me, and I fought the urge to look away from his uncanny stare. He tilted his jaw against my knife, daring me to cut him.

"Go on." His voice was low. "It might as well be you."

"Trust me, I will. But I need to do something else first."

With my second knife, I briskly cut through the layer of gorse and aster chaining his hips. The hilt of his sword slid free—he hadn't had time to unbelt it before lying down. I'd made sure of that.

I unsheathed the weapon. It came free of the scabbard with a sound like surrender—a note so pure it made my throat close with emotion. The black metal vibrated against my palm. Flickering images painted over my vision, vivid yet intangible—iron cliffs and fallow skies, seething seas and windswept trees. I clenched my eyes shut and twisted the hilt in my hand, mastering myself. I swept the blade up to replace my skean. Its kiss raised a line of silvery blood on Irian's throat.

"Tell me how to break the swans' geas," I demanded. "I know a heart is powerful magic. If I take yours, will it be enough to undo the curse?"

"You do not have to take my heart, colleen." He huffed a humorless laugh. "It is already yours."

"Stop *lying*."

"We have both kept secrets, colleen." His brows winged together. "But I have never lied to you."

"You seduced me." Blood throbbed in my ears, control abandoning me with every pulse. "You needed me to fall in love with you. You needed my heart—my *willing* heart."

"Your—" Surprise ghosted across his face. "But why?"

"To set you free." The words jumbled together. "The tithing of the Sky-Sword demands a life, doesn't it? My life, instead of yours. My willing heart, to pay your tithe."

"That is ridiculous."

I pressed trembling lips together. "Ridiculous?"

"The tithing doesn't demand *a* life—it demands *my* life." His eyes flicked between my own, glittering like starlight. "That blade you have at my neck is little more than a symbol, colleen. Like a torc or a staff or a crown. It is as it has always been."

The edges of my vision frayed. "I don't understand."

"The Sky-Sword is not a what. It is a *who*." His mouth curled into a dazzling, desolate smile. "I do not simply wield the Sky-Sword. I *am* the Sky-Sword."

Chapter Thirty-Nine

S top lying." I couldn't muster much venom. I felt dizzy, as if
I were spinning through a sky of falling stars. "That doesn't
make any sense."

"It was the Septs' greatest secret." The sharp, masculine cut
of his jaw tightened against the sword. "For long years, none but
the four chieftains knew the heirs to the Treasures did not simply
inherit the object, but the very elemental magic it represented. We
knew, too, of course—but only after we came of age and learned
that the price of our *great* inheritance was death."

Irony chilled his voice and made a wasteland of his gaze.

"Then the tithing—" I licked my lips, trying to make sense of
this new information. Trying to decide whether he was telling me
the truth. "Not a price, but a mechanism of replacement. The old
tánaiste dies so the new heir may inherit the power."

"Yes. But only if there is a new heir to channel the magic.
Otherwise—"

"The magic goes free." Realization pulsed through me. "The
bardaí discovered the secret, didn't they?"

"They did." His lip curled away from his teeth. "The Septs

already hid their heirs until they could come of age and undergo the tithing. But after Deirdre threw herself from that cliff with no living tánaiste to receive her Treasure, every mother, father, child, and cousin was in mortal danger. Entire lineages were threatened. Family by family, child by child, they were all butchered."

His words drove through me, seeding panic in their wake. I pulled the blade from Irian's throat, leaving a line of silver sliding down his skin. His throat convulsed, but otherwise he didn't move.

"What is this, then?" I hefted the blade of hammered black metal embossed with silver feathers. "I can feel it. The magic—it shows me visions. Of the night sky, of ruffled trees, of storms. I can hear it *singing*."

"It is a kind of conduit, channeling elemental magic between source…and vessel. It is ancient and sharp enough to carve stone, and sometimes I wonder whether it has thoughts and feelings of its own. But it is in essence no more than a sword. I am the vessel—I am *the* sword." His eyes lowered. "And the reason you can hear it singing…is because you are its next heir."

His words slammed into me like a punch to the chest. The sword fell limp in my hand. I pushed back from Irian and stumbled off the edge of the rotting mattress. My Greenmark receded—stalks of flax wilting, bunches of gorse crumbling, fronds of goldenrod sifting to dust.

"No." I was no tánaiste, especially not of magic that sang like the sky and burned like lightning. "You're wrong."

Irian sat up, rubbing his wrists where my makeshift ropes had scored his skin. There were flowers still tangled in his midnight hair—asters and marigolds and hyssops. There was blood on his throat and metal in his eyes. "I am never wrong."

He stood fluidly, stepped toward me. I raised the blade toward him once more, but the gesture was half-hearted, and we both knew it. He plucked the sword from my fingers and tossed it away. He loomed over me. I stood my ground, but I was suddenly very aware that I wore only underclothes. Confusion and lingering hatred and desire and shame burned green and gold through my veins. I clenched my fists and tried not to shake as I met his gaze.

"I guessed it that night on the beach, after you saved Chandika." His voice was dark as midnight. "When I saw your face—so like Deirdre's—it shocked me enough to let my control slip. And the way your magic responded to mine was..." He whistled through his teeth.

I shook my head, remembering high winds and falling water, rattling rocks and groaning trees. "But you—*you* did that."

"The wind was me. The rest of it...was *you*. You rattled the bones of the earth. Pulled stones into the air. Nearly ripped the forest up by its roots." He tilted his head. "It was raw, untethered magic. Pure potential. The kind of potential the Septs would once have battled each other for. And you did not even know what you were doing."

Wordlessly, I shook my head again.

"I was even more certain the night I brought you to my fortress," Irian went on, like I hadn't spoken. "As the tithe approaches, I grow ever weaker, even as the elemental power inside me struggles against its bonds. To anyone else—human or Folk—my touch would be like lightning. But you did not burn, did not scream, barely flinched. You tolerated it."

As if to prove his point, he brushed a scalding hand up my throat, sliding his fingers against my jaw.

"At one point, I even convinced myself you were starting to like it." Devastation marred his gaze. He dropped his hand. "But I see now I was wrong. So very wrong."

Guilt burned bile up my throat. "Irian—"

"You *used* me." His voice throbbed with barely masked pain. "You used my desire—my *love*—against me. You deceived me, seduced me."

"I thought you were seducing *me*!" Anguish painted my tone. "I thought—"

"Ah, yes. The wicked tánaiste who wished to steal your heart."

He turned abruptly away. He leaned his weight against the wall, then sank down until his long legs sprawled out on the cool flag-stones. His head tilted back to rest against the wall. His moonlit eyes were distant. "I suppose it seemed a fitting revenge, to steal mine?"

"That's not—" I bit down on my lip, hard. I remembered Eala's accusations. Chandi's confession—the way her eyes had burned like coals. "Eala told me you seduced the swan girls. One by one, trying to steal their hearts. The eldest first. All the way down to Chandi."

"They were but children when I cursed them, and I was barely older." His mouth curled with distaste. "We raised each other. As they matured, they grew to hate me for how I cursed them. And rightfully so. But I have always seen them as sisters. I would die to protect them. I would *never*—" He broke off, scraped a hand over his face. "It matters not. It only matters that you believed Eala. Over me. When I have spent the last eight moons telling you truths I have never told anyone. Showing you pieces of myself I have never shown anyone. Showing you—"

I didn't interrupt—I didn't dare. His metal eyes slid across my face, too sharp and too jagged. For a long time, he didn't speak.

"The night of the wedding, when you touched the Heart-wood? It sang for you, as it does for me. Then I knew for certain I was meant to tithe the sword to you." His voice was toneless. "It seemed impossible. For thirteen years I have spent nearly every night searching for another heir, and there has been no one. Not in the remaining Folk cities—Falias, Gorias, Findias. Not in the realms of the other Septs—Mag Mell, Ildathach, Tír fo Thuinn. Not even in Emain Ablach, the Silver Isle, where the smith-king Gavida reigns. The bardaí were too thorough.

"And then—*you*. A girl from the human realms with a face like a memory and a tongue like a thorn and a past as broken as mine. And I dared to hope you were my chance for a different ending. I dared to hope my story might be more than pain and failure and ruination. I dared to hope that before I died, I might finally have the chance to live, to—"

He bit down on the words. Stood up.

"It was a fool's hope. I needed an heir—I found one. And we tánaistí are all the same. We were bred to be. Arrogant, to assume we deserve our inheritances. Selfish, to want to keep all that magic for ourselves. And violent, to always protect our legacies. I should not have dreamed you would be any different."

Hurt shuddered through me, and then fury. "I'm not doing this for myself. I'm doing this for my people."

"Your *people*?" He took a step toward me. "And who might they be? Humans?"

"Yes." I lifted my jaw. "The ones who gave me a home. Who raised me. Who loved me."

"Who forged you to be a weapon? Who taught you to fear and revile your most essential self? Who taught you pain was only useful if you were the one inflicting it?" A dark note of irony touched his voice. "If that is love, then I suppose I have known it after all."

He took another step toward me. I retreated. "If you'd let me explain—"

My heels struck stone, and my back hit the wall. Irian stopped half an arm's length away.

"There is nothing left to say." His eyes were empty. "In two months I will tithe the Sky-Sword. If you are not there to receive it, wild magic will go free, and both our worlds will burn. If you are, then you will become as I am. Vilified. Hunted. Powerful beyond measure. You may do with that whatever you wish. Go back to the human realms if you choose—cure your sick and heal your wounded. Or stay here and spend the thirteen years you have left trying to find another doomed heir. It doesn't matter to me—either way, I will be dead. And glad for it."

"You don't mean that," I whispered.

"I do." Carefully, he reached out and brushed his fingertips along my chin, tilting my face up to his. "If you decide to accept your inheritance, colleen, I ask but one thing of you."

My throat was too tight to speak.

"When the time comes, promise me it will be you who strikes me down." He was barely touching me, yet his skin on mine burned. "You have already cut me deep. I know you will not falter."

My heart throbbed, pierced with a thousand biting thorns. *I might not mind oblivion, if you were the one to deliver it.* "There has to be another way."

"Do you think I have not tried everything? Promise me."

"I won't."

"Then you and I have nothing more to say to each other." He moved his hand from my face, placing it on my shoulder. My eyes widened. I reached for him.

"Irian!"

But I was too late. The night sky swallowed me up and spat me out. I fell to my knees in the forest, wearing little more than scraps of golden flowers and streaks of black rot. I rested my head on the dark, warm dirt, reeling from nerves and nausea and the dreadful sensation of impending tragedy. The surrounding trees reached branches down to comfort me. The green of their leaves was tinged with gold. Though the night was warm, a premonition of autumn's bright chill ghosted down my spine, and I shuddered.

I believed Irian.

Morrigan help me, but I believed him. I'd seen the hurt—the devastation—in his moonlit eyes when he became aware of my betrayal. That wasn't something you could fake. He had not wanted me for my heart. At least, not like that.

He had not seduced me or anyone else. If he could not physically touch a human without wounding them...then he could not have laid a finger on any of the maidens.

Which meant Eala and Chandi had lied to me. A huge, egregious deception meant to damn a man I had come to care for—to manipulate me into ruining him. And though I blamed Chandi...I knew which of the two women dictated, and which of them obeyed.

The truth slithered through me and settled heavy on my bones.

My sister, bound in love—perhaps also in blood. Despite the similarity of our appearances, I had always known she and I were not the same. But I had attributed her flights of whimsy and spells of callousness to half a lifetime spent among the Folk. Now I wondered whether her character didn't spring from somewhere more essential—a cold ruthlessness that was both painfully unfathomable and achingly familiar.

Like daughter...like mother.

It felt like the dimming of a light I had thought would always shine. It felt like betrayal.

"Fia!"

I whipped my head around so fast I put a crick in my neck. But it wasn't Irian. It was Rogan, bounding through the forest with dawn at his back. He came at me quickly—something must be wrong. Panic pushed me toward him, and we almost collided. He gripped me around my upper arms and steadied me. The unexpected contact jolted me—he and I had barely touched since we'd ended our dalliance.

"She did it." His river-stone eyes glinted. I stared at him, not understanding. "The translation you gave her—she says it explains everything. About how the Septs are bound to their Treasures. How the bardaí are bound to their Gates. How magic flows through Tír na nÓg. She knows how to set herself free."

His words sent a burst of panic to uproot my thoughts and strew them like leaves. What had she gleaned from the ancient warrior's words that I had not?

"How?"

"To break her from her captor, I must go to the Feis of the Ember Moon on Samhain and declare my love for her before the Folk host." Rogan wasn't celebrating. His mouth was set, his brows were knitted over his blue-green eyes, and his hands still gripped my arms. "We will be wed that night. As she joins the royal house of Bridei, she will be torn from the tánaiste's Sept. She will be free."

Relief coiled with alarm in the thicket surrounding my heart. It was a convenient solution—a declaration of love, an exchange of allegiances. Almost *too* convenient. The same night Irian was to tithe the magic of the Sky-Sword, Rogan was to swear himself to Eala? To buy her freedom with nothing more than his sworn love? It was like something out of one of Cathair's stories.

And Cathair's stories all ended in betrayal, deception, and tragedy.

"Rogan," I said haltingly. After months of pushing Rogan toward Eala, warning him away from her was the last thing I wanted to do. Yet after tonight, I feared I had to. "Do you remember the first time you met your betrothed?"

Rogan's gazed flicked down to mine, gray in the hush of dawn. "Why?"

"I fear that once again, the princess is handing you her doll and telling you to break it."

"Oh?" His mouth twisted. "What will my punishment be this time?"

"I don't know." I swallowed, unsure how much to tell him. "Folk geasa are near-inviolable magical contracts. To break one, an equal magic must be bought and paid for in counterpoise. I'm not sure if a simple vow of marriage is a big enough sacrifice."

Rogan's laugh was grim. "No matter how unwilling the participants?"

Reluctant sympathy sliced through me. "Rogan—"

"It doesn't matter." His hands tightened on my arms, then fell away. "I will do what I am told. If it is the wrong thing, then I will endure whatever whipping comes after. As I have always done."

"Just be careful—"

"I've always known my duty, changeling. And I've never had any choice in it." His voice rang hollow. "So I still have to do whatever I must to free Eala."

A root of sorrow wrapped around my chest and crushed my ribs, making me gasp. I fought sorrow and helplessness and guilt. Was this truly how the story ended? The hero prince ground to dust beneath the boot of duty? The changeling witch made to betray the truest parts of herself? The shining princess so caught up in her own schemes and manipulations that she had lost sight of her own light?

As the sun rose and birds awakened, we walked through the golden forest to Dún Darragh.

There were only two months until Samhain, until the Ember Moon. Only one full moon, as the world slackened, the trees crowned themselves in glory, and winter gnawed at the metal bones of an aging year.

I didn't know what I was going to do. I only knew two months wasn't enough time to decide.

Chapter Forty

Muin—Vine
Early Autumn

With a sigh, summer turned cool and golden.

After the warm season's sweet lull, I was busy in the garden once more. My list of chores expanded as the days cooled. There was weeding and raking and pruning. Next year's bulbs to plant. Pricking out seedlings for the winter crop. Planting new roses, hardy climbers, shrubs, trees, and perennials while the ground still held summer's heat.

Why bother? whispered a tiny voice in my head. Samhain was in two months. Whatever happened, I would soon be gone from here. And without my ministrations, this place would return to the way it was before. The greenhouse would decay, its glass panes splitting and its metal slats warping. The spring-fed grotto would clog with leaves. The flowers would die, and the vegetables would rot in the ground. The earth would go fallow and the forest would creep in, returning this place to nature.

To balance.

But after all the time and effort I'd poured into it over the past eleven months, I couldn't abandon it. Not yet. So I kept working, savoring these last cool sunlit afternoons in the garden. Burying them like acorns to be unearthed later—when frost grew cruel.

For Rogan's part, Eala's dubious revelation was a load lifted from his shoulders. He mended fences and trimmed hedges, bending blackthorn branches and weaving hawthorn. He unearthed a scythe from some forgotten corner of the dún and, after an afternoon spent sharpening its blade, mowed great swaths along the paths and groves. His sun-browned muscles rippled with each stroke, but I didn't like to watch him. Each stalk of golden grass falling before his scythe felt like the moments I had left—moments of sunlight, moments of summer. Moments to decide what I was going to do.

The year was growing old. I was running out of time.

❧ ～ ❧

"Careful, changeling!" Rogan called up to me. "If you fall from that height, you'll break every bone in your body!"

I looked down from my perch near the top of the overgrown apple tree, then ignored him, swinging higher.

The days and nights were almost equal—soon, the year would hurtle perilously toward winter. Leaves had ignited like tongues of flame as trees scattered seeds upon the wind. And the orchard had put forth a bumper crop of crisp, shiny apples. Which was why I was up here and Rogan was down there. Trying not to panic, which was the first funny thing to happen to me in weeks.

"Fia, honestly! Please come down."

"How did I not know," I shouted at him, "that the brave princeling was afraid of heights?"

"Anyone who's not afraid of heights just doesn't have a very good imagination!"

I grinned, grasping the gnarled branch where the sweetest sun-ripened apples stubbornly clung.

"Chiardhubh, chiardhubh," sang Corra, merrily scampering from winking leaf to knotted boll. They teased willing breezes to bend apple-laden twigs closer to my hands. "She'll make us apple pudding and apple pies, apple arms and apple thighs. Teach us the hows and show us the whys!"

"Me, make apple pie?" I snorted, plucking the last few apples and tucking them into my pockets before swinging lower. "Rogan, do you remember the time—"

I landed on solid earth with a thump, my words catching in my throat. Rogan wasn't looking at me—he stared into the bright-dark line of trees, the apple basket forgotten in his arms. I followed his gaze but saw only dying leaves, red as strawflower and yellow as rose mallow.

"What is it?" I laid my palm on his bicep. His skin flinched like a horse's hide beneath a fly. I let my hand drop.

"I thought I saw—" Rogan's hands tightened on the wicker basket.

"What?" I stepped toward the painted forest, my eyes combing through gathering shadows.

What I saw there chilled me.

Leaves crunched as I fell to my knees beside the body of a fawn. Or what was left of it. The juvenile doe's head was perfectly intact, if appallingly lifeless—her slender snout half-parted, pointed ears limp, amber eyes glazed. Her chestnut coat had already begun to thicken for the winter, obscuring the parallel lines of white spots curving down her back. Her front legs sprawled, delicate and disjointed.

Her back half…

Torn flesh and ragged sinew and shattered bone. Flies swarmed, and the stench of decay filled my nostrils. I pressed a hand to my mouth, fighting nausea as I forced myself to look away from the carnage.

Another doe stood in the shadow of an oak, poised for flight. The fawn's mother. Her depthless brown eyes held compassion. But not for herself.

For me. Me, as I knelt weeping beside her dead child.

She flicked an ear. Then bounded off through the undergrowth, her snow-white tail like an omen of the coming winter.

"Changeling?" Rogan crouched beside me, his bulk bleeding heat into the chilly afternoon.

"She was just a fawn," I whispered. "She was so young."

Rogan's hands moved over the torn flesh of the deer's bottom half, fingering the ragged hide.

"These aren't teeth marks," he murmured. "This was no wolf or bear."

"Then what?" My voice came out desperate—as though knowing what had preyed on the fawn would make this death make sense. "What killed her?"

My eyes landed on the scraps of shadow between the fallen leaves. No—they weren't shadows—they were *feathers*.

Stiff pinions scattered between fallen leaves, sharp as swords. Black as the space between stars, with an opalescent sheen that caught the light and turned it silver.

Foreboding loomed heavy over me, creeping close on clawed feet and beating great dark wings around my head. The forest pulsed like a dying heart. Bars of gold and silver striated my vision—sharp swords of light shafting between metal trees. And there were bells, although I couldn't hear them ringing, only feel the sound of them throbbing in my bones.

I knelt on the ground as thorns prickled up my arms. Sudden intuition chilled me.

This was the ending waiting for me.

It wasn't peace. It wasn't home. It wasn't even love.

It was balance. And its other name was *death*.

Slowly, reverently, I placed my hand on the dead fawn's back. Green light rippled from my fingertips, then burst into swift-growing vines twining and braiding over her russet coat. Jasmine and bell-flower bloomed, snow white and rose red. Roots of nearby trees unearthed themselves and clasped the tiny form, drawing it down until there was nothing left of the fawn but a mound of soft brown dirt and a cluster of bright, buoyant colors.

The black sky was vast and alive with stars. The barest sliver of moon hung above the horizon, a smile cut from sharp steel and honed on dreams.

He buried his face deeper into my hair, and I inhaled the cool-bright scent of him, like moonlight and ice water. The long grass itched against my skin.

"There." I traced a line across the sky with my finger, and he followed the arc through slitted eyes. "Did you see it?"

He laughed into my hair. He brushed his lips along the arch of my throat and smiled when I shivered.

"You always see more shooting stars than me." He slid his hand across my chest, fitting his thumb into the hollow where my pulse jumped. "If there were truly so many stars falling from the sky, then the night would be empty and black."

I rolled to face him, curling my arms around his neck and pulling him close. His lips captured mine and I sighed against his mouth. We tangled together in the silver-fretted dark, and there was no yesterday and no tomorrow: only he and me and the blanket of stars at the gateway to eternity.

If only that were enough.

I shuddered awake in the embrace of clammy sheets. Tears trailed cold down my cheeks and soaked the pillow.

I longed to bottle the dream: distill its flavors and drink it like liquor. Savor the warmth of his skin, the distant sweep of constellations I didn't recognize. The lingering taste of his lips.

But it wasn't real. Whatever had existed between Irian and me was ruined. And much as I might like to lay the blame wholly on Eala's cunning, it had been *my* fault.

I hadn't followed my own heart—I'd given in to suspicion and ambition and a lifetime's worth of conditioning. Cathair and Mother had taught me to hate, fear, and mistrust the Folk. But by extension, they'd also taught me to hate, fear, and mistrust the parts of myself that were not human. The shadowy depths of my heart; the spiky push of thorns at my fingertips; my lost memories, dim as a forest path.

I climbed out of bed. The idea stirring in me since Cathair's witch-bird had tapped on my window at Lughnasa raised an ugly, grudging head. I knew what I needed to do.

I had fallen asleep early, which meant the night was late but not too late. The door to Rogan's tower room was ajar, spilling candle-light onto the landing. I slid inside to find him bent over a sheaf of parchment, his fingers black with charcoal as a drawing spilled out below him. He stood up from the table as I stepped in. Pushed the drawing beneath another page. The candlelight played over his features and muddled his expression.

"Changeling?" He sounded weary. I didn't blame him—if his dreams were as unsettled as mine, then he probably wasn't sleeping either.

"Can I have Finan?" The winding stairs had stolen my breath. "Not *have* him. Borrow him? For a day or two."

Rogan's eyes were shadowed. "What for?"

"I'm going—" I hesitated. "I need to go home. For a little while."

Home. It had been a long time since I'd said that word. It grated against my tongue.

"Rath na Mara? Now?" He pushed golden hair off his face and frowned. "Why?"

"I'll explain later," I promised, as if I myself knew.

He still looked bewildered. "It's a day's ride across rough coun-try. And the full moon is two nights away."

"I know."

"All right." He still didn't sound sure. "Finan won't mind the exercise."

"Thank you."

I was nearly to the door when Rogan's voice reached out to stop me. "Fia?"

He stepped toward me. The taper by the door lit his eyes as they searched my face. I wasn't sure what he was looking for.

"Yes?"

"Don't rein Finan too hard—his mouth is sensitive," he told me after a beat. "And if he lathers, rest him. Otherwise you won't have a mount for the ride home."

"Understood." I was restless with the urge to leave, but Rogan's gaze was still heavy on my face. A lifetime of unspoken words swarmed the air between us, but I wasn't sure which of them he was waiting for me to say. "If I don't return by the full moon, go to Roslea without me. The Gates grow ever weaker—you may not need me to cross into Tír na nÓg."

He looked at me for another moment.

"Ride safe," he said.

I didn't need to be told twice. I sped down the stairs, saddled a drowsy, bemused Finan in a hurry, then raced out into the starry night.

Chapter Forty-One

Finan and I moved like ghosts through a sleeping world. The waxing moon provided enough light to see by, but I kept the stallion to a careful pace. The rhythmic beat of his hooves lulled me into a stupor. Thoughts and memories eddied through me, hollowing me out and washing me clean.

From the moment I woke up thirteen years ago in an unfamiliar bed with no memory and no name, surrounded by screaming voices and hate-stained faces, I'd believed that it was my responsibility to earn the love of the people who had taken me in. Maybe if I worked hard enough, my perfection would outweigh my flaws; if I trained hard enough, my strength would outweigh my weakness; if I acted human enough, my conformity would outweigh my Folk deviance. And then—*then* I could be loved.

But I should never have had to work so hard to be loved.

It seemed brutally unfair that love did not follow the same laws of balance that nature did. Love could be offered but spurned; longed for but unrequited. Love could simply end—in heartbreak or triumph or slow, dull fade.

Perhaps, in the end, that was the power of a heart. For love could not be bought or sold or stolen, only given—a magic more profound than any other.

The sun rose in a lavender sky, combing fingers of light over my face. Sweat darkened Finan's chest. With Rogan's warning in mind, I let him rest. I plucked starchy crab apples from overgrown trees and shared them with the stallion. I remounted. We cantered through pastures muddied from too much rain. Past fields where grain rotted on the stalk. Past abandoned farms where the thatch had been burned and the animals had been slaughtered. Grief and worry slinked through me, but remotely—my reactions filtered through a veil of distance I struggled to peer through.

When the sun slid past noon, Rath na Mara came into view, dominating the horizon from its position of power on the ridge above the sea.

I reined Finan to a halt, gazing at my erstwhile home. In the autumn sun, its stone walls and wooden palisade looked so solid, so sturdy, so *human*. I almost couldn't bear it. I swallowed against the weight pressing down on my chest and spurred Finan forward.

The flat plain that had hosted the camps of the Áenach Tailteann now played host to a different kind of encampment. Hundreds of brown canvas tents hunched below the fort. Healers moved between them, unmistakable in their red-and-white vestments. But not nearly enough healers for the multitude of the sick. Plague victims spilled out of the tents onto blankets laid in the mud, skin pocked with lesions and gazes bright with fever and desperation. There was no cure for the wasting sickness. Those who survived, survived. And those who died, died.

Dotted between the sick were the injured. Bloodied bandages. Missing limbs.

The healers seemed little better—exhaustion dogged their footsteps and dulled their eyes.

My chest tightened as I passed the encampment. Beyond, the fortress was heavily guarded. Twice the normal complement stood watch at the gates—sentries stationed all along the stockades, helms gleaming. I glanced over my shoulder, expecting some kind of attacking force, but there was nothing. Only a plain crusted in mud and dotted with dry brown grass.

A guard hailed me thirty paces from the gate. "Halt! State your business."

I reined Finan too hard. He jerked his head, snorting. "I bear tidings for the queen!"

"Your name, wench?"

Wench? I opened my mouth to dress down the sentry. But twenty feet above me, nocked arrows slithered against bowstrings. Eyes glared harder than even I was used to. I scanned the faces, but I did not recognize anyone among the fianna.

This was not the same home I'd left. Just as I was not the same person who'd left it.

I jerked back my hood, angled my face toward the sunlight, and shook out my long dark hair.

"Tell Cathair his little witch has come home!" I grinned, making a show of scanning the faceless guards. "Surely one among you has heard of me?"

Everyone was silent.

"Come!" I shouted. "Tell me I feature in at least one story you tell your children to scare them into eating their vegetables. No? Bedtime, then?"

Finally, the gate cracked open. Ten heavily armed fénnidi tromped out to escort me into the bailey, where I relinquished Finan to one of the stablehands.

"Water him well," I commanded. "And feed him grain."

"We've no grain, m'lady." The groom was young, and one of the fénnidi kicked him for his honesty. "Sorry."

"Then graze him, at least." I frowned at the boy until he nodded.

Assured Rogan's precious stallion would be cared for, I crossed the courtyard. The armed guard tailed me. In the shadow of the keep, I paused, rounding on them.

"I assure you, I can find my way to Cathair's chambers unaccompanied." I flicked my fingers. "You may go."

The rígfénnid gave me a mulish look. The men all clutched their spears and shields. I straightened and prepared to fight for a modicum of independence in the place I'd once called home.

"Gentlemen," said an oily voice from behind me. "Your escort is gracious indeed. But I can take it from here."

The warriors bowed, then trotted to their posts. I turned.

"Hello, little witch." The lines around Cathair's mouth creased deep when he smiled. "I've missed you."

Cathair was as I remembered him—slim, good looking, observant. But he seemed somehow less fearsome. There was more gray in his beard. The trinkets lining his fingers and clinking in his hair looked cheap. Dark circles ringed his eyes. Even so, hatred sent my blood pounding against my eardrums. I dug my nails into my palms, sending semicircles of pain lancing up my arm.

With a sweeping glance toward the sky, the palisade, and the fénnidi ringing it, Cathair stepped back inside the fortress. I followed. Inside, the halls were as I remembered them, if smaller. But that wasn't what gave me pause. The stones, the plaster, the wooden beams—they were all *lifeless*, inanimate. As, of course, they should be. But I had grown so used to Corra's squawking and teasing that Rath na Mara seemed sterile in comparison.

A fortress without a Corra felt like a body without a soul.

Cathair pushed into Mother's throne room, which echoed with emptiness. The door to her chamber of horrors was shut, for which I was grateful. I wasn't sure I could tolerate seeing strange objects ripped from Tír na nÓg—Folk artifacts displayed as spoils of war. The druid helped himself to wine from a decanter, then sat with his bejeweled cup on the plush velvet chair beside Mother's austere throne. It was his customary position, but it left me without a place to sit. Unless I wanted to casually park my arse on the throne of an absent queen.

It felt like an oblique sort of test. So I remained standing.

"Where's Mother?"

"The high queen campaigns against Eòdan. Their king grew

weary of shipping his precious grain to Fannon, where the newly crowned Connla Rechtmar garrisons too many fianna along his borders. Rechtmar retaliated, with Delbhna as his ally. The queen could not withhold aid from her king brother. Bridei remains neutral but has refused to fight the raiders who continue to settle land along the eastern marches."

Bridei was Rogan's kingdom. "Cairell Mòr risks war with Mother? But they have been allies for years."

"Nothing a wedding between a prince and a princess won't smooth over, I'm sure." Cathair's canny hazel eyes fixed me over the rim of his cup. "Is that something we can still expect?"

"A princess may return." I made my voice expressionless. "I may not."

"Hmm." Cathair's fingers tapped his glass. "I'm sorry the queen was not here to greet you. I have sent one of my birds to tell her of your visit, but I imagine it will be a week or so before she returns. You are welcome to wait, although we are on short rations until Eòdan surrenders. Or you can tell me what you came for, and I will pass along the message."

"I'm not here to speak to Mother." I was, of course. There was so much I wanted to ask her. I wanted to ask whether she'd known her husband had seduced and kidnapped a Gentry tánaiste for the power of her Treasure. I wanted to ask whether she'd betrothed her infant daughter four times over for the power and influence it bought her. And most of all, I wanted to ask whether her love for me had been nothing more than a ruse. A manipulation. But in truth, I'd begun to think the main reason I'd come to Rath na Mara was to speak to the serpent of a man sitting in front of me. Of all the wounds I'd borne, his had scarred the ugliest. "I'm here to speak to you."

Surprise flitted across Cathair's face. "Then speak, little witch. You have my full attention."

An hour before, my list of accusations had been a league long. Now, standing before the man who'd tormented, exploited, and abused me, I could barely find the words to tell him how much I resented him. How much his teachings had hurt me. How his influence had shaped me into a person I'd loathed for too long.

"I despise you for what you did to me." My voice didn't shake, and I was grateful for it.

"Yes." Was that regret behind his eyes? "I know."

"Is that all you have to say?" Reflexively, I reached for my wrist, a habit I thought I'd broken. Cathair noticed the gesture, as well as the way I forced my arm back to my side. "You drowned me. Burned me. Cut me. Poisoned me. You made me do unspeakable things to helpless creatures. You filled me up with stories about the heroism of humans and the villainy of the Folk. You took away the parts of me I loved most and replaced them with things I hated. You made me into a weapon, when I was born to be—"

My words failed me. Born to be *what*? I was only beginning to understand what I *wasn't*. I still had no idea what I *was*. I wasn't sure I'd ever understand.

Cathair surged out of his chair. He refilled his jeweled cup, then sloshed wine into a matching one. He pushed it toward me. I didn't move to take it.

"Mothers love their children." His voice was flat. "Fathers make them strong."

Revulsion nearly knocked me over. "You are no *father* to me. And never have been."

"You misunderstand me, little witch." His hazel eyes lifted to mine. If I expected them to be full of cruelty, I was disappointed. They were hollow as an empty grave. "Those are not my words. They were *hers*, a long, long time ago."

The thorns climbing my throat choked me.

"I grew up with Eithne—did you know that?" Cathair leaned against the sideboard. "My father was druid to her father, the late under-king of Delbhna. We were the same age, and there was a time when she and I were inseparable. And she was—" His eyes flew far away, to a past I could hardly imagine. "She was lightness personified. When she laughed, it was like the clouds dispersed, and you could see the sun. She was exquisite."

"That's a poetic way of saying you lusted after her."

Cathair didn't react to my jibe. "We were not made for each other. In time, she was wed to another and grew to love him. I was happy for her. But after Rían was slain by the Folk, Eithne changed. Before, she had been a coddled princess without a care in the world. After, she became a *queen*. All her fear and grief and helplessness transformed into something new. Something with sharp teeth and armored scales and venom. Something that slithered dark as a shadow into her heart. Something named hatred. Something that demanded vengeance."

"I know how the Gate War began. What's your point?"

"Sometimes it seems like mothers and daughters are a wheel that cannot stop turning, rolling through the same insidious cycles." Cathair stared into his goblet. "Eithne had been sold like chattel for peace between warring realms. Eala had barely been born before her mother did the same to her. But Eala was no Eithne. Oh, she was equally exquisite. But only in looks. It was as if the death and darkness that poisoned Eithne had tainted the child in her womb, extinguishing the lightness of spirit before it had even been ignited. Even as a little girl, Eala was cold, cunning, and devious. The harder the queen tried to bring her to heel, the harder she rebelled. The queen fought two wars. One with the Folk. The other at home. Eithne wished to forge Eala into her own image. Eala felt each blow of the hammer and hated her mother for it."

I tasted dirt in the back of my throat. Eala hadn't lied to me about *everything*, then.

"And then you came." Cathair nodded at me. "And although you were the same age as Eala, you were almost like a baby. You were a blank slate. You had no memories, no expectations, no notion of how you ought to act or be treated. You only wanted to be loved. At first, Eithne loathed the sight of you. But then a strange spark of hope struck off the anvil of her keen mind. She wondered whether the Folk had made a mistake in leaving one of their own with her. They might have stolen Eithne's shrewd and crafty daughter. But in her place they had given the queen a second chance at forging a weapon to destroy them."

I digested this, tasting each bitter word, each noxious divulgence. "But she didn't forge me—*you* did."

"Eithne has always known when to learn from her mistakes." Rancor twisted Cathair's mouth. "Do you think I relished tormenting a child? Do you think I was gratified to watch the same lightness I'd seen disappear from Eithne's eyes extinguish in yours? Do you think it brought me joy to sharpen you with malice, harden you with hatred, poison you with someone else's vengeance?" The look he gave me was shriveled with remorse. "It did not."

"Then why did you do it?"

"Because I love her. Because I have always loved her."

"Do you think that excuses what you did?" Now my voice shook. "You did it for love—she did it for hatred. Between the two, you turned me into something I was never meant to be. I *despise* you for it."

"I believe you. If it helps, little witch, you will never hate me more than I hate myself."

Something sticky and cold as sap slid down my spine. Had this been what I wanted when I came here? To hear him tell me he regretted what he'd done to me? To feel pity for a man who'd allowed his love to destroy his morality? To see my own self-loathing reflected in his eyes? I shook my head and turned on my heel. I was nearly to the door when Cathair's voice reached out.

"You have changed, little witch." I stopped but didn't turn. "I believed what we did to you put your light out completely. But something has reignited it. Or, perhaps, someone?"

"What are you talking about?"

"You're in love." He sat down in his velvet chair. Steepled his fingers. "I thought it must be Bridei's princeling. But now I wonder whether it isn't someone else. Some*thing* else. I don't know whether to congratulate you. Or pity you."

My lip curled, renewed loathing creeping through my veins. "I don't want your congratulations. And I don't need your pity."

Cathair shrugged. "Just be careful. A heart is powerful magic."

My pulse dropped out. I turned. "What did you say?"

"In the old stories, a willing heart can do almost anything. Steal magic. Create new worlds. Save doomed men."

I stared at him and wondered how much he knew. Had his witch-birds been spying? Had his fell book been whispering to him as he slept?

"But you only have one heart." His eyes on mine were sharp. "So you'll have to decide which of them you want to save. Choose wisely, lest there be no one left to save *you*."

For that, I had no ready response. Eventually, Cathair picked up his glass of wine to toast me across the dim throne room.

"Goodbye, Fia. I'd say, *May the gods go with you*. But I think we both know you must walk alone."

Chapter Forty-Two

I couldn't get back to Dún Darragh fast enough. But I'd ridden Finan hard—he needed rest. And so did I. I'd barely slept the night before, nor much the last month. So I choked down my half ration of stringy beef and barley gruel, then lay down on the narrow bed in my old dusty chambers.

But sleep proved elusive. At first, I told myself it was the noises of the castle keeping me awake—the banging of shutters and the clank of armored horses and the shouting of guards. But as night wore on and the noises diminished, it proved to be my own noisy head keeping me awake.

I tangled in the rough sheets, voices drifting through my mind like ghosts.

Only I know how to love someone like you. And no one will ever love you more than I do.

You will always have a piece of my heart.

Even loving parents make tools of their children.

I didn't think I had anywhere left to fall. And yet—I've already fallen.

You will never hate me more than I hate myself.

I was glad for dawn. I jogged out into the courtyard, calling for Finan as blue touched the horizon. I mounted. Seagulls and ravens circled high above, shards of black and white against a brightening sky. Their jagged cries echoed in my ears as the huge gates groaned in the palisade.

But the guards weren't opening the gates for me. They were opening them for their high queen.

Eithne Uí Mainnín rode at the head of her fianna, which trailed, battle worn, behind her. Although her figure was hidden beneath chain mail, and a helm in need of polishing concealed her shining hair, she still managed to look both elegant and powerful upon her warhorse. Within moments, the bailey echoed with the ringing of shod hooves. Fénnidi dismounted, Mother in their midst, shouting orders to the guards and grooms and courtiers pouring out of the fort.

No one so much as glanced in my direction. A cowardly instinct needled me, and I almost reined Finan past the milling fianna. Toward the gate. Toward Dún Darragh. Toward Roslea. Toward Tír na nÓg.

But then I hardened my spine with knotty wood and swung out of my saddle, looping Finan's reins around my hand.

I was made of pitted stone and twisted vines and wasted time. I was not made to fear queens. Or mothers.

Divested of horse and shield and helm, Eithne passed a few paces in front of me, already deep in conversation with one of her advisors. The fort and her duties would soon swallow her up. Convention dictated I wait to speak to her until tonight's feast, like the rest of her fawning supplicants. But I was running out of time. I had to speak to her now. Or never.

I pitched my voice to be heard above the hubbub. "Mother."

For a moment, I didn't think she had heard me. But she paused, frowned. Her eyes slid over Finan's imposing bulk, registering familiarity. Then she saw me.

"Fia." Surprise swept across her features, followed by an unreadable expression. Was it . . . *disappointment*? She closed the distance between us. She wasn't as imposing as I remembered. I'd never realized before—she was barely taller than I. "This is unexpected."

"Cathair said he sent one of his birds."

"Eòdan ambushed us at Cluain Tarbh. We changed course and traveled all night by the eastern road." Her eyes raked me from head to toe, assessing. It was the same way Eala had looked at me. "You look tired. And I see you've gained some weight."

The criticism was mild yet powerful—leaden as a rusted shackle around my neck. Part of me wanted to gladly bow beneath its familiar weight. To grovel and cower—to beg for a compliment or a way to atone for my imperfections. But the chain was heavier than I remembered. I found I was no longer willing to be trussed up in Mother's machinations, fettered by her manipulations.

I lifted my chin and met her hard, pale eyes. Behind her, advisors and generals clustered and hovered. Mother would have neither the time nor the patience for the kind of dialogue I'd shared with Cathair. I had to choose my words carefully.

"I will not keep you from your campaigning for long." I lowered my voice. "But a tangle has arisen in the matter you sent me to resolve."

"What kind of tangle?" Her eyebrows lifted. "Could you not have written?"

"And risk sensitive information being intercepted?" I shook my head. "The story is long and winding. It comes down to this— Eala's geas is rooted deep and can only be broken in one way. The destruction of the Treasure you sent me to retrieve. Otherwise she dies at Samhain."

This was a lie. But I wasn't above my own manipulations—I wanted to force Mother to admit her priorities. To show me which she cared about more—her daughter or magic.

Love or vengeance.

Mother's eyes flickered. Her mouth set. "That is an impossible choice."

"And therefore, one I knew you would not want me to make

on your behalf." I bowed my head in a show of deference. "What would you have me do? Save Eala? Or bring you the magical object you have long desired?"

For a long time, Mother was silent. When she finally spoke, her voice was expressionless.

"Since Rían was slaughtered, I never thought to bear another child. But I am still in my prime. Perhaps I will fall pregnant again. And even if I cannot, I have many fosterlings. I may still mold one of them into an heir worthy of the Ó Mainnín lineage." She stepped closer, gripped my chin in an almost painful grasp. The leather of her gauntlets was cold and rough against my skin. "If a choice must be made, I will make it. Our people tremble beneath the weight of war, famine, and plague. Bring me the magic Fódla requires, no matter the cost. But know this, a stór—I consider it a failure on your part. And I will not be quick to forgive."

It was the answer I'd expected. And yet her choice dug sharp into my chest and squeezed my heart—as if I were the daughter Mother consigned to die, instead of Eala. I wrenched my chin out of her grasp, even as her conflicting words jangled in my ears. She called me by the pet name she'd used since I was a child, yet simultaneously told me she could not easily forgive me for failing her. In the same breath, she told me how much she loved me...and how difficult a thing I was to love.

That, too, was the same as it had always been.

And I was finally beginning to realize—it wasn't love at all.

If she registered the defiance beginning to shudder through me, she did not show it. She turned to her waiting cadre of generals and advisors.

"One last thing." I threaded my voice with command and thrilled a little when she stiffened. "Did you never hesitate to make a child into a weapon?"

She looked back at me, very slowly.

"When you told Cathair to make me strong—to forge me with violence, fill me with venom, hone me with hostility—did you never think what that would do to me?" I spoke softly, swiftly. "Or did you think only of vengeance?"

"We did make you strong." She stepped close to me again. This time, she did not touch me. "That is nothing to complain about."

"You told me you loved me, yet filled me with hatred."

"The things we love are weapons to be used against us. Hatred is armor. Hatred makes us invincible."

"You're wrong." I exhaled, releasing memories of rats in buckets and budding flowers tossed on the fire and painful bracelets of nettles and brambles. "The things we love can hurt us, yes. But our capacity *to love* is a far greater weapon."

"If you believe that, then I have failed you." Her jaw hardened and irony touched her voice. "Perhaps you are not such a sharply honed weapon after all."

"Maybe." I flipped Finan's reins over his head. Mounted in one smooth motion. "Or perhaps I am not a weapon at all."

I turned my back on Rath na Mara, Cathair, Mother, and the past thirteen years of my life. I rode toward home.

Dusk was falling when I reached the fort, a chill wind scudding dark clouds across new stars. The air smelled like woodsmoke and fallen leaves.

"Corra!" I shoved into the dún and spun on my heel, scanning the walls for movement. "Are you there?"

"Here, there, everywhere." A squat toad leapt to life on the wall, sliding a long tongue around its mouth.

"Where's Rogan?"

"The rancorous pigeon-egg canker-blossom?" The toad blinked at me with bulging eyes. "Gone. As we predicted."

"He's already left for Roslea?" I cursed. "Donn damn him."

Chapter Forty-Three

Gort—Ivy
Autumn

Finan and I sped toward Roslea. The stallion shook his head in protest but did his best to weave between the trees despite his mounting exhaustion. Contrition rose in me, but I was exhausted too—there was no way I was going to make it to the Willow Gate on foot before the moon rose. Soon, the shadows of stone monsters opened vast jaws to swallow us. The stallion reared up, nearly unseating me. I laid a gentling hand on his neck, careful not to surrender to the forest pulsing green and black through my veins.

My brief time away had dulled the memory of how strong my Greenmark was here at the edge of Tír na nÓg.

I dismounted. Rogan was nowhere to be seen. I led Finan to the stream and let him drink deeply, then tossed his reins over a nearby sapling and loosened his girth.

"Sorry, old boy," I murmured into his mane. "No warm stable or hay for you tonight."

The stallion whickered, shoving his huge black nose into my chest.

"If anything tries to bite you, just kick them. Rogan will take you home at dawn."

The horse bent his head to crop at the grass edging the brook. And I crossed into Tír na nÓg.

———

I stared up at Irian's fortress, which glittered like a dark dream atop a starshine hill. I'd never actually walked up to it—Irian had always flown me inside. I knew it had windows, but did it have doors? If it did, I had no idea where they were. The notion of walking inanely around the fortress looking for entrances made me queasy with embarrassment. But what was I here for, if not to atone? Perhaps I deserved a modicum of humiliation.

I inhaled, flicked the end of my mantle over my shoulder, and climbed. The fort rose up before me, and I found my worries were for naught; it did, indeed, have a door. I put my shoulder against it and pushed.

A stiff gale lashed through the entrance, slamming the door shut and shoving me back. I planted my feet and pushed again. The flagstones shuddered beneath me. The fortress groaned. The door rumbled open. I forced my way inside, even as wind whipped my hair and threw dust in my face.

"Irian," I ground out, "stop it."

The wind died.

Irian stood at the top of the staircase, gripping the banister like he might fall without its support. At his back, shadows coiled in charcoal spirals, lifting the ends of his hair into wings of night. Moonlight spilled down from the high windows, painting his face with bright splashes of emotion: wrath and regret and something akin to relief. His struggle rattled the stones beneath my feet. Howled smoke in the hearth. Shook painted leaves from the living chandeliers.

"Irian." I mouthed the contours of his name like I could reach through the sounds and touch him. "Irian, I never meant—"

His hand made a slashing motion, and my words died in my throat. He came down the stairs two at a time, until he stood before me. His silver eyes writhed with warring wants, warring needs.

"Why have you come?" His hands clenched and unclenched at his sides. He didn't move to touch me. "You should not have come."

"Irian, I'm *sorry*. Please listen to me—"

"Have you decided?" His expression was jagged. "I need to hear you say it."

He was talking about the tithe. "No, I—"

"No?" He rocked back a step. "Then return when you have made up your mind."

"Listen to me!" My guilt twisted into anger. "Once there was a changeling."

Irian stilled. The distance between us felt vast: dark and cold and impossibly huge. "The time for stories is past, colleen."

"She had never known love." I tasted moss and black rot in the back of my throat. "So she searched for it wherever she could. And as the years passed, she was given many opportunities to fall in love. She did so gladly—a hundred times, and then a thousand more."

Irian made a noise deep in his throat.

"Yes—a hundred thousand loves, and none of them real. The girl fell in love with a mother who desired only vengeance, because she did not know the difference between being used and being loved. She fell in love with a fénnid laughing too loudly in the training yard, if only to share his joy. She fell in love with the princeling who snuck her his portion of meat beneath the feasting table. She fell in love with the sweet-faced girl hauling barley down the lane, for to have such simple purpose seemed like bliss. She fell in love with the forest. She fell in love with the night. But she never—ever—thought to fall in love with herself."

Irian was a statue carved from moonlight and marble.

I sucked in a deep, harsh breath. Irian was right—the time for stories was past. "Even as I learned to blindly love the human world

that raised me, so too did I blindly learn to hate myself. I thought—
I thought as long as I despised myself more than they did, I might
one day earn their love. So I taught myself to hate the blood running green and black through my veins. To loathe the way I seemed
made, from rocks and trees and half-rotted memories. To detest the
way the forest called to me, as if my hair were vines and my bones
were roots and my heart was a green stone. But to hate those parts
of myself, I also had to learn to hate the place that had spawned
them. I had to learn to hate magic. To hate Tír na nÓg. To hate the
Folk. To hate *you*, even as I fell for you."

"Colleen—"

"I am trying to unlearn all that hate, Irian. But it is rooted
deep."

Irian's silence was unyielding. My pulse thrummed in my chest.
When he finally spoke, his voice was so hoarse I barely recognized it.

"Once there was a boy. He was not so fortunate as the girl. He
only ever knew one love. One great, terrible, consuming love. A
love that snatched him up and ground him to dust and swallowed
him whole. A love that would blot him out completely if he was not
careful. A savage, scathing, sublime love that only came once in a
lifetime and demanded everything of him. I—"

He broke off. Then he was reaching for me like I was salvation.
He caught me by the waist and dragged me against him, sliding a
hand under my chin to tilt my face toward his. The kiss he brushed
over my lips was hard. Hot. Fragile.

He drew back an inch.

"Have you ever stood at the top of a tall cliff and, though terrified by the height, wildly wished to fall?" His silver eyes flicked
between mine. "That is what loving you feels like. Everything
hurts, and yet I want more of it. To climb a little higher, to press a
little harder, to drive the blade a little deeper. Because being with
you makes me feel so—"

I slid my palms up the front of his mantle, curved my hands

around his neck, tangled my fingers in the silky strands brushing his nape. "What?"

He leaned his forehead against mine and whispered the words against my mouth.

"You make me feel alive, colleen. Even as death looms. If loving you is a cliff, then I have already fallen over it."

He pulled me close and I kissed him back, fierce with hope and hunger. I dragged my hands down his neck and over his arms, his hard, lean muscles contracting beneath my touch. He dropped his mouth to my throat, dragging scalding, shivering kisses against the side of my neck. I hissed as his tongue laved the sensitive spot beneath my ear.

"Apologies." He drew away abruptly, although his words were frayed with want. "I am too forward. We need to talk; we need to—"

"Do you want to talk?" A laugh rasped in my throat, sharp as hyssop and bright as feverfew. "The last thing I want is to talk."

"Good." His eyes darkened to iron. "Where?"

"Bed?" My voice was breathless and my skin was hot.

"You may not have had your way with me last month," he said with a grimace. "But you did my bedroom. My mattress is mulch and flowers. The whole tower has become something of an ... arboretum."

Mortification slapped warmth on my cheeks. But the front of his shirt bled heat against my palms, and his scalding fingertips were buried in my hair—he was too close for me to stay embarrassed for long.

Enough with the logistics. I wanted him *now*.

"Then I suppose *here* will have to do."

I pushed him. He reeled back a step. His calf struck the stone staircase behind him. He sat on the third step, hard. Before he could rise, I straddled him, slinging my thighs around his hips and sliding into his lap. He inhaled, maintaining blistering eye contact. His pupils blew wide—desire eclipsing the moonlight of his gaze.

I arched myself over him, my dark hair falling around us like a curtain of night. His hands found my waist, his fingertips teasing circles of heat against my skin. I leaned down and kissed him—languorously, provocatively. I slid my tongue in his mouth and nipped my teeth over his lips. He made that glorious noise deep in his throat and rocked his hips up against mine. Even through our clothes, I felt the spectacular length of him.

Clothes. I undid the hasp of his cloak without looking, then unlaced the ties down the front of his undershirt, tearing away the fabric to expose the planes of his sculpted body. I skimmed my fingertips down his chest and stomach. His skin shivered and flexed beneath my touch. But when I reached for the waistband of his trousers, he growled and caught my hands in his.

Faster than I could blink, he slid his palms beneath the hem of my shirt and pulled it up over my head, sliding my arms out of my sleeves and mussing my hair. His eyes dragged hungrily over my naked torso. His hands followed a moment later, trailing up my waist and against the side of my breasts. I arched my back, pushing them into his palms. His breath hitched. He leaned forward to take one of my nipples into his mouth, sliding his tongue over the sensitive peak. I moaned into his ear.

The sound triggered something feral in him—he went hard all over. In one smooth, powerful motion he flipped me onto my back and ripped off my breeches. Even with his cloak spread out beneath me, the stone steps cut a chill against my spine. I didn't care.

I watched, transfixed, as Irian unfastened his own trousers, dragging his belt off and tossing the black sword carelessly onto the floor. Moonlight spilled over the angles and curves of his flawless form. His hardness sprang free, kissing the planes of his stomach as he propped himself above me. A thrilling ache tangled in my core, and I reached for him. I brushed my hands up the velvet length of his erection and watched his eyes flash silver before darkening to metal. His hands tightened on my hips, then slid lower, caressing down the outside of my thighs to find my knees.

Slowly, deliberately, possessively, he pushed my legs open. He settled his weight between my thighs, nudging himself against my slick heat. A delicious yearning built in my belly, and I rocked my hips, savoring the feel of him pressed hard against me. But he still hesitated, his eyes roving over my face, my breasts, my stomach.

"What are you waiting for?"

"I am...savoring." His smile simmered with anticipation and desire and unfocused melancholy. "We will never again be able to do this for the first time."

I rose up on one elbow, buried my fingers in his hair, and dragged him down for a wild, seething kiss. "Stop savoring, Sky-Sword. And fuck me."

Braced against the step above me, his forearms grew rigid. Stomach flexing, he pushed himself inside me. Slowly, at first—*so slowly*. The tip of his cock slid into me, stretched me, edged me perilously toward pleasure. I gasped at the hot sensation of him filling me up, and the sound broke his control. I cried out as he thrust into me—he was too big; he burned too hot—but behind the sharp ache a deep well of want rose inside me. A desire that eclipsed everything. A need that had to be fulfilled.

Behind me, the stone stairs shuddered. Cracks burst jagged along the granite, and small plants sprouted in the seams. Stonecrop. Artemisia. Phlox.

Irian's eyes jerked toward the flowers creeping over the steps. But he didn't hesitate, didn't frown, didn't falter. His eyes skated to my face. He curled one hand around my neck, dragged a thumb against my jaw. And smiled.

When he pulled back and thrust again, I moved with him, sliding my hands over his unyielding arms and raking my fingernails down his shoulders. The slippery ache inside me intensified. I clasped my legs tighter around his waist, digging my heels into the small of his back and driving him forward. He groaned against my neck and buried himself even deeper inside me, tangling his hands in my flower-twined hair. He dragged his tongue over my throat, tasting the sweat beading along my skin.

"Colleen—" he growled.

"Don't stop," I gasped out. "Don't you dare stop."

He didn't. He pushed deeper and harder, and the rhythm of our joined bodies obliterated any thoughts or doubts I had left. He pushed me toward the edge of the throbbing, thrumming need consuming me. I surrendered, wild as the dark green earth. I cried his name as I came apart, and the sound undid him. I clung to him as his movements became relentless. With one final, shuddering thrust, he spent himself. He slid against me, breathing hard, then rolled his weight off my frame.

But he didn't let me go. He pulled me to lie with him on the floor below the steps, the cool flagstones littered with tiny blossoms of white and gold. He curled my back against his front, burying his face in my hair and breathing me in. I molded my numb, tingling body to his. His arms curled protectively over my chest as we both gasped for air, shaking with lingering tremors of pleasure.

"Was that all right?" he asked me after a few minutes. "It has... been a long time."

I laughed, still breathless. The afterglow of pleasure and adrenaline made my eyelids heavy, and I fluttered them shut. "It wasn't bad."

He pulled me tighter against him, tucking my rear against his hips. Surprise smoldered through me when I felt him already beginning to harden. His hand curved over my waist and splayed on my stomach, his palm igniting my already sparking nerve endings. A wave of anticipation spangled through me.

"It *wasn't bad*?" His voice was crisp with dark humor. "You wound me."

"So sensitive." I tsked. His hand slid up my waist to cup my breast, his thumb drawing lines of fire around my nipple. "I should have guessed you'd be a perfectionist."

"Not a perfectionist." His growing erection pressed hard against my rear. "Just arrogant enough to think I can do better than *not bad*."

"I remember you mentioning this supposed arrogance." Rose

petals bloomed warm against my skin. "But, if I recall, you paired it with violence and selfishness. Do those traits also extend to the bedroom?"

"Violence? Not without being asked." His hand slid down my stomach, brushing over my navel before delving between my legs. "And selfishness? Well. Where would be the fun in that?"

His fingers were deft, determined, and my desire soon rose to meet his. My breath became ragged as he leisurely pushed me toward the edge of another climax. I caught his hand in the moment before I fell apart, guiding it to my hips. I opened my legs and angled my rear against him, inviting him back inside me. He inhaled and accepted, sheathing himself to the hilt in my slick warmth.

This time, there was no wild release, no loss of control. Irian was slow, careful, *exacting* in his pursuit of my pleasure. He slid deep inside me, building the heat tangling in my core to something almost unbearable. Then his arm tightened around my waist, finding my center once more. He increased his rhythm. My legs stiffened. He brushed the hair away from my face and sucked my earlobe into his mouth, sending sensation cascading down my spine.

I moaned, then shattered, stars falling against the backs of my eyelids as I arched against him. Blackness rushed in, and it was all I could do to hang on to consciousness as he dug his fingers into my hips and followed me over the edge.

Together we fell, like starlight and storms and sunlight on broad leaves. We crashed against each other like a gale against the shore, until the only thing either of us knew was each other.

Chapter Forty-Four

We drowsed. A minute, an hour—I wasn't sure. I only knew that
when Irian pressed a languid kiss below my jaw, slid his arm
from beneath my head, and sat up beside me, I didn't want to wake up.

"Colleen. *Fia.*" My name on his lips sounded like a prayer. "The
sun will soon rise. You should return to the Gate."

I cracked my eyes open. Light spilled dream-soft over the windowsills and painted the flagstones in shades of lily and rose.

"I want to stay." My voice rasped with sleep. I reached for him,
my fingers on his wrist soft, inviting. "I want to stay with you."

"I want that, too, colleen." The hollows of his face were bruised
with dawn. "I want it like a flower wants the sun, like a river wants
the sea. But you should go."

My skin cooled. I, too, sat up. I curled the edge of Irian's cloak
over my nakedness. "Why?"

"Because—" His face contorted. "We are running out of time."

"All the more reason for me to stay."

"Not that. I—" His silver eyes were veined with gold as he
cupped my chin and met my eyes. "I have kept one last secret from
you, colleen. I—"

In a rush, we lost the night. The sun rose in rapture. Brightness curled greedy hands around Irian's silhouette and dragged him back, although his hands still cupped my face and his lips hovered above mine. Tension shuddered through him, bunching the muscles of his shoulders and bucking his spine. Black vines sprouted beneath my fingers, bristling along his forearms and prickling my skin with vicious thorns. Not vines—they were the spines of black feathers, piercing like needles through flesh.

He jerked away from me. His eyes scalded my face, golden as new coins.

"Close your eyes, colleen." He shielded his face from my gaze. His buckling hands were already furred with midnight quills. "Turn away."

"Irian—"

"*Please.*"

The desperation in his voice compelled me to obey. I stared off into the dim fortress. His shattered screams of agony burrowed into the crevices of my heart. I trembled with the torment of his transformation, my heart pulsing in ragged syncopation to his pain.

Finally, it was over. I uncurled myself, forcing my clenched muscles to relax as I opened my eyes.

Irian was gone.

I touched my lips, remembering every stolen kiss I'd shared with him, even as I fought burgeoning betrayal. He'd kept this secret from me, for all these months—

Ah.

It had been a badly kept secret.

The Sept of Feathers.

Swan maidens, cursed and bound by a monstrous magic.

A yearling fawn, torn to shreds by the grasping claws of an enormous aerial predator.

I remembered Irian's voice as he stood upon a high hill and told me about the wild magic that warped him, consumed him, *transformed* him. I remembered lying in his arms while high on the black flower's potent visions and dreaming I was being choked by a monstrous black bird. The following morning, he'd flown me to the Gate only to disappear like shadows in the wind.

I closed my eyes, fighting the cowardly part of myself that wanted to flee. To run back to Dún Darragh and hide inside its high stone walls, its secret gardens. To hide inside myself—inside my *hatred*. My hatred not only for myself, but for all the ugly, imperfect, beautiful things that were also a part of me.

So—Irian was truly a monster. A warped black-winged swan cursed in counterpoise to the white swans whose transformation he mirrored. The geas he had wrought with corrupted wild magic had bound the maidens' lives to his, and his to theirs. A curse for a curse. A price paid in constant balance.

But I had always known he was monstrous, from the first moment I saw his perfect face wreathed in creeping shadows. And I had fallen for him anyway. As he had for me. I met him beneath night's moonlit glamour. And now I'd seen how he transformed by the light of day. In the end, it made little difference to me.

Here, we are all villains.

I dragged Irian's cloak around my chilly shoulders and walked to the window. Tír na nÓg was aflame with new sunlight and autumn's golden glories. The Sky-Sword lay forgotten on the floor where Irian had unbuckled it last night.

I picked the blade up, handling it gingerly. The symbol of the Treasure Irian embodied. The conduit for the magic Irian wanted me to inherit from him. The emblem of the transformation I myself would have to undergo if I wanted to protect the human realms from the unrelenting push of wild magic. From the bardaí, who wanted to break down the Gates and rain slaughter on the people I had once called my own.

In the daylight the uncanny metal shone like sunlight and blue skies. It sang like lightning against my palms, a feeling so different from my own cool, creeping magic. How could I be heir to *this*— cloud and wind and endless skies—when all I had ever known was branches and thorns and the shaded path beneath the trees?

I inhaled crisp autumn air and rested the sword on the window-sill. I counted down the days until Samhain. Until the Ember Moon. Until I had to decide.

Suddenly, every moment—every breath—felt like the ephemeral kisses and scalding touches I'd shared with Irian last night. Fleeting and easily squandered. Only so much could be borrowed—*stolen*—before the balance of Tír na nÓg's magic demanded payment.

And I found I begrudged the cost.

I didn't stray from the fortress that first day. I wandered its halls and admired its intricate, serpentine details, so different and yet so similar to Dún Darragh. I ran my hand over a detailed carving of a creature I did not recognize, and softly called, "Corra?"

I got no answer. But I fancied the barest edge of supernatural attention, an awakening of the stones beneath my feet, a tremor of life along carven spines. A sound caught my ears, like the tolling of a distant bell, but when I turned toward it, it was gone. Nothing more than an echo of a strange, teasing voice.

I had to wonder.

As the days cooled and the trees flamed, I wandered deeper into Tír na nÓg. By daylight, the Folk realms were impossibly, exquisitely unreal. Plains of sunlight. Trees whose fruit tasted like old memories and spiced secrets. Flowers that sang like stars.

I watched the dozen elegant swans ruffling pale feathers over crystal blue water. They stared at me with depthless black eyes before diving for pondweed. I wondered if they knew me. I wondered which of them was Chandi. Which of them was Eala.

I closed my eyes and listened to the trees whispering secrets. They told me of broken magic and rotting earth. They told me of coming winter. They told me of doorways between the realms of the Gates—copses of bloody trees and porticoes of fallen cities and corridors of ravines where the wind eddied crystalline leaves. They were the secret ways Chandi used when she led me through Tír na nÓg.

I began to learn them. I wended my way like a ghost, conspiring with the forest to keep me hidden. I saw ghillies bathing in crystal ponds, cooling their pale, striated skin and damping their mossy hair. I glimpsed colonies of sheeries spinning webs of sunlight designed to catch daydreams. I spied on clusters of incandescent Gentry, but their sunlit promenades looked like battle marches; the cacophony of their fluted voices sounded like a carnyx of war.

I climbed the hills above Murias and stared into the warped cloud of wild magic until my eyes ached. I imagined what it would feel like to be the only force standing against it, and what a toll that must take. I imagined what it would be like to take that tainted power inside myself. I imagined what it must be like to transform, day after day, into something that disturbed me.

When I hiked to the fort, tiny black flowers began to sprout beneath my boots. I paused, then ground them under my heel.

Tír na nÓg by darkness was fragile, intense, heartbreaking. It was the most wondrous dream and the most tragic nightmare I'd ever experienced.

That was when I was with Irian.

Dusk wafted silent across the windowsill, that first night. He rushed in like a nightmare, wrenching shadows from light. Inky feathers scattered across the flagstones. I dived for him as he reached for me. Claws like thorns pierced my palms, even as black feathers receded along his forearms. I locked eyes with him, watching his pain disappear into the murky oubliettes of his geas.

He rested his forehead against mine, sliding his hands around my waist in the way of things held too tightly—as though he feared I might slip through his fingers if he wasn't careful. Heat flared through me, painting my bones in shades of dahlia and rose.

"I hoped—" Irian's whisper cracked. "I hoped you would still be here, colleen."

Colleen. Something about the tender way he said that nickname—that stupid, annoying, perfect nickname—splintered my composure. I breathed in the sharp scent of him and swayed closer. Close enough for our bodies to mold to each other, the hard planes of his torso unyielding through my clothes.

"Why would I want to be anywhere else?"

His lips brushed mine as if he were waking up from a bad dream. My blood quickened at his touch, and I reached up, twining my fingers in the hair curling damp at the nape of his neck. He pulled me closer, tracing the notches of my spine with his fingertips and sending pleasure stitching golden along the fabric of my skin. I fell into his arms.

Maybe if I wished it hard enough, we could have this forever.

"The transformation," I said later, as we lay together, limbs tangled. "Your anam cló. Has it always been that way?"

"When I first discovered my wings, it was the most incredible feeling." He raked sweat-slick hair away from his face. "I used to throw myself off the white cliffs of Emain Ablach at the instant I began the transformation, just to see how far and fast I could fall before the wind caught me up and carried me off." He paused. "Then I tampered with the wild magic. It climbed inside me, warped my mastery of my anam cló. It stole my control. Once, I transformed at will. Now I am myself only by night. By day... I am something else."

He was silent for a long time, lost in the memories.

"Emain Ablach?" I asked gently. "You've mentioned it before."

"It was where I was fostered, colleen." He tensed, his eyes returning to my face. "But it is a story for another night."

I nodded, curling myself against him. We both knew that was a story I might never get to hear.

I soon learned that while all his transformations were bad, some were worse than others.

When he fell into my arms the next evening, his skin was feverish to the touch, yet he quaked and shivered as if he were frozen. His hair was soaked with sweat and jagged with midnight feathers fluttering desolately to the floor. Blood streaked his throat and caked his chin, crusting in the stubble shadowing his jaw. But worst of all were his eyes: no longer the silver of moonlight nor the gold blue of day, but hollow as a dug grave.

"Irian." My hands fluttered around his shoulders. "Tell me what to do."

"*Colleen.*" The word on his cracked lips was an unpolished gemstone: rough but precious nonetheless. He captured my hands in his and kissed them, leaving streaks of blood and sweat along my fingers. "Talk to me, colleen."

I stared into his pain-harrowed eyes, feeling helpless. "About what?"

"Anything," he ground out.

I hesitated. "Once—in a time of sunlight and songbirds—there was a girl. A girl who spent all her days longing for night."

He collapsed against me, curling arms around my waist and laying his head in my lap. "Why would she do such a thing?"

I stroked his damp midnight hair. He shuddered at my touch.

"Because night feels like forever," I whispered. "Even when the crickets rasp their fiddles in the grass, and the wind howls over the moor, sending autumn leaves whispering to each other, there is a stillness at the heart of the night that goes on forever. And when she lets herself drift toward that infinity, she becomes very small. So small that she is everything. Everything and nothing all at once. Like a star that has died and been reborn so many times it has forgotten its own name."

Irian squeezed his eyes shut. "That does not sound real."

"Does it have to be real," I asked softly, "to be true?"

He raised his head. I clasped his jaw and brought his lips to mine, tasting his dissipating pain. He growled, deep in his throat, his hands tightening on my waist as his mouth moved on mine. Stars flung themselves against my skull and burst, scattering down my spine and leaving flaming trails in their wake. I gripped his arms, not caring that they were slicked with the aftermath of nightmares made real, and kissed him, hard.

And before I stopped thinking altogether, I wondered, How long did something have to last before it felt like forever?

Chapter Forty-Five

Every night, he asked me, "Colleen, have you decided what you will do?"

At the Feis of the Ember Moon, he meant. At Samhain.

"Tell me why," I asked one night. "Tell me why it means so much to you—why the Treasure must be renewed, instead of letting wild magic go free. Why I must take this burden from you, instead of letting both worlds burn."

For a long, fraught moment, he was silent.

"I wish I could say I remembered what Tír na nÓg used to be like—before the Gate War, before the bardaí." His voice was rutted with regret. "But I cannot. So I will tell you what Deirdre once said to me, when I asked her why she was willing to tithe the bulk of her life for a destiny she had not asked for. She said, 'I will die sooner or later. Let it be for something greater than myself. Let it be for good. Let it be for magic.'"

His scalding palms curved against my cheeks and smoothed my hair.

"As long as the last Treasure survives, there is a chance things can be better." His face spasmed with that old hope. *It's you.*

"I could never see how. But I am not a good man—I know little beyond violence and vengeance. Perhaps the next heir will find a way to do what I never could. To return balance to our world—to heal the sorrow warping the land."

I held his gaze. "That's asking a lot of me."

"I know." His eyes were dying stars. "If there was a way for me to live—a way for our story to end differently? I would take it in a heartbeat and relish the opportunity to become a better man. For you. For Tír na nÓg. But whether or not I tithe the sword, my death is inevitable. So let me make it mean something. Let it be for good. Let it atone—at least in part—for all the mistakes I have made. For all the violence I have wrought."

But I just shook my head.

Every night, I shook my head. I couldn't be the one to kill him. I *wouldn't.*

And every night, the moon grew a little thinner, until it went dark. And then it began to swell.

The night before Samhain, we made love beneath a nearly full moon. After, we lay together on a blanket in his tower room. His chambers had never recovered from what I'd done to them—his rotting mattress had proved fertile, spawning flax and goldenrod and a thousand waving asters to sway above us in the moonlight. I stared up at the botanical mayhem I'd wrought, and once more imagined what it would be like to be a vessel for the power of the winds, the clouds, the lightning-streaked skies, instead of *this.*

Arms corded with muscle and inked with feathers enveloped me. I nestled against Irian, turning my head for a kiss. He obliged, sliding his mouth deliciously over mine. When he drew away, it was too soon.

"Colleen," he whispered, as he had twenty-eight times before. "Have you decided what you will do?"

I gazed up at him.

"You once said my potential for magic was so great, the Septs would have battled over me." I twined my fingers in his, tracing the raised edges of his markings. "Did the Septs not always select heirs from their own lineages?"

"Not always." He gripped my hand in his scalding palm. "Maintaining a dynasty requires compromise. If a member of the lesser Gentry or even the lower Folk showed great promise, they were encouraged to adopt or marry into a Sept. If they themselves did not become tánaistí, then their children likely would. My mother was such a one."

"But my...*great promise*." I voiced the doubt that had been growing inside me. "I have nothing of wind or air or storm in me. Surely my innate magic is better suited to the element of earth than the element of air—better suited to the Sept of Antlers than the Sept of Feathers."

"Perhaps." Regret made diamonds of Irian's eyes. "Perhaps—had a great many things been different—you might have been heir to Deirdre's Treasure. But the Sept of Antlers is destroyed. Its lineages ended. Its magic broken and the emblem of its Treasure lost. The Sept of Feathers is all that remains. *I* am all that remains. And you, tánaiste of the Sky-Sword by default. I never said it was perfect. But it is all we have."

For a while, we were both silent.

"If I say yes—" His face bruised with wretched hope, and I held up a finger. "*If*. If I agree to take your life, accept your tithe, and become the next Sky-Sword...what exactly will I have to do?"

Irian's heartbeat jolted. Apprehension streaked dark over his silver gaze, touched with a yearning I didn't have to name.

I slid my palm around his wrist and gripped him tight.

"Tomorrow evening, at dusk, we will go together to the Heartwood."

A memory of the giant ancient tree whispered around me like soft leaves—its rough bark beneath my fingertips, the chime of its unearthly music as it sang to me through time and space.

"And then?"

"All you must do is swear yourself to my Sept—to the Sept of Feathers. There are oaths of allegiance. Vows of prostration. But—" A muscle feathered along his jaw. "But the simplest way for us to be bound is a handfasting."

"Irian." I glided my fingers along his jaw, a tendril of delight vining through my dread. "Are you asking me to be your wife?"

"No, colleen. I am asking you to be my widow."

My throat ached. "I can't do it."

"You can. You must." He brushed his lips across my mouth. The kiss tasted like unsung songs. Unspoken regrets. Unshed tears. "I need you to be ruthless, colleen. The girl I met all those months ago—the one who believed that pain was only useful if she was the one inflicting it, who believed her love was nothing but destruction—I need *her* tomorrow night. She must do for me what no one else can."

I choked on a thousand words I wanted to say to him. Stumbled over a thousand lifetimes I wanted to spend with him.

"We've only had a month," I pleaded, as if he could change things. "It wasn't enough time."

"It was more than I ever hoped for." His hand rested across my collarbone, his thumb fitting in the hollow where my pulse leapt. "*You* are more than I ever hoped for. You, I have loved. You, I have lived for. And you, I will die for."

A tear slid down my cheek. "I don't want to say goodbye."

"Then do not." He bent, kissed the tear from my cheek. Kissed the corner of my eye, where more tears trembled. Kissed my mouth, lingering on my lips. "Do not even say good night. I will still be here tomorrow."

His eyes blurred dark. With desire. With memories of lost things. And premonitions of things found, only to be lost again. He deepened the kiss, and I let him, tangling my arms around his neck. He shifted on top of me, bracing his weight on his forearms.

We moved against each other slowly in the dark. But time was a thief, stealing the night from us. Dawn touched the horizon with blue as I curled against Irian, spent, satisfied, but roiling with fury and sorrow and an infinite sense of wrongness.

Why did time keep turning, when the man I was falling for was about to die? Why did I have to be the one to save a realm—*two* realms? Why not let magic run wild and consume it all?

My heart was breaking. And part of me wanted to break the world along with it.

Chapter Forty-Six

Ngetal—Reed
Late Autumn

I pushed open the doors of Dún Darragh with a crash.

That morning, I'd tried to keep myself occupied in Tír na nÓg. But no matter where I turned, all I saw was him. All I could think about was *him*. I'd walked aimlessly through the forest, only faintly surprised when my steps led me to the Willow Gate.

The barrier was weak as torn silk. The full moon would not rise for hours, yet I crossed easily into the human realms, dim and drab and commonplace after Tír na nÓg's splendor. The chilly morning was gray like dried sage as I hiked back to the fortress.

Today felt like an ending. An end to a year. An end to the hopes Rogan and I had carried with us here from Rath na Mara.

I needed to say goodbye. To my garden, going fallow in autumn's chill. To Rogan, who, like me, would not leave the Feis of the Ember Moon the same person he'd come. And, of course, to—

"Corra!" I whirled on my heel, impatiently dredging the fort's gloom for whichever carving the fickle sprite would deign to inhabit this time. "Corra, wake up!"

For the space of a breath, the broad flagstones trembled beneath my feet and the great hall split in half, cracking open like an enormous egg. My breath was gold dust, and the air was sapphire. Laughter chimed, bright as a bell. A breeze curled sinuously between the broad ribs of enormous trees. I tasted sweetness on my tongue, and the tang of scorched metal.

And then it was just me and creeping shadows and a fox uncurling from a nap, sharp-faced with reproach. "Even airy fairy beasties need rest, chiardhubh."

"I take it you didn't miss me?"

"Missing and missing," said Corra, mournful. And then impertinent. "While she was kissing and kissing."

"How do you even know—" I put my hands on my hips and shook my head. "Where's Porridge Face?"

"Does she mean handsome prince Rogan?" Corra's tone was airy. "Gone."

"Where?"

Corra's fox began cleaning a tufted paw.

A thread of worry snagged me, but I tucked it away. Tonight was to be Rogan's wedding night—he was probably in Finn Coradh at the Muddy Ram, drinking away his cold feet. He'd be back before dusk. "I have one more project I need to do. Would you like to be useful one last time?"

Corra helped me scour the ruins of the dún. At first, I despaired of finding anything, but then they began to appear—in shattered niches and broken crooks, behind listing statuettes and beneath broken furniture. The black feathers winked like shards of night, beckoning me with a wicked luster.

Irian's words echoed in my mind: *All you must do is swear yourself to my Sept—to the Sept of Feathers.*

If tonight was also to be my wedding night—if I was truly prepared to tithe my love for magic—then I might as well look the part.

I sat before the roaring hearth. I sewed quickly, the needle darting in and out and in again, threading feathers like the resolve I'd strung on a broken hope. Both were desperate; both were sloppy. But I didn't know what else to do.

"Corra," I said as I sewed. "You either cannot or will not tell me who or what you are. I know that. But will you confirm, if I guess correctly?"

"When seeking answers, keep this in mind." Above the hearth, the arching boughs of a vast tree bobbed with a stout, gnarled figure hanging upside down from its branches. "Things lost to time are not always meant to find."

It was as much permission as I was going to get.

"Once—in a time of disparate realms and estranged lovers—there was a warrior." My hands were clumsy and the feathers were sharp. The vicious vanes cut lacerations along my fingertips and shredded my nails. My blood stained the dark feathers even darker. "He fell in love with a Gentry maiden. Perhaps she returned his love; perhaps she did not. Either way, she returned to her home without him. The inconsolable warrior tried to follow, but the Gates to Tír na nÓg were closed to him. He broke his oaths and abandoned his duties, spending his days building a fortress to his grief and spending his nights writing endless treatises about magic." I paused. This next part was nothing more than conjecture, but I needed an ending to the story, even if it was only one of my own invention. "In his desperation, he wrought forbidden magic. A geas—a binding—unlike anything a human had attempted before. He captured a being, a god—a thing above and beyond both mortals and Folk. A thing of damp earth and endless skies, wild fire and frothing water. And he bound it to the stones, to the garden, to the very earth itself. And with its magic he built himself a bridge between realms, a door between worlds. A door that has never fully closed."

"The magic of nature—you reap what you sow." The goblin shriveled and lengthened, dropping from the boughs of the tree in the guise of a sinuous serpent. "Things given, things taken—always more than you can know."

"Then it was consensual—an agreement of some kind?" My

hands stilled in my lap. "Corra, what *are* you?"

"We are broken hearts and old sorrows." The serpent, now giant, wound around itself in concentric circles around me, until I did not know where its mouth began and its tail ended. "We are open doors and untold stories and the tolling of the bell in the highest tower. We are whatever we need to be."

I supposed that was the answer I deserved for the question I'd asked. I shook my head and kept sewing.

I sewed all day, until a great swath of darkness swept down from my shoulders. I donned one of Corra's ephemeral gowns—sheer black save for delicate silver embroidery that looked like constellations in the night sky. I braided inky feathers into my dark hair, weaving them in a complicated corona around my head until I, too, looked wreathed in shadow.

In the end, I was transformed into the next tánaiste of the Sept of Feathers.

I searched the dún one last time for any sign of Rogan. He still wasn't here. But surely he knew Eala's geas needed to be broken before the zenith of the Ember Moon—he must already be waiting at the Gate.

Finally, I glanced up at the ceiling.

"Thank you for all you gave us, Corra." Despite their mischief and muddlement, I was actually going to miss the fickle beastie. "I hope I was able to give this place something in return."

"Something given, something gotten," Corra sang, unconcerned. "Nothing taken, nothing taught-en. Whatever you need, just ask—and we promise it will be brought-en."

I smiled. If that wasn't an appropriate goodbye from Corra, I didn't know what was. "And a fond farewell to you, too, fiend."

⁓

I stepped out into Samhain Eve. The goose autumn had flown, and stars of frost spangled the grass, bloody where sunset's red-gold stain touched them.

Sunset.

I was late. Irian's transformation would be upon him, and if I wasn't there—

Dread chilled me as I rushed toward Roslea. The gray woods reached for me in the dim, bare branches grasping the hem of my dress and tearing the feathers from my hair. Rooks hopped from branch to branch above my head, curiously silent in the blue blur of dusk. The sheen of their black wings mirrored the burnish on my wretched, resolute heart.

I reached the graveyard of monsters. In the dusk, scales rippled along sinuous limbs, and the groans of sleeping giants rumbled through the earth. Their contorted arms reached for me; their gaping black mouths howled. Beyond, the stream flashed a warning, the last rays of day flaming through the bare branches and striking the stones of the bridge.

I rushed through the Gate. And nearly slammed into a tall frame.

It wasn't Irian. It wasn't even Rogan. It was Chandi.

I stiffened. I'd intentionally avoided the taller girl since my encounter with her and Eala. For a while, I had thought her my friend. It had been nice. But at every turn, she had done Eala's bidding. She'd colluded in the abhorrent lie to damn Irian in my eyes—the lie that had nearly sundered him from me. She was loyal to her princess and always had been.

"What are you doing here?" I asked, cold.

"I know you don't want to see me." She was dressed all in red and gold, her sweeping gown a celebration of autumn's dying majesty. But she was agitated. Her hands wrung together. Sweat beaded on her upper lip, even though the night was cold.

"You're right. I don't."

"I'm sorry about what I did—"

"Which part of it?" I snarled. "Lying to me on Eala's behalf? Or damning an innocent man with a false accusation?"

"I thought I was helping—" She stopped, passed a trembling

hand over her forehead. "It doesn't matter. Listen—Eala would kill me if she knew I was here. But it's the least I can do. You deserve to know."

"Know what?"

"They have *him*."

A premonition of tragedy gripped the back of my neck. "*Who* have him?"

"The bardaí. They know he is at his weakest before the Ember Moon. They trapped him today, while he was...not himself. They will not let him tithe the Sky-Sword to another heir. They wish for the last wild magic to go free—they wish for the Gates to fall, so they may retaliate against the human realms."

"Is he dead?" I gripped her wrist, hard. "Tell me he's not dead."

"Not yet." She grimaced, although I didn't know whether it was from the prospect of his death or the pain of my grip. "They'll want to make a spectacle of it. They'll want to make him pay for his defiance. They'll want to make him watch as his legacy is destroyed forever."

"That's good." Memories and thoughts and half-developed plans blurred through my mind. "That gives me time."

Chandi's lips pressed together. "For what?"

"For everything. For me to bind myself to Irian's Sept. For Rogan to promise himself to Eala, and she to him. For the Treasure to be tithed, as it must be."

"About Rogan." Chandi's face twisted with some new emotion. "You should know—"

But in this particular moment, I didn't care about Rogan. I pushed away from Chandi, back toward the Willow Gate.

"I have an idea." My words were white as frost in the dimming night.

"Should I wait for you?"

"No. Eala will expect you. You've helped me enough. You've helped *him*. Thank you."

I clasped Chandi's shivering hands before climbing over the golden singing bridge. Beyond, Roslea was as I'd left it—grasping, groaning, half-alive with the magic spilling wantonly between Tír na nÓg and the human realms. I kicked off my boots and stepped onto the cool, heaving earth. Power thrilled through me, awaking my Greenmark with a gust of earth-scented wind.

For the first time since I was a child, I let the magic spill over me completely. I reveled in its steady caress of wild growth and unrelenting calm. For years I'd despised it, repressed it, made it my enemy. But this—this magic, this power—had been my one companion, my constant friend. It had lured me, goaded me, pushed me, comforted me. I'd always thought it would be my downfall.

Now I knew, down to my marrow—it would be my salvation.

I closed my eyes and pushed my Greenmark beyond the bounds of my body. It shivered through the earth and sighed through the undergrowth and whispered through the trees.

Hoofbeats on dry leaves. The mare cantered from between the trees, her gait stilted and uneven. I stared, for though she was unmistakable to me, she was not the horse I rode here a year ago. Eimar's dappled gray coat was torn in great swaths, exposing bones of white birch. Supple muscles of clematis flexed. Her hooves were smooth river stones. Her mane and tail dripped with hawthorn and honeysuckle, carrying the scents of Bealtaine in her wake.

"Hello again, swift one."

She lowered her muzzle of coiled ivy and nudged me. I eyed the darkening sky, then gripped her green bridle. Flowers showered to the earth as I climbed onto her back. The boughs of her legs creaked, reluctant; the leaves of her spine rustled, eager.

Massive stone monsters groaned to life behind me. They thronged the dusk, incongruous amid the keening trees. A sleek selkie climbed out of her sheeny skin, her eyes pliant with night. Aughiskies with scales of murky hellebore frolicked beside the stream, their fetlocks like watery foam. A creeping dearg due whetted her teeth on the blades of her hands. And the Fomorians stepped, massive as mountains, toward where I waited motionless before the bridge.

This was my magic—but it was not *only* my magic. I glanced back toward Dún Darragh, even as Corra's last words slid through my mind. I smiled.

I had gotten something out of the bargain after all.

In Tír na nÓg, strains of distant music pooled between the trees. I pushed Eimar across the bridge, into the darkening wood at the edge of elsewhere.

We passed beneath a line of ancient silver beeches, their thick branches pulsing with molten veins. Birds of bone flitted between glass-sharp leaves and pecked at jeweled fruit. Rubies and sapphires and emeralds glinted from their bleached beaks. But no— the ruby was a human heart, ripe with blood, and the sapphire was the seething sea. And the emerald was a whole world, sharp and bright and brimming with promise.

Beyond, the forest. Trees like masts sailed toward a sky splashed with unnameable colors. Trees were forged from iron and hammered from brass. There were trees for every song that had ever been sung. Trees wild as fear, etched with the faces of the long dead. And reaching beneath them, the bones of the earth: roots, an untamed, unseen forest beneath my feet.

And then I saw *them*. The procession of dancing Folk was less strange to me than it had been all those moons ago. Their singing sounded like crackling fire and crashing surf and the wind through wildflowers, but their laughter was just laughter, and their eyes— bold colored and bright as jewels—were just eyes. I edged Eimar to join their parade, and they barely glanced at me or her or the pageant of monsters trailing behind me.

The glade that had once played host to a springtime wedding had been transformed into a revel to celebrate the end of a harvest, a year, a hegemony. Red and orange blossoms splashed the trees like bloodstains. Bold lanterns like faces snapped sharp teeth lit with flickering flame. A stiff breeze needled my skin and scudded clouds across the rising moon. The Heartwood swayed nearby, taller and more majestic than any other tree in the forest.

Something cold lodged in my throat. Night had already fallen with a slow, leaden hush tasting of decay.

I was almost out of time.

I dismounted Eimar, gesturing for my fiann of exhumed monsters to stay hidden beneath the trees. I smoothed the feathers along my brow. I swept my long feathered train behind me, then stepped from the shadow of the forest into the Feis of the Ember Moon.

Only to find Rogan blocking my path.

Chapter Forty-Seven

C hangeling."

His voice was taut with worry…anger…relief. Amid the colored lanterns and creeping shadows, he looked so normal—so *human*—it nearly broke my heart. His golden curls—tamed for the occasion—fell over his brow and shoulders. His river-stone eyes glittered green and blue as they roved over me. He took in my dark hair braided with feathers. My mismatched eyes. My glittering gown and mantle of iridescent black.

"What in Amergin's hell happened to you?" He reached out, caught my wrists. "Where have you been?"

I tried to writhe out of his grip. "I—needed to stay in Tír na nÓg."

He held me fast. "You could have left a message. Unless leaving my horse tethered to a tree at the edge of the Gate was supposed to mean something to me."

I bit my lip with guilt when I realized how little I'd thought of Rogan in the past month. "I was at Dún Darragh all day today. I looked for you, but—"

"I was *here*. Looking for you."

"How?"

"The Gates are weak." His hands tightened painfully on my arms. "After everything Eala and the swan maidens told me, I worried—"

I shook my head, not understanding. "Told you about what?"

"About *him*." Rogan inclined his head.

I followed his gaze. And nearly doubled over from the dread punching into my gut.

Atop a dais before the Folk host, Irian was restrained with metal and malice. But it was not the sight of him on his knees, with his hands caught behind his back, that upset me. It was his expression—cold and hard and storm shuttered. His face alone undid me. In less than a day, he had transformed from the man who had made love to me beneath the moonlight and begged me not to say good night, to *this*. The monster I'd met a year ago, with a face like fear and a mouth like rage.

And he was still so magnificent. Even among this strange revelry, he shone—darkly, insistently. He would not be snuffed out.

And yet, one way or another, he *would* be snuffed out. By their hand or by mine—Irian died tonight.

I started toward him. I had to help him, to hold him, to—

Rogan's grip on my arm whipped me back. Around us, unearthly music swelled. Lithe bodies swirled in a breathless cascade. His hand curled around my waist. He pushed me into the throng of dancers, spinning me through the host like a leaf on the wind.

"What are you doing, princeling?" I craned my neck toward Irian, trying to catch sight of him through the revelry. "This isn't the time—"

"I need you to hear me, Fia." Rogan's voice was low, emphatic. "I've tried to love her. But it's always been you."

The words seized my full attention. "What did you say?"

"You heard me." Our steps slowed but didn't stop. We swayed between the whirling dancers. "For as long as I can remember, I've loved only you. I loved you when we were children stealing sugar from Cook's secret cupboard to feed to the horses. Fighting with toy swords in the yard. Sailing on wooden rafts across the pond. And I loved you more as we grew older. You were the only one who understood me. Who listened to me. Who wanted me to have the life I wanted, instead of the one I'd been assigned. And then we were torn apart."

"Rogan—"

"*They* tore us apart. Your mother. My father." His eyes were dark with regret. "If I could return to that day five years ago, I would. I would fight for you, Fia. I would choose you, no matter the cost. I would tell the world how much I love you, as only I know how to love you. *You* would be the one I wed."

For the barest moment, I hesitated. The lifetime of memories he'd conjured inside me swirled like flowers in a gale. But then his words filtered through my confusion. *I would tell the world how much I love you, as only I know how to love you.*

The words stung. Though Rogan didn't know it, they were too close to Mother's refrain for comfort. *Only I know how to love someone like you. And no one will ever love you more than I do.*

It was those words, more than anything, that drove me toward anger.

Because they were both wrong. They were not the only ones who knew how to love me. Irian knew how to love me, for all that I was and all that I wasn't. And—more importantly—I was beginning to understand how to love myself.

I made my voice hard. "All we had were sweet memories and reckless fantasies, Rogan."

"Then tell me it wasn't real."

The ragged words were cruelly—tortuously—familiar. They yanked me back to that cool blue morning five years ago—my fingertips shaking on his cold stirrup, his drawn white face staring down at me. My resolve cracked as anguish cleaved through me. Rogan's river-stone eyes raked mine, sad and seeking. I looked away, desperate for a glimpse of Irian, but the swirling revel still hid him.

"Don't you have a geas to break?" I tried to sound defiant, but my voice betrayed me.

"Tell me none of it was real, Fia, and I'll let you go."

My heart rattled in my chest. Again, I hesitated. Because for years, it *had* been real. So much of it had been real. I *had* loved him—desperately, finitely, imperfectly. It had been a child's love. But it had been love. And I wouldn't lie to him about that.

I made my face implacable. "It was real, Rogan. But you're too late. I am no longer that girl I once was. And you are no longer that boy. You were never meant for me, nor I for you. That much was always true."

"*Fuck that.*" He surged back, ran a hand through his curls. "What does that even mean? I'm so tired of living my life based on other people's wishes—other people's dreams. Don't I get a say in any of this?"

"You've always known your duty, Rogan—"

"Donn damn my duty." His river-stone eyes flashed green beneath the dancing lanterns. "If I lose Bridei, so be it. If my father wills his precious kingdom to my worthless brother, then it'll be his fault when our people bleed. Not mine. If the high queen decides to hunt me to the end of the earth because I chose to follow my heart, then I will run as long as I have legs to stand on. I don't care if I was meant for Eala, changeling. I want you. If I'm going to give my willing heart to anyone—"

Shock rippled through me. I slapped my hand over Rogan's mouth, silencing the careless words spilling out of his mouth. Surprise stilled him.

"What did you just say?" I lifted my hand an inch off his mouth.

"I said, if I'm going to give my willing heart to *anyone*—"

Again, I covered his mouth with my hand. A cascade of realization rushed over me.

"You said to break the geas, you had to declare your love for Eala before the Folk host," I said hoarsely. "To bind her to your name—your royal house—in marriage."

"That's right." Rogan looked confused. "I have to swear my willing heart to her. But I'm telling you—"

The rest of his words were drowned out beneath the roar of blood in my ears. His *willing heart*. It wasn't a coincidence—it couldn't be. Rogan knew nothing of Folk magic—he would not choose those words at random. He was repeating something Eala had said to him. Something Eala had read. In the journals *I* had given her.

My heart hammered in my chest. Perhaps I was wrong. Perhaps it was nothing. Perhaps it was simply the wording she'd used. But my instincts told me otherwise.

In the old stories, a willing heart can do almost anything, Cathair had said. *Steal magic. Create new worlds. Save doomed men.*

I'd hoped there would be something in those journals she could use. I'd never imagined she would reach for the darkest, dearest magic written in their pages.

But Eala was born a crafty daughter to a ruthless queen and raised beneath her mother's manipulative thumb for years. Then she'd been raised by the Folk, learning their own cold and cunning ways. Never telling a full lie—always twisting words like brambles and briars to obscure the whole truth. Manipulating a situation to benefit her own goals, no matter the cost to others.

This—this was the doll she intended to break. This was her final play. She did need Rogan's help to free her from her geas. But not as a bridegroom. As a willing *sacrifice*.

This time, it was me who gripped Rogan's arm. "Where is she?"

Beneath my fingertips, his bicep jumped. "Who?"

"Eala." My voice was urgent. "Where in the Morrigan's name is she?"

I needn't have asked. Across the Folk host, near the dais where Irian knelt, bound and bowed, a woman with a long, elegant neck stepped to the front of the crowd. She had hair like moonlight and was resplendent in a gown of white feathers. Her gaggle of maidens were dressed in incandescent colors—the blue of swirling water, the red of dancing fire, the gray of swirling clouds, the green of creeping grass. They lifted her up onto the dais, and her feathers fluttered like wings behind her.

"Kith and kin, strangers and friends, I bid you welcome to the Feis of the Ember Moon!" Eala's voice was fluted and piercing, carrying across the crowd. Some heads turned in confusion, but many among the Folk seemed to know her. Uncanny voices rose. Sharp teeth glinted in the moonlight. "You may wonder why it is not Dualtach of the Ivy Gate who addresses you tonight. I hope you will be patient with me instead, and the unexpected joy I wish to share with you." She shaded her eyes against the lanterns and stared out across the revel. "Rogan? My prince? Where are you?"

"Don't," I cried. But Rogan had already left my side. I grabbed for him. My fingertips grazed his elbow, caught on his sleeve.

"I'm done having my choices made for me." He shook me off. "Let me do what I should have done a long time ago."

He shoved through the crowd. I pushed after him, but the Folk host was like a wall in front of me.

"There you are." Eala reached out her slender hands and helped Rogan up beside her. He was golden-haired and strong, effortlessly and undeniably human. Again, the Folk host murmured. I kept shoving my way through their lean, lithe bodies as Eala's laughing voice filtered down toward me. "I have heard it said, *Like calls to like*. Although I have lived among you all these years, it seems I am nevertheless fated to accept the love of a mortal. Is that not amusing?"

An obliging titter sprinted through the revel.

Eala turned toward Rogan. "Is there something you wish to tell me, beloved?"

Rogan leaned down to murmur something in her ear. Eala stiffened. Her expression flickered in the light from the lanterns, and for a split second she looked like one of *them*.

Marble face. Candlelight eyes. Hungry teeth and feral desire.

I wanted to scream at Rogan to get away from her. But he stayed by her side, even as regret pooled in his eyes.

"I am sorry, beloved—I did not quite hear you." Delicately, she brushed blond hair from her ear and tilted her head. "I thought you said you would not pledge yourself to me, after all your fine words and heroic actions. But surely a prince as clever as yourself would not make such a stupid mistake."

Rogan's face hardened. I cringed—if Eala and I had truly been sisters, I would have told her long ago that Rogan hated being called stupid. Hated it even more than he hated being told he was wrong. But she was not my sister. Not in any of the ways that counted.

I pushed harder through the crowd. The Folk host stood transfixed by the drama unfolding before them.

"I cannot offer you my heart." Rogan bowed, princely and penitent, to the seething swan maiden before him. "Not even to break the geas holding you captive. It would not be right—it would not be honest. My heart has long belonged to another. And I bestow it, willingly, to her."

Rogan looked out and fixed his river-stone eyes on me. I froze, a half-dozen paces from the dais. My gaze flew, reluctantly, to Irian. He'd seen me now—how could he not, as I careened through the host in my extravagant gown and cape of night-black feathers, stolen from his own shadowy wings? His eyes held hope . . . sorrow . . . resignation. A cold edge of restrained violence. He jerked against his bonds, sending his torn mantle swinging into the dusk. And waited.

Both of them waited—two sets of eyes fixed on me. One blue-green. One silver. And I—I stood motionless in front of a host of leering, murmuring Folk. My heart throbbed unevenly in my chest. I was running out of time. I had to do something. I had to decide. I had to—

"I did not want to do this." Eala sighed brokenly. "But I'm afraid you've left me no choice."

She lifted her hands to her hair—to her glittering crown of pale feathers and pale flowers. But I saw now—tiny spots of blackness nestled between the white.

Eala plucked one of the black flowers. Blood trickled down her fingertips. Fast as a viper, she stood on her tiptoes. Grabbed Rogan by the stubbled jaw. And shoved her fingers into his mouth.

Dread grasped me. Irian's voice filtered through my hazy memories of the Feis of the Wild Hunt: *The black flowers leave humans...open to suggestion. They overcome loyalty, love, allegiance. Only a will like iron can withstand them.*

Rogan jerked away, but too slowly. Red smeared his lips as his mouth worked. He gagged, spat out mangled black petals. Clawed at his throat. Shuddered. Fell to his knees on the dais.

My dread blossomed into horror as I helplessly watched. When I'd ingested the flower, its effect had taken hold instantly. I had little hope Rogan would be able to withstand its potency.

He had many admirable qualities. *A will like iron* was not one of them.

Finally, Rogan was still. Eala wiped her bloodstained hand down the front of her gown, leaving a smear of red across the white. She gripped Rogan's hands, pulled him to standing. His golden curls hung over his face, and his eyes were lowered.

"You do belong to me, my prince—whether you like it or not." Her words were tender, regretful. Then she turned and pointed straight at me. "Now bring me my sister."

Chapter Forty-Eight

Rogan straightened, following her pointing finger with his eyes.
When they landed on me, I almost screamed. His mercurial
blue-green gaze—like river stones, like oceans, like dusky skies—
was gone. His stare was flat, gray, lifeless. Empty save for a determination that chilled me.

He stepped forward. Jumped down from the dais. And barreled
toward me through the crowd.

Denial and fear warred within me and slowed my reaction. Then
I turned and ran. Or tried to. The Folk host that had impeded my
progress forward hindered it backward. I shoved against slender,
inflexible bodies. Stared pleadingly into faces warped with cruel
amusement or aloof disdain or sneering superiority. Hands gripped
my arms and caught in my feathered braids. Laughter grated
through my ears. Sharp teeth gnashed in moonlight. I spun through
the host like a leaf caught in a gale—forward, backward, sideways.
But I was nearly to the edge of the forest. I reached for the safety
of the trees, conjuring thickets of briars and tangles of greenery to
come to my aid. I silently called to my horde of stone monsters.

A large, hard, familiar body slammed me into a thick trunk.

My skull cracked against rough bark. Colored leaves rained down around me. I reeled, dizzy. My hold on my Greenmark slipped. The forest receded, and my stone army stilled.

Strong arms gathered me up and hauled me back the way I'd come.

The crowd parted for Rogan in a way they had not for me. I fought him as he dragged me toward Eala. I tore at his hair, his mantle. The cloth audibly ripped, his cracked river-stone brooch coming away in my palm. But although I'd sparred with Rogan a thousand times—and bested him often—this was different. He was no longer a man, but a machine. He didn't flinch when my fingernails raised red scratches across his cheek. Didn't blink when my teeth shredded the palm clamped over my mouth. I reached for my Greenmark, throbbing through me with renewed vengeance. Briefly, I considered doing to Rogan what I'd done to Eimar a year ago. What I'd done to Pinecone. To Caitríona.

Then I stopped fighting. Morrigan help me, but even now—with his hands bruising my arms and his eyes empty of any familiarity—I didn't want to hurt him. I didn't know how the magic of the black flowers worked, but he *must* still be in there. I wouldn't destroy him.

Rogan stepped onto the dais and deposited me before Eala. Below us, the Folk whispered and murmured, amused intrigue still holding their interest.

How captivating these petty mortal dramas must seem.

"What have you done?" I ground out.

"I am sorry it had to happen this way." Eala's lovely face was impassive. "I wanted his heart. His *willing* heart."

"So you stole his will instead?"

She shrugged. "I still need him."

"For *what*?"

"Mother was always so shortsighted, allowing her under-kings to keep their power." Eala gave her head a rueful shake. "I never understood why she tolerated their petty quarrels and border disputes. What's the point of being high queen if you must endure the squabbles of men? Why not rule as a true queen, a good queen, a powerful queen? Of everyone?" Her face contorted, then smoothed. "Rogan's *willing heart* would have bought me all Fódla in an instant. But I will make do with his obedience. Bridei will fall easier to me if its crown prince is by my side."

I tried to make sense of her words, but she was already moving away from me and Rogan. She beckoned to one of her swan maidens, a red-haired girl I recognized from the Feis of the Wild Hunt. The girl climbed the stairs toward her princess with a reluctance I didn't understand. She stopped before Eala, shuddering. Eala pulled her into an embrace, kissed her cheek tenderly, sorrowfully, with tears glinting in her eyes.

The knife that appeared in Eala's palm glittered gold in the flickering light of the laughing lanterns. She laid the blade against the redhead's breast.

"Go on." Eala's voice was soothing, gentle, desolate. "Remember, my sweet sister—we do this for Fódla. And for Tír na nÓg. We do this for *us*. And I will see you again."

The redhead closed her eyes. Her mouth moved, as though she was reciting a prayer. Finally, she wetted her lips with a small pink tongue and stood a little straighter.

"By fire and by sky, by fast water and by ancient tree," she said in a trembling voice. "I promise my willing heart to thee, Eala Ní Mainnín."

Eala drove the dagger down. The blade cut her maiden's breast, carving through flesh as the girl gasped and screamed and scrabbled at her chest. A broad red gash opened up. Eala plunged her fist into the shattered rib cage and tore out the girl's still-beating heart. Red coated her arm to the elbow and spattered onto the ground at her feet. The redhead collapsed.

"With the power of this willing heart, I renounce my tie to the Sept of Feathers," Eala cried out. "I declare myself and my maidens free of its geasa, its enchantments, and its bonds of protection and loyalty."

A burst of brutal, savage magic rippled outward from Eala—the magic of stolen love and forced heartbreak. It tore at my bones, nearly ripping me apart. I whimpered and glanced toward Irian, who was thrashing wildly against his bonds. The muscles of his shoulders bulged as he struggled, but there was nothing he could do. He fell forward, limp. I struggled toward him, but Rogan's hands around my arms were like iron.

Not to be deterred, Eala lifted her bloodstained hand and beckoned to her next maiden. "Niamh," she called. "It's time."

A dark-haired girl rose upon the dais. She faltered a few steps from Eala, hesitation plain on her face. Her eyes flickered from the body of her sister crumpled and broken before her, to Rogan, blank-eyed and compliant. To me.

"Please," I begged her. "Whatever she's asked of you, whatever she promised you—it's not worth your life."

But my words only strengthened the maiden's resolve. She crossed the last few steps to Eala. Their embrace lasted just as long, even as the restive Folk stirred below us. The vow on her lips was the same as her sister's.

"By fire and by sky, by fast water and by ancient tree, I promise my willing heart to thee."

Horror burned through me. This time, I refused to watch—I buried my face in Rogan's chest as Eala plunged her dagger into her maiden's chest and tore out the girl's still-beating heart. I cast my gaze over the Folk host, who stood silent and transfixed. None of them seemed to mind this wicked, bloody display. What did it matter to them if the humans they had stolen to be killed wound up killing one another?

"With the power of this willing heart, I claim the Ivy Gate," Eala cried out. "I claim its power, its oaths, and all its supplicants. I declare myself its new and everlasting barda."

Magic once more shuddered outward, slicking my limbs with slit throats and phantom blood. I cried out. This time, I was not alone in my distaste—below me, the Folk host finally rose to outrage. They shoved against the dais and screamed at the sky. Warriors armed with steel appeared among the trees, and hope rose in my chest. But Eala stood straighter, triumphant in the new power wreathing her petite frame.

"Fiann of the Ivy Gate, you belong to me." Eala's voice rang across the clearing. The warriors hesitated. "Guard me. Guard my maidens. Kill anyone who tries to get past you."

Mayhem exploded around us as the Folk fénnidi newly bound by Eala's bloody magic clashed against the revelers swirling angrily toward the dais. Taking advantage of Eala's inattention, I reached my awareness toward my fiann of stone monsters waiting in the trees. But my Greenmark was scattered; my strength, sapped. I could barely feel them. Panic rose inside me, shattering what little composure I had left. I tried to free myself from Rogan's unyielding grip, stomping my heel into his instep. Twisting, I shoved my elbow into his solar plexus. But he barely moved—the pain that must have been coursing up his leg and abdomen didn't register on his face.

Slowly, I calmed. Rogan had always been taller, stronger, faster than I. But there was a reason Mother and Cathair had forged me into a weapon of vengeance. There was a reason I was here, tonight, gowned in black feathers beneath the Ember Moon.

The one thing Rogan had never liked—never *understood*— about me. My Folk blood. My Greenmark. My unknowable, impossible origins. I had always thought that *my* defect. Tonight, I knew it to be his.

I closed my eyes. Forced my breath to slow. Reached for the cool, soothing rush of green leaves and dark earth and creeping roots.

I didn't turn my Greenmark on Rogan. I turned it on myself. Like I had in the graveyard of monsters, I let the full force of my innate power burn through me. Emerald veins branched over my skin, then burst with thorny vines. Greenery rippled up my arms and lapped over my shoulders, tangling in my mantle of black feathers. Flowers of dark red and blinding white burst along my neck and twined in my hair. Twin bracelets circled my wrists—bracelets of brambles and nettles. Of hemlock and poison ivy. Only now they pointed outward.

Blood burst from Rogan's palm. Lesions crept up his wrists. His face didn't change, but his grip slipped. I wrenched my arms free, backed away from him. Without a direct command from Eala, he made no move to follow me.

I scrambled across the dais and threw myself toward Irian. I flung my arms around his neck, burying my face against his shoulder. His arms were bound, so he couldn't embrace me, but he leaned into my touch as I tangled myself around him, heedless of the thorny vines still twining my skin and hair.

"We are running out of time, colleen." His voice was urgent. "The Heartwood—"

"I understand why she needs Rogan," I interrupted him, terse. "Ruling Bridei and commanding its powerful fianna lends her significant power in the human realms. But why the Gates? What is she hoping to accomplish?"

"This must have been her plan all along." Irian's voice was grim. "With control of only a few Gates, she will be powerful beyond measure. She could wage war—hold domains hostage against each other. If the Sword is not tithed, she could gain dominance over both realms, human and Folk. She could control the flow of wild magic. She could become queen of everything."

"We have to stop her."

"The best way to stop her is for me to tithe the Sky-Sword to you. The Ember Moon rises toward its zenith. You must free me from these bonds. We _must_ make haste to the Heartwood."

But I barely heard him. The weight of attention scraped my neck. Eala's gaze was fixed on me. And Irian. Her eyes flicked to Rogan, standing like a statue, with lacerations on his palms and flowers strewn at his feet. Her face grew pitiless. She lifted an imperious, bloodstained hand toward her maidens. She crooked a scarlet finger.

"Chandi, my love," she said. "It's time."

"*No.*" Panic burst through my body. I rose to my feet, even as Chandi reluctantly climbed the dais above the heaving, turbulent Folk host. "Chandi, no!"

Her feet slowed. Hope burst through me. I turned to Eala, pressing my advantage.

"You made me believe *he* was my enemy." Irian glowered from his bonds. "Yet all this time, it was *you.*"

"I am not your enemy—I have never been your enemy." Eala's face warped with sudden emotion. Adoration, consternation, betrayal. "When Rogan first told me he had come to Tír na nÓg in the company of my adoptive sister, I had such high hopes. That I might finally have a true ally, bound in love and in blood, more powerful than any other alliance I could claim." She controlled her expression, gripped the knife tighter in her bloody fingers. "Together, we would have been powerful enough to stand against any who defied us. But you betrayed me. You sided with my captor, instead of me. You let the love of a man overcome the love of a sister. And because of that, I was forced to take more-drastic measures."

"But why?" I raised my voice to be heard over the melee below us. "We could have freed you with less bloodshed. It didn't have to go so far."

"Can't you understand?" Eala's expression was grim. "All my life, I have been used and traded like a coin. Admired. Bartered. Stolen. Desired. Hidden. But I am no coin. I am a weapon, and I am sharper than anyone has ever given me credit for. I want what I've never been allowed—power. My own power. I've waited my whole life for someone—anyone—to deign to give it to me. But no one ever has. So now I have to take it."

"By slaughtering your sisters?" My voice was incredulous. "By stealing the Gates from the bardaí?"

"Whoever controls the Gates controls *everything.*" White feathers floated around her like a halo. "Once the Sky-Sword is destroyed, all the magic the Septs once claimed will be free. But if I hold the Gates, I will decide who comes and who goes. Who trades what, with whom. Who goes to war. Who lives, who dies. I will be more powerful than the Septs. Than the bardaí. And once I use Rogan's fianna to conquer the human under-kings, I will be more powerful than Mother as well. And she will bow to my will, as she once made me bow to hers."

Cathair's voice shivered through me. *Eithne wished to forge Eala into her own image. Eala felt each blow of the hammer and hated her mother for it.*

I shifted my attention to Chandi.

"And you?" I asked softly. "What do you gain from this power grab? Other than death?"

"Once wild magic is freed, Eala will find a way to resurrect us," Chandi told me, with tortured certainty.

"That's not possible."

"She has sworn it."

"And you believe her? She has done nothing but twist the truth with me."

"I know." Anguish contorted Chandi's lovely face. "But she is my best friend. My sister. My mother. My princess. She is the only person who's ever truly loved me. She would not knowingly deceive me in this."

Behind me, Irian rattled against his chains. "Colleen, there is nothing you can do. We must *go!*"

Chandi stepped closer to Eala. With a cry, I swung toward Irian, hiding my face so I didn't have to see Rogan's empty, obedient body...Chandi's heart being torn from her chest...my shining doppelgänger steal magic and plot mayhem.

Relief tangled with resolve in Irian's moonlit eyes.

"The last Treasure of the Septs must not be destroyed. I must not die before I tithe the Sky-Sword." His wrists were raw where he'd struggled against his manacles. "You have to get us to the Heartwood, colleen. I'm too weak to fly us there—you must think of a way to get us past the host."

Behind me, a scream splintered the air, echoing toward the night sky. I closed my eyes as an unbearable wave of sorrow crashed over me. I didn't know what power Chandi's willing heart had bought Eala. I didn't want to know. My blood slowed to sludge. Every muscle in my body grew weak.

Rogan was enchanted, compliant. Chandi was dead. In a few moments, Irian would tithe his own life away. And then I would be alone. Everything I'd ever loved would be *gone*.

A cool, soft palm slid around my elbow. My eyes snapped open, and I stared down at five slender brown fingers ringing my arm.

Chandi stood tall and wistful and determined, her amber eyes golden as the lanterns swinging at her back. Her dress was ripped over her chest, and a thick line of red dribbled from her collarbone to her breastbone. But she was *alive*. Gloriously, perfectly, amazingly alive.

I flung myself up and crushed her in an embrace. She hugged me, then pushed me gently away.

"Go." She flashed me a melancholy smile. In her hands, she gripped the bloodied dagger Eala had tried to take her heart with. "You don't have much time."

Behind her, Eala was murmuring furiously in Rogan's ear. He stirred, muscles flexing as he turned his head toward us.

"You do not have to stand against me, Sister." Eala's voice was even despite the chaos surging in her eyes. "You know I wanted you with me, from the very beginning. Surely we can find a way to work toward a common goal."

"You and I have *nothing* in common."

"You're wrong." She moved toward us, Rogan trailing blankly behind her. "We have everything in common. We are both our mother's creations. Her *weapons*. Let us use that."

"By manipulating those who love us? Coercing their wills? Ripping out their hearts?"

"I once told you, Sister—I am the stronger weapon. If you are determined to make yourself my enemy, then I fear you will find out how sharp my edge is."

"That's where you're wrong," I ground out. "Mother always told me love made me weak. But I believe it makes me strong. Perhaps I am not the sharper blade or the faster arrow. Perhaps I am not a weapon at all. But I am stronger than you know."

Eala glared at me. "Then I suppose we two are at war after all."

She gestured toward Rogan, who lifted his head and moved toward us.

"Go!" Chandi said again, more forcefully. She hefted the dagger and turned away from Irian and me. "I'll hold them off as long as I'm able."

"Thank you." I hoped she knew my thanks were for more than just this.

She wouldn't be able to withstand Rogan for long. It was meant to be only a distraction. So I had to help her with a distraction of my own—and pray she didn't get hurt.

I closed my eyes, bleeding my consciousness into the earth below my feet, the trees ringing the grove, the grass tickling my calves. In an instant, I found them—my army of exhumed monsters, waiting like sentinels beyond the fringe of the forest.

Come.

They obeyed with elation, stomping out into the moonlight and slithering behind the press of angry Folk. They joined the fray, striding strange and huge and stony amid the agitation. The Fomorians gazed down at tiny figures knocking against their boots before beginning to stomp. A bean sidhe keened at the night as she raised shroud-draped arms in promises of death. A dearg due teased bladed claws behind bare knees and across tender throats.

I clasped Irian's hands in my own. I willed tough, spiny brambles to snake down my wrists and tangle around his arms. They burst against his manacles and slid beneath his chains. His hands ripped free. His searing touch circled my waist. His cool breath brushed my cheek.

"The Heartwood. Go!"

Chapter Forty-Nine

We dived into the seething crowd. Faces flickered toward us, strange in the gloom: blood-red eyes and wine-curdled mouths and swelling hate. I tightened my grip on Irian's scalding palm and ran faster, plunging through the night. Black feathers and flowering vines ripped from my hair and gown.

We were trapped in a nightmare. Pounding footsteps echoed close behind us. I tasted rancid breath against my neck. Heard frenzied voices screaming for my life. They would be upon us in moments; they would—

We passed beneath the trees, and the dark forest swallowed us whole. The careful human voice living in my head flung fears to reverberate against my skull. Mortal fears: the forest at midnight, dark with secrets and hungry with the unknown. The shadowed pathway, the twisted tree. The tang of rot, decay…death. But beneath that anxiety my heart began to pulse tranquilly, soothed by the soft promise of growing things. The serene sweep of wind through leaves. The unexplored wilds beyond the calm clearing.

I was coming home.

Instinct carried us deeper. Grass pushed between my bare toes, and petals brushed against my dirt-stained fingers. Twilight hushed between branches; silver antlers chimed against bark.

The Heartwood reached up and up, piercing the vaulted sky before curving down and down to thrust into the earth. Branches—roots—curved around us like ribs around a heart. A breeze sighed, ruffling my hair and scattering the last of my inky feathers across the green growing bower. The moon shone down. High—too high.

We were running out of time.

Irian crushed me against him, his tattooed arms like barely caged lightning against my skin. He brushed a bruising kiss over my lips.

"It is time, colleen."

One of his huge, rough hands gripped mine. With the other, he reached up, tearing a flowering vine from my tangled hair. He wrapped it brusquely around our joined hands, whispering frantic, familiar words.

"Blood of my blood, and bone of my bone, I shall not permit thee to wander alone."

Hesitation and heartache prickled through me, a thicket of grief and yearning. I looked up at Irian—at his silver eyes fastened to my face; at his lush mouth, twisted with duty and despair. Then down at our hands, about to be bound forever. For no more than a few heartless moments.

I inhaled, then repeated the words. Above us, the Heartwood began to sing—an elegy for love found. Love lost.

Next, Irian tore the tie from his mantle, black as night. This, too, he wrapped around our joined hands, as he spoke the next verse of the vow.

"Give me your heart and let it be known: that then, now, and after, you are my home."

It was too late to change course. I repeated the words, although they clawed disconsolately at my throat. The moment I spoke them, magic rippled between us. For a moment, I swore our palms fused together—our skin one skin, our blood one blood. I gasped, and he kissed the sound from my mouth, one last time.

Then he shook off the ties binding us together. He pressed the singeing hilt of his singing sword into my boneless hand. He dropped to his knees before me.

"I need you to be ruthless, colleen." His gaze was parched, pleading. "I need you to do for me what I cannot do for myself."

I stood motionless. There had already been so much violence tonight. My mind swam with images. Rogan's blank, terrible eyes. The expressions on the swan maidens' faces when they'd stepped up to their princess. Blood staining the ground. Their hearts throbbing in Eala's grip. My own fingers convulsed in horrified commiseration, and when I opened the green-veined hand that wasn't holding the sword—that hadn't handfasted with Irian—I saw it still held Rogan's cracked river-stone brooch. Somehow, after I tore it from his cloak, I'd never let go of it.

It throbbed against my palm.

"I told you once, colleen—I would not mind oblivion if you were the one to deliver it." Irian's voice stole my attention. He reached out, grabbed the black blade. Lines of silver scathed his palm as he slid the sword against his own neck. "You promised."

But I hadn't. Amid all this death and destruction and betrayal, I had never promised to kill the man I was beginning to love. I understood his reasons for asking me—I understood them down to my bones.

But I'd never promised.

Above us, the Ember Moon slid higher.

"Our story wasn't supposed to end this way." My words were nearly inaudible.

"Because this was never a story." His voice was hoarse. "I was always going to die tonight, colleen. Let it be by your hand. Let it be so magic survives. Let it be so Eala does not triumph."

I stood transfixed by dark skies and dismay.

"*Please.*" I couldn't stand to hear him beg. "It must be you, Fia. You are my heir. You are tánaiste of the Sept of Feathers."

Lyra Selene

"No." The word crept out of me, half-wondering. "No. I don't think I am."

With those words, the wrongness I'd been fighting against for months laddered waving green fronds through me. It spoke to me of shaded golden paths and flaming forests and cool stones and pliant plants. It reminded me of what I'd always known.

I was made of rot and moss and endless things. I was not made to wield a Sky-Sword.

I glanced down at the veins embroidering green lace beneath my skin. The tiny colorful flowers showering my black gown and dark hair with iridescent petals. The thorns spiking my wrists and shoulders like armor. The shimmering, pulsing stone throbbing against my palm.

A heart is powerful magic.

I lifted the black blade from Irian's neck. I hefted it, slid my blood-slick palm over its hilt until I held it backhanded in front of me. Hesitated one last, longing moment.

I wanted to live. I wanted to love. But more than anything, I wanted to be where I was always meant to be.

I wanted to go home.

I bent the edge of the Sky-Sword to my chest.

A moment too late, Irian realized what I was doing. He stumbled to his feet, lunged for me. But I was too fast. I danced out of his reach, my mouth moving over words I'd never spoken, only heard.

Ancient words. Powerful words. Magic words.

They ripped out of me, an oath I'd always been meant to make. A vow I was destined to fulfill.

"By fire and by sky, by fast water and by ancient tree, I promise my willing heart to thee...O Heartwood."

I plunged the blade into my own chest.

Chapter Fifty

Agony tore through me as the impossibly sharp blade shattered my ribs and wrung a scream from my tattered throat. But even as I twisted forward over the blade splitting me in two, the pain ebbed away, lapping like quiet waves against a pebbled shore until it simply... vanished. Time stuttered, slowed, and then stopped.

I wrenched my eyes open. Irian was gone. The forest was gone. The distant sounds of the Folk-revel-turned-battle were gone.

I was alone with the ancient singing tree.

My chest was torn open but unbleeding. The blade in my hand was the razored edge of a palm frond. My heart, when I pulled it from the branches of my rib cage, was hard and glossy as a river stone. No—it *was* a river stone. It pulsed blue-green in my palms. The crack down its middle shimmered silver in the moonlight.

A great crash stole my gaze. Before me, the Heartwood began to split in two, birthing a figure from the ancient, gnarled trunk.

They waited for me, as I somehow knew they would. I knew them now—I knew their breadth and their height, the sinew roping their muscled limbs. The burnished fur slicking their shoulder blades was leaf mulch on a forest path; the planes of their golden torso were the smooth bark of an ancient oak. Their face was the dimming closeness of a shaded wood. Antlers pierced the sky and smeared blood against the blue.

He—she—*they* beckoned me. This time, I didn't hesitate. I stepped close.

"It's *you*," I said, wondering. Because they *were*. They were the fierce hunt and the wild rut. They were Corra whizzing gleefully between carven faces. They were my garden, growing hungry and fervent over the fertile earth. They were the faces staring from the wood. They were the singing core of the ancient Heartwood.

They were the wild magic of the earth itself. They were...the forest.

"We are one, and we are none, and we are everything together." The voice was the rustle of alder leaves and the chattering of streams and the cawing of rooks. "You have offered your willing heart. We accept. Only, you must choose. What is the tithe for? Where do you seek balance?"

I stared down at my ruined chest. The cool, cracked stone throbbed heavy in my palm. I reached for the steady knowledge growing roots inside me: the ending I had always known but not always wanted to accept.

For so long, I believed my story was tethered in the human realm. The love of a mother, the companionship of a prince, the salvation of a realm. But the mother had not loved me—she had loved only what I could do. The prince might have loved me, but only for what I had been, and not what I was becoming. And the realm—how could I save a kingdom that was forever at war with itself?

There was another story. A story where I could have love, even if it was brief and star-crossed. A story where I could have great magic, even if that magic did not suit me. A story where my fate might achieve something greater than myself. Not just a fate, but a *destiny*.

Cathair's creeping voice echoed from far away.

A willing heart can do almost anything. Steal magic. Create new worlds. Save doomed men.

Both the men I loved were doomed. One had his will subsumed by another, his future bent to her schemes. The other had no future at all. My heart would buy only one of their lives.

You'll have to decide which of them you want to save.

I could choose Rogan—the human, the lighthearted prince, the heart of my childhood.

I could choose Irian—the Gentry tánaiste, the shadowed story-teller, the heart of my future.

Choose wisely, lest there be no one left to save you.

This was *my* story. And for the first time, I didn't want to choose either man. I wanted to choose myself.

"Nature is not good or kind or clean," I said. "But it is fair. It demands balance. Night and day, dusk and dawn. Winter and summer. Death and life. I did not know it, but I have always been that balance."

The figure standing beneath the shadow of the Heartwood waited, as patient as the seasons.

"I cannot understand all the decisions that brought me to this moment. I cannot take responsibility for the actions of Folk who bound wild magic to Treasures, or human kings who seduced inno-cent girls, or bardaí who slaughtered helpless heirs. All I know is this—the balance was broken long before I was born. And though I still do not know who I am, I know this too—I was born with the forest at my fingertips. Though I have often fought it, it is my truest and dearest nature. My heart is of the forest. My heart *is* the forest. I am—"

Once more, I looked down at the smooth, glossy river stone I'd pulled from my chest. The stone that had found me years ago, in the woods below Rath na Mara. The stone I had gifted to Rogan. The stone he had worn upon his chest for years. The stone that had once more found me in Tír na nÓg, through blood and violence and loss. I knew it now for what it was.

It was the Treasure of the Sept of Antlers. I had never asked what it looked like, what shape it took. But as the smooth stone pulsed heavy in my palm, winking up at me like a cracked eye, there was nothing else it could be. Deirdre's inheritance, lost when she threw herself in grief from a high cliff into the hungry forest. The conduit between the vast elemental magic of the earth...and the vessel who could wield it.

I still didn't know whether I was Deirdre's daughter. I didn't know how I'd lost my memories or why I'd been left as a change-ling in the human realms. But it was clear to me now—what Irian believed of me was true. I was heir to a Treasure. But I was not heir to *his* Treasure—not the heir of storm and wind and seething sky. I was the heir of earth and stone and trees of green.

I was the lost tánaiste of the Sept of Antlers. Its hope for renewal. Its hope for *balance*.

I was the Heart of the Forest.

"I will not sacrifice my heart for any of them. Instead, I sacrifice my heart for *all* of them. For Tír na nÓg. For Fódla. For *balance*. I am your heart. And you are mine. I offer my willing heart to the forest, for I *am* the Heart of the Forest." I gazed once more toward the figure at the base of the Heartwood. I lifted the stone nestled in my hand. "Let your lost magic flow through this, to me. Let me mend this broken heart. Let me end this sorrow. Take my life— then let balance decide who else must die. And who else may live."

And then I was running—running toward the antlered figure, who opened leafing arms to embrace me. I wept as I ran. Wept with heartbreak but also with ecstasy.

Great green wings unfurled inside me, sweeping me up even as they rooted me in place. Sap whispered through my veins. Sun-sweet shadows cooled my aching skin. Mud-deep roots dragged me into the dirt. And I remembered the day I left this place.

A note of bright music. A mother's grieving voice, singing one last lullaby. The press of deep green eyes so sorrowful I could hardly bear it.

I tumbled through the twilight, unstitching myself as I fell. Did I die as I came apart? Or was I reborn? The hasty pulse of mortal love pulled free from my throbbing heart. The impossible promise of immortality sang seductive songs in ears that could no longer hear. And then there was only me, and the shaded path between the trees, and the touch of sunlight on my skin.

I was glad to come home.

"A long time ago," murmured that endless voice, "you were given to us for safekeeping. Now we give you back to yourself."

I sifted silver-tipped fingers through a thousand dusk-lit skies, and distant stars stained my branches with the pollen of forever.

After

She preferred the nights.

She liked the moon rising soft and slow, striking silver sparks off the iron anvil of the lough. The rustle of birds in the muffled dark of the trees, their songs fading, then dying in the watercolor sweep of green and black.

She wished she had a voice, so she might join in.

But the nights were punctuated by the days. Bright days—burnished azure. Gilded wings, black feathers fluffed and ruffling in the winter-scented breeze. Diving: a silent susurrus against the pool floor, illuminating blossoms of algae and mollusks curled like fists among greening fronds.

Gray days—polished silver sky and ruffled mirror glass. Head bent against the wind, glass-sharp sand biting against pinion edge. The splash of icy water seeping quiet and strange against the scales of her feet. A feather's touch—a mote of warmth, curling inward; an embrace like the silent forest.

The slow fade of sundown as the sun slipped away, trailing scarlet fingers along the bellies of drifting clouds. Night, long and sweet and lingering. Until dawn once more pinked the horizon.

A flash of green. She splashed to her feet, coughing up water as she pushed dark hair out of her eyes. Black feathers eddied around her hips, cutting silver ripples upon the surface of the lough. For a long moment, she didn't know where she was, only that she was alone.

She wasn't alone.

There was a figure upon the shore, and when he saw her, he strode into the lough, clothes and all. He smelled like moonlight and ice water. He caught her up with strong arms embossed with dark feathers. His hot embrace chased away the creeping chill of the water pooling dark around them.

He kissed her, and kissed her again. But his eyes were the color of the eastern sky, filled with the bitter promise of a day come too soon.

The sun slid up, slicing between them like a fire-fretted blade. They held each other, desperate, as the night faded toward day—their skin one skin, their breath one breath, their heartbeat one heartbeat.

A morning star pricked the dawn, then flung itself down in a line of flame.

She drew back first. Her mismatched eyes shone, huge in her face.

"Irian," she whispered, and then, again: "*Irian*."

He lifted his head from her hair. Slid his hand below her chin. Touched the blue-green stone fixed above her breast.

"You did it, colleen," he murmured. "Fia, you changed our story's ending."

She looked down at the river stone, its crack mended. She slid her hand beneath it, where—impossibly, amazingly—her own heart throbbed a strong, steady pulse. She lifted her arms and saw they were embossed with dark curling vines. Vines tracing her skin like veins, studded with sharp thorns. And tangled in those vines were a thousand sharp black feathers, a near-perfect mirror to the arms holding her now.

Sorrow slid suddenly through her as she remembered. Sorrow for what she'd lost. Sorrow for what she had not yet found. Sorrow for the boy she'd loved, who'd become a thrall for a woman who did not love him. Sorrow for her brave, brazen friend, who'd thrown herself toward an uncertain, violent fate. Sorrow for her mirror sister—her shadow twin—who she'd thought was brightness incarnate but who'd made herself into something much darker. Sorrow for broken kingdoms and stolen Gates and memories lost and not yet found.

But then she looked up. Pulled the man she loved down for a lingering kiss. More than a kiss—a covenant.

Tomorrow they could grieve. Tomorrow they could plan. Tomorrow they could go to war. Tomorrow was more than either of them had ever hoped for.

"Good morning," she said.

A slow smile curved his lush, plush lips. "Good morning, colleen."

And she knew—this was where her story ended.

This was where her story began.

The story continues in...

A Crown So Silver

Book Two of the Fair Folk

Keep reading for a sneak peek!

Acknowledgments

I told this story wrong so many times before I got it right. That never would have happened without so many people cheering me on.

Firstly, to my agent extraordinaire, Jessica Watterson, and the incredible team at Sandra Dijkstra Literary Agency—*thank you* for taking a chance on me and this *very* nascent story.

Orbit Books has been the most wonderful home. To my incredible editor Priyanka Krishnan—your creative passion and constant pride in this story pushed me to make this book the very best it could be. To my UK editor, Nadia Saward—I'm beyond grateful for your diligence in finding places where this story would resonate. Thank you to Bryn A. McDonald and Janice Lee for taming my herd of wild commas and wrangling my dangling modifiers during copyediting. An enormous thanks to Lisa Marie Pompilio for my stunning US jacket cover and to Tim Byrne for the equally gorgeous UK cover. I am indebted to all the wonderful teams in sales, editorial, audio recording, book production, marketing, and publicity—*you* made this happen!

To Roshani Chokshi, who read every single terrible version of this book and always saw the kernel of what it could be, instead of the dumpster fire it was. To Shauna Granger, for fielding frantic brainstorming emails and always encouraging me to make my villains better and my heroes worse. To Kara Quinn, for our wine and writing dates, but mostly for making all my new kissing scenes halfway readable. And to all the far-flung Internet friends and Instagram acquaintances who have been constant cheerleaders for me and my books: Breanne Randall, Nicole Evelina, Brittney Arena, Maya Evan MacGregor, Liv Rancourt, Erin Rose Kim, Naomi Farr, and countless others who have encouraged, supported, or shouted about my books. I love you!

My little family keeps me sane. Kepler, you force me to go outside at least once a day. My dearest Freya, you remind me of how bright the real world is, even when I'm lost in my imaginary ones. And, of course, Steve. Don't lie—you know you're proud *Feather Quack 3: BDEB* finally made it to shelves.

Glossary

anam cló (AH-num klow)—soul form; animal avatar

banfhlaith (BAN-lah)—princess

Bealtaine (BELL-tane)—a high holy day occurring between the spring equinox and the summer solstice; May 1

brùnaidh (BROO-nee), **brùnaidhean** (BROO-nee-in) (pl.)—small, secretive household Folk who tidy homes in exchange for leftovers or milk

cailleach (CAH-lyoch)—witch; a slur

Cathair (KAH-her)

Chandika (CHUN-dee-kaa)

chiardhubh (KEER-va)—sable; nickname roughly meaning *dark-haired*

claíomh (clayve), **claimhte** (CLEV-tah) (pl.)—longsword

Corra (KORE-ah)

darrig (DAH-rig)—a solitary, treelike gnome known to foretell simple futures

dún (dun)—a fort or fortified castle

Dún Darragh (dun DAH-rah)

Eithne Uí Mainnín (ETH-na ee MAN-yin)

Eala (AY-lah)

Fia (FEE-ah)

fénnid (FAY-nid), **fénnidi** (fay-ni-DEE) (pl.)—warrior

feis (FESH), **feiseanna** (FESH-uh-nah) (pl.)—a festival with music and dancing

fiann (FEE-in), **fianna** (FEE-nah) (pl.)—band of warriors; army

Fódla (FAW-lah)—an island nation ruled by a high king or queen, with four major provinces ruled by under-kings

geas (GESH), **geasa** (GES-sah) (pl.)—a magical binding or obligation; a curse

Imbolc (IM-bulk)—a high holy day occurring between the winter solstice and the spring equinox; February 1–2

Irian (EER-ee-in)

leipreachán (lep-reh-HAWN), **leipreacháin** (lep-reh-HAYN) (pl.)—diminutive, mischievous Folk

Lughnasa (LOO-na-sah)—a high holy day occurring between the summer solstice and the autumn equinox; August 1

murúch (ma-ROO), **murúcha** (ma-ROO-a) (pl.)—aquatic Folk inhabiting loughs and rivers

ollphéist (awl-FAYSHT)—wyrm-like Folk creature; a giant serpent

Rogan (ROE-gin)

Samhain (SOW-wen)—a high holy day occurring between the autumn equinox and the winter solstice; November 1

skean (skene)—a small single-edged knife

tánaiste (TAW-nisht), **tánaistí** (TAW-nisht-EE) (pl.)—heir apparent of a Sept's Treasure

extras

orbit

meet the author

Alexis the Greek Photography

LYRA SELENE was born under a full moon and has never quite managed to wipe the moonlight out of her eyes. She grew up on a steady diet of mythology, folklore, and fantasy and now writes tall tales of twisted magic, forbidden love, and brooding landscapes. She lives in New England with her husband, daughter, and dog in an antique farmhouse that's probably not haunted. *A Feather So Black* is her adult debut.

Find out more about Lyra Selene and other Orbit authors by registering for the free monthly newsletter at orbitbooks.net.

if you enjoyed
A FEATHER SO BLACK

look out for

A CROWN SO SILVER

Book Two of the Fair Folk

by

Lyra Selene

Look out for Book Two of the Fair Folk.

Before
Irian

He had watched Fia die.

He would never forget the moment—there, beneath the colossal Heartwood, with the Ember Moon lofting toward its zenith—when she chose to sacrifice herself, instead of him. Bent the sword meant for his chest toward her own heart. Spared his life and took her own.

Paid a tithe that should never have been hers to pay.

For such a palpable decision, it happened so swiftly. Little more than a fleeting stillness, where before she'd trembled. A momentary widening of her lovely mismatched eyes as the terrible idea bloomed inside her. A sudden stubborn angle to her delicate jaw. A flurry of emotion blowing ephemerally across her expressive features—regret, sorrow, tenderness, resolve.

She stepped away. Shifted her grip on the Sky-Sword—*his* sword, *his* emblem, *his* sacrifice—and slid the blade against her chest.

No.

Too late, he realized what she was doing. Horror screamed through him, hollowing his bones and tattering his muscles. He staggered to his feet. Lunged for her. But she was fast—far faster than he, weighed down as he was with the crushing burden of his own dying magic. She danced out of his reach. Lifted her eyes to the Heartwood. Murmured words he could not hear over the percussion of his panicked blood pounding in his ears.

She plunged the Sky-Sword into her heart.

For thirteen years, Irian had been that sword, and the sword had been him. Its curving length of metal—shifting color with the skies—was an extension of his own body, his own mind, his own magic. Its keening song was the melody of his own soul. So when it took his new wife's life, he *felt* it. Felt the razor edge slice into warm skin. Felt the burst of hot blood sliding along its bevels. Felt the blade punch through muscle, carve out bone, bite into her throbbing heart. He felt it as surely as if he had slaughtered her with his own hand. As if he—instead of dying as he had planned—had *become* death and stolen the life of the only person he had ever loved.

He caught Fia in the moment before her body struck the ground. He tore the shard of night from her shattered chest. Pressed his hands over the wound. Tried to stanch the life ebbing from her. It was no use. Her green-dark blood welled slick around his fingers, making his hands slip. It steamed in the cold air, blossoming pale as a ghost above her lifeless form. Its scent filled his nostrils—wet loam and turned earth and the metallic tang of creeping rot. Where the rivulets touched earth, tiny blossoms sprouted—white and black as stars in a night sky.

He gathered her up, clutched her against him. Although she was physically petite, Fia had never struck Irian as small. There was so much of her—so much sharp beauty and biting wit and searing emotion—that it had rendered her more expansive in his mind than her mere body could contain. Yet now, forsaken of all the inimitable qualities that had made her *her,* she seemed impossibly tiny in his arms. Her limbs fragile as birds' bones. Her eyelids the color of bruised lilies. Her skin going gray as the underbelly of a storm cloud. He buried his bloodied palms in her tangle of dark brown hair, brought his lips to her forehead. He clenched his eyes shut, whispered meaningless words against her cooling skin.

"Come back. Let it be me. Please, by all that is holy, let it be *me.*"

The ground shifted beneath him. His eyes flew open. Roots churned up from the dark earth, curling around Fia's limbs. Branches groaned down, bark lengthening to cradle her form. He tried to keep hold of her, but his arms were slick with blood, his limbs sapped of strength, his mind slack with shock and grief. He thought he must have roared as the forest carried her away, but the sound in his ears was hoarse and raw. He did not register it as his own voice, only as the sound of his heart breaking.

The Heartwood carried Fia toward itself, as gently as if she were a sleeping baby. Its roots lifted upward; its branches stretched downward. It opened itself up and swallowed her whole.

Leaving Irian alone.

For an unknowable time, his mind echoed with emptiness. Eventually, thoughts crept in, inexorable.

The Sky-Sword.

He crawled to where he had flung it, took its hilt in his green-streaked palm. It cried out a quiet lament—a threnody of loss. He wondered whether it mourned for him. Or for her.

The Ember Moon.

He squinted up. Between the lofting branches of the Heart-wood, he could not tell whether the moon had reached its zenith. Surely it must be soon. Which meant—

The tithe.

He ran his palm along the sword, letting its singing edge slice his skin. A trickle of his own silver blood mingled with the green already staining its length. The bright line of pain focused his mind, even as it sharpened the anguished elegy screaming through him.

All was lost. He did not know what Fia had meant to do by taking her own life instead of his. Had she meant to pay the tithe on his behalf? To trade her life for his? If so, it had not worked. He could feel the last of the Sky-Sword's strength being sapped from his limbs, its powerful pulse dripping from his veins. He could sense the warped ripple of wild magic pushing at the fraying edge of his consciousness, seeking its freedom.

The tithe had not been paid—his Treasure had not been renewed. And without Fia, there was no heir. Even if he bent the blade to his own chest—paid the tithe as he had intended—there was nowhere for the magic to go.

So—Irian would still die. The wild magic of the Sky-Sword—the last Treasure of the Septs—would go free. The blight of tainted magic would spread throughout Tír na nÓg, warping whatever it touched. The Gates would shatter. Violence would spread through mortal and Folk lands alike. Eala would have her war. Both worlds would burn.

The knowledge should have tormented him. But Irian found he could not muster up the energy to care. About the Gates, about Eala's treachery. About his own worthless life. All he cared about was *her*. About Fia. And she—she was gone. Gone beyond where he could reach her. He could only wait to die, and pray that in death, he would somehow be reunited with her.

So he waited.

But he did not die.

The change was so infinitesimal as to be nearly indiscernible. A slow, silent stirring inside him. A kind of *lightening*—a strange counterpoint to the dimming moon sliding down behind netting branches. He rolled out his stiff shoulders. Shifted his weight on legs numb from kneeling on cold ground. Gripped blood-crusted fingers around a blade that had long gone silent as its magic died.

But no. It *hummed*—so softly Irian couldn't hear it at all, could only feel it purr along his wakening bones. The lightness inside him responded, unfurling soft, slow wings around the painful throb of his shattered heart. A weightlessness—like falling, like flight—lifted him to his feet. When he looked up, he saw a brightening sky painted in broad strokes of vermilion and rose, pricked with distant, dimming stars.

Dawn.

Dread clenched his spine and beat back the growing lightness at his core. Dawn was when he changed—when he became *other*. He did not know why he was still alive, when *she* was not. But he had lived with the cost of his arrogance—the price of his selfishness—for too long to assume it could be wished away. For years, this had been the way—shadow and fury until sunset set him free.

He steeled himself for the pain, for the mutation, for the loss of self.

481

With a distant sigh and a rush, the sun rose.

Irian shielded his eyes from piercing golden light with a hand blackened by tattoos, but not feathers. A brisk wind smelling of frost swept the forest, chasing the last of autumn's leaves and lifting the short hair off his neck. Hair, not feathers. Slowly, he glanced over his shoulder. But the stiff pinions of shadow that had haunted him for years were already beginning to evanesce in the cool bright morning. He reached for them, but they were nothing more than tatters of night; scraps of bad memory; a curse, lifted.

And when the Sky-Sword began to sing—a full-throated aubade to the glory of day—he knew.

Somehow, Fia had done it. She had paid his tithe with her life. She had broken the curse. She had saved the magic of the Sky-Sword. She had saved *him*.

He was not sure he could bear it.

He preferred the days. It had been so long since he had been himself during the day, and he glutted himself on it. He flung himself against the blue sky, the high wind, the rippling sunlight, soaring high and higher. Until the air grew thin in his lungs and flowers of frost blossomed on his inky wings. He screamed at the sky, until he had no voice left to rage with.

Far below him, he watched the landscape of Tír na nÓg shift. Warriors marched across sighing plains, the colors of the bardaí's fianna blending in ways he did not expect. Trees were felled. Camps were pitched, then dismantled. Skirmishes broke out, and the stench of rotting corpses mingled with the carrion reek of warped magic wafting over the hills.

Irian could not bring himself to care. With his Treasure renewed, his borders were secure. His Gate, strong. His magic, unassailable.

And she—she was gone.

One day. Two. Seven. Twelve.

There became a rhythm to the thing: a song of inevitability, notes composed in a nightmare of grief and performed in a solitude of sadness. There were the shadows, creeping long and longer as the light faded. The unclenching grasp of the sun's rosy fingers on the windowsill—the touch of daylight fading. The calls of nesting rooks. The distant yip of kits returning to their dens. The settling of stones into the earth.

And him, alone.

Sometimes, he was calm. He slept and dreamed of never waking up.

Most times he was not calm. A cracked and broken voice dying in a hoarse throat. A spray of glass breaking on flagstones: shards sparkling bright as the tears of those who had died for love. Dim, soft lamplight making that which should be ugly beautiful.

Chairs broken into matchsticks against vine-climbed walls.

Fire-scorched logs scattered from the hearth; palms charred and blackened like overdone meat; the stink of roasting flesh.

Dark, hungry metal against tattooed skin. The lure of steel. But no matter how he wished it, he knew the Sky-Sword would not let him die. Not until he had served his second sentence.

It did not mean he did not try.

⁓

On the thirteenth night—when the sky was black, black without a moon to light it—Irian noticed the swan.

He had tried to stop looking at the lough. The swans were gone—Eala's treachery had torn them all from his influence. He was glad for it. He had never liked the sight of them—it reminded him of all the things he had done wrong. The poor choices he had made. The power he had misused. The years he had squandered—not for himself, but for *them*. He had loved them, in his own way. They were the only things or people who had passed for friends these past thirteen years. But he had hated himself for what he had done to them. As he knew they hated him.

He had spent thirteen years' worth of nights looking out at that lough. Counting. Naming. Worrying. He supposed it was a hard habit to break.

He saw it only in absence, at first. A white ripple against black water. A soft, soundless splash. A vibration in the air as stiff pinions sifted wind. He looked closer, forcing his eyes to distinguish the shape by its outline.

Dark wings, outspread. An elegant, curving neck. A tilted beak. Depthless eyes.

It was a black swan.

A hollow, consuming darkness reared up inside him. For a long, ungenerous moment, Irian thought to run it off. To frighten it so that it took to the air. Let it make some other lough its home—he had had enough of swans for one lifetime.

But then he remembered. Remembered how *she'd* looked that fateful night two weeks ago. What she'd worn the night of her death.

Feathers. Feathers so black they'd stolen the light. Feathers in her hair, on her gown, sweeping down from her shoulders in a magnificent train of night. It had been a statement—a symbol of intent. Fia had meant to swear herself to his Sept the night of the Ember Moon. To declare herself as his heir, his tánaiste. To accept his tithe and inherit the last Treasure, the Treasure of the Sept of Feathers.

But she had gotten only as far as the handfasting. She had wed him, only to tithe herself. She had become his wife, only to die. The darkness inside him gnashed sharp teeth around his heart and threatened to swallow him whole. But in that yawning maw of grief, a tiny star kindled. A spark of light that seemed to sing, *What if?*

He dared not voice the rest of the question.

Irian was not accustomed to hope. He had forgotten how much it *hurt*—a punch to the chest, an explosion behind the eyes, a precipitous tilt toward a future he dared not dream. An unbalancing, a mad slide away from despair toward—

He dared not let himself fall. Not now. Not yet.

Instead, he paced.

For fifteen days, he paced the edge of the lough. He followed the black swan as it sailed around the water. Napped on broad stones. Dived for pondweed. Tucked its head behind ruffled black wings when the wind rose. He stared at it, searching for some glint of recognition, some hint of consciousness. Sometimes, he swore he glimpsed a glitter of green in its smooth, depthless eyes.

All the while, the Sky-Sword sang to him. It sang of heartbreak. It sang of hope. It sang of healing.

He dared not listen.

The full moon sailed up through a cold sky embossed with silver cirrus clouds, and Irian's hope turned feral.

No longer a quiet whisper he dared not acknowledge, it roared inside him—a gale of conflicting emotions lashing his thoughts into chaos. It blew chinks in the armor of grief and rage he had built around his heart. It howled treacherous, wondrous, delirious promises in a voice he did not know if he could trust.

He wildly paced the shore. The night seemed to last forever. And yet as the moon descended toward the grasping forest and dawn touched the horizon with ghostly fingers, he wished it might last forever. He was falling, and if he did not have wings, he did not want to know.

If he was truly alone, he was not sure he could bear it.

The sky turned restless with color. Irian's hope began to die, burning out like a falling star in an endless night. He turned his back on the lough. On the black swan. On his own desperate, foolish hope.

A flash of green split the dim. A breeze kissed his neck, smelling of summertime. He spun.

A splash. A cough. A pale, indistinct form rising from dark water, shedding black feathers as she stood.

He was not alone. Gods alive—*he was not alone.*

Irian strode into the lough. He barely noticed the icy black water biting his thighs—only that it weighed his footsteps and made him slow, clumsy.

He could not reach her fast enough. He gathered her up, clutched her against him. Despite the cold water, her skin was warm. Her heartbeat pulsed strong, her chest against his chest. Color touched her pale cheeks. He buried his palms in her tangle of dark hair, brought his lips to her forehead. He clenched his eyes shut and bent to kiss her, whispering meaningless words against her mouth.

She broke away, stared up at him. A delicate fear crept onto her face—a dread he could not fully fathom. Her eyes jerked toward the horizon, where swords of golden light pierced the canopy of trees. Worry twisted her mouth.

Irian understood.

She did not know. Whatever miracle she had performed—whatever unknowable magic she had wrought—she did not know she had broken the geas. She did not know she had saved the Sky-Sword. She did not know she had saved *him*.

The sunrise was its own explanation. He pulled her close, savoring the heat of her skin, the rush of her breath, the steady throb of her heartbeat.

A morning star pricked the dawn, then flung itself down in a line of fire. Only, Irian no longer felt as if he were falling.

Fia drew back. Her mismatched eyes shone, huge in her lovely face.

"Irian," she whispered. "*Irian.*"

He lifted his head from her hair, slid his hand along the delicate angle of her jaw. Put his hand over her heart, only to touch a blue-green stone hanging above her breast. Wonder rose up in him. He had never seen the Heart of the Forest—he had been a little boy when the Sept of Antlers' Treasure had been lost. But he had heard it described. And even had he not, he *knew* it—knew it by its slow, deep pulse, like dark earth and green growth. Knew it by the way it hummed in counterpoint to the Sky-Sword belted at his waist and anchored in his soul. Knew it by the way it shone the same elusive green as the inquisitive eyes of his childhood friend Deirdre.

The same elusive green as Fia's right eye.

He did not know how or why. But somehow, Fia's sacrifice not only had renewed the magic of the Sky-Sword but had resurrected the lost Treasure of the Sept of Antlers too. She had mended the broken Heart of the Forest. She had ended Deirdre's sorrow.

"You did it, colleen." His voice sounded foreign to his own ears. Hoarse. Hopeful. "Fia, you changed our story's ending."

Fia looked down at the stone shining at her breast, then lifted her arms, which were newly embossed with tattoos like creeping, coiling vines. And tangled amid those vines—feathers. Gleaming, razored pinions, a mirror to his own magical markings. She drew him down, tilting her chin as her mouth parted. She kissed him, and he kissed her back, lingering on lips that tasted of moss and miracles and the aching promise of a future yet untold.

"Good morning," she whispered for the first time.

The smile creasing Irian's face came slowly—not because he was not happy, but because he could not yet forget what had happened. Memories of her death lingered, beating at his head and shoulders like wings of night. Specters of grief clutched sharp fingers around a heart that had not yet healed. That might *never* heal.

Still, he made himself smile. "Good morning, colleen."

He kissed her as dawn bled into morning—kissed her long and slow and deep. And he swore—silently, savagely, solemnly—that so long as he lived, so too would she.

Irian would watch both worlds burn before he would ever watch Fia die again.

orbit

Follow us:

/orbitbooksUS

/orbitbooks

/orbitbooks

Join our mailing list
to receive alerts on our
latest releases and deals.

orbitbooks.net

Enter our monthly
giveaway for the chance
to win some epic prizes.

orbitloot.com